Chasing Charlie

LINDA McLAUGHLAN

BLACK & WHITE PUBLISHING

First published 2016
by Black & White Publishing Ltd
29 Ocean Drive, Edinburgh EH6 6JL

1 3 5 7 9 10 8 6 4 2   16 17 18 19

ISBN: 978 1 78530 013 4

For Gorgi, who never was, and never will be an ex-boyfriend.

ACKNOWLEDGEMENTS

Warm thanks to everyone who has encouraged and supported me in the writing of *Chasing Charlie*. The team at Black & White Publishing have been fantastic, especially my editor Karyn Millar, whose keen eyes and encouraging spirit have been much appreciated. My family and friends helped keep me going every step of the way. Frankie and Billy shifted my focus, while Anne and Jen have been awesome cheerleaders and first readers. Abbie Browne helped brush up my industry knowledge. Gorgi gave precious time, succour and so much more. Finally, I have no idea when this book would have happened without Moo, who is one of the most generous women I have ever met. You all rock.

Leave well alone already.
Traditional

1

SAM

It was about half past five and it felt like most of W1 were on the footpaths that evening looking for somewhere warm, dry and well stocked. Normally, this wouldn't be much of a problem. I'd been in London for long enough to handle a spot of rain and a few extra people about, but that evening my reaction skills were somewhat lacking. My badly chosen pumps were wet for a start. Mara had taken one look at me that morning and her eyebrows had jumped halfway up her head. She was right of course. It was a boot day, not a pump day. But those eyebrows – you know the kind, they say a thousand (mostly patronising) words in the space of a few millimetres. So I left the house without changing my footwear. The roles at 21 Harvist Road, Queen's Park, were clear-cut. Mara was the sensible one; I was the ditzy one. It was an excellent arrangement.

Except, of course, when I lost sensation in my toes. Then it was just bloody stupid.

I was taking my sodden, stupid self to meet the girls at the pub, cursing my feet and all things cold when out of nowhere someone rounded a corner and walked straight into me. A sharp intake of breath and a big splash later, I was on my bum in a puddle.

'Fuck me, it's you,' I whispered, the world tilting (it really was!) as I took in who was reaching out to help me up.

He hadn't changed a bit, and if anything had grown more

handsome since I'd last seen him. He was – sorry, is – excessively good-looking and I would challenge anyone not to find him attractive. He had one of those faces people look twice at and nudge whomever they're out with, murmuring, 'Who's that? Do you think he's off the telly?' His sexy, slightly curving eyebrows sat exactly in the right place on his forehead. His cheekbones were high, his jaw clean-lined, without a smudge of jowl peeking out below. His nose was straight, his lips inviting and his eyes were always sparkling. Was I making him sound like a hero from a Mills & Boon? Perhaps. But I had forgotten his hair. There you had the deal-maker. A warm russety brown, just the right side of boyish and kept just long enough on top to fall into his eyes every so often.

He caught my eye and surprise flashed across his face.

'Sam?' he said uncertainly. 'Sam Moriarty? Is that really you?'

I let him help me back onto my feet and made an ineffective effort to straighten myself out, my heart going nineteen to the dozen. I was vaguely aware that people were swirling either side of us, but I was making no effort to avoid their bags and elbows. I didn't feel like a grown-up Londoner in that moment. I felt seventeen again, flimsy and nervous.

'I'm so sorry,' he said in his creamy Sloane accent. 'I should have looked where I was going. I was in a hurry. Such an idiot . . .'

'Charlie,' I said.

'. . . running late for my meeting, and just came running round the corner . . .'

'Charlie.'

Charlie stopped talking.

'Sorry,' he said. 'Are you OK?'

'I'm all right. More shocked than anything,' I said.

'Seeing me would do that.'

'Yes.' I didn't know what else to say. All I could think about was how close we were standing together under his umbrella.

He glanced at his watch.

'So how long have you been in London?' he asked.

'Four years,' I said.

He looked a little startled. 'As long as that? I thought you were doing Australia.'

'I was there for a couple of years.'

'Then it's amazing we haven't bumped into each other before now,' he said.

'Not really, I doubt we inhabit the same circles,' I said, possibly a little frostily, and he'd laughed then – his big hooting laugh I hadn't heard for such a long time.

'Why, because I'm a toff and you're a woman of the people? Oh, Sammy, you haven't changed a bit!'

'Well it's true!' I said. I was desperately trying to keep my frown on and failing.

He looked at me, his head tipped slightly to the side, as if he was looking at a curious display.

'Look, we should try and have a drink sometime, catch up properly. But right now I've really got to make this meeting. That is, if you're OK?' he said.

'Of course. Go!' I made impatient shooing motions, thinking he'd just go then. But he didn't. He took his phone out, and I took out mine, and he rang my number so I'd have his.

'I'm so glad I bumped into you, Sam,' he said, his voice dropping into his lower register, and he bent down and kissed me on both cheeks. That set off at least a dozen hyperactive butterflies in my chest. I tried to look him in the eye but couldn't manage it.

'All right. Now sod off,' I said.

Charlie laughed.

'I'll call you!' he called as he strode away.

Charlie Hugh-Barrington. I couldn't deny it – a part of me had been thinking about him on and off over the past decade. Sure,

I'd got on with my life, and for large parts of it I hadn't given him another thought. But in my heart there was this teenage girl wearing a hideous gold handkerchief top wondering, 'Will we get back together? Will we?' And now I'd seen him! I had actually, really, truly seen him! Inside, I felt like I had been thrown a mile into the air and left there, hovering, while down on earth my feet walked me mechanically to the pub through the rain. As I trudged, I fingered my phone in my pocket. I had his number.

The door to the pub was sticky from the rain, and I had to give it a good shove to open it. Inside, the air was thick with the stench of perfume, beer and coat after moist coat. I stood there for a moment, still reeling. But I had to pull myself together; it was girls' time now, no time for mooning about. There was a place for that, and it wasn't Friday nights. I took a deep breath and pushed my way to the back. There they were. I could see Claudia's glorious blonde pouf, the perfect beacon, guiding me across the room.

'Sorry I'm late,' I said as I drew level with their booth.

'Would you look at what the cat dragged in?' Claudia's foot-long eyelashes took in the whole sorry sight in front of her, from my scalp to my toes. She paused at my feet. I followed her gaze. The thick grey tights I'd considered the one sensible winter addition to my outfit were wet from my calves down, and were dying a horrible death in the two orange paddling pools that had been my pumps.

'I take it you walked?' Claudia asked.

'Of course I bloody walked,' I answered crossly. What kind of question was that? I peeled my tights and pumps off and left them on the floor. They could produce their own tributary to the Thames without me, thanks all the same. 'And don't bloody say you told me so,' I said to Mara as I squeezed into the booth next to her.

4

Mara grinned at me. 'I really wouldn't know what you're talking about.'

And girls' night began. I held my encounter with Charlie inside like a tiny golden nut. Normally I tell my best friends everything, but he was my secret for the time being.

'You're quiet,' Mara observed at one point. I shrugged. She eyed me with that shrewd 'you can't get anything past me' way of hers, but let it go. I tried to focus on what Claudia was saying. She was telling a story about some calamity her sister had got herself into. I gasped and shook my head and giggled at what I hoped were the right places, all the time feeling like I was going to burst with my news. The only thing that seemed to help was drinking. So I did. Up, down, up went my glass, and the minutes passed. Soon it had been an hour.

Finally I had to use the toilet and I stood, rather unsteadily, and excused myself. At last I could check my phone away from my friends' overly observant eyes.

The door closed behind me, reducing the din from the pub to a dull clatter. The bathroom was cold. A vent, presumably put there to share the smells of the toilets with the universe, was doing a good job of passing on the smell of old chip fat from the kitchen to the bathroom instead. I veered into a cubicle, pulled down my pants and sat down. I rooted around inside my handbag. I hadn't checked it yet, not wanting to give myself away, but it also wasn't the done thing, not with the girls. It was one of many rules that Mara insisted on, completely ignoring popular culture as usual. No phones on the table when it's girls' night. It's rude, it's distracting and it's taking over our whole lives, so shove it in your bag.

There it was. My heart juddered as I took it out.

No new texts. I checked the signal. Four bars. Fuck! What did I expect? I leant over my handbag, my knickers at my knees, and stared at the door, wallowing. It was pathetic. I was pathetic. But then, gradually and quite against my will, my eyes started to focus on the graffiti on the back of the door, and I couldn't help reading it. They stopped at a wriggly heart.

S M

luvs

C H

How immature was that, writing on a toilet door? I rolled my eyes. But they kept being drawn back to the heart. Finally I twigged. Those were our initials, or close enough. And just like that, I was back at the party. The one where it all started.

It was Gavin Mallory's seventeenth birthday party. I was there reluctantly. Annabel Brown had dragged me there to watch her sink a bottle of Cava and pluck up the courage to snog some oaf I had no time for. I stood in the shadows, such as they were in Gavin's parents' garage, and watched the girls swaying and the boys standing around in awkward bunches. I couldn't be bothered with any of them – they were all so samey, talking about nothing, and they bored me. I wanted to be challenged. I wanted to have arguments about stuff that was actually happening in the world, about films, about music. I wanted to be older than I was. I wanted to be out of there.

And then Charlie arrived.

God knows how Gavin knew him – maybe through playing rugby or something – but there was a shift in the air when he stepped out of the darkness of the driveway and into the garage. OK, so the girls weren't overflowing with integrity before, but their preening and tittering took on a whole new lease of life when they clapped eyes on him. The boys weren't sure what to do. Talk to him? Take the piss? But somehow he just melded in, talking effortlessly with whoever had the guts to speak to him. I was transfixed. He had a proper haircut and held himself like a man. Upright, but relaxed. And his voice! The minute he opened his mouth I was done for. Posh, yes, but it wasn't his pronunciation that got to me – it was the texture of his voice that really weakened my seventeen-year-old knees. Like deep red velvet; like black treacle. Mrs Watts, my English teacher, would have reacted violently with her red pen if she'd seen the ardent purple twaddle I wrote in my diary that night and many more nights after that.

At some point during the party, Charlie stopped affably chatting to everyone else and spent the last magical couple of hours with me. Me! He actually fancied me! He could have anyone but he chose middle-of-the-road Sam Moriarty, living in an ordinary semi, in ordinary Petersfield, going to an ordinary comprehensive. From that night on, he transformed my last year at school into something magical.

Of course he was away at school most of the term but our relationship was hot and heavy and meaningful in the holidays, and any odd weekends he was home. And me being me (and an even sillier, seventeen-year-old version at that), I thought that this was it – I'd met The One. We would travel the world together and eventually settle in the country. We would host wonderful parties together, and ride horses across the downs on perpetually sunny days . . . I dreamt up a whole life with him in the year we spent together and didn't have any reason to think he felt otherwise. He was every girl's dream boyfriend, attentive, loving and funny. He pined for me in-between visits home, and couldn't wait to see me again. He was particularly keen on seeing me on a leather couch in his sitting room at home (his brother and him had their own sitting room, if you please), which was just big enough for two teenagers if they lay down on top of one another . . . in other words, he was perfect, we were perfect. Why couldn't it have just kept on being perfect?

It was obvious! I drew back from studying the toilet door. There was no other way of thinking about this. He was the only man I had ever loved. Loved, for Pete's sake. I dabbed cursorily and lunged out of the toilet, all fired up with the zeal of a woman who has finally found her mission in life. I was a complete idiot to let him go without a fight all those years ago. I would win him back, that's what, starting from now.

The door opened then with a bang. In strode Claudia, filling the room with cinnamon and musk.

'There you are!' she said, going straight into a cubicle. 'There's a hilarious guy out there desperate to join our table, but Mara's having none of it,' she said, peeing furiously.

I half listened as I stared into the mirror. So I'm going to win him back, but where to start?

Eyes: definitely my best feature, blue with flecks of green. A bit bloodshot tonight, but we'll brush over that.

Eyebrows: looking a little tatty as usual, but hopefully someone can do something with them.

Nose: Used to be cute and stubby. I turned my head in the mirror – left, right. Left again. Dammit. My nose was starting to look like my mother's, slightly bulbous at the end.

'He's not taking no for an answer. You should see the look on Mara's face,' Claudia continued from behind the door.

'Typical,' I answered. That's the thing about Mara. If I ever started feeling too tragic about my own love life, I could always look at her. She kept a wall so high around her that men probably didn't even realise there was a real, live woman standing behind it.

Claudia joined me at the basin, and took out a compact and lippy from her bag, retouching her perfect make-up with an ease that I had long given up wondering if I would ever achieve. I turned back to the mirror and leant in close. Where were the girl-next-door freckles across the bridge of my nose? There were a

8

couple of blackheads but no sign of the cute freckles, the traitors.

Mouth: lips a little on the thin side, prone to looking worried in repose, not to mention dry. I smiled. At least my faithful pegs were still obediently lined up, only my eye teeth misbehaving, jutting out at a slight angle. The smile would do.

Hair: Christ. I dug my fingers into my greasy roots, attempting to liven it up into something that looked deliberately messy, rather than tragically rained on. I met Claudia's eye in the mirror.

'Darling, your hair looks awful.'

'Do you want to have a go at it?' I asked hopefully.

Claudia came closer and poked an experimental finger into my roots, her face looking as if she was poking something rodenty to check if it was dead or alive.

'No.' She withdrew her finger and washed it under the tap.

'I'm not that disgusting, am I?'

Claudia dried her hands on a paper towel. 'No, darling, you're not. But your crazy hair in this weather is more than I can deal with tonight. I want to relax, not perform miracles.'

'Thanks a lot.'

'You're welcome.'

She was right, of course. And if even my dear Claudia thought I looked a mess, what would Charlie have thought tonight? I doubted I'd looked any more together when I'd seen him. I took one last look at the frizzy-haired face in the mirror. I would need a miracle to whip myself into shape. Amendment: I would need a whole bag full of miracles. A big bag. A mahoosive bag that would be impossible to carry on my own. I could see already those damn miracles were going to put my back out. They would be expensive. They would be elusive. I shook my head and grimaced. What the hell was I thinking?

We went home after that, back to Mara's flat, where I'd lived for the past two years. I was silent on the Tube. All I wanted to

9

do when we got in was shut myself in my room and flick through my memories of Charlie, savouring each sweet moment one by one. I also needed to work out where I could magic the miracles that would help me win him back. I certainly didn't want any more surprises, or anything verging on emotionally taxing. So when we opened the door to the flat and found another gorgeous man sitting in the kitchen, this one brown and lean and smiley, I almost cried.

But Mara didn't. She squealed with excitement.

'Ed! You're back early!'

2

SAM

Mara went straight to her twin and hugged him hard. Claudia followed, clucking like an excited chicken. He was home! Much excitement! But not from me. It's not that he's not lovely, because he is – everyone loves Ed – but I really didn't have the head space. And there was no way I could get away with slinking off to bed now.

Then Ed stepped over to hug me, and it was with a strength I wasn't expecting. Even with my head blurred with wine, I could tell that something was different about him, despite him only having been away a few months. He hadn't put on any weight but he seemed bigger – how was that possible?

I scraped together four clean glasses from the dishwasher and cupboard, and helped Claudia pull the table away from the wall so we could all fit around it. Growing up is such a random business. When I was younger I assumed that you'd just step into adulthood when you left home. But since I'd left that safety net, I was learning that growing up actually happened in little spurts, sometimes when you least expected it, and I definitely wasn't expecting Ed to seem so different . . . so wordly. He'd always seemed so consistent to me, a lanky version of Mara, sweet and quiet and very funny, and kind of – I can't put my finger on it – boyish I guess. I hadn't noticed it until I was sitting there at the kitchen table but before he went away, he wasn't one of those people who took up much space in a room. Not any more. Ed had returned from India a man.

Mara's cat George eyed me from his position at the fridge.

'What?' Bloody thing, he always stared at me, unblinking, like I was the prime suspect in some complicated and extremely dodgy affair.

I couldn't hover in the kitchen forever. Mara would want to know what I was doing, fiddling about with her systems, so I squeezed into the 'wedge chair' (so called because of its proximity to the cupboards) and helped myself to pizza. Not that Mara had noticed what I was or wasn't doing – she was all over Ed, cutting across Claudia's more reasonable questions with an uncharacteristic wheedle.

Claudia: 'When did you fly in?'

Mara: 'You didn't tell me you were coming home early . . .'

Claudia: 'How was your trip?'

Mara: 'Of course it's nice to see you, but why didn't you call me?'

Ed answered each question with that slow, smiley way of his. I put my head down and ate, half listening but not catching his eye. After the whirlwind of bumping into Charlie, and then coming home to Ed being all manned up, I was feeling testosteroned out. I know – that shouldn't be possible, right? A single girl like me, I should have been lapping it up. Ed was looking damn hot but it really was all too much.

Eventually he asked me a question.

'You're quiet, Sam.' I looked up. Yip, he was definitely hot. Even the circles under his eyes were adding something to his face.

'It's been a long day,' I said and shrugged, trying to ward off any more questions. But Ed waited for me to say more, his dark eyes seeing further into my head than I wanted him to.

12

'I wouldn't have said it was possible but you're skinnier now than when you left,' I addressed his chest.

He ran his hands down brown stubbly cheeks.

'I had giardia for the first month.'

'You didn't tell me!' Mara yelped.

'No, I didn't. I didn't want to worry you. It's perfectly normal anyway.'

'It is?' Mara looked unconvinced.

'Was it also normal not to wash?' Claudia sniffed him and made a face.

Ed's laugh showed teeth bright against his tan.

Mara stretched out a finger and scratched at her brother's forearm. 'At least one layer of that tan of yours is grime,' she said.

I laughed then.

We sat and heard about Ed's trip for an hour or so, Claudia starting off the questioning with her easy charm. But after a bit we couldn't help ourselves. Mara, Claudia and I started jumping in and peppered Ed's stories with ones of our own. We have a good-sized shared stockpile of stories – scrapes narrowly avoided and characters met. After all, our friendship was born far away from here. We met each other when we were happily upside down in Melbourne, where we all worked as waitresses in a fantastically grubby steakhouse. We worked together, we partied together, we slept with loud, cussing Australian men – or at least that's what Claudia and I did. Mara fell in love with a small, intense, quiet Australian man who broke her heart and took her spirit for a while. What was I saying? She hadn't had the bottle to trust a man since. But still – we had great adventures together, with trips up and down the east coast, and then through Thailand on the way home. We dragged Mara out of the mire that was breaking up with Mark. And through everything that life's thrown at us since, we'd been best friends.

This didn't mean we always understood each other.

All through the evening, Mara wavered between looking happy and verging on pinched. I may have known her for nine years but she still confuses me. Just when I think she's going to react to something one way, she does the complete opposite. Like now. I know she's been missing Ed like crazy – they've got that whole close thing twins have going on – but here he is in her kitchen and she's tense. What's with that?

Eventually two o'clock rolled around and all I was thinking about was bed. I wanted to be alone and try to straighten out the day in my head in silence. When Claudia left to go home and Mara went to the sitting room to make up the futon, I saw my chance to escape and tried to get out of the wedge chair. But Ed held out a bottle.

'Finish this with me first?' he asked.

And I don't know why but I thought I might as well. He doled out the last drops and I shoved my own wintery hands under the table. They looked sickly in comparison to his.

'You're not tired?' I asked him.

'Too excited to be back,' he said. He leant back in his chair and stretched out his legs, brushing my foot along the way. I moved away from him and waited for him to apologise but he didn't. Before he went away, he used to be so twitchy about physical contact he'd almost apologise in advance.

'I've been talking all night. I want to know your news, Samantha Moriarty,' he said.

My news? I looked at the table. Only Charlie! Charlie! Charlie! Read all about it. But of course I wasn't about to blab to Ed about him. I forced my mind away from him. Think, woman. Here and now remember? Work. I could talk about work.

'Well . . . work is all right, I suppose. Money's tight. I think with the recession there aren't as many commercials being shot

14

at the moment, at least not big-budget ones. I don't know about it really. Sometimes I think I want to eventually move up from being a third to a first AD . . . but other times I just want to tell them all to cock off.' I smiled and then blushed at my choice of words. Move on, move on . . .

'Love life . . .' I paused, my mind being tugged off to you-know-who again. 'Erm, that's non-existent.' For the time being, I added silently.

'Home life . . .' I went on. 'Of course I love living here, having the park just there.' I pointed towards the front of the house, where Queen's Park lay just the other side of the street. Again, he was probably completely knackered but it felt like he was intensely watching every one of my gestures. It was unsettling. It wasn't at all like the Ed I remembered.

'So life's OK I suppose. Just rolling along.'

Ed nodded. The clock on the wall ticked in the pause.

'What about you? What brought you back so suddenly?' I asked him.

He looked at me for a moment before answering. 'It seemed like the right time.'

'Mara's quite ruffled seeing you again,' I said.

Ed looked down the hall towards the front room where we could hear her huffing and puffing over the futon.

'Shall we go and help her?' I asked. There was a pause and then we laughed together. No, of course we wouldn't. That was our favourite game to play, being the lazy, errant children of ever-efficient Mara.

Our sniggering petered out and Ed took a sip of wine. He still hadn't given me an answer.

'Mara's been quite preoccupied lately, a bit on the grumpy side. At first I thought it was me but then I started thinking she might be worried about you. And now you turn up?'

15

He looked at me from behind his Elvis Costello glasses and seemed to take forever to reply. And I don't know why but I was drawn to his mouth. It was as if I was seeing it for the first time and I thought, what beautiful lips. Followed swiftly by: what the hell am I doing? I looked up to his eyes again, feeling a little panicky. I can't be checking out my mate's lips. Ed's eyes were burning and for a crazy moment I actually thought that he was going to kiss me! But he didn't. Thank God.

'Sam, there's something I'd like to speak to you about,' he said, very quietly, leaning in so close to me I could feel the heat of his scalp.

'I'm all ears,' I replied. But I wasn't really. I was all beating heart and breathless chest, all prickly skin and completely and utterly freaked out. I was as far away from being all ears as it was possible to be.

'Well I'm off to bed,' said a voice from the door.

Ed pulled back abruptly then. Mara was standing motionless and pale in the doorway. Guilt washed over me and I tried to smile, but it felt like I'd just bared my teeth. But Mara wasn't looking at me. She was staring at Ed, blinking at the man sitting at the table as if she didn't recognise him.

'All right, Mars, see you in the morning,' he said, his voice strained.

After a spiky pause, Mara turned and went into her bedroom.

I stood up then. Enough was enough.

'Look, I've got to go to bed,' I said.

'Sure,' Ed replied, looking at his hands. He seemed a little defeated sitting there but I couldn't bear spending another second with him, which was unfair on Ed. It wasn't his fault – of course it wasn't. Ed had only rattled me. Charlie had started it all. It was all about Charlie. I had to check my phone.

16

3

ED

From: Ed Minkley <edminkley@gmail.com>
Date: Saturday, 31 January
To: Covington Green <greenworldcov@gmail.com>
Subject: Sam

Cov,

You were right – as soon as I saw her again I knew I was just as smitten and I don't know what I'm going to do about it. Tried talking to her last night but Mara came in and looked at me as if I had my hand in the till and I gave up. It's just like before I left, I'm still just her mate's brother. The good news is she says she's single, so what do I do? I know you're busy saving the planet and all that but what next? You were the one who convinced me to come back and give it a shot – I hold you responsible for my next move!

Ed

4

SAM

Saturday morning. I woke to the smell of coffee and for a moment felt flooded with happiness. Growing up, the smell of coffee always meant it was the weekend, with Mum and Dad at home, slow mornings spent in PJs nagging Dad to leave the paper and play with us. But I wasn't at home, of course. I was in my flat, with Mara, who always drank tea. And then I remembered. Ed was back! And in a millisecond my mind woke up and remembered the day before in a whoosh. Ed surprising us all in the kitchen, we'd been at the pub, I hadn't told the girls something, bumping into Charlie. Charlie! I scrabbled for my phone next to my bed, sending a pile of magazines onto the floor. Nothing. Sweet FA. I groaned.

Mara was in her chair at the table when I went through to the kitchen, her head bent over a crossword. It wasn't until she gave me a cool greeting that I remembered the weirdness of the previous night, with Ed getting all close and serious with me, and Mara looking so freaked out. I hovered in the doorway for a moment, rubbing my eyes. Should I talk about that right now? Get it all out? Probably, but to be honest, I just wanted a cuppa, so I left it. I was probably reading into everything too much anyway.

'Coffee, Sam?' Ed asked. He was smiling an easy smile and I forgot worrying about the twins and me. Ed's coffee is not to be angsted over. It is one of life's true pleasures, to be savoured right down to the bottom of the cup.

'You don't have to ask,' I said, and I sat down in my jim-jams to wait. There was no way I was going to do something as meaningless as showering when there was one of Ed's coffees on offer.

Mara may not drink coffee but while Ed was away she had cared for Ed's coffee machine like it belonged on an altar. Which was perfectly right of her. Ed's coffee machine – like his camera – was like a gift from God to him. Watching Ed then it was as if the squat little machine was the only coffee maker in the whole world. He touched it lightly, almost stroking it, going through the ritual of grinding, packing, cup placing, button pushing, milk frothing in this kind of erotic meditation. That sounds strange, I know, but somehow he made it all look like a perfectly reasonable way to spend your time. And the sounds that accompanied it – sniffing the beans as they were poured into the grinder, happy little grunts as the metal coffee holder clicked into place, the quiet 'ah' as he added the milk to the silky blackness. It was better than television.

'Here's one for you, Ed. City in India, home to the Red Fort,' Mara cut across Ed's blissful little moment.

He answered absently. 'Delhi.'

'Delhi.' Mara wrote it into the crossword.

'OK. Another word for earache. Seven letters.'

'Earache?' I offered, knowing I shouldn't. She never normally asked for help when it was just me – I rarely had anything of value to add. She looked up just long enough to wither at me. I poked my tongue out at her.

My phone beeped. I opened the message in lightning time, then threw the phone on the table in disgust when I saw who it was from.

'Watch out!' Mara said as it skidded dangerously close to her crossword.

'Keep your hair on, it's just a phone.'

19

'Do you have to text at the breakfast table?' Yes, she really did say that.

'This isn't the bloody breakfast table – it's just a table. Do we have a dining table hidden away somewhere, in a hidden dining room perhaps? Or even better, a table just for texting, in a hidden texting room perhaps?'

'Sounds rude.' Ed came over with my coffee then, just in the nick of time. It wasn't fair of me to take out my disappointment on Mara. I took the coffee gratefully.

'Who was it anyway?' he asked.

I took a sip before I answered, closing my eyes as the bitter syrup slid over my tongue. Beautifully textured, just the right temperature, with hints of smoke and caramel undertones. Fuck me, that's good. When I opened my eyes, Ed was smiling and Mara, bemused, was looking at me like I was a nutter, a look she gives me a lot.

'It was the silly cow herself,' I said.

'Who's that?' Ed asked.

'Rebecca,' Mara and I answered at the same time. Mara smirked in my direction.

'How did you know?' he asked Mara.

'Lucky guess,' Mara answered, and returned to her crossword.

'She's the only silly cow we know,' I explained. 'It's just a pity I have to be related to her.'

'Oh, your sister.' Ed finally caught up.

'Unfortunately.'

Mara smirked at her paper again.

'She's not that bad. In fact, she's quite fit if memory serves,' he said.

'Fucking typical.'

'What's that supposed to mean?'

'I mean you're a typical man, sees a skinny girl and thinks

she's hot. Did you not notice that she doesn't have the beautiful personality to go with it?'

'She's amiable enough.'

I choked on my coffee. 'You've got to be joking!'

Ed grinned. 'Maybe I find her calculating gaze mysterious?'

'You're bloody winding me up.'

I started smiling with him then. For a moment I was worried. I'm not sure I could be friends with someone who actually did like my sister.

I took another sip. 'It wasn't actually Rebecca. It was Mum, texting me about Rebecca. Apparently she's split up from James. Mum wants me to check up on her.'

Mara groaned.

'Exactly,' I said.

'Exactly what?' Ed asked.

I caught Mara's eye again. We were forgetting to translate. The few months Ed had been away were obviously long enough for him to forget how the shorthand Mara and I use – built up over years of muttering semi (or otherwise) bitchily about other people – works.

'Well?'

'Sorry, Ed. When Rebecca breaks up with someone, we usually see more of her.'

Mara groaned again.

'And that's a bad thing?' Ed asked.

I got up then. 'Basically, Ed, you're too bloody nice.'

It was time for a shower. I went to find some clothes to take to the bathroom. That was the crazy thing about Ed – he was a seriously nice person and I'd never known him to judge someone else harshly, especially if he didn't know them well. Being so nice was bound to get him into trouble one of these days.

5

ED

From: Ed Minkley <edminkley@gmail.com>
Date: Saturday, 31 January
To: Covington Green <greenworldcov@gmail.com>
Subject: Sam again

She sits with knees resting on the table, her hair all over the place, and yawns. Her pyjamas give away hints of her curves below.

Ed

PS She still isn't noticing me. Need some help here, mate!

PPS About now would be good.

6

SAM

Where had all the blinking razors gone? Placing my left foot on the side of the bath, I ran my hands up and down my leg. Then I swapped them over. Yup, both the same – you could exfoliate your hands on them. There must have been at least a week's growth on the buggers. And they were sickly January white. I leant out to open the bathroom cupboard, dripping water over my cast-off PJs. Perhaps there was one in there? But of course there wasn't. Not even on a day off, when I have more time for things like grooming, do I manage to actually do something about it. I took my foot off the side of the bath and put my head back under the shower. When was I going to be a woman who was organised and cared about this stuff enough to be on top of my beauty regime? Actually, when was I even going to have a beauty regime?

Two years ago, when we had first moved in, it was close to Christmas and I had a bountiful supply of razors from Santa. The fancy ones, with the soapy strip and everything. When they ran out, I moved onto Mara's supply. Mara had tried to put her sensibly shod foot down about this issue, citing personal hygiene, respect for personal property and textbook taking-the-effing-piss as reasons why I really should stop but I ignored her. I didn't mean to piss Mara off (much). I just never got around to buying some of my own. And after a while Mara gave up and started buying packs of ten throwaway plastic jobs. I suspect that Mara kept her own fancy razor in her bedroom, buying the cheap ones as decoys to keep me from sniffing around. Fair play to her, I suppose. I had proved, yet again, that I couldn't even keep on top of my razor supply.

I stood under the water, gently rocking from side to side, letting the hot water scorch one shoulder then the other. Annoyingly, once I'd stopped beating myself up about my lack of a beauty regime, my mind moved swiftly onto Ed. I would much rather have been fantasising about seeing Charlie again. But every time I fixed Charlie's face in my mind it would be replaced by Ed, with his stubbled face and cheeky grin. Of course it was nice to have Ed sitting at the kitchen table, slotting back into our little family again, but I didn't want to be thinking about him in the shower. I turned round, letting the water pelt my front. I thought back to the previous night. Ed wanted to talk, obviously without Mara. And Mara had been so flipping prickly. What the hell could that be about?

And then I clicked. How could I have been so stupid? There must be something wrong with her! He'd want to talk about it while Mara wasn't in the room to deny it. I ran through Mara's behaviour leading up to Ed's return. She'd been grumpier than usual, definitely preoccupied with something. I'd assumed it was just Mara doing what she does best – worrying. He was in India, after all, where anything could happen to him. But could I have missed something else? It was possible. Mara was a shocker for fussing over everyone else and ignoring her own needs, and it was virtually impossible to get any information out of her about how she was. Blood from a stone doesn't come close.

I was so occupied chewing over these worrying thoughts that for a second, possibly two, I didn't register my phone vibrating enthusiastically on top of the curved cistern. But then I did.

24

And although everything happened very quickly, it felt like it happened in slow motion.

My brain registered . . . that's my phone!

I looked wildly through the steamy gloom . . . Oh my God, it's wobbling on top of the toilet.

I stepped over the side of the bath . . . stumbling a little . . . Fuck! What are my shoes doing right there?

I lunged for the phone . . . which fell – plop! Into the toilet.

'No!' I shouted and fished it out quickly. There on the screen was the blissful yellow envelope that signified a text message.

Please be him, please be him! I dabbed at the phone perfunctorily with a towel and jabbed the keys.

> Pompous ex requests company over a beer this
> afternoon, u free? Cx

'Yes!' I closed my fist and pumped my elbow into my side, immediately grateful no one was there to witness the toilet dunking or the childish arm pumping. There was a tentative knock on the door.

'Are you OK in there?'

It was Ed.

'Brilliant, thank you!'

'Oh.' He sounded confused. 'But you sounded like you'd hurt yourself.'

I was rifling through the cupboard in a frenzied attempt to locate some forgotten Veet. I had to remove hair. Now.

'Actually can you get Mara for me?'

'Sure.' Ed sounded relieved.

A few moments later I heard a decidedly unsympathetic Mara at the door. I opened it a crack and put on what I hoped was my saddest puppy-dog face.

'Can I please borrow a razor?'

'Why?' Mara narrowed her eyes.

'Why do you think, to write a novel with?' I jiggled up and down with excitement. 'Mara, I've got a hair-removal emergency going on here!'

Mara sighed.

'Look, I've got to meet someone later.' I didn't want to tell her anything more.

Mara lowered her voice and glanced towards the kitchen, where we could hear Ed washing up.

'Ed and I need some time together this afternoon. We haven't seen each other for ages.'

'Well I won't be around. I've just told you, I'm meeting someone. Now can I please, please, please borrow your razor?' What was the matter with Mara – had she become stupid all of a sudden as well as poorly? Confusion, followed by what looked like relief, passed over her face and she disappeared. I continued to jiggle, all thoughts of Ed well banished now. It was Charlie a-go-go.

As Mara passed her razor reluctantly through the gap in the door, she started to say, 'I thought—'

'Yeah?' Come on, Mara.

'Oh nothing. Just wash the razor properly when you've finished,' she said, boring little holes into my eyes with her fierce brown ones before marching back to the kitchen.

7

MARA

Eventually I gave up waiting for Ed to return and set out for the supermarket. I was trying very hard not to feel hurt and failing miserably.

'I don't want to sponge off you, Mars, and I'd rather see him in person to see if he has any shifts,' he'd said.

Of course Ed was right. Max was his best friend and had been his main source of income for the past couple of years, so why shouldn't he see him today? It wasn't fair on Max for me to feel jealous. Ed was damn lucky to have him in his life. He could ask Max for any shifts on his coffee cart when he needed them, fitting his photography in around it. We could spend time together another day.

My brother the photographer! I felt a flutter of excitement every time I said that to myself. I loved that he was following his dream, even though it meant pulling coffees just to get by when we both had turning thirty just around the corner. Yes, I worried about how he would survive when he was old. Would he have enough of a pension to live comfortably? Maybe. Maybe not. Did it matter? Wasn't it more important that he was doing what felt right today? Puff puff went my breath as I strode out, and I pushed those thoughts out with it. Photography was Ed's gift. Of course he was doing the right thing.

Before he went to India, he'd become more and more interested in documentary photography, spending hours and hours in one area of London at a time, shooting people going about their everyday business. Maybe he'd invite me along to do that soon. I don't know how he did it – the idea of taking photos of strangers made my blood run cold but I loved watching him. People didn't seem to notice him, and if they did, he just chatted as if he'd known them forever, his lovely smile illuminating his face. Sometimes it felt like he got all the social skills that were being dished out to us in the womb, leaving me with nothing.

I was halfway across the park. The sun was actually managing to brighten the wintery yellow grass. My cheeks were cold but I was snug inside my duffle coat and couldn't help but feel lighter as I walked along. Sainsbury's wasn't far away, and I never tired of the simple pleasure of being able to walk there and back with my shopping bags. I'd always been partial to a bit of efficiency. Sam teased me, but she just didn't understand the pleasure of something working. Walking to the supermarket with a couple of jute bags – and walking back – worked. She didn't even do the shopping most of the time, which was no bad thing really. Left up to Sam, she would – admittedly warm-heartedly – march off to the supermarket for supper and come home with Jaffa Cakes, Gorgonzola and crisps, when what I really would have liked was a nice piece of haddock. I ran over my list again: ham for sand-wiches, rice, milk, mustard and chocolate. There was something else. Oh yes, razors for Sam. Some things never changed.

Sam. God only knows who she was flitting off to meet this time. He'd be one of two varieties:

1. The Handsome Rogue: funny and charming, usually swept Sam off her feet, spent a lot of time in bed with her, she wanted him to meet her friends and family (which he avoided), allergic to commitment, invariably broke it off with her within a few weeks.

28

2. The Handsome Better-off-as-a-Friend: sometimes younger than Sam, funny and kind-hearted, she swept him off his feet, he spent a lot of time in bed with her, wanted to spend time with me and meet Sam's family (which she avoided), fell in love with her, but Sam broke it off with him within a few weeks, saying they would be better off as friends.

I'd been watching Sam hurtle between the two varieties like a thoughtless pinball for years; bouncing from one or two handsome rogues in a row into the arms of a better-off-as-a-friend, then back to another rogue. She knew the rogues were no good for her so, bless her, she tried to be with a good man, but she was never attracted to the better-off-as-friends. So surprise surprise, she then fell for the next rogue that crossed her path because he was exciting. Round and round the same old circuit. It was deeply tedious.

And the blame for this cycle I placed fair and square on the palatial doorstep of Charlie Hugh-Barrington, Sam's first – and as far as I could make out only – love. The inaugural handsome rogue. I would have loved to take him down a peg or two. The guy sounded like a complete and utter rake. Thank goodness Sam wasn't in touch with him. He was the last thing she needed in her life.

I crossed the road. Not far now. My mind flipped back to Ed again. Specifically Ed and Sam. With Sam's chequered history, a series of pointless and inevitably flawed dalliances, I had always been clear that he mustn't go anywhere near Sam romantically. It was obvious which category he fell into, and the last thing I wanted was to be comforting him as he licked his wounds. I would be so cross with Sam too, so flipping cross it made my stomach churn just thinking about the possibility. It would wreck everything.

I had hoped that India would get Sam out of Ed's system. He'd never spoken to me about it but it was obvious how he felt. He'd always lit up when she was around, and the year before he went away he might as well have had his tongue hanging out he was so besotted. But for lots of reasons we'd never quite got around to discussing it. Mainly because I didn't want to make it any more real than it was. Amazingly Sam hadn't noticed. So far. But he'd returned from India still daft about her. Daft about her, and more determined. Or something. I couldn't figure out what exactly. There was an urgency to Ed that concerned me. He felt . . . complicated. And there was still the mystery of why he was completely out of touch for the last two months of his trip, save the odd email to let me know he was still alive. I should have been able to feel how he was, even long distance. But this time I couldn't feel a thing.

The supermarket was quiet. Ham first, then the condiment aisle. There it was. I reached up for some mustard. A couple next to me were discussing what sauces were missing from their cupboard. Neither of them could remember what they needed. They were pale, half awake and completely at ease with each other.

'I don't know, some horseradish, let's try that,' the man yawned.

'OK.' The woman sounded doubtful but was reaching for the shelf. 'Why not?'

Why not? Why not? I know I needed a bit more 'why not'. I'd kept myself carefully packaged up, safe and sealed from another relationship since Mark. I caught the man's eye. He smiled in a friendly, relaxed way, no agenda. Just a 'hello stranger, I'm wandering round the supermarket on a Saturday evening' kind of way. No hint of darkness below. No hint of Markness. I lowered my eyes and walked down the aisle towards the bread. Yes, there are nice men out there, Mara, but you can't trust them. It was always the same old voices, the same old battle inside. Stop it! This was dangerous territory, worrying about myself. Focus. I would go home and make a nice supper, and have a chat with Ed, try to find out what was going on with him in India and why he was home now, so much earlier than expected.

8

SAM

By the time I got to the pub, the butterflies in my belly were frantic. I stood at the door and swallowed a few times, trying to keep them inside, along with the contents of my stomach. But he was there, smiling warmly at me across the room. HE'S PLEASED TO SEE ME! my seventeen-year-old voice shrieked in my head.

He was sitting languidly at a small table, his long legs crossed, a bottle of wine and two glasses in front of him. He stood (stood!) as I approached and kissed me on both cheeks. I'd expected this greeting to be more awkward than it was, but Charlie made it seem like the most natural thing in the world. His hands felt warm through my sleeves where he'd held my arms. He smelt of antique furniture, brandy and the beach, and the smell went straight to my you know what.

'Sam, it's so good to see you,' he purred.

'You too, Charlie.' Stop grinning. Stop it. Play it cool.

He pulled out a chair and I sat down and willed myself not to stuff this up. He poured another glass and handed it to me. My hands were shaking.

'So . . . Sam Moriarty,' he said.

'That's me.' I took a quick sip and for the second time in twelve hours, hid my hands under the table. God, he was handsome. Those cheeks. You could land a plane on them.

'You haven't changed a bit,' he said, leaning back in his chair. 'Still as cute as ever, with that wild-around-the-edges look.' I touched my hair compulsively. What did he mean? Women – and men for that matter – kept glancing at him from other tables. Beautiful women without a hair out of place. I gave him a tight smile. I had to get this conversation started before I bolted out the door.

'So you're a doctor then,' I stuttered, immediately kicking myself – couldn't I come up with a more interesting question than that?

He smiled. If he noticed my nervousness he wasn't showing it.

'A surgeon actually.'

'Oh!'

'It's only one step up from a butcher really.'

I winced.

'That doesn't sound good, does it? I don't mean we butcher our patients. But it's fairly straightforward most of the time. Single-focus stuff.' He leant forward then and said in a provocative whisper, 'Good for men.'

'And not for women?' And there it was, the conversation had ignited. There was nothing like a good bit of fighting to get rid of nerves. I may overuse it a little and yes, it is how seventeen-year-olds interact, but it works. Suddenly my nerves were gone. And the stupid grin that replaced Charlie's more controlled charming smile showed he'd just been waiting for it to kick off.

'I knew you'd say that!' he almost crowed. 'Still the feminist are we, Sam?' He leant back again and pushed his hair off his face.

'The feminist? What, I suppose you only know one?'

Charlie ignored me.

'What I mean, Sam,' Charlie continued, 'is that it suits men because we just get on with the job at hand without too much multitasking. It's just a series of steps really.'

'What if something goes wrong?'

'Well, then things get a little more complicated, but you've got a whole team supporting you.'

'Very impressive.' I raised my glass to him.

'No need to be sarcastic.'

'I'm not!' I hadn't meant to sound insincere actually. Well, not much. 'You've worked hard to get to where you are and I'm impressed, honestly.'

He paused, assessing me across the table.

'What about you, Sam? I'm sure you're up to something interesting. You were always so . . . creative.' I felt myself colouring under his gaze, and the few remaining butterflies left in my stomach set off again.

'I was?'

'Sure. Don't you remember that sculpture you made of that headless girl, an arrow through her heart?' He mimed plunging an arrow into his chest.

Oh no, not that. Why did he have to remember that?

'What was it about again, something Greek?'

'Yes. Something like that.' I laughed, hoping he wouldn't pry further. The sculpture had actually been my way of expressing how I felt about him at the time: utterly brainless with Cupid's arrow lodged in my breast.

'You were always so intense, Sam.'

'Was I?' I may have been a tad on the dramatic side as a teenager, but wasn't everyone at that age?

'So what do you do now?'

Oh thank you – let's talk about now.

'Nothing great really. I work in the film and telly world as a third AD.'

'Really?' Charlie's eyes lit up. 'That's much more exciting than cutting people up.'

'I don't know about that.' My face felt like it was on fire.

'Of course it is. Tell me about it.'

And we talked, and we drank, and we laughed. And then we drank some more, and leapt through the last decade. My cheeks toned down to what, in my tipsy state, I thought was a pretty pink, and I stopped feeling like I was going to career out of my chair with nerves.

As we chatted and the afternoon slid into darkness, I began to see flashes of his younger, softer face, the one I'd caressed and spent hours looking at. It kept peeking out of this grown-up, more chiselled version, giving me a little shock every time. He asked intelligent questions about my work, leaning in to hear my answers, and seemed genuinely interested. His hazel eyes, only slightly crinkled around the edges, didn't leave my face for a moment.

And then, when I'd stopped wondering if we would ever talk about that night, he said, his face serious for the first time all evening, 'Sam, I want to say how sorry I am about how it ended. I've always felt bloody awful about it.'

'It was pretty shitty,' I murmured as I took sip number fifty-five of the evening. I was warm and drunk and felt ridiculously attractive. I rooted vaguely around inside to find the anger that had been simmering for all those years. Here? No. What about here? No. The anger wasn't there at all. But he was.

'Hey, we were young, what happened happened. Life's gone on. Cheers!' I raised my glass to him, aware of the naughtiness in my eyes. His eyes glittered back at me.

'But I was a complete sod,' he persisted, his fingers resting on my arm. I looked down at them. God, they were sexy.

'Yes, but you were young,' I insisted. I wanted to keep this high going and enjoy the lack of antipathy I felt. But he wouldn't leave it alone.

'The thing is, Sam,' he said, leaning in closer, 'I've often wondered what happened to you. You've been at the back of my mind. Not always, but there, you know?'

Do I what? My heart was in my throat.

'It's really, really good to see you again. I didn't think I'd get the chance to see you before—' But he stopped himself, settling back into the chair. And even in my drunken state I could see he was battling with himself.

'Before what?'

He shook his head once, then leant in again. 'Oh, I don't know. Before life gets all serious, you know.'

'What, wife and kids?'

'Yes. Or perhaps we settle somewhere else in the world?'

He'd suddenly faltered, not so smooth after all.

'Are you seeing anyone now then?' There, I'd said it.

Charlie hesitated, ever so slightly, but then reached across the table and took my hands.

'I'm so happy to have bumped into you, Sam. This means so much to me,' he said, his face utterly earnest.

'It's nice to see you too, Charlie.' My face was heating up again.

And then it happened. My eyes locked with his, the noisy chattering around us stopped and we became completely lost in one another, the years folding up neatly until there was nothing at all between us.

A moment passed, then another, and then he opened his mouth and sang 'Da da da – da!' like we were in some crazy opera, and we cracked up laughing and broke away from each other, returning to the frolicking conversation of before. But it had happened – we'd shared a moment and it meant something, and my heart soared for the rest of the night.

9

SAM

There is a certain kind of magazine that I often found myself reading and loathing. You know the kind – glossy, aspirational and filled with gorgeous people living amazing, fulfilling lives in beautiful homes. They never make you feel good. They make you feel like you aren't worthy of these people, in all their polished fabulousness. But the damn things are compulsive. You just can't help but pick them up. I don't get it at all. But, sucker that I am, I found myself sitting in my favourite café in Notting Hill on Sunday morning, my cheekbones resting on my cupped hands with *House & Garden* open between my elbows. I was reading about an artist in Cornwall, and the 'light and airy space' that was her studio slash home. Apparently this woman had 'eclectic furniture and nick-nacks gleaned from junk shops scattered randomly . . . sticking to a muted palate of neutrals with an occasional flash of crimson'. Oh please, give me a break. With great effort I pulled my head up from my hands and looked out the window onto the street. No flashes of crimson to be seen there. Just grey, grey and more grey. Oh hang on. I squinted. There, far above the shops, was a tiny patch of blue.

It was enough. The hungover shoppers shuffling along outside disappeared. In my mind, I was noodling on the beach at Studland in the middle of an endlessly sunny Sunday afternoon – yellow sand, mellow sun, seagulls wheeling and chattering overhead, fighting over the last of the fish and chips, the sharp, salty tang in the air. I wished I could be a child again, before everything got so damn complicated.

The door to the café opened, letting in a burst of cold air, eddying around the legs of those closest to the door. People shifted slightly in their seats and glanced up, waiting for whoever was coming in to close the door. Would they have to shut it? No. Good. The woman closed it firmly behind her.

It was Claudia.

She saw me and lifted her eyebrows. 'Can I come too?' She could be scarily perceptive could Claudia.

'To the beach?'

'Sounds good.' Claudia took off her coat with the spiky collar. The cold had formed perfect shiny beads on the wool. Now Claudia was one person who would never feel swamped by the fabulousness of other people's lives. She slid in opposite me and grabbed a menu.

'So . . .' Claudia said, 'what did you do last night to put you in such a dreamy state, young lady?'

'You mean, what was the girl who looks wild around the edges up to last night?'

'What are you talking about?'

I groaned and she slapped the menu shut.

'She was up to no good!' she proclaimed.

The stubble-cheeked Mediterranean waiter appeared at her elbow and she gave her order hastily.

'That was quick,' I said.

Claudia looked at me blankly.

'You usually string it out, you know, cos he's so scrummy?'

'I have no idea what you're talking about. Anyway this is much more exciting, so come on, tell me.' She did know damn well what I was talking about, of course. She was the world's best flirter. Especially with waiting staff. It's a pity there isn't an Olympic event for it really – she could double England's usual medal total easily.

'Well?' She was also persistent. Perceptive, flirtatious and persistent, a killer combination.

Well, here goes.

'I saw Charlie.'

'Charlie? Who's Charlie?'

'My first love, you know, the Big Teenage Romance.'

Claudia's eyes widened. 'Really? Isn't he the one you never wanted to see again?'

'Yes. And no.' I avoided her eyes. 'It's complicated.'

'I didn't know—'

'No one knew.'

I waited for her to say something but she didn't. And then my cursed blush began.

'Oh, something happened!' she squeaked.

A couple of people turned their heads towards the noise and I blushed harder.

Claudia lowered her voice. 'Was it good?'

'I didn't sleep with him.'

'Sure.'

'I didn't!' I took a sip of coffee, playing for time. I still wasn't sure what to say but there was no way I could go through the day without telling someone something.

'He did give me a lovely kiss goodbye.'

Claudia's eyes glittered with amusement. 'That makes for a nice change then.'

'What do you mean? I haven't been completely idle on the kissing front, thank you very much.'

'Last year was fairly quiet, Sam—'

'Thanks for the reminder. Anyway you're distracting me from the story!'

'Sorry, go on.'

I took another sip of my coffee and Claudia waited.

'It wasn't just that, Claudia, it was just that . . . we made a connection last night.'

Claudia threw back her head and hooted. 'Ooooh, the girl's in love!'

'Keep your voice down!' I hissed. God, she could be so embarrassing.

'What does Mara make of it?'

'Are you kidding? I'm not telling her. You know what she'll say, she can't stand him.'

'But she hasn't met him, has she?'

I shook my head. That was the problem. Mara's strongest opinions were about people she didn't know.

'It won't take her long to be on to you,' said Claudia. 'You're not exactly hard to read.'

'I'm not?'

'Definitely not. But it's one of your charms, my love.' Claudia smiled kindly at me and rubbed the top of my hand. It occurred to me she had probably said this to me before but like all the little observations friends make about each other, this one felt brand new, given my new situation. If I was so easy to read, wouldn't that mean Charlie could see right through me last night and see how desperately excited I was to see him? And wouldn't that send him running?

My phone. A text.

'See? That's probably Mara now, just confirming that when she looked in your eyes this morning, she could tell you'd been with Charlie the night before.'

I laughed and swiped my screen.

40

'I didn't see her—'

I stopped. My heart stopped. It was him.

> Thanks for a great night. It was gorgeous seeing u
> again. Hope we can do it again soon Cx

'Nice!' Claudia pronounced. She had leant over and read it upside down.

My heart was racing and my finger was so shaky it could barely make contact with the screen to press reply.

'Uh-uh,' Claudia said. 'Not yet.'

I withdrew my finger. 'Not yet?'

'Make him wait until you've finished breakfast.'

'After breakfast,' I murmured. I read it one more time. OK, five times.

It was *gorgeous* seeing you again.

BANG! BANG! BANG! went my heart.

But Claudia was right; she was the mistress of this stuff. So reluctantly I flipped the cover on the phone shut.

Claudia's breakfast arrived, pancakes with blueberries and maple syrup. I stared at it.

'What? A girl can't have a little comfort now and then?' Claudia asked me, sounding slightly defensive, something she never is. Strange.

'I wasn't thinking about your food, Claud,' I said. 'I just don't know what to do about Charlie.'

'What do you mean do? Just enjoy it.'

'But what will my Mum and Dad think? They weren't exactly devastated when we broke up.'

Claudia laughed. 'What's there to tell? You're not about to walk down the aisle – you're just having a little fun. God, Sam, lighten up.'

'I'm not uptight!' I resented that.

'Well, maybe not compared to your sister or Mara but, babe, you could just let yourself go and have a bit of fun without worrying about the future.' Claudia waggled a finger at me.

Rebecca. I grimaced. That mincing, eyelash-batting minx of a sister. When Charlie used to visit, Rebecca was nine and known as Becky. She would watch out for him arriving and rush upstairs to put on her prettiest dress, a pink tutu. She would then make her grand entrance, twirling into the room and ending, without fail, on Charlie's lap, her famous eyelashes going nineteen to the dozen. Those damn eyelashes – I ground my teeth – have remained the only generous thing about her. What would Rebecca do these days around Charlie? And then I smiled. Actually telling Rebecca about who I was seeing again could be fun. If indeed I was seeing him, of course . . . But even to casually mention I had been out on a date, implying there had been smooching, would be very satisfying indeed. Have some fun, Claudia said. Oh yes, I thought, I think that could just be possible.

A little later, Claudia put her knife and fork regretfully onto her plate.

'You haven't finished!' I was shocked.

'I know.' For a moment, Claudia looked almost . . . well, you could only describe it as sad. And Claudia was never sad.

'Are you OK, Claud?'

Claudia took a deep breath and she straightened her shoulders.

'Of course I am,' she said quickly, 'I just haven't got my usual appetite at the moment. Now how was Mara yesterday?' She was changing the subject.

'Mara?' I asked. 'She was still jumpy yesterday. I don't know what's going on. Actually I was wondering if she isn't well and that's why Ed's home early?' I suggested, remembering the brainwave I'd had in the shower.

Claudia frowned. 'It doesn't sound right to me. I think it's Ed she's worried about.'

'Yes, I thought that too but now I'm not so sure.' I pictured Ed twinkling at me across the kitchen table. He didn't look like someone who needed worrying about to me.

'Do you think it could be drugs?' Claudia asked.

'Drugs!' I squawked, my turn this time to get people turning their heads. 'No way, he's too smart for that.'

'Yes, that's true . . .' Claudia paused for a moment and looked at me as if she was searching for something.

'What?'

Claudia lowered her gaze and took a sip of her coffee. 'Oh nothing. I just think he's lovely.'

'You don't fancy him, do you?' Surely not. Claudia seemed so much more grown up than Ed. I couldn't imagine her ever seeing him as anything but a friend.

'Me? No, I don't fancy him.' Claudia looked me in the eye again. 'Do you?'

'Ed?' My head hurt. Do I like Ed? That wasn't even something to try thinking about. 'He's Mara's brother, and he feels like my brother too, I think,' I answered eventually.

Claudia lifted her shoulder in a tiny shrug.

'Me too,' she said.

10

SAM

Who am I kidding? I wondered, as I positioned my lamp to shine more directly onto my face. It really was too late to improve my looks at the ripe old age of thirty. Why hadn't I invested more time and money in looking after my skin in my twenties? More to the point, why hadn't I invested in a lamp that stayed in one place and didn't keep falling down? Of course I hadn't given a toss about my skin until I bumped into Charlie. I have, as a rule, looked down at the sad girls who spend too much time looking in the mirror when they could be doing more important things. Playing frisbee in the park, for instance, or drinking. Or both. But overnight the stakes had escalated and I had already spent a shameful number of minutes checking out every pore and hair on my face.

Specifically I was looking for my freckles. When I came back from breakfast with Claudia, I had shut myself in my room and spent minutes, several of the bastards, looking for signs of the cute freckles I was sure I'd had once upon a time. They had to be there somewhere but, after some time, I had to admit it. They'd gone. I'd lain on my bed in despair then, and the 'who was I kidding?' whine started in earnest in my tired, freckle-free head. That was when I spied my lamp. Sessions under a sunbed weren't an option. I couldn't even afford breakfast that morning (Claudia had paid, again). But the lamp might just be worth trying . . .

I wriggled as close as I could to the edge of the bed, my arm teetering on the side, and finally the lamp behaved itself and stayed in one place, shining directly onto my face. I was soon asleep.

★

I woke to a sharp voice.

'What on earth are you doing?'

I sat up and my head banged into something hard, making a loud 'clang'. Instinctively, I reached out and grabbed whatever was in the way.

'FUCK!' My hand registered the pain from holding hot metal in the same moment I remembered what I was doing. What a nightmare, and on top of it all I was dreaming that Rebecca was . . .

In my room.

Fucking brilliant. It wasn't a dream.

'What's that smell?' Rebecca squawked.

I shoved my hand into my mouth and then waved it in the air.

'Fucking hell that hurts!'

'It smells really wrong.'

She was right, of course. With the smell of burning paint in my nostrils, I gingerly reached out with my good hand and turned the lamp off. Perhaps a hundred-watt light bulb in there wasn't such a great idea after all.

'You should really put that under water, you know,' she said. So helpful, my sister.

'You think?'

I rushed past her and into the bathroom and thrust my hand under the cold tap. How many varieties of idiot was it possible for me to be in one day, I wondered. Damn my hand hurt. I braved looking in the mirror. I looked awful and—

45

'Your face is all red and blotchy, Samantha.'

She'd followed me into the bathroom. Awesome. And she was right – I was all red and blotchy, with dark circles under my eyes and a most tragic, pained expression on my face. I looked back down at my hand. I was in pain. Stupid, stupid Sam.

'I haven't seen you for a while, Rebecca.' I looked in the mirror again. There was a total of zero freckles.

There was a small pause as Rebecca no doubt considered whether or not to return to her original question of why I was asleep with a desk lamp pointed at my face, minutes away from burning the house down.

'I was in the area,' she sniffed.

Good, she was dropping the lamp. But I could hear her 'poor me' tone loud and clear. I was in the area because I wasn't with my boyfriend. If I was, I'd have no reason to come to this dump but as it is I'm terribly lonely. Yes, I could imagine exactly what was going through my sister's mind.

'Right.' My hand was freezing cold and starting to cramp up. I had a headache. Rebecca wasn't going anywhere fast. I turned the tap off and dried my hand. That would have to do.

'Shall we have a cuppa then?' I sighed and motioned Rebecca out of the room ahead of me. If I was sure of one thing it was that I wasn't entertaining Rebecca on my own. Mara and Ed could damn well help water her down. It was the least they could do, having lucked out so ridiculously in the sibling lottery.

The windows in the kitchen were fogged up. A cauldron of soup was simmering away on the hob, and Mara was at the kitchen bench surrounded by mounds of vegetables and dirty dishes. She withdrew her hand from inside the carcass of a chicken and waved fingers smeared in stuffing at Rebecca, who gave her a strained smile.

'She rises,' Ed said cheerfully.

I grunted at him.

'What happened to your face?'

'Don't talk to me.'

Ed shrugged and turned his attention to Rebecca.

'So what are you doing with yourself these days?' he asked her, pulling out a seat for her. I saw Rebecca relax instantly. Not a lot of course, because she never does relax like normal human beings, but Ed was definitely making her feel at home. My memory of him being a bit awkward at times really was way off. I glanced at Mara but she had her back to everyone, quite obviously trying to ignore the polite murmuring at the table while doing something complicated with the chicken.

'I've applied for a new job, for the firm Claudia works for,' Rebecca said a little louder, glancing at me briefly to make sure I was paying attention, and added, 'as PA to the head of marketing.'

I was lining cups along the bench with my left hand and concentrating on counting them to keep my mouth shut.

'Sounds exciting,' Ed said, actually sounding interested.

'Yes, he seems like a really nice man.'

'What's his name?' I asked.

'John Morgan.'

A snort escaped. John Morgan! I couldn't believe it.

'What's so funny?' She honed in on me then – she would love nothing better than some juicy gossip.

'Oh nothing.' I wasn't about to give away Claudia's connection to him. Especially not to Rebecca, who would surely manage to make it work to her advantage. She stared at me as I set her tea down in front of her.

'Is that skimmed milk in there?' she asked.

I didn't answer her. There was an uncomfortable silence as I picked my own cup up and joined them at the table.

'Are you staying for supper?' Ed asked her then.

47

I froze, my cup hovering between the table and my lips.

'Well, I only popped by for a cup of tea really . . .' Rebecca smiled sweetly at him, more than a little expectantly.

I tried to think of something to say to put her off.

'Well, I'm sure there's enough. Mara?' Ed bowled on. Scrap that assessment of him being Mr Social. The guy was a lunatic.

Mara paused. Please be in a straight-talking mood, I thought.

'That's fine, there's plenty to eat,' she said curtly.

Damn.

Ed helped pass the time before supper by showing Rebecca photos from India on his laptop, which helped make up for his brash invitation earlier. Any time I tried to talk to her I ended up feeling run over. But Ed was managing her beautifully and Rebecca – who, incidentally, had never shown any interest in life outside London before, let alone in what she would call a dirty third-world country – appeared to be deeply interested. In fact, if I hadn't known her better, I may even have said she was flirting with him, leaning in close to look at the screen, her dainty ankles crossed beneath her chair. 'Oh, she's pretty, isn't she? Those Indian girls have such lovely skin!' she cooed.

There was no way she would like him. He was too nice for her, for a start, and the guy didn't even have a job. He'd certainly never worked in the City. I watched him closely for signs of reciprocation. He was being very warm towards her, lots of smiles and charming, clever comments. I felt uneasy, remembering him remarking on Rebecca's looks the day before. But he was joking then, wasn't he? He couldn't possibly be attracted to her, could he? Not that I cared. Of course I didn't. As I sat with them, I thought about how satisfying it was going to be to wipe that pretty little smile off Rebecca's face when I told her about Charlie.

Eventually there was food on the table. Rebecca put a ridiculously small portion of everything on her plate.

'Hmmm, delish, sis,' Ed said through a mouth stuffed with roast chicken.

Mara raised her eyebrows. She wasn't into being called 'sis'.

Ed just grinned back, his lips oily with gravy.

Mara met my eye with a stony 'oh my god, they're both annoying' look.

'What did you get up to last night, Samantha?' Rebecca asked then, in-between one of her mouse-like mouthfuls.

A snuffly giggle escaped through Ed's nose.

'Samaaaaantha,' he drawled, in a bad imitation of Rebecca's cut-glass accent.

'Hey!' Rebecca dug him in the side.

I felt Mara flinch next to me. I couldn't believe it – they were definitely flirting. It was almost enough to put you off your food.

'So, sis?' Yuck, now she was imitating him.

'I was just out,' I said, fervently wishing this meal was over already.

'Very late,' Ed added.

'Yes, we got a bit carried away.' I felt myself blushing. Had I really just said that? I caught Ed's eye. He had gone quite still. I glanced at Mara, who had the same expression, and in that moment my glee at telling Rebecca about Charlie evaporated in front of the twins' concern. Dammit, I couldn't gloat in front of my friends, who actually cared about me, when I knew they'd disapprove.

'We?' Rebecca persisted.

'It was just a workmate I hadn't seen in a while. We had a lot of catching up to do,' I said quickly, willing my blush to bugger off.

'Anyone I know?' Rebecca's eyes glittered with interest.

'I'm not going to talk about it.'

'Oooooooh!'

'Just drop it, Rebecca.' I tried to give her a hard look then returned to my plate, forcing myself to eat a large piece of roast potato that took about fifty chews to get down.

'Leave her alone, it's her business,' Mara cut across Rebecca's cackle.

Rebecca giggled and put her hand over her mouth, and tried to engage Ed in some whispered, witty banter but he just laughed politely and didn't take the bait.

I took the gap in the conversation as the perfect time to change topics. It was time to see how upset Rebecca really was.

'So Mum told me you and . . .'

'James,' she said, her amusement evaporated.

'Ah yes, you and James broke up?'

'Yes.' Rebecca looked at her hands.

I waited for her to say more but she'd gone quiet, her eyes not moving from her hands.

'What happened?' Ed asked her.

Rebecca opened her mouth to say something but instead her hands flew to her face. Her shoulders were shaking. I leant forward in my chair and tried peering up into her face. Could it be? It was. Real tears. Impressive. I hadn't seen such a stellar performance from her for some time.

'Amazing,' Mara muttered.

Ed glared at us and put an arm around Rebecca when it was clear that I wasn't going to. I exhaled noisily through my nose. The tears might be wet, Ed, but I'd put money on them not being real.

'What happened, Rebecca?' Ed asked her again.

'He . . . he . . . he says he's . . . not ready for a commitment!' she gasped in-between jagged, teary gulps. She was really laying it on nice and thick now.

'Surely you didn't take him home to meet Mum and Dad?' I had to ask. If it ever got serious enough to meet the 'rentals,

Rebecca would usually ask them up to London for lunch. She was too embarrassed to take them back to the red-brick semi we grew up in. With its small garden and lack of antique furniture, it was way off the image Rebecca had been carefully cultivating for herself since childhood.

Rebecca shot her a poisonous look. 'Don't be a bitch!'

Bingo.

'All right, Sam, can't you be nicer than that?' Ed gave me a stern look. I sighed.

'Sorry,' I said. And I was. I didn't like how uncomfortable I felt when Ed looked at me like that. Like he was disappointed in me. It didn't sit right. So I tried again.

'How long have you been with this guy anyway?'

Rebecca blew her nose. 'Four months. I've told you about him!'

'You did?'

Rebecca scoffed. 'Typical. What do you care anyway?'

'I do!'

'Strange way of showing it,' she muttered, looking down at her hands again.

And finally one of my heartstrings was genuinely pulled, and against my better judgement, I softened. I felt the familiar, sinking feeling that always occurred when spending time with Rebecca and I knew there was no point resisting it. There was no way but Rebecca's way. I sighed.

'Would you like to stay tonight?' I asked her.

11

CLAUDIA

I didn't have my usual get-up-and-go today. My fingers were struggling to achieve anything near their usual pitter-patter speed, and had been petering out into far too frequent pauses. I kept finding myself just staring into the middle of the office. It wasn't like I hadn't made an attempt at cheering myself up this morning either. I'd poured myself into my current fave suit – a charcoal pinstripe pencil skirt, teamed with that gorgeous peplum (I loved that word) jacket that cinched in my waist and then flared out in pleats. It was a sort of modern Edwardian number I liked to think. All the accent on the rounded buttocks. But it wasn't working today. I still felt rubbish and I kept shuffling in my seat trying to get comfortable. I was itchy down there. Yuck.

I refused to be ill. Other people may get colds and flu and whatever else and retreat to bed, buried in sodden tissues. But not me. If a tickle dared to form in my throat, I just slugged back some Jägermeister and got on with it. I was sure that self-pity simply made things worse, and good health simply relied on having the right attitude and the appropriate liquor. But this was different. This was all wrong. Whatever this was, it was giving the old Jägermeister the fingers and burying in further. A dull ache that had been niggling inside since before Ed got back hadn't subsided either, and I couldn't bear to think about what was happening to my thirty-quid underwear. Whatever it was wasn't shifting with Persil alone.

Anyway back to the office. At some point I had kind of given up on trying to concentrate and was standing at my window, gazing over Canary Wharf, when a voice at the door startled me.

'Claudia?' It was John Tightpants, or John Morgan, Head of Marketing, as he was known to everyone who wasn't me (and Sam, and Mara, and Kate – oh and of course that time I was at the pub when I told almost every person I met that night about him).

'Sorry, is this a good time?' he asked.

'Yes, it's fine, John, have a seat.' I crossed the room to join him. I wanted to say no, John, it isn't all right at all. But I didn't. I can't say that to the head of marketing, can I?

He sat down and patted the vacant spot on the sofa. I pretended not to notice and sat down in a seat adjacent to him. I asked him what I could do for him.

He sat there, knees apart, his groin straining for attention in those irresistibly tight pants beneath his trousers. Behind his back, people around the office (mostly women) call him Daniel Craig. But, just quietly, I think he's actually more handsome than Mr Bond: his face kinder, his lips more generous. He is, in fact, the best-looking man in the building with a panting following from women and men of all ages, and as he bulged in front of me this morning, I tried very hard to push away the memories of the incredible sex I'd had with him. Because we can't be together – I will never let that happen.

'I've had a look at your shortlist for the assistant-marketing-director role.' John smiled confidently at me, his eyes twinkling. He, of course, being so confident, had been ignoring the fact that I'd been avoiding him for a month, and at every meeting he still managed to talk shop and scream sex with his eyes.

I took the offered sheaves of A4, the five excellent CVs of two men and three women who'd applied for the role, and flicked through them briefly.

'So these are the ones you'd like to have back in for a second interview?' I said, risking a quick glance at his face.

'I think so, the very top five you had on your preference list. You have great judgement, Claudia.'

No, I haven't, I'd thought then. It wasn't good judgement to get over-excited at Hadyn's leaving do and go home with him. It wasn't good judgement at all. The sex was amazing, incandescent, but so stupid. Worse than the sex, I haven't been able to get him out of my mind, which makes me feel exposed somehow. *And* it was against my rules to screw men on the same or higher management level as me. That was an absolute no-go. I was happy to turn on the charm to help me get up the ladder, but no one was going to say I slept my way to the top!

I wished he'd stop looking at me like that. Like he was sure there would be a repeat performance some day.

'Well then, I'll get Susie to get them back in,' I'd said brightly, standing up as if I was in a huge hurry.

John stood too.

'Right. Good,' he said.

He paused, and honestly it felt like he was trying to twinkle his way inside me.

'By the way, Susie's found me a very good PA too. Very professional,' he said.

'Excellent.' I opened the door for him and stood back to let him out. 'I'm giving Susie more reign to recruit on her own without me looking over her shoulder, so your PA wasn't under my radar. I hope she works out,' I said.

'I'm sure she will,' John said, and slowly walked past me to the door. 'See you soon then.'

He was gone. I leant against the door. I'd held my breath in an effort not to smell him as he walked past me but it was no use. His scent lingered on in my office for the rest of the day, teasing me.

12

ED

I watched Mara set off to work on her bike. She'd just picked up speed when some idiot stepped out onto the road without looking a few yards ahead of her. There was plenty of time for her to brake but in the end she had to swerve to avoid them.

'Whoa!' I shouted into the silent room. What was up with her? Did she have so much on her mind she didn't see that guy? Or were her brakes too soft? I waited until she'd completely disappeared from view, imagining she was surrounded by a protective shell. If only she was. The reality was so different. She always seemed so tough but she was just as fragile as everyone else inside and who other than me could really look after her? Mum was off in her new life, Dad was too sad and Kate had the kids to look after.

After a bit I went and stood in Sam's doorway again. I had started doing this whenever both the girls were out. I didn't ever go in – that would feel too pervy. It was sad enough standing and looking into her room. Sam's bed was unmade and I could just make out the impression her body had left behind, indicating she either got out of bed in a hurry or was a lazy so-and-so. The clothes lying across the end of her bed, all over her floor and disappearing under her desk like children trying to hide, pointed to the latter. On her desk was a framed family photograph, peeking out from behind a tower of magazines. I guessed that

Sam must have been about ten when the photo was taken. She was standing with her family in front of a tent: Richard in shorts, his beard just starting to grey; Alison in a lemon dress, peering out from under a Lady Di fringe; the girls both brown-limbed and grinning. They looked untidy and relaxed, with no sign of the polished Rebecca that existed now. Sam looked as if she was enjoying a good joke.

I stood at her door and wished I was a less principled person. I wished I was the sort of person who could march right in and start rifling through her stuff. But I just couldn't. I wandered back to the sitting room and stood there for a moment, lost in one of those all too frequent moments, not knowing what on earth to do with myself. I stared absently at the bookshelves. Novel after novel by extremely clever women: Margaret Atwood, A. S. Byatt, Barbara Kingsolver, Toni Morrison, Joyce Carol Oates. All Mara's obviously. I tried to picture a time I've seen Sam holding a book. Nope. Nothing doing. There was a whole shelf of DVDs. Then there were Mara's photo albums. I paused. If Mara's photo albums were there, then maybe . . . I moved closer to the shelves. There, shoved on top of Mara's photo albums, was a tatty cardboard box with 'random photos' written on the side in Sam's writing. Of course Sam wouldn't have her photos all neatly displayed in albums like Mara. I couldn't believe my luck! I took them out, my heart racing. This wasn't snooping, I told my conscience. The sitting room is communal. No it isn't. Yes it is! Oh shut up.

I sat down on the futon and took the lid off. They were Sam's all right – loads of them. I took a stack out. The first one was of Claudia, Sam and Mara raising their glasses to the camera in front of a eucalyptus. That must be Melbourne, where they met each other originally. Sam and Claudia had obviously drunk enough wine to look all loose around the eyes. Mara was smiling her closed-lipped little smile, her eyes unreadable, not letting herself go. Who took the photo? Mara's expression would point to Mark – her one-time shit of a boyfriend.

I kept flicking. There were endearing photos of a badly dressed Sam as a child, photos of her as a teenager with too much hair and awkward posture, all muddled up with photos of her as an adult, her arms flung around this person or that. There were a lot of photos of her travels. Lush rice paddies in Thailand. Long, empty beaches in Australia. That glacier she visited in New Zealand. Then I came across a photo of me and the girls, taken three or four years ago. Sam was in-between Mara and I, with only half of Mara's face in the frame. She had an arm around both of our necks, pulling us in, squashing our faces against hers. My glasses were askew, making me look goofy, and my smile almost took up the whole of my face. I placed my thumb over Mara so it was just Sam and me. I felt an ache in my chest. I remembered that time well. It was around the time I started admitting to myself I was in love with her.

The doorbell jangled me out of my dream and I looked up sharply. I shoved the other photos back into the box, returned it to the shelf and hurried to the intercom with the photo still in my hand.

'Hello?' I answered, my heart pounding.

'Ed? I was about to give up.'

It was Rebecca. What the hell was she doing here at ten o'clock on a weekday?

'Erm . . . hi,' I said.

'Can you let me in? I think I've left something there.'

And curses, I couldn't think of a good reason to say no.

I checked the sitting room, scanning it quickly to check I hadn't left any photos lying around. And then Rebecca was there, about to knock on the front door. I reached for the lock, remembering just before I opened it to stuff the photo into my pocket.

'Hi!' Rebecca said brightly.

'Come in, come in, it's freezing out there.' I motioned to her to come inside. Nervousness always makes me talk about the weather and I despised myself for it.

'Horrible day,' Rebecca said gaily as she walked towards the kitchen, turning her head to look into Sam's room as she passed, and I got this horrible feeling she knew I'd been standing there only a few minutes before.

'Yes, it does look awful. I haven't been out yet,' I continued. Pathetic.

'Been catching up on your beauty sleep then have you?' She stood next to the radiator in the kitchen and warmed her hands. I laughed uncertainly.

'So . . . how's the job-hunting going?' she asked me.

'Ah, OK. My friend has some hours next week. I don't really feel like I've arrived yet,' I answered.

'I know how you feel.'

Somehow I doubted that. I put the kettle on, and turned and leant against the worktop.

'What have you left behind?' I asked her, wondering how long I would have to make this painful small talk before she would leave again.

'My address book – I'll check her room in a minute. Thought it would be nice to see you while I was here.'

'Right.'

The kettle growled in the awkward silence. I was suddenly hyper aware of the photo in my back pocket and I moved away from the worktop slightly so I wouldn't crush it.

'Have you seen James this week?' I asked her.

Rebecca's face darkened for a moment and then cleared, as if she was pushing away any negative feelings by force.

'No. I'm not chasing him either. A bit of distance is probably the best thing.'

I nodded. Now I was all out of questions.

'Kettle's boiled.' Rebecca pointed behind me.

'Ah, yes.' I busied myself with making her tea.

'Are you not having one?' she asked.

'I've just had a coffee.'

'Ooooh, would you make me one of your coffees? I've heard they're amazing!' Rebecca's gushing chafed my nerves but I found myself obediently lowering the kettle and moving to the coffee machine instead.

'I'll have a quick look then. While you make that,' she said.

'Right.'

After a bit, she came out of Sam's room holding the photo of them camping and my stomach lurched when I saw it in her hand. For a crazy moment I thought she was going to ask me why I had been looking at it myself.

'It's not in there, so that's a mystery,' she prattled away. 'Found this though. Didn't notice it the other night – it must have been hiding.'

I really hoped I looked surprised.

'Look how skinny we were!' she said, her eyes wide.

'You're still thin!'

'I am.' Rebecca smiled coyly.

'So is Sam.'

'In a size twelve sort of way,' she said, looking at the photo again with her head to the side and then turning to me, a conspiratorial look on her face.

I looked at the photo again, too cross to answer her. Sam's got a gorgeous body, a damn sight more attractive than the head on sticks standing in the kitchen next to me. I am constantly amazed at how two sisters can be so different from each other. What was it that Sam told me about her? Something about Rebecca pretending when she was little that she was actually a royal living with the Moriarty family in Petersfield, placed there to give her a normal upbringing. When she turned eighteen, a Rolls-Royce would come and collect her, to take her to the life she was always destined to lead. She must have had quite a shock when the Rolls didn't turn up.

'So . . .' Rebecca looked mischievously at me. 'Have you found out who she was with the other night?'

'No, and it's none of my business!' I said, too quickly to be very convincing.

'Whatever! She'll spill the beans before too long, she can never keep anything to herself.' Rebecca laughed a hard little laugh that didn't match her carefully groomed exterior then stared into her coffee. For a moment, she seemed to have forgotten that I was sitting there in front of her. But then she shook her head, clearing the thoughts from her mind and looked up.

'Not like you, Ed. You're quite the dark horse,' she said.

'I am?' I squirmed under her steady gaze, my mouth dry with dread.

13

SAM

Wrangling annoying extras, trying to keep children warm and having to be polite to their overbearing parents was difficult enough on an average day. It was even more difficult when a girl felt compelled to check her phone every half hour, without anyone noticing. It had been three whole sleeps since our date and the text he'd sent about how gorgeous it was to see me. My patience was almost broken enough to contact him. I wasn't going to though; I'd promised myself I wouldn't be that weak. I would have some fun, like Claudia said, without throwing myself at him. I did have *some* pride. I'm not completely sure where exactly . . . Anyway it was hard to check for text messages when everyone was meant to have their phones off. Especially when I'm essentially another set of eyes and ears for the first – who had to have a quiet set.

Today I was working on a commercial for an insurance firm. Most of it was inside, in a pretty grand house in Highgate, but there were a few set-ups on the driveway outside. The script went: family (the children overexcited, the parents looking harassed) are leaving a children's birthday party, they pile into their car and then the father reverses – crunch – into the fence. The ad ends with the rest of the children spilling out of the house when they hear the noise, yelling in unison, 'You should have insured with Carsure!' It was riveting stuff.

All morning there had been much umming and ahhing over the weather, which had completely buggered up the proposed schedule. We were meant to shoot the exterior scenes last but as it had been threatening to rain all morning, the decision had been made to push on and get the outside shots done before the rain made it impossible. Unfortunately for me this had meant keeping fifteen extras, all aged around eight years old, plus their parents, quiet and happy inside all morning, while they waited for the scene when they were all due to emerge from the house, yelling about insurance – obviously the first thing on every eight-year-old's mind. Whatever bright spark had written this script and thought they needed so many kids at this party (couldn't they tell it with, say, six kids?) had obviously never been a third. And the extras! They weren't the usual, well-behaved lot from an agency or a drama school or whatever – they were the children and friends of the client. A few of them were plugged into screens of one sort or another but most of them were horsing about and looking at me with an insolent eye, while the mums (with a couple of exceptions) gossiped and flicked through magazines.

'Come in, Sam, over.' The radio crackled on my hip.

'Receiving, over.' At last, the first! That had to be the call for my extras to stand by for their scene surely. Or, even better, we were wrapping for lunch. I glanced at my watch – one o'clock already, no wonder I was hungry. I watched a heavyset boy get up onto a chair and prepare himself to jump off into an area of floor littered with discarded shoes and toys, most of them with wheels.

'Stand by for updated schedule. We're stopping now to discuss, over.'

'Roger, over.'

Crap. I shoved my radio back into its holster and reached the boy just before he jumped off, taking him by the arm and guiding him firmly to the ground.

'Ow, that hurt!' The boy shook off my hand. I looked at his flaccid face and saw a boy who didn't get enough exercise or the word no. I sighed noisily – it was either that or scream.

'I want Dad!' he demanded, rubbing his arm some more.

A pretty Asian woman appeared then. 'Don't worry, Henry. Daddy's busy being big man outside right now, you see him soon.'

Big man? Did she really just say that without any irony at all?

'But I want him now!'

'Come on, Henry, come and see what Nanny Chu has for you in her bag, it's your favourite,' and she took him out of my reach, thankfully, before I banged their heads together.

Taking a chance that no one would come looking for me, I quickly popped out of the back door of the house (the extras and I were holed up in the family room slash conservatory at the back of the house, out of the way of the camera at the front) and walked quickly to the corner of the building to peer around. The camera base was under a pop-up gazebo on the driveway at the front of the house, a good thirty yards from where I stood. Even from this distance I could tell that the tension on set had moved up a few notches from edgy (fuelled only by adrenaline) to unpleasant (fuelled by fear). Overhead, the clouds loomed darkly, while on the ground, the director, DOP, first, gaffer, producer and client were huddled together. Ridiculously, the producer still had his 'client smile' plastered on his face, although the stress had frozen it into a frightened rictus. He would look so much more convincing if he just frowned. But who would have the balls to tell him that? I watched the gaffer break away to peer at the sky through a gaffer's glass, looking for the position of the sun behind the clouds. My heart sank.

That would indicate they were discussing the next shot, not lunch. My tummy rumbled.

I turned to go back to the conservatory of hell when a boy shot past me, running straight for the gazebo. It was Henry. I was wrong about the lack of exercise – he could move.

'Henry! Come back.' Nanny Chu staggered past me in her heels, her hands pawing the air in front of her, looking a little like she was practising her doggy paddle in what I can only assume was an attempt to make herself go faster. Henry wasn't listening; he was hell-bent on reaching that gazebo in record time and he was going so fast he looked like he was going to run straight into the meeting without stopping. My hand reached for the radio but wavered, not sure if a message on the radio would serve to warn my first of the incoming spoilt missile or distract her. As it was, it all happened too fast for me to stop it. Henry went to barrel into his father from behind but in the second before he made contact, his dad must have heard him – or more likely the squawking from the nanny – and half turned, just as Henry made contact, his dad's elbow fitting neatly into the socket of Henry's right eye. Henry reeled back, clutching his eye and screaming. Only then did my feet get into gear and I ran over to join the chaos. As I pulled up short of the group, the first fixed me with an icy stare.

'Get back to the extras, Sam,' she said, before motioning to the runner to fetch an ice pack from inside. I turned to go but she said my name again. It was really noisy with Henry going on and on, the producer flapping about apologising to the client and no doubt bitterly regretting his poorly thought-out 'sure, what a great idea to have your son and his friends as the extras – he'll love it!' But I heard her all right. I could probably hear her 100 yards away, just speaking in her usual voice. There was something about firsts that always made you hear what they had to say. Something to do with consequences and all hell breaking

65

loose, and being ever so slightly terrified of them at all times – something like that.

I turned back. She wasn't looking at me but at the ground. There, just behind Henry's anguished stomping feet, was my phone, the screen all lit up and blindingly bloody obviously *on*. Oh crap.

I scooped it up, fumbling to press the off switch.

'Oops,' I said, cringing. The first didn't say a thing; she didn't have to. Her look, cutting straight through my flaky ex-boyfriend-stalking bullshit was cold and clear. Sort it out, Sam. Now.

14

MARA

Kate kissed Rosie and Luke as they sat on either side of Ed like two wriggling bookends.

'Kids, listen to me – you be good kids for Aunty Mara and Uncle Ed,' she said, trying to get one of them at least to look her in the eye. 'Lights out at half past seven, no later!'

'You're in the way, Mum,' Luke whined. He tried peering around her to see the television.

'Charming.' Kate gave up and turned to me. I was standing in the doorway, watching the little scene with amusement. 'There's a treat in the tin for you two in the kitchen and wine somewhere. Cook yourselves whatever you want. Sorry I haven't got anything prepared,' she said to me, glancing at the book I was holding. 'They might not want to read, Mars, not when the telly's on, sorry.'

'I'll give it my best shot. Anyway, Ed will listen, won't you?' I said, waving the book at the sofa. 'It's *The Tiger Who Came to Tea*!'

'Ooooh, my favourite!'

'Favewit! Favewit!' Rosie chorused and jumped up and down next to Ed.

'Well, that one might work,' Kate conceded. 'She's completely obsessed with cats at the moment.'

'See? Now push off out of here before you're late, don't worry about us.'

We walked to the front door together.

'Have you heard from Dad lately?' she asked, pulling on a rose coat that hugged her slim frame.

'No, have you?'.

'Not a squeak. It's like he doesn't have grandchildren,' she said bitterly.

I took her arm. 'Don't take it personally. You know he just shut down after Mum left. He isn't in touch with anyone, it's not just you.'

'I know.' Kate threw her handbag over her shoulder, frowning. 'I just worry about him.'

'There's only so much we can do, Katie.'

'I suppose so.'

'Ed hasn't seen him properly yet. When he does I'll tag along and check in on him, how about that? Now, you stop your worrying.'

'I'll try.' Kate opened the door. 'Thanks for everything.'

'There's just one thing I need to tell you,' I said.

'Yes?' Kate turned, still looking worried.

'You look beautiful.'

Kate's pretty face broke into a smile, her chin falling to her chest in the bashful expression she'd carried over from child-hood. I hugged her. Dear little Kate, she deserved the best after the crap she'd endured through the break-up with Martin, that slimy excuse for a human being.

A little under an hour later, I was starting to envy Kate's night out.

'Upstairs now, Rosie. No more arguing.' Was that the millionth time I had said that, or the millionth and one? Rosie responded by jumping from one sofa to the next, squealing in delight. I was sure I had never seen the kids so wound up, thanks to Ed. There I was thinking it would be a perfect opportunity for having a heart to heart with him by bringing him babysitting with me. What a joke.

'Come on!'

Squeal, squeal, squeal.

'Ed, can you grab her? This is all your fault.'

'How so, sis?'

'Don't call me that!'

Ed tucked Rosie under one arm and left the room.

I stared at his back disappearing up the stairs. When exactly did he become so annoying?

Eventually I had Ed to myself. I pushed aside the domestic detritus on the table to make two plate-sized spaces. A plastic duck hovered close to the side of the table. I considered moving it but decided, on balance, that I was too exhausted to care. I'd assumed the kids would get less tiring as they got older, but it appeared the opposite was true. How did Kate cope? I sat down and groaned.

Thankfully Ed put a plate of food in front of me in record time. My favourite slap-up supper – poached eggs on toast. And look, the dear thing had tarted them up with chilli.

'Sorry if I was grumpy before.'

'It doesn't matter.' Ed smiled reassuringly. In a light voice – as if it didn't matter at all – he added, 'Rebecca came by today.'

'What?' The idea of that piece of work sneaking around my home outside chaperone hours almost had me shouting.

'She thought she'd left something behind, an address book, I think she said.'

'Riiiight . . .' My fork still hovered over my food. I hoped Ed's story was going to get better.

'She's a strange girl, isn't she?' he said.

I exhaled and stabbed my knife through the egg and toast. 'Strange is one word you could use. I could think of several others more pertinent.'

Ed picked up the plastic duck and turned it over in his hand.

'It was almost as if the address book was just an excuse to come round . . .'

You don't say. I knew I had to pick my words carefully. 'She was being very friendly with you the other night,' I said finally, not quite able to meet his eye.

'She was,' Ed addressed the fridge. 'But I'm not actually convinced that was why she was there. I can't quite work it out . . .'

I waited for him to say more but he didn't.

'Well, you know I don't trust her, Ed. It always feels like she's got some kind of agenda. It usually involves having something over Sam.'

'Why would she want to do that?' Ed frowned.

'I really have no idea.'

There was a small silence as I chewed my last mouthful. Ed continued to frown.

'Ed?' I had to ask him. I just had to.

'Yes?'

'What brought you back from India so quickly?'

Ed let out a long sigh and started building a tower. I waited. I knew trying to hurry him wouldn't help. On the bottom went two pieces of oversized orange Lego, followed by a stack of junk mail, a book and a small bag of lentils. The plastic duck was placed on top.

'It's a long story.'

'I'm not going anywhere.'

He looked at me and sighed again.

'I thought that going away would make things better . . .'

But he got no further. From the top of the stairs came the sound of Luke roaring.

'Rosie, you can't poo there!'

ED

'Grab that table, Ed. I'll get us some food.' Claudia pointed to somewhere right over on the other side of the café. I looked across the sea of office workers and took a deep breath before wading in. As I wove between tables, it became very obvious to me, and most likely the entire bloody café, that I was the only man in the room not suited and booted. The men's glances only grazed me as I passed them. He's obviously not worth networking with, I could hear them thinking. But perhaps I was being unfair. They probably weren't even thinking about work at all. In fact, the conversations I heard snatches of were mostly about games played at the weekend. Of course they were. But the women were different. I could feel their glances burning holes through the back of my trousers. I was a bit of rough standing out in all the suits. Ha! That improved my mood.

Claudia brought over a mountain of food.

'Thanks! What do I owe you?' I asked her.

'Absolutely not, this is my treat.'

I knew better than to argue. Claudia is aggressively generous and there is no point fighting it.

'So what brings you down here? I presume it's not the fishing?' she asked as she passed me a plate.

'You're right. Although if I was in the mood, Canary Wharf

wouldn't be a bad place for it,' I said, bending my head to a table of women nearby.

'I didn't know you were into the polished variety, Ed. Wouldn't have picked them as your type at all.'

'No. You're right.' Of course she was. She usually was, which is why Claudia was such a good person to talk to. She didn't bend anything to make it easier to hear.

'But it has been a long time between drinks, has it not?' Claudia asked.

Oh, and she never edged around a topic.

'It's Sam,' I said.

'I thought so.'

'Have I been that obvious?'

Claudia put down her sandwich and looked at me with pity. I didn't like the look of that at all. 'Do you want an honest answer?'

'I suppose so.' Yes, of course I did, but for a moment I wasn't sure if I was ready for whatever she had to say at all.

'It's obvious to me but I'm not entirely sure if Sam has figured it out yet.'

I supposed that was a good thing in some ways, but the whole reason for coming back from India so quickly was to see if she would notice, wasn't it? The café clattered with chatter and metal on china and suddenly it seemed too loud in there, like everyone else was having important conversations, living their important lives, while I was there to ask my friend a question that had no point to it at all. It was obvious Sam was never going to look at me as important, never see me as central in her life. I would remain on the outside, just like my scruffiness set me apart in this company. Suddenly all I wanted to do was leave.

'Tell me what you want to know, Ed. You can't come all this way and then look terrified.' Claudia reached out and laid a hand on my sleeve, as if she knew she had to keep me sitting there for a few more minutes.

'Why can you read me so easily?' I said.

'It's a gift, one of my few.' Claudia grinned at me. Was I seeing things or could I see a hint of sadness behind that smile? Maybe, maybe not. But she was right – I did have to ask her.

'I wondered if you knew who she was seeing,' I managed to say, my voice coming out all quiet and uncertain.

Claudia raised her eyebrows at me, took another bite of her sandwich and chewed it slowly. I tried again.

'She was out really late on Saturday with someone . . .' My voice petered out. I sounded like a petulant child who wasn't getting what I wanted, which I was really.

Claudia finally put down her sandwich.

'Are you asking me to tell you something that Sam told me in confidence?'

'So you know?' My heart beat faster.

Claudia sighed.

'Ed, I will tell you, only because you're going to have to be patient with this one. He's a biggie.'

'A biggie?' I didn't like the sound of that.

'Her first love.'

I racked my brain for a name.

'Charles Hugh-Barrington. Otherwise known as Charlie. Saw him in her last year at college.'

It wasn't ringing any bells but all the same my hands suddenly felt slick.

'Ed.' Claudia reached across the table for the second time. 'I don't know what's going to happen with this but I've got a feeling that Sam might need to get him out of her system. And she may never move on from him,' she added.

I looked at the cheesecake I knew I couldn't possibly eat.

'Were you finally going to do something about her?' she asked me.

'About who?' said a woman's voice.

Out of nowhere, standing next to our table, was Rebecca.

'Jesus!' I recoiled from her.

'Sorry, didn't mean to give you a fright!' What was with this girl? She was everywhere.

'What are you doing here?' Claudia asked.

'I work here!' She was glowing with pride.

'You do?'

'Yes and apparently you know my boss? A certain John Morgan?'

Claudia looked shocked. 'You're his new PA?'

'That's me! Exciting, isn't it? Mind if I join you? You could dish all the dirt on him.'

'Actually . . .' Claudia stood up and shot me an apologetic look. 'I've got to get back. Have my seat.'

'Oh are you sure?' But Rebecca sat down before I'd even had time to blink, let alone say goodbye to Claudia. This was too much to take in. Now I really had to get as far away as I could from this hive of chirpy office workers, particularly the one beaming at me across the table.

'I wasn't interrupting anything, was I?' Rebecca asked brightly.

I started getting out of my chair.

'Actually, I really need to go. Sorry. Running late.' It was completely against my nature to be so rude but I really couldn't do this.

Rebecca looked a bit shocked but then stood with me.

'Of course, sorry, I shouldn't have just barged in like that.'

'Oh you didn't, honestly, I just have to go.'

Rebecca motioned to my food. 'You've hardly eaten anything.'

'You can have it!'

Rebecca looked blank. Of course she wouldn't eat my leftover food. God, this was awkward.

'I mean . . .'

Rebecca smiled brightly. 'Look, you go, Ed, but before you do I was just this moment wondering who might come to a party I've been invited to on Friday night.'

I was doing a bad job of putting my jacket on. I couldn't seem to negotiate my left arm into the armhole. I was distracted. I was in a hurry.

'Oh, right.'

'Would you like to come with me?'

She totally nailed it. All I could answer, before my mouth could engage with my brain was – 'Sure, sounds great. See you soon.'

16

SAM

From what I could see, Mara seemed pretty healthy. She was sipping slowly on one of her careful little halves of Guinness. She hadn't lost any weight. I looked at her tummy. Seemed the same size as usual. I remember when Mum's friend Chrissy was really sick with something – maybe cancer – her stomach became really bloated, like she was pregnant. It looked horrible. Unnatural on a fifty-something-year-old. But Mara's tum looked like it always did. Sturdy I'd describe it as, but not to her obviously. I returned to her face. Maybe she was paler than normal? But it was winter, and she was usually the colour of a freshly painted white wall anyway. Mara was listening very closely to Claudia talking quietly about her dad's gall bladder. It looked like her ears were operating as normal. I was probably worrying about nothing, I told myself, and drifted back to thinking about Charlie. Mara had other ideas.

'Sam, have I got something on my face?' she said a little crossly.

'No,' I replied.

'You're staring at me.'

'No I'm not,' I said, denying it out of habit. I really wasn't in the mood for getting into trouble with her again.

She held my gaze.

'Maybe I was a little bit,' I conceded. I stammered on, 'I-I was wondering if you're all right.'

'I'm fine,' she said frostily, frowning at me.

'Are you sure there's something you aren't telling us? Something to do with your health?'

'Of course there isn't, I'm very healthy!' She shot a glance at Claudia, as if questioning my sanity.

'Well, that's good then.' I looked at my hands. I wasn't getting very far here.

Then she softened her voice slightly, 'Honestly, I'm fine. What made you ask?'

I caught Claudia giving me an encouraging smile so I braved meeting Mara's eyes again.

'It's just that, well . . .' It was no use; I was floundering around like a tongue-tied teenager. I had never made much of a point of confronting Mara about her moods, generally because she was pretty constant. She was . . . well, she was just Mara most of the time. But it was pointless even going there with her. She was useless at talking about herself, bloody useless.

'Spit it out, Sam.'

'All right. Sheesh.' I took a deep breath. 'It started when Ed came back. Before, in fact. You seemed a bit . . .' I tried to think of a kinder word but couldn't. 'Uptight before Ed came back, and I thought you were worried about him, but now he's back . . . well, he seems all right to me but you're still jumpy,' I ended in a rush.

Mara looked at me with her hard stare, her flaring nostrils the only thing moving on her face. But she still didn't say anything.

I plunged on. 'It, erm, got me thinking that maybe it's yourself you're worried about, rather than Ed. I mean, he's OK, maybe a bit lost, not sure what to do next, but he's in good shape, right?'

'Good shape?' Mara asked and raised her eyebrows.

'His mind,' I clarified. I looked from Mara to Claudia. Mara looked like she was steeling herself for something and Claudia was leaning forward a little, her eyes wide open, in an almost . . . expectant way. Strange. Oh my God. Surely not!

'You don't think I like him, do you?' I almost shouted in disbelief. 'You've got to be joking!'

Mara's eyebrows lowered slowly. I looked at Claudia but she didn't say anything, just sat back in her chair and hid behind her drink.

'I mean, don't get me wrong, Mara, he's a great guy and everything . . .' I paused, giving Mara another chance to say something, any bloody thing. No wonder she was so tense! You'd have be Mother Bloody Teresa to be good enough for Mara's twin. But she was staring at her drink now, not saying a thing, not even looking like she was about to say anything. She looked all hard and disapproving and something else, something that looked a lot like fear . . . There was only one thing to do. It looked like I'd have to put all the cards on the table. Mara needed to know what was happening then she'd know for sure she had nothing to worry about.

'Well, aside from him being your brother, Mara, I'm actually seeing someone.' This wasn't a proven fact yet, of course, but I was desperate.

'You are?' Mara said. She looked shocked. Good. A good start. Definitely a step on from looking scared.

'I am, and you won't approve!'

'Go on.' Mara reached for her drink.

So I told her all about Charlie and rather than being painful, the conversation I had been dreading having with her actually turned out to be a rocking good time. OK, so it was only because, in comparison, the horror of me seducing Ed seemed like much the greater evil. It was so much fun talking about it that I threw myself head first into the telling, really playing up the role of the stupid girl who can't think straight when she's infatuated (I didn't have to pretend that bit, of course), tossing my hair about and everything. Mara listened to every word with just the odd exclamation of 'Sam, you silly girl!' and 'What a smarmy tosser!' and other pearls in gruff, disdainful tones, while her body language showed loud and clear what she was actually feeling – sweet fucking relief.

The evening took a distinct turn for the better after that. I was very glad not to be talking about Ed any longer. It started to turn into a relaxed Friday-night drink. It obviously wasn't going to be a big one. Claudia wasn't drinking (watching the calories apparently), Mara always drank modestly and I wasn't really in the mood for a big night. We were just getting to the yawning-let's-go-home-to-the-telly part of the evening when Mara, who had the best view of the pub, said, 'What's he doing here?'

A moment later, standing next to our table in his signature Howies jacket, his faded olive-green satchel slung across his chest, was Ed.

'Good question, what are you doing here, Ed?' I asked him.

'You sure know how to make a girl feel welcome,' he said, sitting down.

'You're a pretty funny-looking girl.'

'Full of compliments, Sam, as usual.' He reached across the table and took Mara's drink.

'Oi! That's mine. A drink being drunk by a girl because this is a girls' night out!'

'Don't worry, sis. I'm going to a party, I only popped in to say a quick hello.'

'Don't call me that!'

'Thanks very much!' Ed raised Mara's glass at her and took another big glug.

I was shocked. I had never seen him act so arsey with Mara before. He was acting very strangely. Then it dawned on me that he looked like he'd had a few too many drinks.

'Whose party is it?' asked Claudia.

'I don't know,' Ed shrugged. He looked nonchalantly at each of us in turn. As his eyes met mine, I felt a tug at my belly. The awkwardness with Mara and my blustering explanation played out in frenetic fast forward in my mind. God, I wished he'd just piss off. I really didn't need him muddying things up. Why was he here anyway?

'Sounds intriguing,' said Claudia.

'Maybe.' He shrugged with more irritating nonchalance that seemed wrong coming from him. 'It'll probably just be a bunch of boring City workers, knowing Rebecca.'

'Rebecca?' I almost shouted again. 'Are you feeling OK?'

Ed looked at me but didn't say a thing.

'It's certainly not my idea of a good time,' I added crossly.

'No, I've gathered that.'

'What's that meant to mean?'

But before he could answer Mara butted in and asked Ed if Rebecca had been the one to invite him, and her voice was quiet and hard. The pub was bustling with noisy Friday drinkers all around them but there was no mistaking the seriousness of her tone.

Ed looked irritated.

'Does it matter?' he said. When Mara didn't reply, he continued, 'Chill out, Mars, it's only a night out. Just something to do, nothing more. I'm not going to go home with her, if that's what you're worried about.'

'It's none of my business who you go home with,' Mara said primly.

Ed laughed and Mara's cheeks coloured with indignation.

I couldn't really believe what I was seeing. Ed was never this hard. I didn't like seeing him like this. It was a bit sad.

Thankfully Claudia managed to break the tension and pull Ed out of his mood a little by telling some tall tale she'd heard through the week. My phone buzzed in my pocket and I was grateful for the distraction. Discreetly, I took the phone out of my pocket and swiped the screen. Two unread messages!

Hope yr week's been better than mine. Haven't stopped.
Enjoying beer o'clock. You?

And then:

Scrap that. Beer o'clock would be better with you.
There's no one to argue with here.

I sniggered.

'What?' Mara asked.

'Nothing!' I replied.

She narrowed her eyes. Then she stood up and leant over the table between us.

'You've got your phone out! Who do you need to be in touch with? We're all here!'

I shoved my phone back in my pocket and grinned. Mara could chastise me as much as she wanted. I didn't mind; I was flying high. He was thinking about me! About me!

'Not everyone,' Ed said. 'Your special someone isn't here, is he, Sam?'

'Shut up, Ed,' I replied. I hadn't told him about Charlie and I wasn't about to now. Not when he was in such a grumpy mood.

Ed replied by draining Mara's drink and standing up. He picked up his satchel and swung it over his head, a rather insincere grin on his face that didn't suit him one little bit.

'Well, that's me. Thanks for the drink, Mars. Have an enjoyable evening, ladies.'

I tried to think of a suitably cutting retort but couldn't think of anything, so I had to settle for glaring at him instead. He ignored me, blew a kiss to Mara and then winked at Claudia. Claudia gave him an amused smile back. I made a mental note to ask Claudia about it when he'd gone.

'What the fuck are we going to do about that, "sis"?' I said, chucking my thumb over my shoulder, where Ed had disappeared into the throng at the bar. Mara gave me a tight smile and let out her breath, as if she'd been holding it for the duration.

'Well, I'm going to get a round,' said Claudia, standing up.

'Make it a lime and soda for me,' Mara said, 'I want to go home soon.'

'Me too.'

'We're really pushing the boat out tonight, aren't we?' she replied and joined the crowd.

'What the hell is going on, Mara?' I leant in towards her. Surely Mara would know what was going on with Ed. They've always seemed so close, had the kind of relationship I've always wished I'd had with a sister or brother growing up. They made the sibling thing look so effortless, so natural – nothing like the awkwardness between the little minx and me.

'I don't know but I don't like it,' Mara answered and bit the side of her thumbnail thoughtfully. Suddenly her face cleared as she remembered something. 'Rebecca came to our house during the week.'

'You're joking.'

'It was during the day, the day after she stayed the night – Monday, was it? Or Tuesday . . . Anyway she said to Ed she'd come to find her address book or something.'

'I never saw any book.'

'No, neither did I.'

That little tart. She'd come when we were at work and Ed would be home alone.

82

Claudia bustled back with the drinks. She set them all down and then busily distributed one to each of us. This was usually when she would take charge of the situation and chivvy us all into having a good time again. But she didn't look like she was about to say anything; in fact, I was sure she looked more like she was holding her thoughts in, keeping them to herself.

'Claudia, you've been very quiet all evening, what do you make of Ed panting after that little snake in the grass?'

Claudia sat down and took a long sip of her water and looked at Mara and then me, as if she was turning her thoughts over in her head carefully before she opened her mouth.

'Actually, I think it's the other way round,' she said, her eyes shining with amusement, or tiredness. It was hard to tell.

'Rebecca's throwing herself at him?' I asked.

'Something like that,' Claudia replied from behind her glass.

I turned it over in my mind. Yes, she was flirting with him the other night at our place. Yes, she's just broken up with James and is probably in need of some distraction. But Ed? Really? It didn't feel quite right, and I was sure Claudia was holding something back. There was something in her eyes, like she knew something we didn't. But first things first – we had to come up with some sort of plan to keep Rebecca away from our home. It was enough to endure being in the same room as my sister at family gatherings; I couldn't bear the thought of her impinging on my social life too.

Then my phone buzzed again. I took it out before I could think about it and had the message open in a flash.

It wasn't Charlie – it was Ed!

Stop looking at your phone. It's girls' night.

I snorted.

'Your Casanova again?' Mara asked wearily.

I was giggling so much I couldn't get my words out.

'It's—' I met Mara's eye. And with a flash of inspiration I answered, 'It's Rebecca. Wondering if we've seen Ed.'

After all, half an hour ago Mara still thought I was after her brother. She can't know he'd just texted me and made me laugh, no way.

'Told you!' Claudia said.

Mara shook her head and half laughed with the shock.

'This is all your fault, Sam, she's your sister.'

'Sorry. I'd send her back if I could.'

'She would too,' Claudia laughed.

'There's only one thing for it,' Mara continued. 'As soon as Ed's got some work, he can move out. At least that way if they do become . . . friends,' she said the word delicately, as if trying it out in a strange language for the first time, 'we won't have to be involved. He's planning to do that anyway. I wasn't really looking forward to him leaving but I'm quickly changing my mind.'

'Hear hear. Not that I want him to move out,' I added quickly. 'He's OK but I can't abide her.'

'We know!' Mara and Claudia said at the same time and we laughed together. Quite frankly, it was do that or cry.

17

ED

From: Ed Minkley <edminkley@gmail.com>
Date: Saturday, 7 February
To: Covington Green <greenworldcov@gmail.com>
Subject: Trouble
📎 Minkleys.jpg
📎 Trouble.jpg

Hey Cov,

That new project sounds amazing. Mara wonders if you've heard of these guys – asiacleanwater.org. She said it looked like they were also working in Tamil Nadu so maybe you could hook up. She loves hearing about what you're doing. In fact, your Minkley fan club is growing, you flash bastard. It would do her so much good to get away and do some NGO work like you're doing sometime.

On to more pressing matters. As you suggested, I did my hard-to-get act last night. I was nervous so I had a couple of jars before, poss one too many. I only meant to be Mr Hard Man towards Sam but as she was with the others, I managed to not only annoy her but also piss Mara off. Quite crappy of me, I think. Maybe not your best advice. Or, more likely, not my best move putting it into practice right at that moment. Anyway I went on to that party with the crazy vixen girl. She was all right in the end. Wasn't all over me like the proverbial rash the whole evening. Actually I got chatting to some suits about what you're up to. They might be keen to kick some funds in – so my night wasn't a complete waste of time!

As requested, I've attached a photo of sisters with crazy niece and nephew. You must be really desperate, mate, to want to see a photo of my family though. We're nowhere near as flash as your one ;)

Oh, and one of the vixen. See what I mean?

Ed

18

CLAUDIA

I left Hampstead tube station walking briskly but as I neared the surgery, I slowed right down, and the walk that should have taken five minutes took at least ten. If only I hadn't watched that damn programme last night, I could still be burying deeper into snuggly denial.

The programme in question, *Embarrassing Bodies*, was exactly the vapid watch I needed. I got home early from the pub. I had my hot-water bottle. My phone was off. I was all set to escape. But then the spanners started coming, fast and furious.

First up: Dr Jessen. A big blonde hunk. He looked so much like John Morgan he could be his brother and I couldn't believe I hadn't noticed this before. My finger hovered over the remote for a moment. It was escape I was after, not art imitating life. Or, more to the point, not a probing medical series into other people's unfortunate ailments imitating life. The whole aim of this show was to gasp in horror at some woman's elephantine knees, murmuring to oneself, 'That poor, poor woman,' while quietly feeling comforted that your own knees are really quite supermodel in comparison. Wasn't it? You weren't meant to recognise the symptoms that other people – always other people – had as yours.

But that damn chisel-faced doctor had fixed me with his unflinching gaze and spoken to me directly. The remote slipped, forgotten, onto my blanket while I started comparing my symptoms to those on the TV. Sore down there. More *scheidenausfluss* than usual (I hate the English word, won't even think it if I can help it). And itchy.

So I was on the phone booking an appointment with my GP first thing this morning, and a few hours later I was walking down the quiet residential street I'd walked down countless times before, watching my royal-blue Pollini peep-toes taking one step at a time and wishing it was further away from the station so I wouldn't be there any second. But there it was. Number twenty in a well-kept Victorian terrace. One freshly painted door to open and I'd be inside, no turning back. I paused, just for a moment, and walked in.

The waiting room was warm and smelt clean and reassuring. Sitting at the reception desk was a woman with a neat dark bob and glasses, and I was pleased to see I didn't know her. I checked in and took a seat, picking up a *Vogue* from a coffee table on the way. The table looked spotless, as did the chairs and carpet. I breathed in deeply and started flicking absently through the magazine.

Gradually my eyes started wandering, taking little sideways peeps at the other people waiting. I was careful not to catch anyone's eye. Any one of them could be someone I knew or, worse, someone my parents knew, waiting to have their boils inspected or moan about their IBS or to be told to lose some weight. I had no doubt there would be no one in their social circle here for the same reason as myself.

The decor had been updated since I'd last been and it was definitely an improvement. The walls had been painted deep terracotta, and the lighting was what my mother would refer to as thoughtful. Which sounds so pompous but I have to say, in this setting, it was just that. There were a couple of standing lights tucked into corners, and spotlights beneath a handful of well-executed (another word overused by Mother) oils. The room somehow managed to feel open and cosy at the same time. There was soft music – Bach, I think – playing in the background. All very lovely. If I could have erased the underlying tang of antiseptic, I could have been visiting Aunt Vivian, waiting for her to prepare a G&T. I took another breath. My nervous stomach had settled a little. This was do-able, and practically five star compared to my last experience of the world of all things medical.

The last time was seeing Kate and a brand-new Rosie in hospital. I couldn't get there fast enough – although my imagination had heaved with Dickensian images of what an NHS maternity ward would look like. I had imagined far too many mothers and babies crawling with germs, dilapidated buildings, exhausted under-resourced nurses walking around in a sleep-deprived daze, and I wasn't disappointed. The ward was full of women and babies, copious tears issuing from both. The paint was faded and worn. The staff looked peaky. But then I saw Rosie. She was a perfect little bundle, so beautiful she eclipsed her surroundings, and as I looked down at her in her little plastic crib, I almost forgot to breathe.

I turned a page in the magazine. It was strange I hadn't thought about having my own children very often, considering I'd entered my thirties. But I really hadn't. At least not until this all started rumbling. I put my hand on my belly. The night before I had lain awake churning everything over in my mind. What if my fertility had been affected? And I thought about it and thought about it and realised I was scared witless, and all because of a brief moment of pleasure. Was I missing the point here, after all? I have always enjoyed my body without shame, always seen it as mine to enjoy, one of life's pleasures. Like hot chips, walking at the seaside, chocolate in front of a film. But as I had tossed and turned past one o'clock, past two, past three, I wondered for the first time in my life if I wasn't a woman making choices but actually an irresponsible slapper.

The day before I'd had lunch with Jill at work.

'What's eating you, Claudia?' she'd asked in her Afrikaans accent. 'Scowling doesn't suit you, you know.' There wasn't much that passed Jill by. She'd been round the block and back again. Her teenagers were convinced she could read minds.

'Oh women,' I'd replied, rolling my eyes. 'Our place.'

Jill raised her eyebrows. 'Our place?'

'The good woman. This stupid world,' I continued, scrabbling around for tangible examples to describe the sudden swell of indignation I was feeling. 'All around us, blocking out perfectly good sunlight, are billboards of sexy women selling bloody anything and everything with their tits—'

'You've only just noticed?' Jill asked.

'No, of course I've seen them. It's just that I've never minded before. I've always taken them for granted. They do their job . . .' I paused; I still couldn't quite get to my point. 'It's not them I've got a problem with – of course tits sell stuff, why wouldn't they? They're fabulous!'

'Speak for yourself.' Jill looked down her top. 'Mine are dropping out of sight rapidly.'

'Your fault for breastfeeding,' I said.

'Charming!'

I flapped my hand at her – I didn't want to get distracted from my train of thought.

'I think that what's eating me is that despite all the sexy images of women, in real life we're not really allowed to be sexy, not in the full sense of the word. We're still expected to stay in our place, be good women. Look sexy, act sweet,' I said.

'Oh listen to her. You'd better watch out, you'll be burning your bra and marching the streets if you're not careful.'

'But that's the thing I don't get. We had feminism. Our mothers—' Here I paused again. 'Well, maybe not my mother, but other women's mothers marched the streets demanding equality, and got labelled men-hating dykes.' I'd have to ask my mother if she'd ever been mistaken for a lesbian. I tried picturing her protesting in her Louis Vuitton suit, her thin, elegant legs, and her perfect ankles. Hmmm, difficult. Then I tried to imagine my father, in one of his beautiful suits, cheering her on. No. Despite his liberal political views, I just couldn't picture it. I kept on.

'These women did so much. Gave us "women can do anything". And now we wear whatever we want, study what we want, pursue careers, travel the world and go out with whoever. Do all of that. But we can't dress up like sluts, enjoy it and garner any respect for it.'

Jill started shaking into her sandwich.

'What?' I frowned at her. I wasn't joking.

'Shame!' That was Jill's favourite saying, said swiftly, almost swallowed. She put her sandwich down. 'Look at you, most often dressed in a miniskirt and tarty heels, cleavage fit for a high diver to land in, bleached blonde hair, Angelina pout. You're gorgeous and you're respected, with a great job. You're the envy of most of the women who work here and fuelling fantasies for most men. What's the problem? Where's this all coming from?'

I sighed. 'Oh I don't know. Maybe a dormant feminist gene is finally coming to life and telling the other genes committed to being a siren that they aren't self-respecting enough.'

Jill shook her head again. 'Poor sexy Claud, my heart bleeds for you, it really does.' She paused and then her voice became serious. 'Is there something really concerning you, Claud?' she asked, her brown eyes trained on me like two searchlights.

I struggled to meet her gaze. Could I tell her? Maybe I could. I opened my mouth to speak but a bulging crotch caught my eye. It was hovering just above the table, looking like it was going to plop down onto it. It could only belong to one person. I looked up – it was Tightpants himself.

He stood there grinning, with a big tray of food. 'Can I join you ladies?' he asked.

'Ah . . .' said Jill, looking at me for an answer.

'Of course you can,' I said quickly and motioned for him to sit down. Jill didn't need to hear about my problems anyway. She had a hard enough job keeping her fourteen-year-old from falling pregnant.

'Thanks.' John sat down opposite me, his cologne wafting gently over the table. I looked at his tray of food rather than look at his face. Bouillabaisse and the cheesecake, exactly what I'd almost finished eating.

'So what have the ladies been talking about?' he said.

'Oh this and that, nothing really,' I said quickly.

'Nothing important?' Jill raised her eyebrows again at me and then turned to John – the last person I wanted to discuss this with.

'It's not important that women get to dress and be who they want to be without apologising for it?' she said.

'Sounds serious.' John grinned.

'It is serious,' I found myself saying.

'Do you mean women should be able to wear their trackies into work?' John asked.

'No, the opposite. That women should be able to dress like saucy tarts and not be thought any less of,' said Jill.

John said nothing for a moment and then said quietly, 'Do women really get that much grief when they look hot? Or are they just appreciated more?'

I didn't say a thing.

'According to Claudia, possibly not,' Jill said for me.

I shot her a warning look, which she pretended not to see.

John feigned shock. 'Claudia? Since when did you worry about such trivial things as what people might think of you? You're a confident and intelligent woman who knows who she is. There isn't anything more attractive than that.'

We were both silent then and I saw him colouring slightly. He tucked into his soup.

Jill looked at me questioningly then, finally twigging that perhaps there was more to this strange conversation than met the eye, and I – the coward – kept my eyes on the table. Dammit, I could feel my cheeks colouring slightly too.

'Claudia Myers?' a soft voice broke across my thoughts. It was Dr Epstein. I smiled nervously and followed his slow steps into his office.

'So how are you, my dear?' he asked through a cropped white beard, once he'd lowered himself into his chair, more creakily than when I'd last seen him. How old was he now? It felt like he'd been old forever.

I sat in front of him, clutching my handbag. I did wonder, not for the first time that day, why the hell I was coming to my family GP when an anonymous private doctor would have done the job perfectly well, but for some reason I'd felt drawn here. I swallowed, acutely aware of how dry my mouth had become.

'I haven't seen you in a long time. Still working in HR?'

I nodded.

'I bet you're just great in that job. They're lucky to have you.'

I managed a small smile. Dr Epstein's kind blue eyes were crinkled with genuine delight at seeing me all grown up, a girl whose leg he'd stitched and temperature he'd taken and whatever else throughout her childhood. I knew in that instant why I was there. I wanted to share my fears with someone older than me, someone I looked up to. I couldn't tell my parents what I was afraid of, and I loved my friends but they didn't feel older and wiser most of the time. Dr Epstein, however, would take it all in his stride.

'Well . . .' I swallowed again. 'I'm worried about symptoms I've been having lately and wanted to get them checked out,' I finally managed to say.

'Yes . . .' Dr Epstein sat perfectly still, as if he had all the time in the world to wait for me to elaborate.

'My—' I motioned in a vague circular motion down there.

'Uterus?'

'Yes. That. It's aching on and off. Mainly on, actually.' I kept my eyes on his tidy desk.

'Have you noticed any abnormal discharge?'

My stomach turned over. I couldn't say it.

Dr Epstein waited quietly.

And suddenly I felt really flustered. 'You must have seen this all before,' I blurted, and then almost stood up to leave. I felt out of control. What was I blethering on about? Even Dr Epstein didn't have time to listen to my neurotic babble . . . but I didn't. I took a deep breath.

'Sorry,' I said. 'That was my mind speaking without permission. I'm a little nervous.'

Dr Epstein adjusted position in his seat.

'I have seen a lot of things, Claudia, and every day I see nervous people here. Most importantly, though, we're going to try to find out what's going on so we can treat it.'

'OK,' I said, and I managed to look up at him and hold his gaze for a millisecond.

'So tell me about your' – the doctor paused – 'what's going on down below.'

I took another deep breath.

'I'm having a lot of . . . stuff come out down there,' I said.

'What colour is it?'

'Yellowish,' I told my nails in a quiet voice. My squeamishness was turning into nausea.

'Right. Any spotting of blood between your periods?'

'No, I don't think so.'

'And how long have you had these symptoms?'

'A month or so I think. I've really only started noticing it properly in the last couple of weeks.'

'OK.'

He wrote some quick notes and then looked up.

'Tell me a bit about your sexual history. In strictest confidence,' he added.

'Have you got all day?' I laughed, a touch closer to hysterical. But I pulled myself together enough to cast back into my dodgy history and gave him a summary. It really would have taken all day to tell him about every single one of my partners, so I skipped over a couple of them (perhaps a dozen). Dr Epstein wrote notes as I spoke, not appearing to judge me, but midway through hearing about the tenth man, he put his hand up and cut in brusquely,

'And what about lately?'

'Lately?'

'Yes, do you have multiple partners at the moment?'

The way he said the word multiple made me want to disappear into my chair.

'I . . . I really haven't felt like it for a while now. Since all these symptoms started I guess,' I stuttered. My safe feeling had gone; Dr Epstein was judging me after all. This was a monumentally stupid thing to have done. What if he felt obligated to tell my parents?

He breathed heavily through his nose and looked up from his pad.

'When did you last have sex?'

'Ah—' I looked at the ceiling and struggled to think back. I felt so overcome with a sense of failure, of letting Dr Epstein down. The appointment was turning out to be exactly how I imagined it if my parents knew about my real life – all the men, all the fun and games. Eventually I whispered lamely, 'I guess that would have been six or seven weeks ago now.'

Dr Epstein nodded and then stood, indicating the bed.

I tried to stand up but found my legs weren't cooperating. He must have noticed because as he was pulling the curtains, his voice sounded soft and kind again.

'I just need to take a swab to send off for testing. It won't take a moment and it won't hurt, Claudia.'

I stepped behind the curtain while he called in a nurse to chaperone.

Thankfully it was over within seconds, and when I was dressed again and he had washed up, Dr Epstein motioned for me to sit down. He sat down carefully again and entered some information into his computer, stabbing the keyboard with his index fingers. My heart pinched watching him do what he obviously had to do but was clearly inept at. He turned to face me.

'First things first: we'll check for a number of diseases and conditions. I suspect it could be chlamydia, but we'll test for a range of other things just to make sure. If you have tested positive for anything, we'll call you to make an appointment to discuss it further and start treatment. Chlamydia can be treated effectively with antibiotics. If it's caught early, it can be cleared quite quickly with minimum long-term damage.'

I stared at him, my stomach in free fall from fear. Had I heard him right? Did he actually think I might have one of those STIs, one with a horrible, dirty name? I mean, I did come in here to check if I had one but it still shocked me to have it confirmed.

'Do you have any questions?' he asked.

I couldn't think straight. I never got sick; I just didn't. How was I meant to know what to ask?

Dr Epstein sighed a small sigh and continued. 'You're lucky, you know. You're having symptoms and most women don't have any at all. If it is what I think it is, we've hopefully caught it early enough and there will be little to no damage to your fertility.'

Fertility? Another swoop of fear deep in my stomach. I was right to be worried about that. I pulled at my skirt, as if by doing so I could make it longer.

'Will you be able to tell how long I've had it?' Would I be able to guess who passed it on, I meant.

'Not really. We could have a guess but it could be inaccurate.' He paused. 'Is there someone that you suspect may have given you this, someone recently, or in the past?'

The picture of a dozen men lounging in my bed flicked through my mind, ending in that vision of John in his tight Calvin Kleins. I shrugged.

'I'm not sure.'

I reached down and picked up my handbag and tucked it under my arm, suddenly desperate to be in the fresh air, away from this small room with its fake calm and freakish instruments for poking into orifices. I wanted to scream and I wanted to walk, really fast. But Dr Epstein hadn't quite finished.

'Just one more thing, Claudia.'

I looked at him, my whole body quivering now with the effort to stay still.

'I know it's none of my business but when I was your age, I buried myself in work, and when I wasn't working I had a lot of fun.' He paused and looked at me to make sure I understood what he meant. 'I told myself that I was perfectly happy running around, that I didn't need to have a long-term partner, that it was

97

boring, restrictive and somehow' – he tapped his finger against one cheek – 'demeaning to chain yourself to one person. That was how I thought about it, chaining myself. It took me a long time to be honest with myself – that I was actually scared of trusting someone with my heart.' He paused again, shaking his head and glancing at a photograph on his desk. 'I am so glad I realised that and finally took the plunge with someone special. It was the single most important thing I've done in my life.'

I sat there blinking at him. I'd heard him speaking but I couldn't take it in. I stood, something tugging at me, urging me to say something, but I only managed an awkward thank you before walking stiffly out of the room.

19

SAM

I waited for the question. It'd be any minute now. Mum was setting cups of tea down on the twenty-five-year-old coasters ('Haven't they've lasted well – you get only the best from Sheila'). When they were all placed just so, she sighed happily and backed herself down onto the sofa, all ready for a girly catch-up.

'So what's new?'

There it was. Christ, it irritated me every single time. It also annoyed Rebecca and was possibly the only thing we had in common. We sighed, heavily, in unison.

'You go first,' I said through my teeth.

Mum smiled encouragingly at Rebecca. Rebecca gave me a look that said it was my bloody turn to go first next time but obediently opened her mouth and started broadcasting.

'Well, I heard from Miranda through the week, you know she's getting married this year . . .' I tuned out and saw my chance to escape, and although I'd only just sat down, I took my tea to the kitchen to 'help' Dad. Not that he would accept any help – it was his way or the highway – but hanging around him as he finished off lunch was infinitely more preferable than listening to Rebecca's perfect vowels.

Dad had a new apron, green and white striped. It was tied very snugly around his body and highlighted his gradually increasing middle. He was moving around slowly and happily in his favourite room in the house. Chopping carrots and cabbage to go on to steam, checking the pork roasting in the oven, preparing the gravy. Small tasks, strung together to make a little symphony of small tasks, made Dad very happy. He was a potterer extraordinaire. Bumbling from one thing to the next in small steps. Always the same things, for it was the familiar little tasks that made up his life. Other men worried about what they'd do when they retired but not Dad. Mum often commented that she could hire him out to lonely old men and women on their own. Someone to get under their feet and fill their home with the happy, small noises of rubbish bins and dishwashers being emptied, kitchen benches wiped down, bird tables replenished. They could make a fortune!

'How are you, love?' he asked me in his quiet voice.

'Oh, the usual, Dad. Not sure what I'm up to but trying to enjoy the ride.' Where did that came from? But I always found myself telling him what was really on my mind.

'Work OK?' he asked, wiping the kitchen counter for the three hundredth time that hour.

'Not too bad. I've got some bookings in for the next month. All commercials. They pay well but are only a day or so, though sometimes as much as a week for the really big ones. I would love to get more work on films. They're less bitty.'

Dad nodded.

'Hopefully Vic will get one soon.'

'Vic, she's the first AD you work with a lot, isn't she?'

'Yes. She's my favourite, a good friend. She always books me if I'm available.'

'Any work as a first or second on the horizon?'

'No, not yet.'

'You'll get there. It takes time. You're going in the right direction.'

'Yeah.' Dad was right; it did take time. Careers aren't built in a day, and when you're driving it all yourself as a freelancer it will take time. He always helped me remember there was a context to everything.

'It was really nice to see you and Rebecca together this morning.'

I didn't have the heart to say that it was an unhappy coincidence we'd caught the same train down, that we didn't even know we were on the same one until we got off at Petersfield. Dad had looked overjoyed when he saw us waiting together outside the little white station. He was always hopeful that his girls would grow to appreciate each other and have the kind of close relationship he enjoyed with his sister. He waited for more but I couldn't go there, so he rinsed the cloth slowly and carefully hung it over the tap.

'Well then, can you call the others to sit down?' he said.

Lunch was delicious and although I had to endure sitting opposite Rebecca, I couldn't help but mellow as the perfectly cooked pork, crunchy roasties, just-steamed veg and the world's best gravy, all cooked with love, warmed me from the inside out. I even forgot to avoid looking at Rebecca during pudding and managed to tell a couple of silly stories about people I'd worked with instead. I should make it home for Sunday lunch more often – Mum and Dad either side of me, genuinely caring about what I had to say. I sat back in my chair in satisfaction. Even Rebecca seemed less fatuous than usual. It was all really rather lovely.

'So, Samantha, anyone special out there?'

I felt my goodwill pop like a balloon. Mum just had to go and spoil it all by asking the second-most annoying question in her repertoire. I felt my smile slide off to be replaced by an unwelcome blush that only fuelled Mum into further excitement.

'Oh she has, look she's going red!'

'I am not!'

'You are.' Rebecca regarded me with cool eyes.

I glanced at Dad who smiled warmly and gave a little 'what can we do? Mum can't help herself' shrug, and I chuckled, in spite of myself. Here they were, my family, sitting around the table that had seen many an awkward conversation in the past. What was the harm in telling them?

'Well . . . I did see someone the other day. An old flame actually.' I could feel Rebecca's eyes trained on me and I kept my gaze steadily on Mum's plate.

'It was Charlie Hugh-Barrington.'

'Really?' Mum looked confused. 'But . . .'

'Yes, Mum, we broke up eleven years ago but we bumped into each other in London and ended up going out for a drink.'

'Oh!' I saw her looking at Dad, bewildered. Of course I had to be landed with the only two people who came through the free-love seventies completely straight-laced. Mum had met Dad at sixteen and married him three years later, and that was that. She found it jolly hard keeping up with all the comings and goings of her daughters and their friends. I could see I might have to explain that it was possible to meet up with someone you used to go out with but I wasn't sure I had the energy and was glad when Dad chipped in.

'What's he up to these days. Is he a GP yet?' I could hear the tiniest tight nuance in his voice. I turned my head from Mum on my left past Rebecca, who was continuing to stare hard at me, and stopped gratefully on Dad's round, goateed face.

'He's a surgeon.'

Dad looked impressed. 'Well well. What kind of surgeon?'

I tried to remember. I'd never excelled at knowing the details of other people's careers. And before I could answer Rebecca asked another question. It was a second or two before I could take it in and then, once I'd registered it, I had to ask her to repeat it. It couldn't be true. It just couldn't.

'How are things with his girlfriend?'

It felt as if all my blood had been sucked out of my feet, leaving a hollow shell behind. She didn't just say that surely?

'He didn't mention he had one,' I eventually mustered.

'Maybe they've broken up,' Mum added bouncily.

'I don't thing so.' Rebecca's tone was even harder than normal. Emphatic was the word that sprung to mind. Fuck.

'How do you . . .' I faltered.

'Oh I bump into him at parties from time to time. His girlfriend went to school with a friend of mine.'

'Oh.'

'I can show you a picture on the computer if you want.'

I nodded dumbly although what I really wanted to do was throw myself onto the turquoise bedspread still on my old bed and weep.

It took forever for the computer to wake up. I stood there like a lamb to the slaughter, wanting to see the picture but at the same time wanting to run and hide. Rebecca's beautifully manicured nails tapped away confidently. Maybe Mum and Dad's internet would be down, I hoped, or failing that Facebook would have crashed, for good. Maybe aliens would arrive right now outside 31 Durford Road and take me away.

'Here we go . . .' Rebecca logged in. I couldn't help glancing at her friends total – 878 friends. Who were all those people? 'Let's have a look at Bindy's page, she's got a good one of them together . . .' Rebecca's tone had lightened considerably. She was probably enjoying this; in fact watching her sister suffer was Rebecca's ideal way to spend a Sunday. I became aware that my nails were digging into my palms. Click click click went Rebecca's finger on the mouse.

'Here we are!'

And there he was, smiling at the camera, his arm around a tall, beautiful blonde woman with perfectly straight, impossibly shiny hair and a lean-machine body, looking like she'd just walked out of a fashion shoot. I recognised her as one of the many women he had photos with on his home page.

'That's her. Her name's Lucy,' Rebecca said gleefully. I stared at the photo in shock. Not again. Not another elegant girlfriend on his arm. Where the hell did they all come from?

I remembered when I couldn't wait for the first holiday to arrive in my first year at university. As luck would have it I finished a day earlier than Charlie and had decided to travel to Warwick to surprise him. I could barely sit still on the train on the way there, imagining the look on his face when he saw me. It had been weeks and weeks since we'd seen each other, and we'd been missing each other so much. It was true his emails hadn't been as frequent the longer we were apart but he was really busy doing his medical degree and I wasn't worried. I found him in a pub full of students rowdily drinking their parents' money. He was leaning nonchalantly on the bar, managing to look debonair even in that student drinking hole.

'Sam!' He looked surprised to see me. Not quite the elaborate ecstasy I'd imagined but he seemed pleased.

My face was glowing with excitement and the anticipation of being enveloped by him. His hug came. Hmmm, that unforgettable smell of man, beer and cigarettes. And something else. Chanel? But I was determined to hold onto the dream and gaily chatted on to him about my trip to see him, my course, and this and that. Charlie smiled his devastating smile and nodded and chatted with me. He bought me a drink. His friends melted away, leaving us alone. I was trying very hard to ignore the way his eyes flicked backwards to the door. To the door, to me, to the door, to me. I was just asking about his family when the smell of Chanel seemed to fill my nostrils. Charlie was looking at the space next to my stool.

'Penny!' he exclaimed in a strained, jolly voice.

I turned and saw her. A tiny creature wearing something charmingly understated. Despite the wind outside, her hair was glossy. I felt extremely uneasy looking at her.

Penny went to kiss Charlie hello, aiming for his lips, but he went for her cheek. It was awkward and her composure faltered slightly but it only lasted a second. When she turned enquiringly to me she was the picture of well-bred confidence.

'Sam, this is Penny . . . Penny, Sam.'

'Pleased to meet you.' Penny offered her beautiful hand to shake. It was cold.

'Are you at university with Charlie?' I enquired, not particularly interested in the answer.

She gave me a puzzled look. 'Of course we are,' she said.

Charlie swallowed and managed a tight grin.

'Drink?'

'Yes, please,' we answered at the same time.

'Sauvignon.'

'Same again thanks.' I offered him my pint glass.

Penny eyed it coolly. 'So, Sam, what do you study?'

'Media studies. Not here though, I've come up to surprise Charlie. He seems pretty surprised.'

Penny's perfect eyebrows lifted slightly.

'Oh? That's . . . nice. How do you know him?'

How did I know him?

'I'm his girlfriend.'

Penny looked at Charlie, who had returned with the two drinks, and keeping her eyes on him asked me querulously, 'What did you just say?'

I looked at Charlie. His mouth was open. His eyes flicked between us, for once unable to come up with a single word.

I repeated myself, slower this time, because it looked like Penny was having a hard time understanding me.

'I'm his girlfriend.'

'No you're not.'

'Ah . . . yes I am. We've been together for over a year.'

With that, Penny's creamy complexion flooded beetroot red and she turned to Charlie with tears pooling in disbelieving, furious eyes.

'You' – she stuttered, finally spitting out, 'Bloody bastard!'

Then she snatched the drinks out of Charlie's hands and poured beer over him (the cashmere!) and wine over me. I gasped and watched her turn on her petite heel and storm out. Charlie followed her, running out on me without a backwards glance, let alone some sort of explanation. I was left alone with the wine starting to seep all the way through to my skin. I looked around at the bemused faces of the students, not a single one of them familiar, and felt, for the first time in my life, utter miserable loneliness. I didn't wait for long. Something told me Charlie wouldn't be back and I stumbled into the night, hot tears mingling with the Sauvignon. Somehow I made it onto the train, and I went straight home and cried for the whole of Christmas. I swore I'd never see him again.

20

SAM

'I can't bloody believe it!' I said as I wiped the tears furiously from my face. Mara sat next to me, her feet tucked up underneath her, her hand on my shoulder. It felt warm and reassuring but it wasn't stopping the tears. Or the snot for that matter. She passed me a tissue.

'He's not worth the heartache, Sam.'

'I just can't believe I've fallen for his bullshit again! One' – I raised a shaking finger in the air – 'he didn't tell me he had a girlfriend! Two' – second finger up – 'I had to hear about it from my frigging sister!'

'Oh Sam,' Mara murmured as I buried my face in my hands again.

Not long after the bombshell from Rebecca, I'd asked Dad to drive me to the station.

'But what about going for a walk?' Mum had asked desperately, as if the Facebook episode wasn't the end of the world.

But I couldn't bear being around any of them, particularly Rebecca's smug face. Neither could I be in that house, the place I'd cried myself sick the last time this had bloody happened. I sat on the train, staring at the landscape passing by the window, stripped bare of any life or colour, turning the evening I'd spent with Charlie over and over in my mind, trying to remember when I'd had that conversation, the bit where we talked about his love life. But I couldn't remember it. Surely I hadn't been so stupid as to not ask him? By the time the train was coming into London, passing brick terrace after brick terrace, I had to acknowledge that perhaps I hadn't asked the question old muggins should have asked first. I mustn't have wanted the answer. I was pathetic. A weak, pathetic excuse for a woman.

I blew my nose some more and eventually the tears stopped. Mara made me another hot chocolate and put the telly on. George came in and kindly chose my knee to knead, spin and then settle on, and started dribbling in earnest. I felt washed out and raw but much calmer. This was Mara in her element and I was quite happy to go with it. It was like having a really competent mum take care of everything and, at that moment, it was exactly what I needed. The silly sitcom on the box flickered, highlighting Mara's small, heart-shaped face. It took me a couple of seconds to work out what was different about her and then I clicked. It was her mouth. It was the first time since before Ed came home that her mouth wasn't a tight, little line.

'Where's Ed?' I asked.

'Seeing Max.'

'I've got some work for him on Tuesday,' I said, suddenly realising I hadn't told her.

'Really?' Mara said brightly. 'That's great!'

'I was in seeing Katherine at her office the other day and she happened to get a call from a client asking if they could have some photos taken of the commercial we're shooting this week. I showed them some of Ed's work on my laptop and she agreed on the spot.'

'Is it paid?'

'No, unfortunately not.'

'It's a start though. Nice work, Sam.'

'I can't believe I didn't tell you.'

'Doesn't matter, we've been distracted by other worries with Ed, haven't we?'

I must have looked nonplussed because Mara arched her 'wake up, slow coach' eyebrow.

'Rebecca?' Mara said.

Just hearing Rebecca's name tightened the anxious belt around my middle again, bringing the rawness of that day's discovery straight back.

'She is such a bitch.'

'Really? Tell me something I don't know.'

'She was so pleased to see the look on my face when she told me about Lucy!' The audience on the telly laughed stupidly as one.

'That's Rebecca for you, the epitome of compassion.'

'As if it isn't enough for her to tell me about his girlfriend, she has to gloat over it too.'

Mara patted my arm kindly and I felt more tears well up. God, where do they all come from? I hadn't cried this much since . . . since . . . well, since the last time this all happened. More laughter erupted from the telly. It was as if they were laughing at me, the sad sack on the sofa crying over the same man for the second time, while my self-satisfied sister was no doubt gleefully telling the story to her friends across town. It just wasn't fair!

'Did Rebecca say anything about that party they went to on Friday night?' said Mara.

'Who went to?' I asked distractedly, too busy concentrating on my churning belly to listen.

'Ed was meeting Rebecca at a party, remember?' Mara said. Her voice was gentle but her body language gave away how anxious she was to know the details.

'Oh that! I completely forgot to ask her, sorry.'

Mara shrugged and let her head fall back into the sofa again, turning to stare at the television.

109

'Ed didn't give anything away either,' she said, her lips no longer soft and relaxed. I couldn't think of a single positive thing to say and sat there awkwardly for a few minutes. Then my phone beeped and I gratefully reached for it.

I couldn't believe whose name had come up.

'It's Charlie,' I whispered. And despite it all, my stupid heart leapt as I opened the text quickly.

Hi sexy, fancy coming to my birthday party Sat the 28th?
Whitehall Club, 8pm Cx

'Oh my God.'

'What's the slimeball got to say for himself?' asked Mara.

'He's invited me to his birthday in a couple of weeks,' I answered, distracted.

Mara's face darkened. 'What a louse.'

I flinched. Suddenly the care and attention of mother-hen Mara felt more like control and repression. And in that moment, it all became clear to me. These past few weeks, where she'd been so uncomfortable with Ed around, were all about Mara not being in control. Ed was daring to do things Mara didn't approve of (granted, I didn't approve of him hanging out with Rebecca . . .) and now I was doing things she didn't approve of either, so Mara was getting cross. I sat up straighter on the sofa. What the hell would Mara know about love anyway? She never allowed it to come close to her.

'You know what, Mara? I am bloody well going to go to that party!' I blurted. Mara's face dropped in disbelief and for a moment I wavered but then I ploughed on.

'I am going to go, and I'm going to look amazing, and I'm going to bloody well show him!'

Mara sighed and slumped back against the sofa, shaking her head.

'Show him what?' she asked wearily.

Yes, good question. I huffed and puffed for a moment.

'Show him who the most beautiful, funny, real woman in the room is ... Show him ... show him that the person he keeps mucking around isn't a mug, she's a living, breathing, gorgeous woman!'

Mara sighed a resigned sigh.

I would show him all right, I thought. I almost slapped my own thigh I was so fired up with determination. I was damn well going to look the best I'd ever looked. He was going to be so bowled over he wouldn't be able to help himself. He'd forget about his girlfriend – she'd be so fucking boring and lifeless she'd fade into the curtains. It would be as if only I – hopefully standing under a suitably flattering light – existed. I got up off the sofa, far too revved up to loll about feeling sorry for myself and went directly to my bedroom to look through my wardrobe, knowing full well there was nothing glamorous in there. As I marched into my little hovel, two thoughts jostled for space in my racing mind.

1. Charlie couldn't really be serious about that stuck-up tart if he'd invited me to his party surely?

2. How the hell was I going to afford a new dress?

21

SAM

My alarm woke me while it was still dark. I sat up and groaned. What a bloody awful night. All that fervour at proving myself to Charlie had lasted about five minutes in the end and I'd spent the last two nights worrying about Charlie's party, and what the bloody hell I was going to wear. I padded down to the sitting room to wake Ed up. For once he responded straightaway to my quiet knock. Without talking much, we took a quick shower each and grabbed some toast to eat en route on the Tube. Not for the first time I wished I had a car. Getting to set on time was always a mission for me without one and this time I also had Ed's kit to help carry down the road. It was heavier than it looked.

Outside, the sun hadn't even started thinking about getting up. The wind had died down overnight and taken the sharp edge with it. I hoped it would stay that way, as I would be spending most of the day outside. I liked the company we were going to be working for today and usually I looked forward to working with them. They were young and imaginative, always coming up with interesting concepts on limited budgets – and they paid on time, which was always a plus – but today I was struggling to muster any enthusiasm. On top of the worrying I was doing about Charlie, I was also feeling tense about Ed. I'd wrangled this job for him and if he stuffed up it would reflect poorly on me. Katherine, the producer, had told me that she had another job

– that one paid – lined up where the photographer had just pulled out, so this could mean a few weeks' work for Ed on location in Scotland if he performed well that day. He'd bloody well better.

To top the morning off, Louise Laverell was due on set in half an hour. Ms Laverell was basically made up of a body into which a bunch of sharp and prickly words and thoughts had been poured and kept all tense and spiky by far too much exercise and not enough food. She was struggling to keep her head above the dangerous water forty-plus-year-old female actors swam in and was high maintenance, grade eight. Laverell had starred in a long-running whodunnit series for ten years, gone on to dabble in theatre, bit parts in television dramas and a role in a Film Four film. In my opinion (far too humble, obviously), she'd done pretty well for herself and should be happy. Unfortunately for everyone around her, she wasn't. Quite the contrary. Laverell was extremely bitter and twisted about her perceived sidelining by the industry, and people not appreciating her enormous talent. It wasn't money she wanted – she was married to an exceedingly rich investment banker who hadn't appeared to be even remotely affected by the banking crisis. But she would do anything to get on the telly, which was great news for a company like Katherine's, who were working on a tight budget. Desperate actors can be very amenable to heavily negotiated fees but unfortunately with Louise, it was impossible to negotiate her attitude once she was on set.

At Archway, Ed led the way up to the surface of the earth. Commuters pushed up behind us and I was forced to walk very closely behind him. I was surprised that he smelt of freshly washed clothes and soap. The funky stench of the backpacking photographer had well and truly gone. Hang on – I couldn't help but sniff harder – there! Underneath the floral detergent, I caught a whiff of his tangy manly odour. A brief vision of his chest, lean and hard, flashed across my mind. I pulled away from his jacket. Whoa, Sam, I thought, that was a bit random for half six in the morning. I looked around furtively. Had anyone actually seen me lean in to sniff a man's jacket? But the bland, shuttered faces passing us on the opposite escalator didn't flick a single eye my way.

Out of the station, we turned right and right again. Ahead I could see a couple of trucks parked up.

'Cool.' Ed grinned at me. I smiled back. Even after a few years in the industry, I couldn't help feeling excited when I saw the big trucks parked up. They always look like they mean business – something about their size and numbers, I guess.

'What did they have to do to get all this parking?' Ed asked.

'Hand over a hefty wedge to the local council,' I replied. 'These are only the ones that need to be close to set, most of the trucks are parked up the road, a couple of minutes away, in a car park they've leased for the day.'

'So which ones are here then?'

I counted them off as we got closer. 'Looks like camera, gaffers, grips and . . . make-up maybe? Although usually they're parked with everyone else down the road.' Then I remembered about Louise Laverell. Of course that would explain the position of make-up so close to set. Louise's proximity to set is always a deal-breaker and a total headache for everyone.

'Which one's which again?' Ed asked.

'Gaffers look after lights, grips look after the movement of the camera.'

'Cool,' Ed said again and I hit him, instantly regretting it because my arm had gone weak from his kit weighing me down.

'Don't be such a kid!' I said and he grinned some more, point-ing at a car parked right behind one of the trucks.

'What happens if someone is away and they've left their car in the way?'

'Well, it means the location manager has a thumping big headache. Although not the one on this job. Smooth Pete doesn't do headaches, as far as I know.'

Speaking of the devil, I spied Pete ahead on his phone, standing beside a svelte little car. As we drew closer to him, we could see it was a Porsche. Pete's face was tight. Like a man with a headache threatening. Oh dear.

'Yes, I've tried that, it was a pittance to them I think so he's not budging . . . aha . . . OK, I'll see you soon.' He turned to look at us and gave me a hug. He smelt of cigarettes.

'Sammy, great to see you!' Pete's social skills made him an exceptional location manager. He could literally charm the pants off anyone. Something I knew from experience.

'Likewise,' I answered and stepped back slightly, suddenly uncomfortable that there was history between us with Ed standing right there.

'You're looking a bit stressed out there, mate,' Ed observed.

Pete looked at the Porsche. 'Yes. An uncooperative member of the public won't move their car.'

Ed and I studied the car with Pete for a moment, looking up to the house it was parked next to. It was a detached Georgian. A magnolia tree reached over the clipped box hedge with bare knobbly branches. The house they were filming in was next door.

'Have you tried bribing them?' I asked.

'Oh yes, with Katherine's amazing vouchers, tickets for two to IMAX, off peak. They said no.'

'They've probably got their own IMAX inside,' Ed mused.

Pete chuckled. 'Well, it means the diva won't be parked close to set. This spot was going to be for make-up. She'll have to – shock horror – walk down the street to set.'

'Isn't that make-up, just down there?' I pointed to the truck about a hundred yards down the road.

'Yip, that's the one, about eighty yards too far away for madam.' He pulled a face and then turned to Ed, his hand extended. 'I'm Pete by the way.'

'Ed.'

'Oh, sorry,' I said. 'This is Ed.'

'I gathered that,' Pete said.

I blushed, glad it wasn't quite light yet.

'Well, best be off. Everyone will be arriving shortly and I definitely need a coffee before I see Louise.'

'We'll come with you, I need to get the radios out.'

Together we walked a couple of blocks up the road where the rest of the trucks, including honey wagons, wardrobe, unit and numerous crew cars were parked up, and the unit truck was in full swing making coffee. I left Ed catching a quick coffee, grabbed all the radios, gave a few to the crew I could see who needed them in the car park, and headed back to set to give the rest out to the camera and lighting crew.

An hour later, I heard the low hum of a car slowing down outside the house. That had to be Louise. I nipped to the edge of the Porsche still parked up and held up my call sheet so the driver would see where to stop. Louise always wanted to be met by the director or, failing that, the producer, which was a right pain in everyone's bums. There was no way the director would have time, and neither would the producer. It was part of the third's job, getting the cast onto set on time, so it should always be people like me meeting Louise. In fact, I knew exactly what time Louise had got up that morning. Katherine had reminded her over the phone the day before. Actors, honestly! I'd learnt early on that it was best to approach them with flattery slathered generously with professional jargon, to make them feel part of something very, very exciting. I almost always deployed that tactic when I had to dig the buggers out of make-up. They often felt they weren't pretty enough yet so when it came to knocking on the door of the make-up trailer, I would say, 'This is your five-minute call. Camera is standing by, grips and gaffers are on final checks and the director is looking forward to seeing you on set.' And that usually did it. The actors would be ready to go when I returned four minutes later.

I hoped Louise had behaved herself this morning. This was a big job for Katherine and it was so important that everything ran smoothly, and the client went home happy. It was six forty-five. I opened the passenger door.

'Good morning, Ms Laverell. I'm sorry we had to get you out of bed so early this morning. Make-up is this way.'

Louise looked at me haughtily and sighed. 'And you are?'

'Sam Moriarty, third assistant director, Ms Laverell.'

'And you are?' What a line. It was so tedious that Louise couldn't, or wouldn't, remember me from other jobs. I'd worked with her on several occasions in the past. Of course, I would always be invisible to her. She would never consider a third someone worthy of speaking to, let alone remembering. There were far more important people locked into Louise's one-track mind. People who talk to other people like her at exclusive private parties, at openings, at awards ceremonies. It was people like Louise that had my enthusiasm for my job hanging by a thread some days.

Louise contemplated her options. A cab beeped angrily behind her car, which was – surprise, surprise – blocking the way. Blocking the road as if Louise was more important than anyone else in the entire city in that moment.

'Marm?' the unit driver queried, looking rather anxiously into his rear-view mirror. I glanced at him. He was a pimply little beggar, with no discernable chin, his young hands clutching the wheel anxiously. I didn't recognise him and he didn't look like he'd been in the job for long. I felt a pang of pity for him. He'd obviously be much happier breeding Labradors or pet bunnies or something, not cowering in the seat in front of Louise, his vulnerable neck just there for her to sink her nails into.

'Fine,' Louise huffed. She placed an elegant shoe onto the road and stepped out, coming up to my shoulder. I took one step back and opened my arm, directing her to the footpath, not unlike an aircraft marshaller minus the ping-pong bats. You could never be too careful with actors – they might not be able to make it to the footpath without being shown the way. Once I was sure Louise had stepped safely onto the footpath, I stepped back quickly to shut the car door, leaning in to offer a 'Good luck, mate!' to the relieved driver.

Louise stood on the footpath. It was early dawn but nonetheless she wore dark glasses, the collar of her large woollen coat turned up against the potential invasion of fans or paparazzi. I looked around. The crew were exchanging rude banter while they lugged equipment into the house they would be filming inside that day. No one was even looking our way. Poor Louise, I smirked, no attention for her at all. All that money spent on her Armani sunglasses for nothing. But below her glasses her mouth looked sad, and I reminded myself of the other thing about actors. At the end of the day, they could be staggeringly insecure. I sighed. I couldn't really feel animosity for this woman. She was someone to be pitied rather than intimidated by. I took another look. Written on that mouth was a whisper of what I'd seen in Mara lately: Mara the worrier, trying to keep it together; Mara, the one who just cared too much about the tiny circle of friends and family around her. I cursed myself for my mean thoughts about Mara being a control freak.

I was so lost in these thoughts that I walked straight past wardrobe and had to pull up abruptly.

'What!' Louise snapped.

'Sorry, Ms Laverell, I was thinking about something else, wardrobe's just back here.' I retraced my steps, walked over to the trailer and stood next to it. Louise's lips pursed as she marched past me to the door, her coat bristling with disdain, but then she stopped. I wondered what she was up to for a moment until I realised she was waiting for me to open the door.

'You don't want to make me late, do you?' Louise demanded.

'Sorry,' I muttered to Louise's shoes as I opened the door. 'I was just thinking about a friend who's worrying about things too much at the moment,' I added under my breath. I'd said it aloud without thinking and I was sure she wouldn't hear me but Louise's heels stopped their click-clack mid-step. She turned to me, standing by the door beneath her, and took her glasses off.

'What did you say?' she said, her tone much less biting.

'Oh.' I bit a suddenly wobbly bottom lip and looked up to meet Louise's eye for a second.

'Nothing really, it's just things at home have been a bit strange lately. One of my best friends hasn't been very happy,' I found herself blurting out, wondering why of all people I would be sharing this with Louise Laverell?

Louise looked at me, her face softening the tiniest bit. 'I'm sorry to hear that, Miss Moriarty.' And then she turned and went into the trailer, leaving me to shut the door behind her. I stood blinking on the footpath and pressed my fingernails into my palms, then forced myself to take three slow breaths.

In. You are pathetic! Out. In. Pull yourself together! Out. In. And bloody well get on with your bloody work! Out.

Vic was coming up the road, her jaunty step obvious even in the half-light. I meant it when I told Dad that she was my favourite first. In her late thirties, Vic was fairly formidable at times of stress and took no nonsense, but she was rock solid and

119

had a wicked sense of humour. She also made me feel calmer just seeing her.

'You all right?' Vic asked as she gave me a brief, hard hug.

'Fine, yes. Just being a girl over something. Nothing important.' I waved my call sheet under Vic's nose. 'Can we talk through a couple of things on this?'

Vic didn't press me and got straight down to business, running through who was due where, when and discussing the weather. Then Vic spied Ed and blew slowly through her teeth.

'You didn't tell me that photographer friend of yours was so hot.'

'He's Mara's twin brother.'

'He's gorgeous.'

'Yeah, he's all right.' I kept looking at my call sheet, fiddling with the bull clip holding it onto my clipboard. Vic waited for me to say more but I kept studiously fiddling. I couldn't find it in myself to meet her eye but there was no mistaking the smile in Vic's voice when she said, 'Right then, let's get cracking.'

The first couple of hours passed quickly. I watched Ed from the corner of my eye as I worked and quickly realised I had nothing to worry about. He looked every inch the professional photographer. I'd never been concerned about the images he would take but I had wondered how he'd cope with the dynamic of a shoot. How the machine worked. How everyone was integral to making it work smoothly, with everyone dependent on everyone else working hard without faffing about, or getting in anyone else's way, and adhering to the many unspoken rules of how close you can get to certain people. I was relieved to see Ed just getting on with it, occasionally checking with the producer or the production manager but not once disturbing the director, the DOP or the talent. All of whom were susceptible to having a major sense-of-humour failure if they were bugged by underlings.

A bit harsh if seen from the outside, I suppose, but they did need to focus completely on what they were doing.

Ed's job for the day was to take photographs for the client to use in-house. They wanted a record of the day to use for training in their marketing department, and also as a record of things achieved, I supposed. Thinking about it, most of the clients who came along to the shoots spent their working lives in an office somewhere, stuck in front of a computer. They were happy occupiers of Squaresville, white men in ties, who drove nice cars, had matching sofa sets and sent their children to good schools. Sometimes they were uptight on set. Overseeing their employer spending tens or hundreds of thousands of pounds in a day or two all for thirty seconds of airtime would do that. But in the end they couldn't help but enjoy themselves. They were around funky film-crew types, people who never wore suits, who wore trainers, who smoked. Men and women who had exciting-looking boxes and kit in big shiny trucks, and crackling two-way radios on their hips. Burly grips who carried around the camera, laying down track. Gaffers who confidently set up expensive lights in places that didn't make sense to the common man. And actors lurking in make-up trailers – or on bigger productions, in their own trailer, waiting to be called. They added the glamour, the pizzazz, that these square suits just loved being around.

I noticed Ed unobtrusively taking photographs of the clients, who were speaking with the producer and director, and Louise. She was smiling and gesturing to the client, knowing perfectly well what side her bread was buttered on. Nice one, Ed, keep it up, they'll love that.

Lunch arrived and was set up on a trestle by the caterers. Lamb meatballs with couscous, beetroot and rocket salad, and crusty sourdough. I waited outside the house, listening for the call from Vic. When the director was happy, Vic called a wrap

121

on the current scene and the crew piled out for lunch. Ed came out ahead of them into the weak sunshine, taking photographs of everyone lining up for the food. He looked as if he was going to take photographs all lunchtime so I went and tapped him on the shoulder.

'Hey!' He turned, his eyes bright.

'Get some food – they won't need a million photos of them eating. It'll just make the poor sods stuck in the office jealous,' I said.

'True,' Ed said. 'If you're sure? I am hungry,' he said, eyeing the table.

'Come on then, let's get a plate before these greedy buggers eat it all.' We made our way to the table, passing crew crouching on the edge of the footpath and on the backs of trucks, their plates piled high with food.

'This looks amazing,' Ed said appreciatively, and then leant in close to whisper, 'The men inside were grumbling about what they were going to have for lunch!'

'Oh, they always do, Ed, it's part of their job description.'

'But why? This is great food, and they don't pay for it.'

'Good question,' I said, piling food onto three plates, one for Louise, one for Vic and one for the director. Ed took one out of my hands. 'It's one I've never found an answer for. I mean, how many people do you know outside hospitality who get fed at lunch, with really high-quality food at that?' I asked him.

'I know people who work in restaurants where they have to buy their food.'

'Exactly.' We took the plates over and handed them to the director, Vic and Louise. I pointed to a spot for Ed to eat and went back to get a plate for myself.

I'd met other ADs over the years who were so busy at lunchtime they didn't get any food themselves. It was a critical point in the day to assess the schedule with the first, make any changes for the afternoon and touch base with the second in the production office. It meant having several intense, important discussions with people, so for ADs it wasn't really a break, but I always made sure to get some lunch. I knew from bitter experience that if I didn't eat, come mid-afternoon I would simply cease being any use to anyone. I loaded up my plate and looked around for Ed. There he was, eating with one of the runners. He looked at me and grinned and my tummy fluttered a little.

Damn hunger pains. I walked off in the opposite direction to find Vic, the sound of Ed's easy laugh rising over the rumble of the crew chatting.

Vic and I were only halfway through discussing the afternoon's schedule when Katherine joined us in a flap.

'You won't believe it,' she said breathily, her usually composed face flushed.

'What?' we chimed, looking at each other. What crisis needed to be solved now?

'The MD is coming this afternoon.'

'Fine,' Vic said. 'What's the problem with that? Is he a particularly difficult man?'

'She is an exceedingly particular woman – a very busy woman, who's on crutches.'

Vic and I looked at each other again. Katherine was really getting her knickers in a knot over this. What was the big deal?

'We can accommodate that,' said Vic.

'I could get her a chair,' I said, shovelling in food while I could.

'Yes, yes, that's great, ladies, but the problem is that she's on crutches!'

Katherine was uncharacteristically not making any bloody sense whatsoever.

'That's OK – we can meet her cab here' – Vic gestured to the road in front of the house – 'and help her out of it.'

Katherine sighed. 'Yes, but she's being driven here in her own car from another commitment.'

'So the car stops here and we'll help her out,' Vic persisted, her face puzzled.

'But she wants to keep working on her laptop in her car. No, she won't work anywhere else, Vic, I don't know why. Like I said, she is a very particular, very busy woman. She wants to be parked close to set, so she can hobble up to the house a couple of times to watch, and return to her car in-between.'

We looked at the trucks parked nose to tail down the street. There were absolutely no spaces available as far as the eye could see. At the far end of the street, Georgia the production manager was officiously bobbing along the footpath towards us, her phone jammed to the side of her face. Without thinking about it, we moved closer together, ever so slightly, huddling in for safety from her confident posh squawk, fresh-faced good looks and, above all, her very bouncy ponytail.

'Kaarthrine!' she squawked as she was ten yards away.

'Georgia?' Katherine frowned pensively at her.

'I've jarst gort orf the phone with Ms Hawthorne's secretary,' she announced.

'Yes?' Katherine cringed.

'She's going to be here in fifteen minutes,' she said, as if she was announcing the start of World War Three.

'Christ.' Katherine's eyes rolled heavenward.

Vic thought quickly. 'Sam, grab a runner or two and check the street again to make sure there are no more spaces. I'll talk to Pete about possibly moving trucks. Let's meet here in two minutes.' And they dispersed, leaving Katherine with the pony-tailed seagull.

I went to grab the runner next to Ed.

'What's going on?' Ed asked, looking concerned.

124

'We need to find a parking space for the MD of Steins ASAP,' I snapped, not meaning to sound so sharp.

He put his hands up. 'OK, just asking.'

'Sorry, it's a nightmare,' I called over my shoulder as I followed the runner down the street.

When I returned, Ed had disappeared. As expected, there were no car parks to be found within two blocks, and I returned to Katherine and Georgia with the bad news. Katherine was biting the side of her finger, looking up and down the road, her eyes wide with fright. I wouldn't have been surprised to see her start foaming at the mouth. Fair enough too – if she stuffed up in the eyes of the MD, then Steins wouldn't be up for their advertising agency suggesting they use Katherine's production company again in the future.

I was madly trying to think of a solution but nothing was presenting itself. For once, not even Georgia was saying anything. She tugged at her ponytail instead, stroking the shiny beast as if it were a talisman.

Vic returned then, looking fierce. 'I've spoken with the HODs and Pete. There's no way we can shift trucks, the schedule is too tight this afternoon to allow extra time to move equipment from further away. You'd be running into overtime if you did that,' she said.

'Fuck,' Katherine said from the side of her mouth, the side of her finger taking up the front of it. Vic, Georgia and I looked at her to say more. 'Fuck,' she said again, retracting her finger from her mouth and holding it behind her back with her other hand, as if to keep it from intruding embarrassingly into her mouth again.

Then Vic asked the question no one dared to ask.

'What about moving the make-up truck further away?'

'No fucking way,' was the reply. I couldn't blame her. Last time Katherine asked Louise Laverell to accommodate a change on

125

shoot day – something to do with sharing make-up with a couple of extras or something – Louise threw such a big wobbly that the shoot was taken into overtime by an hour, costing Katherine's company an easy £5,000.

Then I caught sight of Ed – where the hell had he been? – coming out of the gate of the house next door with a rotund little man in his fifties. They watched in silence as the man opened the door to the little Porsche and drove off.

Vic ran to grab a cone from the back of a truck and stuck it in the car's place. Instinctively we all moved into the space where the car had been, hovering around Ed as if he were our saviour, which, after all, he was.

'What happened? How did you do that?' Georgia asked. Ed put up his hands and smiled, trying to bat the questions off. But then Vic joined the happy little scene.

'What the hell were you doing next door, Ed?' she barked.

His face fell. He wasn't expecting that reaction. Katherine made sympathetic, don't-be-so-harsh noises but Vic was unrepentant.

'Liaising with the public should be done by the location manager or the producer only, Ed, not the photographer.' Lesson number one, Ed – never, ever bend the rules with a first. Watch out, here comes her lecture.

'Rules are there for a reason, Ed. If just anyone took it upon themselves to talk to the public, we'd have chaos,' Vic spoke sternly.

Ed looked at her, his bright eyes a little jaded now, quickly learning this film business really wasn't all glamour and warm fuzzies. 'He's my uncle,' he said.

'Oh.' That put Vic back in her box. 'Well, that's different.'

'Your uncle?' Now I was really confused. What would an uncle of Mara and Ed's be doing living here?

'He's my mother's brother. He's always been a difficult man.

126

Mum never had much to do with him. I saw him last at Gran's funeral but he left straight after the service.'

'I'm sorry, Ed, for jumping down your throat,' said Vic, contrite. I was amazed – I don't think I've seen her apologise to anyone, ever.

'That's OK, Vic. I didn't speak to him at the start of the day because it was so early, and anyway I didn't want to upset protocol. Then, sometime in the morning, I thought it was probably worth a go knocking on his door. He didn't answer it though, probably expecting it to be one of the film crew. I didn't persist because at that stage it seemed people were managing without it. Anyway, I really don't feel that loving towards him so I was happy to keep my head down.'

Pete had joined them, and he listened with rapt attention to Ed's story.

'Then, when it seemed like you could really do with a parking space close by, I went and knocked again, this time on his conservatory door at the back. He saw me standing there. Gave him quite a shock, I did.'

'Wow,' said Katherine. She was transfixed. 'Thank you so much, that's really saved us a pile of stress.'

'No problem.' Ed shrugged. Good one, Ed, I thought. If anyone had any doubts about him before, they certainly wouldn't now. He'd been utterly professional and then went out of his personal comfort zone to ask a favour of someone he felt uncomfortable about.

On cue, there was a short honk from a car in the street, and Katherine personally removed the cone and waved the MD's car in. I touched Ed lightly on the arm. He looked down at my hand, and then into my eyes.

'Good one, Ed, that was brilliant.'

'Thanks, Sam,' he replied, his gaze lingering just a little longer than completely necessary.

After we'd wrapped, Louise had been ushered safely back into her car and Ed had been thanked again by the production staff, Ed and I walked back down the road towards the Tube. Dusk had passed without us noticing and the city had slipped into darkness. The wind was cold in our faces but we didn't mind – we were too busy going over the day, the highs and lows. Ed made me laugh more than once at his bang-on insights into my workplace.

We were close to the Tube when Ed put his hand lightly on the small of my back and steered me down a side street and into a little bar I've never noticed before. It was tiny. Round, French-style tables down one side, a bar with stools on the other.

'What can I get you?'

'Definitely a gin and tonic after a day like that,' I replied. Ed gestured that I should sit down and wait, and then he came over with the drinks.

'Cheers,' he said, passing me one.

'Cheers, Ed!' I touched his glass with mine and grinned.

'We need to celebrate!' he said.

'We do?'

'Firstly, we need to toast the fact I didn't stuff up today!'

'Cheers to that.' I raised my glass. 'A small miracle.'

'Indeed . . .' Ed paused. 'And Katherine said she'd call me tomorrow about the job in Scotland!'

'Really?' I felt my mouth hang open. I couldn't believe he'd pulled it off.

'Don't sound so surprised.'

'Oh, I'm not surprised at you, Ed, more surprised at Katherine saying that today – you must have really impressed her!'

'Well, it's all because of you, Sam. I wouldn't have had the chance to impress anyone without you getting me on the shoot in the first place.' Ed held out his glass to me again. 'To you!' he said.

'To me!' I replied. His eyes were burning with excitement, so much so I had to look away. They made me feel a bit weird. The G&T was going straight to my head.

I remembered the last time we'd been out in the evening together. It was the night he was off to a party with Rebecca, ugh. I didn't want this lovely warm feeling to leave but I had him in front of me – trying to get some details out of him was the least I could do for Mara.

'So are you going to tell me how your night with Rebecca went the other night?' I launched in. I hoped he couldn't see through my stuck-on bright smile. I didn't really want to know how their evening went. I didn't want to be speaking about my sister at all.

Ed groaned.

'Do I have to?'

'You know what, Ed? I'd rather not know but I know someone else in our house who is pretty keen.'

Ed drained his glass and glanced over to the bar, assessing how quickly it would take to get refills.

I leaned in.

'Look, give me something and then I'll get us another drink before we go home.'

Ed groaned again but his eyes twinkled at me.

'OK, for you I will, Sam. To be honest, it was better than I thought it would be. I met some guys and got chatting to them about the project my friend Cov is doing in India – you know, the water one – and they made pretty enthusiastic noises about putting some money into it.' A shadow crossed his face. 'Actually I really need to crack on with following that up. I've never asked people for money before. I feel really uncomfortable about it.'

'But you're not asking them, they offered, right?'

'I think that's how the conversation went. It was noisy, we'd had a couple of drinks . . . but yes, you're right, they did get quite excited about it. I think they wanted to support something that didn't have expensive bureaucracy attached to it, and Cov is such a dude, just throws himself into whatever he's doing. These guys wanted to back something where they would know the money was going straight into making a difference.'

'You'll be fine, Ed. You're such a natural with people.'

'I am?' Ed looked open and vulnerable in that moment, and so much younger.

'Totally! Look how you impressed everyone today – you were fantastic.'

And we launched back into reliving the day without mentioning Rebecca's name once. We talked through one more drink and all the way to the Tube before sitting in exhausted silence together on the way home. I fell into bed that night, glad that Ed had been his usual mellow company again. Best of all, I was so tired from the day I had no energy to lie awake fretting about Charlie and the dreaded party.

22

ED

From: Ed Minkley <edminkley@gmail.com>
Date: Wednesday, 11 February
To: Covington Green <greenworldcov@gmail.com>
Subject: Progress, I think
📎 DSC_345.jpg
📎 DSC_349.jpg

Hey,

You're like a dog with a bone, aren't you? Here are a couple more pics of Mara. I had to pretend to be testing my lenses – she hates having her photo taken. I passed on your thanks to her for telling you about that organisation. They sound really great. She is so massively interested in what you're doing . . . but, mate, if you're asking for more photos of her, aren't you taking this interest in her a little bit too far? I have told you about how much she trusts men, right? I'm shaking my head in worry here.

Oh yeah, thanks for the reminder about talking to those guys with the money who I met with Rebecca too. I must chase them up for you. I was just speaking to Sam about it last night, as it happens. We were out having a drink together. Yes. Not a date, exactly, but I could be making progress. Maybe. She did get me a job, though, working on set with her, so she must have been happy to spend all that time together – not that we saw each other until the end of the day. We were both really busy. Man, she nails her job. And seeing her marching around with a two-way radio on her hip all day. There's definitely something about a girl with a radio on her hip . . . Listen to me. I'm getting off on communication tools. Worrying.

And you think I should find out more about this Charlie Posh-whatsit? I don't know, mate, I'm not sure I can see the point of doing that but as you say, knowing more about my competition might be helpful. Either that, or it will make me want to go and deck him. I'll report back.

Gotta scoot,

Ed

23

MARA

I almost tripped over a pigeon on the way home. It was crouching a few yards from the flat, with its feathers all fluffed up to make itself look bigger. I saw it just in time and stopped. At first glance, it looked like a grumpy old man, like he was sitting there in the way on purpose, making a statement. He could have looked quite amusing but that first glance of mine with the ridiculous storyline quickly turned into reality. The pigeon wasn't just having an off day. He was on his last legs and his eyes had a sickly glaze. I tucked my chin further into my scarf and hurried the last bit home. It only occurred to me later that I hadn't even contemplated bringing the bird inside. But I was looking out for enough creatures already, I reasoned.

And every one of them was completely ignoring my good intentions, as per usual. I was getting nothing out of Ed about what had been going on in India and now that Rebecca was hanging around like an expensive bad smell, I had a terrible feeling I wasn't going to get many chances to press him further. To top it off, I was worried about Sam setting herself up for yet more disappointment with Charlie. So much to worry about – all on top of always worrying about how Dad was, and if he was looking after himself and wishing he could be happier. The only saving grace amongst all this was that Kate and the kids seemed to be OK, no need to worry about them for a change. And Claudia, of course. But I didn't tend to worry about her very often. She was generally able to look after herself, that one. In fact, Claudia was quite possibly the only friend I had that could be defined as a fully grown woman. If only there were more of those around!

I was really hoping to have the flat to myself but as soon as I put the key in the lock, I could hear Sam singing tunelessly to herself in the shower. Since the invitation to Charlie's party – only going to end one way, that one – she'd become somewhat obsessed with exfoliating and almost living in the bathroom. No doubt hoping for miracles where he was concerned, the silly girl. Ed wasn't due home until later. He was meeting with that producer to discuss more work. Which was a good thing, I tried to tell myself. I took off my coat. Sam had yet again flung her coat on my coat hook, so I stood on my toes to unhook it and hang it on Sam's. Mine on the left, Sam in the middle, visitor on the right. Simple. I went to my room, put my shoes away side by side under the bed and sat down to put my slippers on, pausing to rub my feet first.

Ed had come home shining last night, looking so alive, and I'd felt so pleased for him. It was so right for him to be following his dream. But later in the evening I'd caught him looking with such longing at Sam that my gut had twisted with . . . what? Jealousy? No, surely I was more mature than that. I could share my beloved brother with someone else, of course I could. I am an adult, after all. I straightened my shoulders and looked sternly at my reflection in the mirror. It was simply a case of not getting lost in the worry. And anyway, Sam's head was filled to bursting with Charlie – she wouldn't be noticing anyone else. That I was one hundred per cent sure about.

After supper, I settled into my favourite chair in the sitting room and the latest Margaret Atwood. You don't get many perks managing a library. In fact, having free access to recent releases is pretty much the only perk. And I like to make the most of it.

Soon I was well and truly lost in Atwood's terrifyingly resonant future, meandering off occasionally to think about how lucky Ed's Covington was to actually be working on a project where he was making a tangible difference to people's lives, instead of what I was doing, sticking my head in a book and not doing a thing! And then Sam slapped barefoot into the sitting room, her legs bare under her miniskirt, clutching a collection of tools and nail varnish and breaking well and truly into my thoughts.

'I can do yours too, if you want,' she offered.

'Aren't you going out?' I said.

'Do you want me to?' Sam's face dropped. She looked disappointed, which surprised me. Surely she wanted to be out with Charlie, or one of her friends who'd be happy to talk about how much fun this party was going to be, not old stick-in-the-mud me. I smiled at her apologetically.

'No, of course not. It wasn't meant to come out like that.' And that was true, I didn't really mean to be that harsh, I just didn't want a pedicure when there was Margaret Atwood to read. Sam should know that. In fact, she was quickly morphing into someone I didn't recognise. Sam had always thrown herself into the world unkempt and unpolished, and had never a problem attracting guys. She was gorgeous, and if you asked me (which no one does) I would say that a large part of her appeal was her random, tomboyish appearance, with hair that tended to frizz and feet that for the most part were ignored. But all this stuff that I love about Sam was quickly evaporating. She was becoming more immaculately dressed by the day, her make-up getting more sophisticated – even her hair was being tamed! And now she was scrubbing away violently at her heels with the kind of instrument that looked as if it belonged in an archaeologist's toolbox. She was turning, in front of my alarmed eyes, into a girly girl.

The doorbell broke through my thoughts, and I went to release the downstairs door. Just in time, Ed, I thought. I was in danger of really disliking the person I care most about in the whole world. As I pressed the button for the street door, I fleetingly wondered why he hadn't used his key. Perhaps he'd lost it. I opened the door to the flat to let him in, suddenly remembering he was coming home with news of one sort or another. But it wasn't Ed. Around the corner of the stairs came the unmistakeable neat little frame of Rebecca.

'Mara!' she trilled.

'Oh, it's you.'

'Did you think I was going to be someone else?'

I tried to rearrange the disappointment on my face into something more palatable but couldn't help standing in her way for a beat longer than was polite before I motioned for her to come inside.

Sam looked shocked to see her, which was initially satisfying to me – at least her descent into pedicure land hadn't changed how she felt about her sister. But then I thought if Sam didn't know she was coming, who the hell invited her over?

'Have we heard yet?' Rebecca asked brightly as she took off her coat.

'Have we heard what?' Sam asked, raising an eyebrow in my direction.

'If Ed got the job, of course,' Rebecca answered, taking her coat off and looking around for somewhere to put it.

'Not yet,' I said tightly. I took Rebecca's coat and hung it up on the right hook, then took a couple of deep breaths before returning to the sitting room.

'Did Ed ask you to come over?' I asked her.

Rebecca wavered. 'No, but I knew he was meeting with Katherine tonight and I was just passing, so thought I'd pop in to hear the news.'

I caught Sam's eye.

'You don't mind, do you?' Rebecca asked innocently.

There was a pause and then we answered together in voices heavy with untruth, 'That's fine.'

Before the atmosphere become too brittle to breathe we heard Ed bound up the stairs, noisily fight the door with his key and come in. We all turned to the sitting-room door as it opened.

Ed walked in. 'Hi! Oh.' He looked startled when he saw Rebecca. That's good, I thought and then kicked myself inwardly. Never mind about that – what about the job?

'So?' Rebecca got there first.

Ed's face fell as he lifted his bag strap over his head.

'The thing is . . .' He looked morosely at us. I held my breath.

'I GOT THE JOB!' And he cracked into his widest, shiniest grin. We all cheered and got up from our chairs, or in Sam's case her little patch of old heel skin and gave him a hug each.

Thank you, thank you, I thought, as I returned to my seat. Thank you for getting my brother away from these crazy sisters for a bit.

'How long will you be away for?' I asked when the cheering had died down.

'Three weeks. But I'm not leaving for another couple.'

I smiled at him. Three whole weeks. Pity it wasn't going to start sooner. I glanced around the room. Sam was back to scraping her feet, while asking him more questions about the job. But Rebecca looked odd. Her face didn't match the cheering she'd just been doing. She looked . . . what was it? Crestfallen, yes that was it. Ed going away for three weeks obviously wasn't what she wanted to hear. I don't think Ed saw her face; he'd loped off down the hallway to find his supper. I sat back in my chair and picked up my book again. Run while you can, my brother, I thought to myself, run as fast as you can.

24

SAM

'This way.' Claudia marched through the racks of clothes like a sergeant major. I trailed behind her. A hundred yards in and I was already feeling like I might drown in garments. Was that possible? I imagined being smothered by the row of purple dresses we were passing at speed, or there, those black trousers. There must be at least a hundred pairs all lined up. It wouldn't take much to kill me. Just the size eights and tens would be enough, wrapped around my face. The size twelves wouldn't even be needed. They and the fourteens would just be waiting for their next victim, appearing so innocent.

'Come on, you're not after trousers. Keep focussed.' Claudia took my arm and dragged me deeper into the shop.

I could do charity shops fine. They were small, with such limited choice it was like finding treasure when you found something – you could really feel like you'd achieved something. Not so on the high street and definitely not in H&M or Topshop. No, then I just started feeling panicky. Having Claudia at my side was the only way I could brave them.

'This, this and . . .' Claudia flicked through the hangers at speed and pulled out a bright blue dress, 'This.' She looked at me. 'What's wrong with you? Shopping is meant to be fun, you know.'

'Whatever.'

Claudia shook her head and strode off to the changing rooms and I almost had to run to keep up. The last time I'd tried shopping here, I'd got as far as choosing something to try on then had become so disorientated trying to find somewhere to change I'd given up and left. But I couldn't do that today. No way. I had to find something to wear. There was a gaping hole in my wardrobe that had to be filled by something fabulous. I was sure my confidence would be boosted just knowing it was there. If I made it out from this sodding shop alive, of course. We reached the changing rooms. There were enough cubicles for half of Petersfield to change in there and still have room for a picnic. I dithered for a second. There was too much choice again: which one was I meant to use?

'Come out when you've got something on!' Claudia ordered and hustled me into the first one on the left.

'What's wrong with the mirror in here?' I whined. Claudia didn't reply.

I sighed and started peeling off layers. Jacket, hoodie, top. I tried to avoid the mirror, as I seemed to consist almost entirely of dark bags and dry skin.

'Try the blue one on first,' Claudia said behind the door. 'And take your boots off.'

I looked down. 'How do you know I haven't taken them off already?'

'I can't smell your feet.'

'Right. Thanks for that.'

I pulled my boots off obediently and took the blue dress down and peeked at the price. Shit. I'd never spent that much on a dress in my life. But I held it up in front of myself anyway, concentrating on the dress itself and avoiding looking at my face. It was a shame about the price – it was such a nice colour. My phone beeped then. I was expecting Vic to be in touch about a

139

job so I quickly scooped it out of my pocket and checked it. My heart skipped a beat – it just couldn't help itself.

Can't wait to see you. Cx

I tapped out my reply and pressed send recklessly. Another reason why I don't go shopping very often: I am likely to make rash, spur-of-the-moment decisions.

You're not going to know what hit you.

He replied instantly.

Oh really?

'Sam? What are you doing in there? You're not on your phone, are you? We're here to do a job, stay focussed!' Claudia tapped her fingernails on the door.

Just one more.

Yes, really. Gotta go. Got a job to do.

I snapped my phone shut and shoved it back in my bag. With shaking hands I pulled the dress over my head and opened the door.

'Oh my!' Claudia beamed. 'Don't you look amazing!'

'I do?' I smiled, feeling all stupid and shy for a moment.

'Go on, have a look yourself.' Claudia pushed me towards a large mirror at the end of the room. The dress was made of some sort of floaty fabric – I never know the correct names. It crossed over at the breasts, drawing in tight under them, and then fell to just past my knees. It was beautiful. I forced myself to look at my face, steeling myself for disappointment. There, in the mirror, a proper woman looked back at me.

'Oh my God.'

'Here.' Claudia lifted my hair off my shoulders and held it up on top of my head, 'What do you think?'

I tried responding but I could only make a strangled squeaking sound. Maybe this hare-brained scheme could actually work. Maybe I would look good enough to eat, good enough to leave your girlfriend for!

It was only when we were on our way to the checkout that I remembered the price. My heart sank. I couldn't bear the idea of going back through the racks for cheaper dresses. Maybe, oh maybe, one of my cards would work? Perhaps some central computer at the bank would be down and they wouldn't realise I was already over the limit on my overdraft? The queue snaked twenty people deep to the row of cashiers and I had plenty of time to worry as we edged closer to the front. I tried engaging Claudia about work. Any more stories about John Tightpants? But Claudia wasn't playing ball. She just gave me some one-line answers and then went all quiet. I was left to worry about the dress in silence. I handed over my first card with wet palms.

'Sorry. Declined,' said the girl behind the counter. She stared at me blankly, waiting for my next move. As I thumbed through my cards I could feel the eyes of the queue on my back. I handed over another one. Maybe the bank hadn't cancelled this one after all, maybe, by some miracle . . .

'This one too,' she said, just the wrong side of withering.

'Bother,' I said quietly. I shuffled my cards some more. Library, out-of-date gym card, supermarket loyalty cards, unread business cards, all useless. Not a healthy bank balance between them.

'I'll get it.' Claudia handed her card to the cashier just as I started pulling away from the counter, defeated.

'Are you sure? I'll pay you back.' I felt like a heel.

'You have to have that dress.' Claudia smiled at me.

'Thanks. And sorry, again.'

My cheeks burnt as the patronising cow behind the counter passed Claudia the bag. Another thing Claudia had paid for, another bloody thing. Out on the street, I started to thank her again but Claudia cut across me.

'Actually, I've got to get moving, sweetie, but I'm so pleased you found a dress you love. It looks really good on you. I'll call you soon, OK?' And with another kiss she was gone, disappearing into Oxford Street, six deep with bustling lunchtime shoppers.

25

CLAUDIA

Finally the day was over and I was home. I dropped my keys on the table and stood and stared, unseeing, at the rooftops out my window. The word inside my head sounded dirty and fungal and seething. I felt as if my whole being was infected, as if I couldn't form a single thought that wasn't poisoned by it. I don't know how long I stood there – it could have been a couple of minutes or half an hour – but it was long enough for every one of my demons to come out from whatever rank hole they usually lived in. They took up with that horrible word and started a violent party in my head, singing along to their favourite songs about how awful and unworthy I was. No, not singing – shouting. I swear I hadn't felt this dark for years. Eventually I made my way to the kitchen and dug around in a cupboard until I found a bottle of whisky, some cheap crap Sam had brought round months before. I'd drown them out. Pour shot, tilt head, bang. I shook my head from side to side, the fiery liquid scorching my throat. 'Ahhhhh!' I shouted at the nothingness around me and my stupid, hot tears ran down my face.

For a moment that afternoon, I had felt quite serene sitting in that civilised waiting room again. I even found myself admiring the decor again, my head desperate to be taken along some inane thought process that involved colour combinations and fabric textures and la-di-da-di – anything but reality. It didn't last.

Reality kicked in when I walked back into Dr Epstein's consulting room. Then I'd felt nauseous and nervous as hell.

'Have a seat. We've had your tests back,' Dr Epstein had said. And was I imagining it? Was he more formal than when I'd last seen him? I took my seat.

And then he dropped the bombshell.

'You have tested positive for chlamydia and negative for all other tests.'

Chlamydia. Chlamydia. That word. As soon as he said it, it stuck in my head. I felt cold and scared, with only one word inside me. Chlamydia. Dr Epstein started speaking but he sounded like a bee in the corner of the room. A bee with a German accent. He buzzed away about antibiotics and effectiveness and timescales and frequency of doses, but none of it made any sense.

Until he said, 'Ah so the next step will be notifying your sexual partners from the past six months.'

'All of them?' I gasped. Chlamydia shrunk while I started counting back, trying to tally how many awful conversations that would entail. Too many to bear – I couldn't count them, couldn't even begin to. Dr Epstein was buzzing again and this time I forced myself to listen to what he was saying.

'. . . if you want, we can contact your partners on your behalf, telling them that they may have been exposed to the infection and that they, and their partners, should get tested. Your name wouldn't be mentioned . . . buzz buzz buzz.'

I swallowed. Bloody hell, I didn't even have a last name for some of them! Oh, Claudia, you idiot. It was one thing to enjoy sex like one might enjoy a sweetie; it was quite another thing to have the whole sweetie jar tipped onto the table for all to see.

'The woman who does this job does it in complete confidence. There isn't much she hasn't seen.'

Suddenly I bristled. He was patronising me! I clenched my

144

hands in my lap. I was being tossed from indignation at the situation to deep insecurity about my choices. Furious, I felt tears well up. Dr Epstein passed me tissues, and his small act of kindness made me weep even more. I stabbed at the tears and blew my nose noisily, trying to regain some composure.

'I'll need to get some of the contacts from home,' I said eventually.

'That's fine. If it's possible, please drop them in tomorrow.' He passed me a card. 'Actually, I think there's an email address on there. You could email them to her.'

'I'll see what I can do,' I said, my voice tinny.

Back at the office, I was completely distracted. I tried to bury myself in work but it was useless. Even though I had a pile of tasks waiting for me, I couldn't focus on a single one of them. The knot in my stomach tightened as the minutes ticked over. I kept coming back to the gruesome reality of having to tell all those men about the infection. I had questions now too – of course they'd started bouncing round and round my head, competing for space with that word, once I'd left the surgery. If they told my partners, would I be told which one of the bastards gave me the infection? Of course not! Damn patient confidentiality. I got up from my desk and stood at the window, resting my forehead on the cool glass. I could see the logic of having a service to tell my partners but something didn't quite sit right. Of course it didn't sit right. How could news like this ever sit right? I needed to know who the culprit was, that's why! I stared out the window at the Thames, glinting in the early spring sunshine. Sunshine – I hadn't even noticed there was sunshine.

'Everything OK?'

I swung around, my hand on my chest. 'Jesus, John, you gave me a fright!'

'Sorry, I didn't mean to.'

145

He offered a soft smile.

'Why didn't you knock?'

John looked a little sheepish. 'I don't know really. I didn't really want to disturb you, in case you were on the phone.'

What was he talking about?

'You could have been on an important call!' he said defensively.

'People usually knock on my door.'

'Sorry,' he said again. As he stood there, his solid frame seemed to take up more room than usual and it was as if he wasn't quite sure where to put himself, as if he couldn't remember exactly why he was there.

'You were looking thoughtful, Claudia.'

I wished he'd get to the point and then leave. I didn't have the energy for small talk. I wasn't even fit for work.

'How long were you looking at me?' I asked him.

'Not long. Long enough to see you didn't look very happy.' He really was making an effort – that much was obvious. I took a deep breath and all of a sudden felt like I needed to talk about this awful situation right there and then.

'I'm not happy as it happens, John,' I said, fighting back yet more sissy tears.

John nodded slightly, waiting for me to go on.

'Actually, it's something I'd like to talk to you about.'

But John held a finger up to his mouth. 'Can we talk about it outside of the office? Let me buy you dinner tonight,' he said.

I paused, looking around my office for evidence that this wasn't the place to discuss this.

'Somewhere private, where we can have a good talk,' he insisted.

And for a moment, I weighed up my need to be at home against my desire to share. Home won. I couldn't have been ready to talk quite yet, after all.

'I can't.'

'How about tomorrow night then?'

He wasn't going to give up until he had a date. 'OK, tomorrow night then,' I said, knowing that I'd have twenty-four hours to come up with an excuse not to.

'Great!' His face lit up and he paused on the ball of one foot as if he was about to – horror of horrors – cross the floor to join me at my desk. But he stopped himself and left the room with a wave, closing the door quietly behind him.

26

From: Ed Minkley <edminkley@gmail.com>
Date: Monday, 16 February
To: Covington Green <greenworldcov@gmail.com>
Subject: Dodgy
📎 Charlie.jpg

Cov,

Here he is, Charles himself. I feel awful but I had a quick look at Sam's account when she left her laptop lying around. If this comes back to bite me on the bum, it'll all be your fault! So the competition . . . must be from a nice resort somewhere hot. See how the dapper mug's eyes are slightly hooded, as if he is so relaxed he can barely open them. Don't tell me, you've probably been to the same resort, you preppy bastard. Of course occupying the moral high ground means I wouldn't ever consider visiting such a place. I know – they're probably fantastic. Yada yada. There were loads of pics of him with the same leggy blonde thing, probably the girlfriend. I just don't get it – this is who Sam is chasing? There were loads of other pics – of Charlie on boats, on waterskis, drunk Charlie, Charlie with a series of ladies who all look the same. All meaningless bullshit – playboys and empty-headed women having their jollies, completely oblivious to how the real world lives, their lifestyles revolving around having fun, fun and more fun. Fuck, they looked like they were having a bloody good time doing it! Can't they look miserable now and then? Just for my sake?

Anyway, when I was on his page I saw his party invite and a list of people going to it. There was Sam. Seeing her name there made me feel like shit. I wished it was my party she was coming to. Get the violins out, mate!

But back to business – I've made a note of the place and time of the party and also the name of Charlie's work . . .

You are making me feel extremely dodgy, mate. For a guy who likes saving the planet, you sure lack moral fibre.

Ed

27

SAM

I was texting at the table, and without Mara there to tell me not to, I could fiddle with my phone all night if I wanted. Mum, bless her, had requested a girls' night out with her daughters. And like many of the barely concealed plans to get Rebecca and me to spend time together that Mum had tried over the years, this one was bound for failure. She was bustling – in fact she was even managing to bustle while she was sitting down, for Pete's sake. She was on a mission and I had a terrible feeling the mission was that this girls'-night malarkey would become a regular occurrence. Right on cue she began gushing once the preliminary – and in both Rebecca's and my case begrudging – hellos had been dispensed with.

'So Suzanne has this thing with her daughters.' She paused and looked at each of us in turn, making sure we were paying attention. I lifted my head from the phone long enough for her to stop looking at me. I had no desire to hear anything more. It was Suzanne who inspired Mum to enthusiastically slap up friezes, a different one for each room, throughout the entire house, a good five years after they'd gone out of fashion. Suzanne, whose hair was so emphatically blow-dried it should come with a public health warning. Suzanne, who generated a special, Suzanne-sized sigh from Dad every time she 'popped in'. Suzanne, who lived next door.

'Once a month, they meet for a night together. A girls' night,' she added, hooking her fingers around the imaginary sentence hanging in the air in front of her.

We were silent.

'So I thought that might suit us.' She made big rotating motions with her hands. 'I mean, I know you're both really busy.' She shook her fingers in Rebecca's general direction. Oh yes, it was the full repertoire of her bustling plan-making. Lots of arm motions, lots of trilling. Way too much trilling.

'What do you think?'

'Well, it's a good idea in theory, Mum, but as you say, we're very busy,' Rebecca said, while I sort of hmmmed in half-hearted agreement.

'Great!' Mum beamed. 'Now let's have a look at this menu. It certainly is different, isn't it?'

We were eating Lebanese food, on account of Petersfield not having any, so in Mum's book that definitely counted as 'different'. Anything that wasn't curry or Chinese would probably fall under this bracket. And different is what Mum loved. She wasn't a small-town bigot, no way. She always got very excited about new experiences.

'Look at that lovely picture!' (A faded, slightly food-spattered print of a hubbly-bubbly pipe.)

'These cushions are nice!' (Running her multi-ringed fingers over cheap velveteen.)

'Do you think these people are all Lebanese, you know, to get some authentic food?' (Said in a stage whisper, as she peered around at the other diners, none of whom jumped out as particularly, or even partly, Lebanese.)

Once through this little routine she settled back in her chair, happy as anything. Here she was with her girls in an interesting place. What could be better?

151

'So James hasn't returned any of my calls,' Rebecca stabbed across the table.

'Oh dear, that must feel awful for you, darling,' and the conversation galloped off around the rocky, windswept terrain that was Rebecca's broken heart. And as nauseating as it was I didn't mind it that much, at least not for the moment. I tuned out and tuned back into checking Facebook and noticing (not without considerable relief) that there were no new photos of Charlie with any beautiful women on there from today. In fact, I was discovering quite quickly that Charlie wasn't really on Facebook much. Most of the photos posted were uploaded by his friends, not by him, which was probably a good thing. I was trying to see it as a good thing anyway. He was too busy doing other things – that was good, right? Of course it was. The problem with him not Facebooking of course meant that I started imagining all of those other things he was too busy doing and it invariably involved him looking all sharp and gorgeous, with some silky stick on his arm who wasn't me.

'Ooooh! Here comes the food, girls, put your phones away!' Mum shook her hands and the waiter looked worried for a moment. I think he may have thought she was about to break into song or, worse, dance.

'Delicious! Girls, doesn't it smell amazing?'

She was right. Tantalising dishes smelling of garlic, mint and warm spices were placed on the table, and I quite happily dropped my phone into my bag. My mouth was watering. I piled my plate up high with a bit of everything and dug in.

After a bit, Mum turned her attention to me. 'How's Mara?' she asked.

I nodded, not wanting to let any of the bulgar wheat escape. It was too good! How come I can never get it to turn out like this? I thought. I could never get bulgar to do anything but sit in a wet cardboardy lump.

'How's her job at the library?' Mum was insisting. She had

heard all about Rebecca's life – now it was my turn. This was what Mum called fair. Personally I called it annoying.

'Good, I think.' Dammit, some of the out-of-this-world salad escaped into my lap – a double waste, as I wasn't actually sure if that answer had been correct. I realised, as I tried unsuccessfully to rescue the tiny grains from beneath my crotch, that I actually hadn't asked Mara about work for a long time. She could be having a really crap time and I wouldn't know. God, I could be a shit friend sometimes.

'And is Ed still staying?'

'Yes but he's off up to Scotland for some work a week on Monday.'

'Is he well?'

I shovelled another forkful in and nodded at Mum. Of course the parents loved Ed; after all, being Mara's twin was all the credentials he needed. In fact sometimes I did wonder if Mara and I were ever to stop being friends which of us my parents would rather keep.

'He's very dry, isn't he?' Rebecca chipped in. 'As in, his sense of humour.'

'Sorry?'

Mum looked at Rebecca. I could see by her expression that she was surprised Rebecca even had an opinion about him. I groaned inwardly. Next thing would be Mum getting her hopes up that Rebecca and I were actually spending time together and enjoying it. But I wasn't expecting what came next.

'I went out with him the other week,' Rebecca explained, glancing across to make sure I was listening.

'You what?' Then I twigged – the party.

'He's a clever guy,' she said, as if that was a surprise.

'Of course he's clever,' I snorted. 'Mara's smart!'

'Yes, she is smart, but Ed, he's very social, isn't he?'

'What do you mean by that?'

153

'Well, he's very charming, very amusing. Easy to be around.'

'So is Mara.'

'If you're her friend, perhaps,' Rebecca said, after a small pause.

I glared at her. I knew how awkward Mara could be socially but I was the only one who was allowed to point that out.

'Well, it's nice you're getting to know him. Maybe it'll take your mind off things, darling,' Mum said brightly.

Rebecca put her head on her side and looked at her plate, arranged so carefully with careful little heaps of food. It was her cute-coy look. My least favourite. I moved my head around to look at Mum instead before I reached out and wiped that stupid look off Rebecca's face. Mum smiled.

'How about you, darling? Have you seen Charlie again?'

I wished I didn't blush so easily.

'He's been really busy . . . and so have I,' I stammered.

'Right . . .' Mum said, waiting for more.

I didn't have to look to know my stuttering would be giving Rebecca huge satisfaction. But I honestly didn't know what to say. I wanted the conversation to move along but all I could do was worry the skin on the sides of my nails. But then I also couldn't let an opportunity to surprise Rebecca pass.

'I haven't seen him much but we'll catch up next weekend. I'm going to his birthday party,' I said in the most nonchalant tone I could muster. As if it was, in fact, an afterthought, something I'd only just remembered then – not something filling my whole fucking being every fucking second of every fucking day.

'That's lovely!' Mum said.

Rebecca looked confused, almost agitated.

'But I told you he's got a girlfriend!' she squeaked.

'I didn't invite myself. He asked me. Anyway, what's wrong with me going? I'm just an old friend he bumped into – what exactly is the problem with that?'

154

'The problem is you're his ex-girlfriend!'

I held my hands up. 'Settle down, petal. What the hell is your problem?'

'Girls, girls, please!' Mum hissed at us, flapping her hands around in the air between us, as if trying to disperse smoke.

Rebecca glared at me for a moment more and then I could see her reining herself in. Back, back, back she retreated, her emotions back in their metal box, her mouth a thin line.

'I don't have a problem,' she said icily, 'but I doubt Lucy will appreciate it.'

I gazed at the hubbly-bubbly pipe masterpiece on the wall so she wouldn't see how much I had thought about this. 'Well, either Charlie doesn't think it's an issue or, if you're right and Lucy will care that his ex is there, he obviously doesn't think much of her.'

'He doesn't care for her much,' Rebecca said quickly. My head whipped away from the picture. I just caught the regret in her face before she tried covering it up with some story about how he'd let her down recently but then made it up to her . . . blah blah . . . but I wasn't listening. I'd heard all I needed to hear. Inside I was beaming. In fact, I was so pleased I could have almost kissed Rebecca. Almost, but not quite.

Mum had to leave early, as there was a limited service on the trains to Petersfield that night, so everyone was spared any more awkward conversations about Charlie. The bill came and both Rebecca and myself insisted on splitting it three ways, both vying to prove to Mum who was more grown up. But the waiter came back with my card, a look of apology on his face, and my heart sank. Oh crap.

In a flash, Rebecca was pressing a note into his hand and shooing him away.

'No, no, I'll get it,' Mum objected, fumbling for her purse. But it was too late. The waiter inclined his head in thanks and

155

disappeared with the money. He knew better than to argue with a woman like Rebecca. She looked stronger than most of the men he'd done his military service with and he couldn't get away from her fast enough.

I couldn't get away fast enough either. I said my goodbyes and walked briskly to the Tube, trying to shake off the smarting shame I felt with Rebecca covering me. Now I owed money to her on top of Claudia, Mara, and God knows how much to Mum and Dad. Claudia insisted I needn't pay her back but I could sense Mara was getting tense about the money I owed at the flat. I'd been short on my rent the previous month and had forgotten to contribute to food for the past couple of weeks. Damn money, I hated it. I felt ashamed and disorganised and weak. It was always such a mystery – I'm paid a chunk of money, not bad money either, for every job I do, and every time I think brilliant! Now I've got loads of cash, I'll be able to this and that with it. But then it goes. All of it and then some, and I'm in the bloody red again. Again and again and again.

I ran up and down every step at every Tube station, to try to burn the shame and anger away, finishing with a jog down Harvist Road. The house was silent when I crept in. The doors to the sitting room and Mara's bedroom were closed. On the kitchen table I found a note from Mara.

Sam –
Some bills have come in, and I did some sums tonight –
Food £66.50 (last couple of weeks)
Electricity/Gas £58 each
Thanks,
M x

Bloody brilliant.

28

SAM

I flicked through Mara's newspaper, occasionally glancing at the clock as I waited for the buzzer to the street door. I was having trouble focussing on the words. I needed a coffee for them to start stringing together into something that made sense but I'd have to wait for Ed for that. I hadn't made a single cup for myself since he'd arrived home – his were too good.

I was waiting for Kate. She'd called that morning and Mara had said yes, she was sure that Sam could have the kids and, if not, Ed would be able to. Just bring them around.

'Thanks for offering my babysitting services without consulting me!' I'd grumped at her before she'd left for work. I'd instantly regretted it though. Of course I'd be happy to have the kids. We all did what we could to support Kate since Martin had left her. Out of Mara's family, Kate was the one that everyone – not just Mara – felt a little protective of and went out of their way to help. She was so nice, and her kids were such fun anyway. It never felt like you were doing them a favour. Seeing them always cheered me up. They didn't give a rat's bum what I looked like, or what I said or didn't say. I didn't have to be anyone but myself around them. The buzzer blurted across my thoughts. I crossed the kitchen and pressed the talk button.

'Hi, it's me, sorry.'

It was Kate. I could hear Rosie whining in the background.

'Don't apologise, come on up.'

I went down the hall to the front door and after a few moments I could see the outline of Kate and two small heads. Even through the door I could hear her trying to control Luke and Rosie, asking them to calm down before entering the flat. The sitting-room door was closed; Ed must still be asleep. Not for much longer, I thought. I smiled at them as I opened the door.

'Hi, guys, come in!' Nice and loud, that'll do it.

'Now, don't forget, we're playing quiet little mice.' Kate walked through the door and crossed her eyes at me. 'Thank you so much for this, you're a lifesaver.'

'No problem, it's my pleasure.' And it was. Kate knelt down to give each kid a squeeze, her thick dark hair wrapping around each child's head and obscuring their mussy blonde tops. Why do the Minkleys have such amazing hair? I thought for the millionth time. The girl could pass as Kate Middleton. So friggin' beautiful it was almost painful to look at her. And she was a genuinely lovely person. I shook my head.

'Come on, monsters, let's go down to the kitchen. Mummy, you push off,' I said, holding the door open for her. 'Go on, you. We'll be just fine.' Kate hovered for a moment, looking uncertainly at me in a way that just made me want to hug her. So sweet and earnest, her worries and pleasures passing across her fairy-fine features like the weather. I bent down and scooped Rosie up before she started grizzling and pretended to eat her pudgy little arm.

'Thanks, Sam. I really appreciate it.'

'Go on, you'll be late!'

Kate went to leave, and then turned and smiled. 'You're a real natural with kids, did you know that? You'll make a great mother one day.'

I snorted. That was the silliest thing I'd heard all week. A mum? I was barely an adult.

Kate left and I put Rosie down to roar down the hall, no doubt to see what there was to eat in the kitchen, with Luke right behind her. For a moment I thought they were heading straight for the fridge (maybe letting them drink milk straight out of the container last time I looked after them wasn't so hilarious after all), but instead Rosie surprised George, who had chosen the wrong moment to settle down for a nap on Mara's chair.

'Cat, cat!' Rosie reached out her hand to pat him.

'Hold up, Rosie.' I knelt down beside her. 'I'm not sure if George feels like cuddles. Just look, no touching.' Rosie's chin wobbled a little and her mouth turned down while she tried to decide if she would get upset about this. I took her hand.

'Look. Let's do it really slowly.' I guided Rosie's hand onto George's back. Her chubby fingers disappeared into his coat.

'It's all right, George, it's only Rosie,' I said to him, my voice soft and my gaze stern. He looked at me briefly and then graciously lowered his eyelids in pleasure, his head retracting into the puff of his body. Rosie was entranced and I felt my heart melt. Maybe I could do this one day after all, I thought.

Then, at the top of his voice, Luke yelled, 'I wanna go!' and pulled Rosie's arm away. Rosie screamed in protest and George leapt off the chair with a wail and disappeared into the hallway.

'Luke! Look what you've done. Say sorry to Rosie!' OK maybe I wasn't ready just yet.

Luke frowned at us, his hands thrust deep into his pockets.

'I was waiting for ages!'

I had plenty to say in return but miraculously I remembered the namby-pamby counting to ten in your head that Kate talked about doing. Eventually he spat out a quiet, angry sorry, as if he was emptying his pockets and letting a little stone fall to the floor. I did wonder at that point how on earth I could have been looking forward to seeing them a minute ago. God, I really needed that coffee now.

'I've got an idea. Why don't you go and wake your Uncle Ed up?' I suggested.

That did the trick – it was as if I'd mentioned Christmas. Luke's face lit up and he ran down the hallway with Rosie following.

I nipped to the loo and moments later found them body slamming Ed.

'Charge!'

'Aaaaaahhh!'

'Hey, that's en— oomph.'

I stood at the door grinning. My vision of enjoying one of Ed's coffees while the children quietly drew at the table with me was perhaps, I thought, a little ambitious.

'Thanks for my – umpf – wake-up call. Remind me to get some alarm clocks like these for your birthday,' he said.

'My pleasure. So, kids, who wants to come to the park?'

Ed looked up to say something but was smothered by a flying Rosie.

'Hello? I said who wants to come to the park with me?'

The children continued to ignore me. Ed's head was nowhere to be seen.

'What if Ed came too?' I tried. There was an almost deafening roar of approval. I covered my ears. At least I'd finally got their attention.

Ed looked at me questioningly.

'There's coffee near the park, lazybones, come on.'

Ed looked doubtful.

'It's quite good actually. It is!'

'All right, all right. You kids get out and let me get dressed,' he said.

'We'll meet you outside,' I said, suddenly aware that I had

160

no idea what he had on underneath the duvet.

I took the shirt Rosie was holding out to Ed from her hand. I was going to give it to him but halfway through passing it to him I was overcome with awkwardness, and threw it on the bed instead. I clattered down the stairs with the kids, the vision of Ed's naked torso sitting up in bed imprinted, unbidden, on my mind.

We walked to the park through empty Monday streets. The sun shone weakly as if it was calling London to imagine what spring would feel like in a few weeks. Ed seemed more relaxed, walking with slow strides while Luke tried to match him with his much shorter legs. I felt happiness well up inside me. The day felt full of possibilities.

Rosie held my hand and half skipped, half walked as she pulled me along. She sang little songs to herself and stumbled sometimes in her excitement to keep up. And before I could edit my thoughts I blurted out happily, 'Well, isn't this a lovely family outing.'

Ed looked at me quizzically, his eyes glinting darkly against the blue sky. 'Really? I didn't know we were playing mummies and daddies.'

I felt my cheeks warm. 'I, uh, ha ha ha,' I laughed nervously. 'I didn't mean it like that.'

'Like what?' Ed asked.

'Like you and me. I mean . . .' I glanced at him again. He was smiling a closed-lipped smile, his mouth twitching. 'Oh, Ed, you're laughing at me!'

His laugh escaped then, joyful and infectious. I couldn't help but join in, not exactly sure about what we were laughing at exactly – the idea of us together? At me being such an awkward twat? Who cared! It was all hilarious and my laughter spewed out like a geyser. Ha ha ha, I rattled, clutching my stomach, tears

161

running down my cheeks. Hee hee hee, I shrieked, as Luke and Rosie joined in with their easy giggling. It lasted the length of the walk and it wasn't until we were opening the gate to the park that I downgraded to sputtery little after-laughs that fell out every now and then.

Ed had always been able to do that – make me laugh at the weirdest things. Sometimes when I was with him it was almost as if I was in a whole other reality. I know that sounds all New Agey and naff. And I don't mean I'm high on drugs with him either. It was something else, as if there was always this possibility that we could be tipped into some parallel universe by one comment from him, where everything was nonsensical yet at the same time made complete sense in its craziness, if you know what I mean. I'm not really explaining myself very well but it was just something Ed did. I never felt like this with anyone else.

Luke was off like a fighter jet and was up the ladder to the slide in moments, yelling for us to come over and watch his mega sliding skills. Rosie wanted a go too so I stood behind her as she negotiated the ladder, reaching up so my hands formed an emergency backstop in case Rosie needed it. I could feel my top riding up, exposing my belly. I retracted one arm to attempt to pull my top down, suddenly conscious of Ed standing a few yards away at the far end of the slide, waiting for Luke to descend. I glanced at him but at that moment Luke barrelled straight through the tunnel Ed had made from his long legs.

'That was crap! I could go faster than that!' he yelled at Luke. Luke grinned and ran around to the ladder again, jiggling to reach the top of the ladder in impatience behind Rosie, who was still on her way up.

There was slide after slide after slide, and all the time Ed stayed focussed on the kids as they came down while I stayed at the ladder to make sure Rosie got up safely. I'd felt so euphoric, laughing so hard, and then so much lighter afterwards, a bit like I did after a good cry. But weirdly now I felt flat and a little awkward again. Had Ed actually been laughing at me the whole time? The kids moved on to the swings and I stood next to him as we pushed a swing each and wondered what to say. In the end all I could come up with was a rather lame, 'Um, so what are your plans, Ed?'

'Ooooh, look, she's getting all serious,' he said.

'I was just asking—'

'Sorry, I didn't mean it to sound like that. What plans do you mean?'

'You know, work, life, a place to live . . .'

'You kicking me out?' Ed asked, a little sharply.

I coloured. 'No. It's just a question.'

There was a small pause, then he answered, 'I know one thing. I'm bloody sick of making coffee.'

'Language!' I pointed to the kids.

He grimaced guiltily. 'Whoops, sorry, Mum.'

'Shut up!'

'Sorry.' He paused again. 'Well, I loved the day on the shoot and I can't wait for Scotland.'

'You did a great job.'

'Thanks.'

The swings squeaked as we pushed.

'So take photos,' I said.

'And live in London? Yeah, sure.'

'You could live with your dad for a while, while you get started.'

'I thought about all of that a lot while I was in India. I could do it but could I cope with having my will to live sapped from me in Bexley?'

'It's not that bad,' I said, more than a little uncertainly.

'I don't see you living there, Sam.'

'No, that's true.' I tried imagining Ed coming in every night to beans on toast in front of *Corrie*. I pictured his long legs ending in brown pseudo-suede slippers, exactly like his father's, the television flickering light onto his shut-down face. The image faltered and fell apart in my mind. It couldn't work. Ed loved a good debate over some hot and spicy food and vehemently loathed television. And I'm not sure I'd ever seen him in a pair of slippers.

'What about staying with us for longer then?' I said before giving it any thought. Did I really want Ed living with us full-time? He'd only been here ten days and everything seemed more complicated than it had been before.

Thankfully, before I was forced to hang out with that thought for any longer, the kids ran off to the sandpit and we followed them slowly. Ed joined them and started pushing sand together to make a castle.

I hesitated before joining in too. There was a seat nearby; maybe I should sit there? But I wanted to sit near him for some reason. I started pushing the wet sand around and hoped he wasn't sick of me pestering him. We didn't speak for a few moments and the kids warbled away. I'd forgotten that Ed hadn't answered my question and was startled when he started talking.

'I might ask Kate if I can stay with her,' he said.

I looked up. 'Oh right, yes.'

'I think, in the circumstances, that would be better.'

'In the circumstances?' What circumstances could he mean?

'She's got a box room I could sleep in,' he said.

'Oh yes, of course.' A room of his own of course.

'What did you think I meant?' Ed asked, and I looked up because I could hear that his voice was sweet and open, not laced with sarcasm. He was looking at me intently over the top of the children's heads and for a moment I felt as if my chest was caving into my stomach.

'ROSIE!' The children erupted between us, Luke roaring in indignation as Rosie stomped all over the castle.

'Get off it, Rosie, get off.' He lashed out with fists flying but Ed held him back. Rosie burst into tears.

'Come on, monsters, let's see what treats are on offer at the café.'

'Yay! Café!'

Kate complains about never getting a sentence finished with the little interrupters around but right then I was stupidly grateful to them for interrupting the weirdness. There was some pretty strong coffee withdrawal going on here. Why hadn't we stopped at the café on the way to the park? That was a serious error in judgement. I stood and gathered up discarded gloves and hats.

We walked to the café, grabbed takeaways and then walked home without talking any more between ourselves. I was happy to listen to the kids prattle. I couldn't help stealing glances at Ed's face now and then but it looked like the Minkley shutdown was in action. I wouldn't be getting any eye contact from him now. Which was a good thing, of course. I'm nowhere near his type – far too ditzy – and anyway, it was Charlie I wanted to impress. I watched my feet walking one step in front of the other all the way home.

29

CLAUDIA

In the end, I couldn't seem to come up with an excuse not to have dinner with John. I saw him in the corner as soon as I walked in and my tummy did a little flip. He had chosen a beautiful restaurant to meet. I wasn't sure what was worse: telling him my sordid news in a place like this – candles on each table, murmured conversations peppered with the chink of fine glass, the chip-chip of silver on bone china – or a fast food outlet with fluorescent lighting. How was I meant to say chlamydia in this room? Then again, I hadn't set foot in McDonalds since I was a teenager and I wasn't intending to any time soon, so this wasn't actually an argument. He had also seen me. I took a deep breath and walked across the room.

He stood up for me as I took my seat. I wished he wouldn't. Not tonight.

'You look lovely,' he said.

'Thank you.' I picked up the menu. I had really thought I could do this. I thought I wanted to but now I wasn't at all sure how I was going to get the words out.

I had left work early that day and sat in a hot bath at home for twenty minutes, hoping to boil my nerves into submission. It worked long enough for me to dress and get out of the door but as I travelled across town, they started writhing away in my belly again. I tried to ignore them, to take control of the situation.

In the back of the black cab, I wrote down a list of all the men from the last six months in careful script. I reached twelve but I had a feeling there were a couple missing. I could sense them rather than remember who they were. But my head was noisy and not behaving. I snapped my notebook shut. There was the restaurant. First things first, I had to tell John.

'So . . .' John put his menu down. I waited for him to ask me how I was. That was when I was going to tell him the truth. Straight into it, get it over and done with.

'Have you heard about Greg and Laura?' he asked.

Oh, thank you! He knew some office gossip and it became clear to me that he was easing me into the evening. It could be possible that I had never spent time with a man with better social skills. We chatted about our colleagues and the starters came, were eaten and were cleared. The elephant in the room sat politely a little out of view and my nervous tummy settled down a little.

Over the main course we stayed on another safe topic: sharing tales of woe and stupidity from holidays. John told me an elaborate tale from his last holiday, when he found himself stranded in a small village in France waiting for his motorbike to be fixed. The locals were about as welcoming to this large Englishman as Mrs Thatcher was to the miners. He was a natural, spinning out the story bit by bit, making himself the self-deprecating hero who tried every way he could to ingratiate himself with the locals and failed. I almost forgot why I was there and was surprised to find myself laughing. I reached for my mineral water.

'You're not drinking?'

'I don't really feel like it,' I answered, trying to brush him off. He smiled, as if me not drinking was something to be excited about.

Finally, as we were drinking coffee, I invited the elephant to come and join us.

167

'John, I need to talk to you,' I said.

John put his cup down on its saucer, linked his fingers together and rested them on the table. That's weird, I thought. He's reminding me of someone.

'I'm all ears.'

'Right. OK.' I paused and took a breath. 'I went to the doctor last week.'

John smiled again, as if I'd just given him a present and he was about to open it.

'Yes?'

I paused. I wished he wouldn't look so expectant.

'I . . . ah . . . I found out yesterday that I've tested positive for an STI.' There, I'd said it.

John's face stopped shining abruptly. 'Y-you've what?' he stammered.

I sighed. I didn't want to have to say it again. 'I've tested positive for an STI, chlamydia to be precise.' Argh, wash your mouth out.

'Oh dear,' he said evenly, blinking as if that would somehow make his brain take in the information faster.

'Yes,' I said. I couldn't think of what else to say so I took another sip of coffee. It was lukewarm and tasted stale. I realised in that moment that I'd expected to feel relief when I told him but now I just felt tired.

'So,' I prodded after a bit, 'you'll need to get tested for it too.'

He looked at me, his mouth grim. 'Yes, of course.'

We sat in silence until I couldn't bear the tension any longer, at which point I excused myself to a thankfully empty bathroom and leant on the basin to stare in the mirror. A very jaded Claudia looked back. My lips were flat and turned down at each corner, drawing down my cheeks, my eyes, my nose and making me look much older, beakier even. And sad, so sad. What did John see in

168

me in the first place? All I could see now was a washed-up old hag. I felt overwhelmed with loneliness.

The waitress was taking John's card when I returned. We were off then. I hovered next to the table, my handbag in hand and waited for the waitress to leave.

'So I'd better go home,' I said.

John didn't look up. 'OK,' he said to his fingers. And then I had it – Papa linked his fingers together like that. My gentle, darling father. Hot pain stabbed my belly and tears welled, threatening to overflow. There was no way John had given me this horrid STI. How on earth could I have thought he'd given it to me? He was a tart, sure, but it took one to know one. Yet seeing his fingers quietly interlocked with those big hands, I could see he was also a gentleman, a solid, self-aware man. I choked out a quiet goodbye and hurried out into the dark night, running down the street, trying to run from the disappointment, the dreadful realisation that I'd met my equal at long last, slept with him, brushed him off and then told him he might have chlamydia.

30

SAM

I yawned. I'd been chasing Charlie all night in my dreams, and now my eyes felt dry and gritty. Behind my forehead sat a sluggish tiredness. I tried rubbing my face in a pathetic attempt to invigorate myself but it was no use. It was as if concrete had been poured into my head, smothering all useful brain activity. All that was left was a feeling of stolid dullness. I was drowning in dullness – what a lovely way to spend your day. This could top shopping in H&M.

Thankfully I didn't have to think too much for myself. Keeping my eyes and ears open and being sensible were the key skills required on set, which was lucky considering that was all I could manage. Late the previous night I'd said yes to a job as a runner on a commercial the next day, starting at six in the morning. I really didn't want to do it but I didn't have a choice. As my grandfather was fond of saying (usually when I was broke), when the wolf was at the door you just had to feed it. It was just a pity that keeping the wolf from the door started so early in the morning.

The shoot was on a pedestrian-only street so most of the day had been spent on one side of the set-up directing shoppers around the scene, making sure they didn't walk straight into shot, but also, more importantly, making sure they didn't stop and gawp. Somehow the minutes and hours had ticked over. Now it was mid-afternoon and all I wanted to do was lie down and sleep. I could do it right here, I mused, staring at the now-very-familiar footpath under my feet. In fact, the longer I stood there, the more I was sure that if I lay down I would go straight off.

'Can you take this to the production office?' I jumped. The production manager, clutching a small package, was suddenly at my elbow.

'Sorry,' he said.

'Oh no, I'd love to.' I couldn't wait to have another job to do.

'I meant, I'm sorry for making you jump.'

'Yes, of course.' I glanced at his hard face, his mouth pinched with tension, and had one of my moments of utterly despising the whole stressed-out world of film and TV, where too many people took themselves far too seriously. But although I couldn't wait to get away from him, whatever his name was (concrete head couldn't recall it), my damn professionalism stopped me from taking off straightaway.

'Who's going to direct people while I'm gone then?'

'I will, so make it snappy.'

'Right.'

I set off at a quick march. Soho wasn't far away and I trotted through the narrow streets busy with creatives coming back from lunch. It was good to be on the move and to get away from the boredom of being on set.

The office was a postmodern number that the architect had forgotten to give windows to, tucked in-between two older buildings. At reception, what looked like a fourteen-year-old girl sat at her desk, trying to look busy. The intern, no doubt. As I got closer, I noted the girl was dressed head to toe in something exceedingly expensive, and so cutting edge it made the office furniture bought all of six months ago look desperately uncool.

'Can I help you?' she asked politely. I smiled. The vowels

171

confirmed it. Here was a fine specimen of the trust-fund intern. I waved the package at her.

'I need to give this to . . .' I looked at the package again. 'Caro Schneider?'

'One moment.'

The girl picked up the phone, listened and then replaced the handset.

'She's on the phone right now. I'll let her know that you're here.'

'I'm from the Moore & Tyler shoot.'

'Right, thanks. Take a seat.'

I knew if I sat down I'd have trouble staying awake so I remained standing and paced the small foyer. The open-plan office behind the receptionist was empty but at the back of the room were a couple of small rooms walled off from the rest of the space with their doors open. Through one of them I could hear a woman talking animatedly on the phone, presumably Caro. After a couple of minutes it was clear Caro was organising a dinner date with a friend. Good, I thought. She won't be long then. But the minutes ticked by and soon two minutes were five. I briefly wondered if I should just leave the package with the intern. Surly old whatshisname hadn't specified that I give it to Caro in person. But he hadn't said give it to just anyone either. I decided that, on balance, I'd rather return to a grumpy production manager a few minutes late than find out tomorrow that the rushes from the morning had been lost and it was all my bloody fault.

I checked my watch again. I'd been waiting seven minutes.

'Look, can I just pop my head in her door, please? I really need to get back to the shoot.'

'She's quite particular about not being interrupted.'

Caro's words came out of her door shrill and clear, 'But,

darling, we can't invite her, she spends the whole time in the toilet doing who knows what and then falls asleep in the meringue. What was that? Oh no, darling, I work far too hard to make them myself, there's this darling little patisserie round the corner from work where I pick them up but I'm not doing them this time . . .' On and on she went, chirruping away about dessert after dessert.

I met the intern's eye. The girl grinned, which made her look reassuringly older and slightly cheeky.

'I'm sure she wouldn't mind me interrupting pudding, it'd only take a moment.'

'Go on then.' The girl motioned towards Caro's office, giggling quietly, and I marched quickly across the floor, knocked once and placed the package squarely on Caro's desk. She looked at me in surprise but didn't stop talking. I smiled at her without warmth, patted the package with emphasis and left, winking at the intern on the way and jogging down the stairs onto the street. Somehow I'd been away from the shoot for ten minutes already – great. Mr Surlypants was not going to be pleasant when I returned. I felt my phone vibrate and I hoicked it quickly out of my pocket, hoping it wouldn't be him. I didn't recognise the number so I answered it quickly.

'Hello?'

'Sam.'

My heart dropped.

'Hi, Rebecca.'

'How's your day going?' This wasn't a good sign. She was being nice.

'Pretty shit to be honest and I can't talk for long, I'm working.'

'That's OK. I was just checking in.'

Checking in? Rebecca didn't check in. Check up, yes, but not check in.

'Right. Yeah. I'm OK, just tired. You OK?'

'Oh yes, thank you,' she said brightly, 'it was a nice evening the other night with Mum.'

If you say so, I thought.

'I just wanted to say that you don't have to pay me back that money you owe me.'

'That's not necessary, Rebecca, I will pay you back once I've been paid for this job.'

'No, really, it's nice to help out. I've just got this job so I'm doing OK.'

You mean you're doing better than I am, I thought.

'I will pay you back.'

'No, please don't, honestly. Anyway, gotta go, hope your day gets better!'

'Bye.' I shoved my phone back in my pocket. A generous Rebecca was even more annoying than the usual nasty one. It's because, I fumed, she doesn't genuinely want to help – she just wants to gloat. Left, right, right, nearly there. Fucking money, I thought as I stomped. Fucking smelly old wolf at the door.

Then I was back to the production manager, puffing slightly and frowning significantly and, no surprise, he echoed my expression minus the panting.

'I know, I took my time!' I barked before he could open his mouth. 'Caro made me wait while she discussed what dessert to serve at some dinner party. Eventually I gave up and put it on her desk.'

'There was no one else there?'

'Yes, the pretty thing manning the phones. But you didn't say drop it off to just anyone.'

'Well, that's fine then.' He turned to go and then turned back. 'Dessert did you say?'

'Yes.'

'From the darling little patisserie round the corner?'

174

'That's the one.'

The corner of his mouth was twitching into a grin and I couldn't help but join in.

'You shouldn't have been listening in, of course.'

'I wasn't listening in, it was more like the office was being addressed by tannoy.'

The PM laughed then, a big barky laugh that squished his shrewd little eyes into raisins. 'You're funny, Sam,' he said, then he turned away and went off to boss someone else around.

Eventually the day was over and I was paid in sweet cash. I stowed the money I owed Rebecca and Mara into a separate part of my wallet and counted the rest. That would keep the wolf from the door and maybe even buy me some shoes for the party. But shoes could wait. I just wanted to get home. For the first time all day I actually felt slightly relaxed, maybe even a little happy. Perhaps Mara would be home when I got in, with some food ready. We could have a nice catch-up and then I could have a bath and go to bed, safe in the knowledge I had enough money for a few days.

But the flat was dark and quiet when I got home, with a note from Mara saying she and Ed had gone to stay with their dad for the night. I felt very alone. Next to the note was a single, pathetic bill addressed to me. It was from EE. I sighed and opened it, knowing what it was going to say. There it was in black and white. I was overdue with last month's bill and if I didn't pay it in the next week, my phone would be cut off.

31

MARA

I insisted that we sit at the table for tea. Dad just grunted in response but I was determined to ignore him. It was usually the best thing to do. Dad's grumpiness was barely skin-deep, an annoying habit rather than his nature and is best sidestepped. It was a crutch, really – unfortunately one he'd become very reliant on over the last couple of years. A little like the newspaper he refused to move while I laid the table around him.

'Could you not move that?'

Dad sighed and in painful slow motion folded his newspaper in half while I put the food on the table but not without me catching sight of him smirking. Oh, you are a belligerent old sod, I thought as I slipped a coaster under his can of Fosters.

'I don't bother about that, love.'

'You don't usually bother with the table at all,' I said, a little more sharply than I'd intended. But any contrition I felt at snapping at him was short-lived. I watched him and Ed share a complicit snigger. I frowned. It was meant to be Ed and me enduring him, not Dad and Ed putting up with me!

'It's been ages since I've had a home-cooked meal, love,' Dad said, wiping the look off his face.

'Don't you go next door on a Monday any more?'

'Oh yes, but that was Monday, wasn't it?' And for a moment, his long-dormant cheekiness twinkled in his eyes. My heart

176

softened. It was always like this, visiting Dad. Feeling full of love and empathy one moment, sharply irritated the next, then settling on a general feeling of sadness and regret.

Two years on, Dad hadn't really moved on after Mum up and left him for Roger – some man with a tan who seemed to come out of thin air. None of us had ever heard of him, that was for certain. When we questioned her, all she said was that she'd had enough. Actually, it was more along the lines of – 'Why? Why? Isn't it obvious? I've had enough! E-bloody-nough! I want more from life than sitting around watching the bleedin' telly!'

She packed her clothes and jewellery into two suitcases and went to live with Roger in Tenerife. Just like that. Thirty-five years of marriage and she left with two bags. It broke Dad's heart, it did. And it broke my heart to see him like this, the sad old sack. But he was also the sad old sack that Mum had got completely fed up with, and more and more I could see why, though I wished I couldn't.

After dinner, Ed started on the dishes and I switched from thinking about Dad to thinking about how I would broach the subject of Rebecca. Ed would have his hands busy and he wouldn't have to look at me as I did the drying up. Dad would be settled in front of the telly so no need to worry about him.

'I'll put away then, shall I?' Dad said.

'You don't have to Dad, you go and relax.'

'No, I'd like to. I spend too many evenings alone in front of the box.'

'Right. Of course.'

I wished I didn't feel so disappointed. Of course he wanted to spend time with his twins. I shouldn't feel upset about it. What kind of daughter would feel upset about that? So, very slowly, Dad put the dishes away in the tiny cupboards. Usually I found the pokey little cupboards, unchanged since the sixties, comforting. I was proud of them and their history and lack of space for big modern plates. But I opened them and felt slightly depressed that evening.

Dad told us a story from the garage. I wasn't listening properly to start with, too preoccupied with wanting to speak with Ed. But, as he spoke, he became perkier than I'd seen him in months. His brusqueness fell away and he was as grateful as a puppy for the company. The guilt of not visiting more piled up on my shoulders as I dried and by the time the dishes were done, I heard myself saying I'd join him in front of a *Top Gear* rerun.

'A Jeremy Clarkson fan are we now, Mars?' Ed asked me, his head in a cupboard looking for biscuits.

'You know perfectly well I am not a fan of Jeremy twatting Clarkson.'

Ed withdrew his head, a packet of Penguins in his hand and a big grin on his face.

I snatched the biscuits out of his hand and marched into the lounge.

I amazed myself by lasting twenty whole minutes in front of the television without throwing a single Penguin at the screen. I was sure that the more Penguins I ate, the less guilty I felt about not coming more often. It didn't stop anyone on *Top Gear* being a complete jerk, of course, but I made a mental note to eat chocolate before I pitched up to Dad's. But twenty minutes was still my absolute limit, and I kissed Dad on the forehead and went upstairs to find Ed, who had disappeared after only ten!

Ed's door was shut. I knocked softly and opened it. There he was, sitting on his old single bed with a box half unpacked all over the bed.

'Taking a walk down memory lane?' I asked him and closed the door behind me.

'Something like that,' he said, looking a little sheepish.

I sat down on the bed with him and picked up a 1998 *Face* magazine and flicked through it absently.

'Dad enjoyed the evening,' I said.

'Yeah.' Ed was quiet for a bit. 'It makes you sad though, doesn't it? Seeing him light up like that makes his sadness look much bigger in comparison.'

'Definitely.'

I forced myself to flick through to the end of the magazine before I spoke again.

'How are you anyway?'

'Oh, good. Can't wait to go on this job.' He wasn't looking at me, just shuffling through shoebox after shoebox filled with photos.

'Bet you can't, you're going to love it.'

I watched him lean forward and grab another handful of photographs and then said, as casually as I could, 'Rebecca looked upset that you'd be gone for so long.'

'She did?' Ed looked at the door, shrugged and returned to the pile of photographs. Not a flicker of guilt on his face. But he didn't look at me either.

'I don't like her, if that's what you're worried about, Mars,' he said, not looking up from whatever photo he was holding.

I felt myself blush. I didn't really have anything more to say. Although I hadn't had the backbone to look him in the eye, I could hear that his voice was straight and honest and I'd heard what I needed to hear. So I picked at the knobbly green bedspread that had been on the bed for as long as I could remember and enjoyed the sweetness of relief. When the green bobbles had been picked enough, I lifted my head and peered over the rim of the box.

'So what treasures have you got in here anyway?' I took out a handful of photographs and started flicking through them. They were mostly arty ones he'd taken years ago. I smiled as I saw the

179

familiar images, reminding me of times past, and also charting the development of Ed. They were little windows into Ed's mind as it grew through his teens and twenties. There were images of graffiti (anarchic phase); homeless men huddled in shop doors (social consciousness growing); the obligatory headstones (every photographer has some); and the start of his street scenes: people going about their business in various neighbourhoods. Then, after a couple of photos of blank walls, came a crumpled photo of Sam and I, arms thrown around each other's shoulders, our faces turned to the sun laughing. It was in the summer, in Hyde Park, at a music festival. I smiled. That was a good day. But then I realised.

'Ed, where did you get this?'

Ed glanced at the photo and hesitated slightly before shrugging his shoulders. He returned to flicking through the stack he was looking at but I could tell he wasn't really looking at the photos. He looked uncomfortable. And well he might, I thought. This photograph had been on the fridge in the flat for a few months before disappearing. I'd assumed it had fallen underneath the fridge and I'd forgotten about it. But here it was amongst Ed's things, of all places! My unease returned and flooded my body, bringing with it a heavy weariness. Maybe I wasn't in the mood for talking after all. I stood up. Maybe I wasn't ready to hear what was going on at all.

'I'm off to bed now.'

'OK, sleep well,' he replied, his head still bent over the photos. I stood there waiting for him to look up at me and when he finally did his eyes met mine for the briefest of moments. He wasn't letting me in.

'Night, Mars,' he said.

32

SAM

By lunchtime on Saturday, I was filled with that wormy boredom Saturdays are prone to producing – especially ones that aren't spent hungover. I had more energy than I knew what to do with and zero motivation to use it.

Without Mara and Ed around, the flat was far too quiet. Now and then, George would mew anxiously, calling for Mara. His cries seemed to magnify how lonely I felt and also how crap I was at spending time alone. I picked up a magazine but I couldn't concentrate on it. I'd done the little housework there was to be done; the kitchen counter was clear, the floor was swept. I checked my phone for the thirtieth time that morning. Nothing. From. Nobody.

Fuuuuuck.

Sort it out!

Just bloody text someone.

Him.

No, not him.

OK, him.

My fingers hovered briefly over the keys but only briefly.

Am free this afternoon, fancy a lazy drink? S

I hesitated over how to sign the text, almost adding a kiss; I usually did on texts to friends. But was Charlie a friend? No. He was an ex. One of those people in your life that don't really have a place. Can't file them into the friends drawer – not if you were being completely honest with yourself. Some you can just chuck into the enemies drawer but it's never that simple.

He'd replied straightaway.

Great. How about the Cock & Bull in Notting Hill? Cx

Was he for real? I laughed and it seemed to reverberate around the quiet room. Mara would find that hilarious. How apt, Charles, and how typical. He'd never been one for irony. But I couldn't show it to Mara, of course. I couldn't show the text to anyone because there was no one there to show. Nothing for it but to go out.

I marched down the street towards the Tube. The day was brightening and I was glad to leave the dead air at home behind. I was expecting him to be late but there he was at the bar when I arrived. I watched him for a moment before joining him. He took off his long black coat and laid it on a stool next to him. It was lined with salmon satin, the very edge of a gilt-edged label peeking out. I swallowed and crossed the room and watched with satisfaction how his face lit up when he saw me. I took a seat one stool away from him, the coat an island of fine tailoring between us, and took the glass he offered me. His eyes were loaded with innuendo.

We chatted about this and that. I could see an extra line under his eye I hadn't noticed a couple of weeks ago.

'You look a little tired.'

'I've been manic at work,' he said. Work! Why hadn't I thought of that all this time I was worrying he didn't want to see me? I nodded and took a sip, glad I hadn't asked him about his silence outright. It was strange but, for the second time, any annoyance I had been feeling for him dissolved. I shrugged away his behaviour. He couldn't help it really. He was my shitty ex. I supposed everyone would have one in their closet. An ex who was a bit – or a lot – of a bastard. A bad boy. Or in Charlie's case, a bad boy with a really good haircut.

'So what's new with you this week?' he asked, flicking his floppy fringy thing out of his eyes.

I paused. Other than thinking about you? I thought. Worrying about money. I opened my mouth and shut it again. No, I would not discuss that with him. I scraped around for something else . . . Ed. I could tell him about Ed.

'My flatmate's brother is home from India and is staying with us.'

'Oh yes, touring or working out there?'

'Taking photographs. Opening his mind, that kind of thing, I think.'

'Lucky chap. I'd like to take a photographic sojourn somewhere one day—'

Sojourn, what a pompous fart.

'—although you wouldn't catch me in India.'

I stiffened. Here we go. 'Why not, Charlie? Too many Indians?'

Charlie responded by laughing and holding his hands up in the air. 'You said it, not me.' He was loving this and it felt very familiar.

'You thought it.' I glared at him.

'How do you know?' He took a graceful but manly, practised sup from his pint and eyed his loafers. 'I could have been about to say that I don't have the right shoes.'

I struggled to keep a straight face. Damn you, Charlie. I could never work out if his prejudices were for real or not. I'd always thought he wasn't really as conservative as he made out but perhaps that was wishful thinking on my part. It didn't matter anyway. He was gorgeous and charming and twinkly-eyed. No matter what we argued about, we always used to end up laughing. He always charmed his way past the words into my heart, into my pants.

And as we sat there, at four o'clock on a Saturday afternoon, Charlie's eyes bored into me as ardently as they ever had before. His intention was very clear. I wriggled on my stool. My jeans were skintight, and I was becoming acutely aware of how tight they were at the very top of my legs.

'Fancy a stroll?' Charlie asked me.

The air cut into my cheeks so sharply it felt like it was taking a layer of skin off. Charlie pulled on soft black leather gloves and we marched down the road, my hands stuffed deeply into my pockets. He seemed to have a plan of where we were going and I was happy to go with him. At first I thought we might be going to Hyde Park but he turned down a residential street with white Victorian terraces running down both sides. The entranceways alternated between shabby chic and shipshape smart. They all appeared to be single dwellings – not carved into lots of little flats, like the street that Mara and I lived in. I was lost in a daydream imagining living in one of these beautiful homes when Charlie slowed down abruptly, took my elbow and steered me through a gate. A short black-and-white-checked walkway led up to a glossy black door, complete with a shiny brass doorknocker in the shape of a lion's head.

'Oh,' I said in surprise.

'Tea time.' Charlie twinkled at me, flicking his hair out of his eyes again.

'Oh?' Couldn't I say something else?

He took keys out of his pocket and opened the door.

'Welcome to my place,' he said. He stepped inside and waited for me to join him.

I eyed the brass lion as I passed; it returned my gaze imperiously. 'Beware, shabby intruder,' it seemed to be saying. I swallowed and followed him up the stairs.

His place was simple and orderly. A cream leather sofa sat next to a glass-topped coffee table with an enormous vase of lilies. An ultra-thin television sat sleekly in one corner. On his dining table, a bowl of fruit and piles of magazines. It felt tidy and calm, and lived in.

My mouth felt dry and my stomach bubbled nervously. We hadn't discussed his girlfriend and if the flowers were anything to go by, we should.

'So how's Lucy?'

There. Said it.

Charlie's shoulders stiffened and he looked at me, obviously trying to remember when he'd told me about his girlfriend. But you won't remember, I thought, because you haven't got around to telling me.

But with a shrug as if to say to himself, oh well it's probably better that she knows, he replied, 'She's away skiing at the moment with her family.'

'Nice.' I tried to smile like I cared. Of course I didn't care what fun Lucy was having. I wished she didn't exist at all. But at least she wasn't in the same country right at that minute. I didn't think now was the time to meet her, not in Charlie's living room. Not in the lion's den.

Charlie was putting biscuits on a plate and setting out cups while the kettle boiled. I watched him from the door to the kitchen, my arms crossed. I'd never seen him do anything domestic. We never played house as teenagers. Any eating without parents had involved wall-to-wall pizza, with either Wotsits or Frazzles on the side. Now, as I watched him, I felt something more than plain desire kindle inside. A softer, deeper drawing through my veins.

185

He was making me tea and he wanted me to be in his home! In his life? Be quiet, I told myself. Not in his life – I'm having some fun with him on the edge of his life. On the side. A bit on the side. Which is a start, isn't it?

We sat, one at each end of the long three-seater, and drank our tea. Charlie slipped his shoes off and stretched his legs out towards me, tucking his toes in behind my back.

'Oi!'

'What?' he asked me, as he slid onto his back, his arms up behind his head.

My mouth became dry again, my tummy fluttering with excitement. I kept my eyes straight ahead, my tea cupped in my hands, and looked out the window. I felt enormously self-conscious as he watched me sip. My lips. My tongue. I wanted to put it down but it was giving me something to do. Charlie was gently rubbing his feet up and down the small of my back and I felt the heat rising in my face again. Eventually I couldn't bear it any longer and took a deep breath, set the tea down in front of me on the table and turned to him.

It didn't take long and afterwards I lay on top of him, panting for several moments.

'Jesus,' I finally managed to say, and I picked my head up off the cushion next to his and looked at him. He was strangely unreadable. I lifted my bum into the air and he inhaled as I left him. I retreated to my end of the couch again, putting my boobs back into place, and pulled my top down. I fished my pants off the floor and put them on but waited to put on my jeans. I didn't quite fancy squeezing myself in just yet.

Charlie lay there completely relaxed, making no effort to put his bottom half on again.

'Do you recognise this sofa, Sam?' he asked me after a while.

I looked at it. 'It's not . . .' I trailed off, rubbing my hand across

186

the leather. I hadn't noticed it to start with but it had obviously had a life.

'The very same. Dad gave it to me when I bought this place.' He looked down the sofa at me. 'Do you remember fucking like rabbits on it when we were together?'

'I remember your brother walking in on us.'

'Which time?'

'What do you mean, which time? I only remember it happening once – that was traumatising enough!'

I remembered one Friday night when Jimmy was out at a party, and Charlie and I had the boys' den to ourselves. We'd been watching something . . . what was it? Ha, I almost laughed out loud when I remembered. *Mission: Impossible.* It wasn't the first time we'd seen it, so most of our time had been spent . . . well . . . our hands had been occupied elsewhere. The film was only halfway through when I was on top of Charlie, the light from the screen flickering on my bare bum as it rocked back and forth. It was at that moment that Jimmy stumbled in, pissed as a fart.

Charlie and I froze, in a position I have seared on my memory for life. He stared for what felt like a long time but was probably only a heartbeat, and then hiccupped, 'Whoops! Don't mind me,' and stumbled out again. I had collapsed onto Charlie in embarrassment, wanting to giggle and talk about what had happened – which I did – while Charlie continued with the job at hand.

'What did you mean by which time?' I asked.

'Oh nothing,' he said lightly.

I persisted. 'What did you mean?' I stared him out until he closed his eyes and sighed.

'Oh, I think there were a few other times that he saw us.'

'How do you know?' I heard myself squawking.

'Oh, I saw his little eye peering through the door a few times.'

'I don't remember that!'

187

'You were usually on top, Sam, as you like it so much.'

'No!' Not sweet little Jimmy! Two years younger than Charlie, he had a floppy mop of hair like his brother's but much blonder. He idolised Charlie and was always trying to impress me, saving up little stories from his week, hoping to make me laugh. I knew he had a crush on me but I'd assumed it was a sweet and inno- cent crush, based on mucking around together, both showing off in front of Charlie, teasing each other. It wasn't, I thought, based on any first-hand sightings of my private parts.

'Why didn't you tell him to go away?'

'Oh, I told him all about it after you'd leave. He never looked for long anyway, just long enough to refresh his memory.'

'Refresh his memory!' I threw a cushion at him. 'That was my bum he was looking at!'

'And your breasts.'

'You shit! You're nothing more than a pimp!' I leapt onto Charlie and we wrestled until he pinned me on the floor.

Later, we finally extricated ourselves from each other and dressed. Charlie made another cup of tea and we sat at the table, absent-mindedly reading the paper together. I felt warm and filled up. I'd forgotten completely about the existence of Lucy until the sound of footsteps on the stairs had Charlie jolt upright and look, confused, towards the door. My heart leapt into my stomach, creating a shock wave that I was sure was going to have me off my chair.

In she strode, even more beautiful in person: tall and thin, wearing skintight white jeans and a full-length Puffa, and holding a large black tote.

'Hiiiii . . . oh.' She looked at me and then at Charlie.

He found his voice quickly. 'Hi, babe, you're home early! This is Sam, an old friend.'

'Oh, hello.' Lucy crossed the room to shake my hand. All very formal. I offered a reluctant hand, wishing I could have found an excuse not to touch her. I was sure I just reeked of sex.

Lucy walked to the sofa – Charlie and I watching her with horror – and slung her jacket over the back and wandered into the kitchen. Good, that must mean we put all the pillows on the floor back on the couch again. I moved my head around, catching a strained glance from Charlie as I did so.

'So . . . I thought I'd come home a day early and surprise you.' I had missed the first bit of the story; my head was full of white noise, pure panic.

'Well, I'm surprised, darling,' he called into the kitchen, as if she was more than a couple of yards from his seat. Strange how fright can make people louder and brighter – you'd think they'd get quieter. I swallowed.

'I hope I haven't interrupted anything,' Lucy asked.

'No, nothing exciting, babe. Sam here is an old friend, a bit like a cousin in a way. We've been putting the world to rights.'

'Oh? I don't think you've mentioned her before,' she replied coolly, bringing her tea to the door of the kitchen.

A bit like a cousin? My face was going to crack with this smile. I dropped it for a moment although that was probably the wrong thing to do. Now I probably looked upset as well as guilty.

'Don't lump me into your family, thank you very much. I've got a perfectly respectable one myself.'

Lucy smirked and I relaxed, ever so slightly. But I had to get out of there. I felt sick. I stood up.

'I should get going really, get home for supper.' I picked my jacket up off the back of my chair and put it on, my heart thumping loudly enough to be heard.

'Oh, don't let me change your plans,' Lucy said.

'No, really, I should be going. I just popped by for—'

'A cup of tea,' finished Charlie. No, that wasn't a good look.

Hesitation over explanations was dodgy. God, could this be any worse? I walked over to the couch to find my handbag and there I saw that yes, things could get infinitely worse. Slumped quietly on the floor, down the end that Charlie was sitting in originally, was a condom – a white, shiny bomb. My stomach was in my mouth instantly, along with my heart, my morals, my backbone. It was very crowded in there and for a moment I was sure I was going to empty everything all over the cream sofa but I swallowed it all down. How could Lucy have missed seeing it when she put her coat down? And how the hell was I going to pick it up without being noticed? Lucy and Charlie were standing yards away, watching me. My handbag was sitting uselessly on 'my' end of the sofa. Perhaps . . . my mind raced . . . yes, it could work. I braced myself; I didn't have an option. I walked around to get my bag from the sofa. From here, it would have made sense to the onlooker for me to walk back around the back of the sofa and go to the door. Instead I awkwardly manoeuvred my way through the small gap between the sofa and table, bending over as I did to smell the lilies. I could feel them watching me, no doubt bemused by my strange actions, and I hoped Lucy couldn't see me shaking as I inhaled the pollen deeply. There . . . and here it comes, a rushing, bubbling *a-tish-hoo!* that forced me to drop me bag.

'Bless you!' came the beautifully intonated vowels from behind. Eyes streaming, I bent down to retrieve my bag, scooping up the condom as I did so. I straightened, holding my bag close to my body in one hand, like a little dog, with the squelching condom wedged wetly between my fingers and the bottom of my handbag. I prayed it wasn't slipping between my fingers and wouldn't dangle into view. I turned back towards the kitchen, my vision blurry and sinuses still buzzing. I went to rub my eyes with my free hand and discovered I had somehow got pollen on my hand. I looked at the orange on my fingertips. I'd probably got it smeared all over my face. What a muppet. I felt completely out of my depth. I had no place here in this smart house with my falling-apart cheap pumps, my unbrushed hair and my orange-smeared face. I longed to be home in the safety of Queen's Park.

'Well, bye then, see you again, nice to see you both,' I said, cheeks burning. Lucy came over to say goodbye, offering her hand again, but my right hand was full of hidden bagged semen and my bag. I held up my left hand to show her the pollen on my fingers, as if to say, sorry, really messy, darling, can't shake! And then I disappeared down the stairs, my heart hammering under my ribs, with Lucy calling out behind me, 'Bye, Sam, nice to meet you.'

33

ED

I stood across the road from the hospital, watching the faces leaving the silent, revolving doors. Now and then I would glance quickly at the pic on my phone from Charlie's Facebook page, just to refresh my memory. But when he appeared I realised immediately that any concerns about not recognising him were pointless. I would have recognised Charlie on a dark, foggy night. He stood tall and confident, and that haircut was for real, straight out of *Four Weddings*. Charlie paused for a moment, as if thinking about what direction he was going in, and then set off down the street. I followed him at a discreet distance, feeling full of fizz. It was the same buzz I felt when I was on the scent of a strong image.

Charlie reached a cluster of upmarket bars and restaurants, which even on a Monday evening were starting to fill up with City workers. He entered a dark bar. I followed. It was warm inside. A curved bar in dark wood stretched down one side of the room, with most of the punters milling nearby. A few small round tables on tall legs were dotted down the left-hand wall. I clocked an empty table at the very back of the room and I headed for a space at the bar closest to it, passing Charlie greeting a couple of suits on my way. Once I had my pint, I took up a seat at the table and pulled out my phone, keeping my head down as I pretended to be immersed in it. No one seemed to even notice me as I sat in the shadows. Surreptitious glances clocked Charlie greeting several other men and women, his smile wide and gestures expansive. I counted three pints going into his mouth within half an hour. 'Thirsty are we, Charlie boy?' I muttered under my breath.

After about forty minutes, a woman came through the door and I watched as nearly every man, and most women in the room, looked her way. She could have stepped out of a fashion magazine. Long graceful legs, thick, shiny blonde hair, and a porcelain face with arched brows framing perfectly proportioned features. She was, without a doubt, the most beautiful woman in the room. And she walked straight up to Charlie and kissed him on the mouth. He put his arm around her proprietarily (as well you might, Charlie boy – every man in this room would have her if they could), and put his face close to hers as she spoke to him.

His girlfriend looked like she'd been made especially for Charlie – beautiful, well dressed and obviously not short of a bob or three, and I asked myself yet again why he was mucking around with Sam – in fact, why he would want to play away at all? It could only be for the thrill of getting away with it – Charlie must get off on the duplicity. I studied her some more for a bit. She looked elegant and self-contained standing with the rowdy suits, their body language cocksure, their feet planted wide apart, oozing confidence, and the most sickening thing to me was that even from across the room, I could see that she was a nice person, with a good heart. It was disgusting that Charlie was cheating on her, and how could Sam think this was OK?

I'd had enough of all this. I had to get out of there. I slid off my stool and took a couple of steps towards Charlie and the exit but then stopped in my tracks. There, coming through the door, was Rebecca. I quickly turned on my heel and headed into the Gents. Why, out of all the bars in London, did she have to choose this one to come to at this moment? I went into a cubicle and shut the door.

Shit. Shit. Shit.

I lowered the seat lid, sat down on the toilet and tried to think of a plan. I twisted around and looked behind me – no window to climb out of. I ran my hands through my hair. I couldn't just sit in the toilet all night waiting for her to leave. I would just have to get out there and 'bump into her' and act surprised. I took a deep breath and stood up, unlatched the door and then changed my mind, locking it again before undoing my fly. I'd relieve myself first, that's what. As I peed, I wondered to myself what it was about Rebecca that made me unsettled. It wasn't like she had anything over me.

Did she?

I shook my head; I couldn't bear analysing her any more than necessary. All I wanted was to get the hell out of there.

I opened the bathroom door a crack and spotted her in the middle of a group next to the bar. So far, so good. I may yet slip past without her noticing. I took my phone out again and set off through the bar, studying it intently as I weaved my way through the crowd. I sensed the door getting closer and was almost going to breathe a sigh of relief when I heard my name being screeched above the bubbling, barking voices.

'Ed!'

I turned – what else could I do? – and forced myself to look distractedly across the faces of the crowd before finding Rebecca.

'Rebecca?' I said, hoping I looked surprised.

Rebecca pushed past her friends and threw her arms around me when she reached me, her body pushed up against mine. I had to shift my body to accommodate her weight and, in doing so, put my arms around her waist to steady her. As she drew back, her tipsy state was confirmed by her eyes, which looked a little dislodged, as if they'd been shaken violently and hadn't quite returned to their accustomed position.

'Erm, hi, Rebecca, fancy bumping into you.'

'I could say the same. What brings you to the City?'

'I, um, I was meeting a friend, but they' – I waved my phone pathetically at her – 'can't make it after all.'

'They?'

'Ah, no, I mean he.'

'Aren't you the mysterious one? Well, let me buy you a drink, we can't have you on your own.'

'No, really, I should get going . . .'

But it was no use – Rebecca dragged me into the thicket of City slickers at the bar and started introducing me to everyone, somehow producing a pint for me in record time.

I smiled and nodded and smiled some more and shook hands with half a dozen men as they grilled me about how I knew Rebecca, and she stood next to me, far closer than I was comfortable with, with her arm on mine. Then she shrieked again, 'Charlie! Come and meet Ed,' and waved furiously until he broke away from his leggy girlfriend and joined us.

This can't be happening, I thought.

'Charlie, this is Ed. Sam's flatmate's brother. Ed, this is Charlie.'

Charlie's face lit up. 'Ah, the photographer!' he boomed. 'Just returned from India, haven't you?'

'That's me.'

I glanced at Rebecca, about to tell her off for gossiping about me, but she looked blank. She obviously hadn't told Charlie about me. The only other person who knew Charlie was Sam. She'd been talking to Charlie about me! I grinned and felt filled with largesse about life. Maybe it wasn't so bad after all.

Another drink appeared and another and another, and I melted

195

into an affable drunkenness. Like the party I'd been to the week before, I found that as I chatted to Rebecca's friends, I started thinking they weren't all that bad – in fact some were actually quite interesting. One of them even reminded me I'd met him before. And after a while I didn't even mind Rebecca's arm on my sleeve. She needed it more and more, as the night wore on.

But then I came to a point where I just wanted to be in bed. The spying and then several pints on an empty stomach were suddenly and deeply tiring. Rebecca came outside with me to say goodbye.

'It was great to see you, Ed,' she slurred.

'I had an enjoyable evening.' I reached out and held her up as she swayed. 'Are you sure you're OK to get home?'

'Are you offering me a bed for the night?'

'No, and I'm afraid I can't even pay for a cab for you either. I'm fairly useless, really.' I watched her closely for signs of disappointment, relieved to see there were none.

'Oh don't worry, they'll get me home OK, they are all,' she waved at the bar, 'all perfect gentlemen,' and she grinned, delighted at herself.

'Well, I've got to go, thanks for the great night.' I took a step away from her tentatively, testing her to see if she'd stay upright.

'There is one thing before you go, Ed.'

'Yes?' I asked uneasily. I was really rather keen to get away now.

'Would you come to Charlie's birthday party with me next weekend?'

'Charlie's birthday? Don't you have a date?' My heart was thumping again; this was too good to be true.

Rebecca screwed up her face. 'No, not really. It'd be fun if you came and Charlie obviously likes you.'

'Well, I'd love to. Which night is it on?' I asked, knowing

perfectly well which night. It was only the most anticipated event this year in my temporary home, casting a shadow over almost every room and inspiring record hours of bathroom use.

'Oh goodie, I'm so pleased!' she gushed, threatening to topple onto me again. 'Itssh on Saturday night.' Rebecca's face lit up and for a moment I glimpsed the uncomplicated girl beneath the strange, polished face she presented to the world.

'Well, thanks for a good night, I've got to go,' I said, picking Rebecca's hands off my arm and setting them back beside her body. I took some experimental steps away from her and looked back to check she wasn't following me, raising my arm in a wave. 'See you then!'

'If not before!' Rebecca called after me.

34

SAM

The morning after the afternoon shenanigans with Charlie I woke cursing myself. He made me feel so good, so so so . . . dammit, I hadn't felt like that for years. Not since him all those years ago! But it wasn't meant to have happened like that. I wasn't meant to sleep with him now. I was meant to knock him dead at his party then he'd break up with Lucy, *then* we'd hook up. That was the order of events. What was I thinking yesterday? Sitting there in his flat saying to myself it was OK to be his bit on the side then fucking him at his house, just before his girlfriend came home? I didn't want to be the other woman. As much as I disliked Lucy, I didn't actually want to be sleeping with him while he was still with someone. I shuddered when I recalled Lucy coming in. And that condom. Oh God, that condom.

I stood in front of the mirror naked. I saw a pale-skinned woman who should have known better. I saw a strong body with faults. I saw thighs that cosied up together; I saw arms that were a little too robust. I looked sad and hard. My hair was oily. I probably stank.

I was seconds from pulling out of the whole ridiculous quest and then I glanced at the list I'd written in a fit of enthusiasm and stuck to my mirror.

Exfoliate elephant heels
Learn to put on make-up
Hair – WTF?
Buy dress – Claudia?
Tone up!

I pulled it off and considered it. I ticked off dress. I had endured shopping and actually had a dress – one that Claudia would be sad if I didn't wear. I had spent hours grating my heels. Tick. My hair had almost been tamed. Tick. I could actually put make-up on now without looking like a clown. Double tick for that, as that was a small miracle in itself.

And then my phone beeped.

My heart flipped.

It was him.

> Sorry about yesterday. It was so good to see you – all of you. Cx

'Wasn't it,' I said to the sad face in the mirror.

I took a deep breath. Come on, girl, you can do better than this. This is just a little passion getting in the way of carefully laid plans, that's all. You've got one more thing on your list.

I swiped my phone. Charlie could wait.

★

Later that day in the changing room of her gym, Claudia leant over to tie her trainer, one long leg up on the bench. She wore black leggings with a matching sports top and her hair was held back in a girlish ponytail.

'Are you sure you're feeling up for this, Claud?'

Claudia did look a bit on the pale side. She'd been reluctant to meet me here, something about feeling a bit under the weather.

Claudia addressed her laces. 'I'll be fine. It's good for me to do something other than work and go home anyway.'

'What do you mean? Aren't you out most nights, Miss Social Butterfly?'

'Not at the moment.'

Claudia put our bags in a big locker, put in a pound coin and turned the lock. She didn't explain herself any more. Sometimes she was like that, Claudia. She wasn't always in the mood for chatting about herself. She straightened up and gave me a small smile. Even though she was pale and wearing sportswear, she still managed to look glamorous. I looked down at my own faded leggings, which were bagging at the knee, and noticed my vest top had a stain near one nipple. Fucking fantastic.

'Chin up, darling, it won't hurt that much.'

'I'm not worried about the exercise, it's my outfit.'

'There's nothing wrong with it.'

But Claudia didn't sound convinced.

I followed her swinging ponytail reluctantly into the gym.

'Christ, Claud, I never realised that the term smart casual applies to working out.'

'What do you mean?' Claudia looked around her.

'Claud, these gym outfits cost more than the stuff I wear to work!'

'Sam, do you or do you not want to get in better shape before the weekend?'

'Do,' I mumbled.

'Well, you'll have to get over your silly inferiority complex and get on the machine. It's really easy, you just push your feet down like this – it's a little like riding a bike.'

Claudia set off, her body rising up and down as her feet went round and round, her hands clutching two large poles that went rapidly back and forth, her bosom flumph-flumph-flumphing onto her chest. I eyed up the machine with suspicion. It didn't look like riding a bike. It looked ridiculous. But I sighed and clambered on, acutely aware of how amateur I looked, placing my feet in the oversized foot shapes and hoisting myself up onto the machine. Holding onto the bar in front of me, I gingerly tried moving my feet like I was on a bicycle.

'This feels really weird – my body doesn't feel straight.'

'You'll get used to it, now grab hold of the poles,' Claudia said briskly, not breaking her rhythm.

I kept my feet moving and looked at the poles going forward and back, forward and back, on their own. I took a deep breath and lunged for the right one as it came close. It hurtled away from me immediately, taking my body roughly to the right. I lunged for the left one and grasped it tightly. I felt like I was being taken for a ride, not the other way around. Claudia snorted with laughter next to me.

'Shut it!' I hissed.

'You could just stop your feet, darling, and then grab the poles.'

I sensed Claudia stopping next to me and turned my head just enough to glance at her as she showed me, with exaggerated moves, how easy it was to reach the poles in a stationary position.

'Well, great, that's really helpful now, Claud.' I caught the eye of a man, easily ten years my senior and as fit as a fireman, running on a treadmill nearby and obviously tickled watching me. I gritted my teeth and kept moving. This fucking machine would not beat me. I would slim down. Charlie would look at me and swoon. I would create a new me.

'So has he been in touch since?'

I couldn't understand how Claudia could chat and work out at the same time. My side of the conversation came out in sad little puffs.

'Oh yes . . . lots of texts . . .' Gasp. 'He says . . . he doesn't think he's in love with her any more . . . that they're more like old friends . . .' Back, forth, back, forth went the poles. Round and round went my feet. Burn burn went my thighs!

'That old chestnut, eh?' Claudia smiled at me and raised her eyebrows.

'Yes, that's what I . . . said. He insisted it was . . . true . . . says he wants to see me at his party.'

Claudia's eyebrows were still halfway up her forehead.

'I thought you were meant to be playing hard to get a bit, you know, holding out for the big reveal at this party?'

Round and round, round and round. I hated this machine so much.

'You know . . . what?' I gasped. 'Having the third degree while . . . trying to make this . . . fucking thing work . . .'

Claudia glanced at me as I slowed down. Her lovely cheeks had acquired two little circles of pink.

'Giving up already?' she asked.

I leant on the bar, my legs shaking.

'What did you say this thing is called again?'

'It's called a crosstrainer.'

'I'm not sure I need any training in being cross, you know.'

I stepped down off the foot platforms onto the floor. It appeared to be much harder since I'd last stepped on it.

'Maybe I just need to make the most of my outfit instead, Claud? This body can't hack the pace.'

Claudia nimbly stepped down off her machine.

'I don't know why you're worrying about your body anyway, Sam. You've never worried before – why start now?'

'I know. I didn't have Charlie in my life again, though, did I?'

Claudia looked at me for a bit without saying anything. I couldn't tell if she was looking at me with pity or confusion, or something else completely. Whatever it was, she stopped thinking it, gave herself a little shake and said, 'Come on, let's just call it a day and go home. I'm wiped out.'

'What a bloody good idea,' I agreed.

★

The following day I had a couple of meetings in Soho in the afternoon, and was at Kate's by four o'clock. Why I hadn't come to see her earlier had stumped me all day. Girl has big date at weekend, girl wants to get thinner, girl asks ex-model friend for advice, right? No, girl flaps around panicking about what to wear first, spends way too much time in the bathroom, girl mortifies herself at a poncy gym. Honestly, I thought, you are a prize idiot sometimes.

Kate put a cup of peppermint tea in front of me and sort of wafted into the seat opposite me at the kitchen table.

'Sorry, I can't find the normal tea.'

I smiled thinly but my stomach turned at the thought of drinking it. Kate was a dear thing but she really was missing out when it came to food and drink. Far too many pulses and herbal teas, and not enough hamburgers and milky cups of builder's.

'I don't know how I can help you, Sam. I can't even find basic food items in my cupboard.'

'You probably didn't have them there to start with.'

Kate glanced over to the chaos of her kitchen bench.

'No, you're probably right.' Her voice was so soft it was almost ethereal. She turned back to look at me and waited.

'The thing is, Kate, I've got Charlie's birthday party coming up on Saturday night and I want to look my best. I tried the gym with Claudia last night and it was awful, and I've met his girlfriend, and she's gorgeous and skinny—'

'No.'

203

I looked at her, bewildered – how did she know what I was going to ask her?

'I'm not going to.'

'Not going to do what?'

'I'm not going to tell you how to lose weight between now and Saturday.'

'How did you know I was going to ask you that?'

Kate frowned a small frown. 'Of course you were going to.'

I sat back in my chair. 'You're right,' I relented. 'I'm sorry. It's really pathetic of me. I just feel out of my depth a bit and I really want to make an impression.' I was aware I was whining.

'You're gorgeous just the way you are!'

'That's kind of you to say, Kate, but I don't feel that way. I feel like a frumpy, clumsy, plain commoner. And I want to look special that night, and feel like I'm worthy of him.'

Kate looked at me thoughtfully. 'What's so special about this guy anyway?' She pushed a bowl of Bombay mix towards me.

I took a handful and tipped it into my mouth, looking up at the ceiling at a damp spot where it met the wall, and then down at the table. I pushed a drip of tea along the grain of the wood.

'I don't know what's so amazing about him actually. I just know that I feel different when I'm with him. I feel like I'm sharp, amusing, unique—' I stopped and shook my head. 'Christ, listen to me drivelling on. You don't need to hear this. I'm not even making sense.'

'Yes, you are,' Kate replied. 'I'm not sure I'm convinced he deserves the attention but I understand you feeling like that. I used to feel like that around Martin.'

I couldn't believe she'd said that – she couldn't compare Martin to Charlie! Martin was a sleazy, two-timing, shallow, selfish . . . Oh.

'I'm not saying that what happened to me will happen to you,'

Kate said, as if reading my mind. She drew her finger absently across her bottom lip and then laid it on the table. 'I suppose you're going to sit there until I give you some of my evil dieting advice, aren't you.'

My face lit up. 'You bet!'

'You've never been interested in this kind of thing before. I thought you were more down to earth than this.'

I squirmed in my seat, aware that embarrassment was twisting my mouth into a funny shape.

'All right,' Kate said reluctantly, 'I'll give you something to do through til Saturday.'

'Thank you!'

'But there is one condition.' She gave me a severe look, looking less fairy-like and much more like Mara in her scary bossy mode.

'Anything.'

'You don't do it again after this week. Ever. You don't need to – you're in great shape and you'll have to learn to love yourself the way you are.'

'Yes, ma'am.' I saluted.

'You won't need to write anything down,' Kate said, as she saw me rummaging in my bag for paper and pen. 'It's quite simple – all you're going to eat are grapes.'

'Grapes?'

'That's it. As few as possible. Some women get by on one a day.'

My jaw dropped.

'But you're to eat more than that and drink loads of water. Black tea and coffee, no sugar obviously, no juice and definitely no alcohol.' Kate stood up and picked up her large Cath Kidston tote, which was slung across the back of a chair. 'I've gotta go get the kids now. Hopefully they've given their dad and his tart their bug.' She walked down the hall with me.

'Bug?'

'Oh yeah, nothing too crazy, just a bit of vomiting.'

She caught the look on my face at the door and laughed.

'Oh don't worry! I cleaned the kitchen.'

Somehow I found that a little difficult to believe. Thank God I hadn't had any of my tea.

After kissing Kate goodbye, I wandered down the road in the direction of the fruit shop where Kate was sure you could buy grapes with pips in them ('None of that genetically modified rubbish!'). It wasn't until I entered the fruit shop and saw bags of Bombay mix lined up that I recalled both my own and Kate's hands dipping into the bowl of nibbles.

35

CLAUDIA

All week I immersed myself in work and kept banter with colleagues to a minimum. I avoided eating lunch with Jill. I didn't go out in the evenings – except for a quick visit to the gym one evening with a very amusing Sam, who proved to be welcome light relief. I had never seen anyone take to a crosstrainer quite as unnaturally as she did.

But that was only one night. More typically in the evenings I went straight home, took my pills and curled into a ball in front of the TV. It was the slowest week of my life.

The only thing of note I had achieved was getting in touch with the two men I had slept with before John. Marco was first. He was a buff bouncer from a club I often go to, his olive skin stretched taut over his biceps. I had known him for years and our relationship was a warm friendship based on mutual respect and understanding for each other's sex appeal. He had been very blasé about it and promised me that he'd get tested as soon as he could.

'Oh, my darlin', don't you worry your pretty head any more. Marco will find out the facts and get straight back to you.' He was obviously well used to the procedure and completely unfazed by it all. It was slightly comforting to think I wasn't the only woman in London going through the torment of contacting lovers. Marco wouldn't be the only lover in London getting tested. In fact, he was probably a regular at his local clinic. I could just imagine Marco happily calling into a clinic on the way to work in the early evening and flirting with the receptionist. Then I swung back to feeling cheap. The voices in my head, in their roles of 'Daddy's little girl' and 'woman of the world', were conducting an epic conversation in my head.

I'm sharing this experience with sleazy bouncers – that's crazy!

Stop being such a snob.

But I come from a good family. It's not meant to be like this.

You come from a sperm and an egg, get real.

Papa would hate this if he knew.

Your daddy tried keeping you in a box away from other people.

He didn't mean any harm!

No, but he's a snob and wanted you to be better than everyone else.

He was just doing what he knew was best.

But you love knowing all sorts of people.

But I don't have to sleep with them all!

Life's for living, stop giving yourself such a hard time.

But I caught a *bug*!

On and on it went boiling away quietly in the background as I wrote emails, took meetings, went to the toilet and collected documents from the printer, keeping my head down and my hands busy. The busier I was, the quieter the argument in my head, but when I left the office it ramped up into a full-blown barney. Claudia has chlamydia. Claudia has chlamydia. Only whisky would dampen the noise. Shots, two minimum, downed as quickly as possible. The orders from Doc not to drink on top of the medication were too hard to stick to. It was only a couple of drinks, I reasoned, and it lowered the volume of the voices in my head enough for me to fall asleep.

It was at the end of one of these short evenings that instead of passing out directly, I picked up my phone to call David, the second man before John. David was in insurance, a brisk, extremely clean man who I'd met one night at a party.

'Yes?' he answered his mobile, obviously frightfully busy at nine thirty on a Tuesday evening.

'It's Claudia.'

David paused although why he had to I had no idea. My name would have come up on his phone anyway. Unless he'd deleted my contact details of course. Pity he was hearing from me with such bad news.

'Claudia.'

'Yes, I'm sorry to bother you—'

'Yes, I am rather busy.'

I could hear the sounds of a restaurant in the background. He was out for supper. He was probably with a woman. Not the best environment to hear you needed to go and get tested for an STI. But you shouldn't have answered your phone during supper, you rude man. I remembered his air of self-importance – I was momentarily attracted to it until I realised (unfortunately post-coitally) that he didn't possess a smidgen of warmth to coax his confidence into charm. He was a cold, calculating, vain bore. Which was why he would have answered his phone. If my name hadn't come up, he would have answered it in case it was someone important. If my name had shown it would demonstrate to whomever he was dining with how important he was, receiving calls even during supper.

Plonker.

'I won't keep you for long. It's just that I've had a bit of bad news, which may impact on you.'

David was silent, waiting for me to go on.

'Um, I, um, I've just found out I have an STI – chlamydia – and that means that you'll need to go and get tested too.'

Again, David was silent.

Oh this is fun, I thought grimly.

'Are you there?' I asked him.

'Yes, one moment.'

I heard muffled voices and the sound of clothes rustling, and then the sounds of the street.

'Are you there, David?'

'Can you repeat that for me please?' His voice had become decidedly less confident.

'Do I have to?'

'Yes!' he said crossly. 'I'm a little shocked.'

I sighed. 'You need to get tested for chlamydia,' I repeated, 'either at your GP or a sexual-health clinic. The results come back quite quickly.'

'Is it curable?'

'Yes, usually very easily with antibiotics.' My head was clearing a little as the conversation went on. I knew the script so well by now though I could have been asleep, if it didn't make me feel so churned up inside.

'It better be,' he said, with a menacing edge to his voice.

'If you have it, David, I'd really like to know. I'm trying to trace it back to the source.'

'It won't be me!' he said, defensive.

'I hope it isn't. If you don't have it, it narrows my search considerably. If you do have it, that means I need to talk to men before you.' The conversation was sobering me up quickly.

'Right.'

'I hope you don't have it, David, I really do, but if you do, you'll need to tell the partners you've had since me.'

'My fiancée.'

'Oh! Congratulations, that's great news!'

'Not the engagement gift I was planning.'

'No.'

There was a pause while a siren passed David by in the background.

'So let me know the result will you? And, David, I'm really sorry.'

'Sure you are, Claudia.'

'Bye!' I attempted brightly but the phone was dead.

★

I wasn't expecting to see John back in the office until Thursday, as he was away in Brussels for the first part of the week. So when I heard a soft knock on my door on late Wednesday afternoon, I didn't look up to see who was coming through the door straightaway.

'Claudia?'

I whipped my head up from my computer in shock.

'Oh, it's you!'

'Don't sound too glad to see me.'

'Sorry, I didn't expect you,' I said, flustered.

'No, we finished earlier than expected. I caught an earlier train back.'

'Oh good, how was the meeting?'

'Productive.'

I waited for more. I didn't want to speak to him but if I had to I wanted to talk about work. Anything but the thing lurking in the background. But John just stood there, his hands in his pockets. Refusing to talk about work at all. I tried again.

'Simon was expecting the MD to put up a lot of opposition to our proposal.'

'Hmmm,' he mumbled, almost as if he wasn't hearing me. He had crossed the room, his feet quiet and quick on the oatmeal carpet, to stand at the window. I felt like a junior secretary who

211

wasn't being included in the big boys' club. I would normally get bolshy when I felt excluded from information sharing but right then I just felt small and useless. I looked at my screen. An email from Jill had just come in:

I know you're in here somewhere, lovely. What's up?

What's up? What's up indeed, I thought. What am I meant to say to John? Think of something. Anything.

He strode over to my desk and laid his hands on top of it, leaning in and then pulling back from me, as if he was stretching his wrists or something. His big torso so close to me wasn't helping my brain function any better.

'Claudia?'

'Yes?' I answered in a small voice.

'Are you busy tonight?' He stared at me.

'No,' I answered, completely forgetting my week-long pact with my television.

'Good,' he replied. 'Why don't we go for a drink straight from work?'

'OK.'

'I'll come past you,' he said. He stopped his strange moving back and forth, and looked as if he wanted to say something more but stopped himself, and abruptly left the room.

I let out a huge sigh of relief, as if I'd been holding my breath, and my shoulders dropped about a mile from my ears. Oh dear, I thought. What am I doing? I looked stupidly at Jill's email that sat there, demanding an answer.

Hiya,

I tapped out, trying to sound breezy.

Hiya, hon, I'm here somewhere.

Now what? How much of the truth can I bear to share.

Hiya, hon, I'm here somewhere. Buried in work, a bit self-inflicted. I'll come up for air one day soon and tell you all about it. Thanks for asking. Claudia x

That felt a little better. I'd felt awful shutting Jill out all week.

I was waiting for John from about half past five. And I waited, and waited, and waited. I knew he had a difficult meeting last thing and assumed it was running over but it didn't stop me putting on my coat three times and almost leaving. By the time he arrived at my door, full of apologies at seven, I felt almost sick with nerves.

'It'll have to be dinner instead now it's so late. I'm starving,' he said curtly as he ushered me into a cab. We sat in silence as the cab wended its way through the city, each of us lost in our own thoughts. I felt like I was on my way to be told off by the headmaster and John . . . well, who knew what was going on in his head. I was certain it wasn't generous thoughts about me, that was for sure.

The silence was broken when we pulled up outside a Japanese restaurant I'd been meaning to try for ages and I gasped, suddenly feeling enormously grateful and even more emotional than before. I didn't feel like I deserved to be brought to such a lovely place.

'Everything OK?'

'Yes. It's just . . .' I put a tentative hand on his offered arm as I came out of the cab. 'Thank you for bringing me here.'

He looked at me, puzzled, then took me inside and shepherded me into my seat. From the start, I desperately started

213

searching for something to talk about, deciding on work again as the easiest subject, but John gave me one-word answers. We lapsed into uncomfortable silence too quickly. I looked around us at the tables of couples or groups of friends speaking effortlessly, laughing together as they tried different pieces of the exquisitely presented sashimi and sushi in front of them. I felt we were marooned at our silent table and I was trying desperately not to care, to nonchalantly study the wood panelling that divided the room into several little areas, the plants placed just so. I even twisted around to study the water feature behind me, its perpetual gurgling as peaceful as the traditional music being piped out to diners discreetly from well-positioned speakers.

'You can't beat the Japanese for excellent design,' I offered, a last-ditch attempt at generating much-needed conversation. But John just looked blankly at me like he hadn't heard anything I was saying.

'Claudia.'

'Yes?'

'I've had my results back and I've tested positive.'

'Ah,' I replied, the colour draining from my face, then flooding it again with an unwelcome blush.

'I, ah . . .' I took a deep drink of water, overcome with thirst. 'I didn't expect you to know so quickly.'

Of course it couldn't have been any other outcome – John had to have it. I hadn't slept with anyone since him – but I was still shocked to hear it.

'I was tested in Brussels and they turned it around quickly. I found out on the train on the way back today.'

I nodded, looking at my fingers. I wished I could wave a magic wand and make this all better. What he must think of me now he knew he was infected. I felt tears of self-loathing and pity well up and excused myself, walking quickly to the bathroom.

I almost threw myself into a cubicle and sat down on top of the toilet, suddenly completely overcome with emotion, balling my eyes out, the tears hot and ferocious, full of all the sadness and frustration I'd been feeling for days, for weeks, forever. Fuck you, Claudia with chlamydia, fuck your choices, my head screamed at me, the snot running over my fingers, which were trying to muffle the raw sound coming out of my mouth, my heart. It's so unfair, I raged. I had no idea how long I was in there. It could have been three minutes or thirty. When the tears finally stopped I took several deep breaths, trying desperately to compose myself. I fished around at my legs for my bag and realised, with a sinking heart, that I'd left my handbag at the table. Never in my life had I committed such a heinous crime against my appearance. How the hell was I meant to make myself look presentable now?

I took a long length of toilet paper and opened the door, then let out a short scream. A woman stood there, looking as if she'd been waiting for me.

'Sorry, sorry, I didn't know you were there,' I flustered.

The woman didn't flinch but looked at me calmly. She obviously worked at the restaurant but I didn't remember seeing her in there earlier. She was dressed in a dark blue kimono, her hair up in a classical bun with ornamental chopsticks poked through. She was so peaceful it was almost as if she was floating next to the hand basin.

I avoided eye contact with her as I dabbed away at my face with the toilet paper, making very little progress with the black rivulets staining my cheeks. After a little bit, I felt a light tap on my shoulder and turned to find the woman passing me a cotton pad and a bottle of Clarins cleanser, a small smile on her lips that was somehow insistent and unobtrusive at the same time. I looked at them for a moment and then took them, whispering my thanks.

The cleanser made quick work of my recalcitrant make-up and I very quickly looked a lot less like Alice Cooper, though still a lot more like my mother than I was comfortable with. I sighed and looked at the woman again. Her hands were inside the folds of her kimono. She withdrew them, miraculously flourishing a Chanel compact, the exact shade that I used. I couldn't believe it. I took the compact from the woman, murmuring a heartfelt thanks. Strangely, I didn't feel the need to make idle chatter with her. There. I was finished. Now I could face John again. I gave the compact back to the woman, who smiled at me and opened the door.

John's face was full of concern as I crossed the room. His tender gaze was almost more than I could cope with. I didn't need pity right then – I was trying to hold it together. I held the menu up over my face and pretended to study it.

'I ordered for us, I hope you don't mind. You were in there a while,' he said. 'Are you OK?'

'Oh, right. Thanks.' My eyes focussed on the writing in front of me. It appeared that I was holding the now redundant wine list. I set it down with as much dignity as I could muster. I cleared my throat. 'There was a woman in there. We got . . . chatting,' I answered, aware of how unconvincing I sounded. I knew too that as patched together as my face was, my puffy eyes would be giving me away.

'Claudia, I'm really sorry,' he started to say.

'You're sorry?'

'Yes, I am.'

He sounded so sincere but still I didn't dare look at him. I wanted to be able to talk about and really engage about the whole sorryness but thinking about it all was too hard. I felt so fragile, as if at any moment I would dissolve into a tragic, Claudia-sized puddle. Which would be a real shame for my lovely shoes, not to mention the upholstery. I was saved by the arrival of food. It was her, the woman from the bathroom, hovering next to the table with an array of tiny pieces of seafood. Very quietly she placed each dish onto the table, her head bent. As she turned to go, she caught my eye. Don't fret, she seemed to be saying. Just breathe.

'Did you hear that?' I turned to John, suddenly feeling a little freaked out.

'Hear what?'

'That woman, the one that served us.'

'Not a thing, she was as quiet as a mouse.'

'Right.' I turned and looked across the restaurant uncertainly. No sign of her. I turned back to John and found myself inhaling a massive lungful of air and then letting it out slowly. Some of my tension left with it. I may have blown any chance of having a relationship with John but he still cared – you could tell by the look on his face. That kind woman in the kimono cared too. And of course the girls, the Queen's Park girls, and Jill at work, they all wanted me to be happy. I realised, with a pang, I'd been feeling wretchedly lonely through all of this. No one but John knew – not the girls, not my family.

Finally, the food in front of me could be ignored no longer. I crammed in rice, wasabi, tuna, salmon. All the crying and deep breathing had left a massive, hungry hole. As I ate I finally felt happy to be there. John grabbed two pieces of sashimi and stuffed them into his mouth, mimicking my squirrel cheeks, and I laughed so much I almost choked. It all felt so much easier after that. We giggled about people at work, talked more seriously about the direction of the company and dissected the Brussels meeting comprehensively. By the end of the meal I felt that perhaps we'd work out as friends, and be able to hang out like this from time to time. I'd like that.

I was chortling away about a particularly suave operator from the HR team when I burst out with, 'Oh, that reminds me, I've been in touch with a couple of the men before you about this thing,' smiling away as if I didn't have a care in the world.

'Speaking of Casanovas?'

'Well yes, one of them is a darker version of Randy Steve in the office. His name is Marrrrco,' I giggled.

'I was meaning you.' He raised his eyebrows at me.

'What do you mean?'

'Don't feign innocence at me, you slapper,' he said, grinning mischievously.

'*Moi*? I don't know what you're talking about!'

'It takes one to know one, Claudia,' he said, looking at me steadily.

I didn't reply, just leant back in my chair and stared back at him. I could do this talk, this easy flirting banter. I felt at home with it, leaning in my chair the same way I had leant a thousand times before, with dozens of men. Foreplay given with glinting eyes, falling lashes. I set my glass down in front of me.

'I think Marco may have done this before. He was quite happy to go off and get tested. Straight old David was unimpressed and not relishing telling his fiancée either.'

'Ouch.'

'Indeed. He was such a bore about it I almost hope he's got it.'

'I didn't take you to be vindictive, Claudia,' he said, laying his fingertips together. 'You're many things but you're not a bitch.'

'You're right.' I looked up at him and because I'd had two wines said, 'You're quite perceptive, aren't you?'

'I am?'

'Definitely.' And before I could self-censor said, 'I've been quite disarmed at times with how you seem to understand me.'

'I think we're quite similar, you and me. We're ambitious with our work, without being grasping. We relish using our senses in our playtime – all of our senses,' he added.

218

'You mean we're a couple of lushes who eat too much and sleep around?' I said.

John shrugged. 'If you want to look at it that way. I was choosing words more fitting to this classy restaurant – and the company of course.'

'He adds hastily.'

'No, I mean it, you're a classy bird, Claudia.'

'Not so classy I can't pick up an STI,' I said.

'Bugs don't care how refined you are. They can't see how much you have in your bank account. They don't care if you wear Prada or Primark.'

I sipped my drink thoughtfully. We didn't speak for a moment or two. I looked around me and was surprised to see the restaurant almost empty.

'We should get going and let these people go home,' I said.

But John didn't make any effort to move.

'Why haven't you settled down with one man?' he said.

'You're the perceptive one, you tell me.'

'My mother has always said that about me.'

'What, being a mind reader?'

'Yes, she also said I wouldn't find someone to settle down with until quite late. Which is nice, because she's never bothered me about it. Do your parents bug you about your love life?'

I looked at my nails. 'It's complicated. They don't bug me as such – at least Papa doesn't, because he's so proud of my career. But Mother, I think she'd like to see me with someone but she's too well mannered to pry into my private life. She prods for information indirectly, almost without me knowing she's doing it.'

'Sounds like a clever woman.'

'She is. They're both clever.'

'I don't doubt it.' Again he was staring right inside me. Warmth

219

bloomed inside my chest. I was kidding myself. We couldn't possibly be friends in the long term. There was no way I could be friends with someone who made me feel like this.

'Mum was on the phone just last night actually. She was asking me about my love life.' He paused for a moment.

I waited for him to continue and hoped my chest wasn't flushed.

'She was asking if I was seeing anyone.'

He looked like he was waiting for me to respond but what the hell was I meant to say to that? I panicked.

'Really?' I said, my voice quavering feebly.

'It was strange her asking. As I said earlier, she never does ask. It must have been something in my voice,' John said, pausing yet again for me to say something.

But what do you want me to say? I thought. I've ruined any chances of seeing you!

'Am I seeing someone, Claudia?'

I found it difficult to meet his intense stare.

'Erm, are you?'

'I'm asking you,' John insisted.

I went to reach for my water but misjudged the distance and knocked it over, sending water all over the table and onto the floor.

Within a heartbeat, the woman from the bathroom was there, mopping it up while I apologised with small squawks.

John reached over and took my hand. 'Don't worry,' he said, and I sat there, my heart thumping, until the woman had finished. She flashed me one more be-calm glance and we were left alone.

'I think we should go, it's getting late,' I said.

'We will when you've answered my question. I'm only going to ask it one more time – am I seeing anyone, Claudia?'

'I . . . I don't know the answer to that, John. I didn't think you were. I . . . ah, with everything that's happened, I thought that meant that maybe you weren't, rather *we* weren't, but . . .' I stuttered.

'But?'

'But?'

'But – could I be seeing someone? Could that be possible? Could you at least think about it and get back to me?'

I let out the air that seemed to have been trapped in my chest for a minute or more and nodded inanely, as if I had no control over my head.

'I could . . . think about it,' I said.

36

SAM

On Friday morning I opened my curtains to find the sun streaming in gaily though my window and it made me want to sing. I
was feeling excessively pleased with myself, having managed to
get through the whole of the previous evening eating a total of
thirty grapes. The day stretched ahead of me, hours and hours
of uninterrupted preening. Finally, my two-week beautifying
regime would be coming to a flurried conclusion. The list on
my mirror had grown. I had a mud mask to apply, yet more
exfoliating and a detailed analysis of my eyebrows to complete.
Possible toenail painting – I thought I'd leave my fingernails until
the following day. I thought I'd also pepper the day with toning
yoga stretches and eat a suitably tiny amount of grapes. I patted
my stomach happily. I was sure I was feeling lighter already.

I spied my oil burner almost buried on my desk and unearthed
it. It had a thick layer of dust coating the bowl so I picked a
pair of knickers off the floor and wiped as much off as I could. I
poured a little water in from the glass next to my bed and, after
rummaging in my drawer, I found a tealight and some lavender
oil. As I dropped a couple of drops into the bowl, the clean, sharp
scent filled my nostrils, lifting my virtuous little spirit further.
Lovely. I smiled.

I found Ed reading the paper in the kitchen.

'Morning! What a day!' I said.

'Indeed.'

'Can I borrow your lighter?'

'What for?'

'Just to light my oil burner.' I looked at him, hands on my hips, but I was smiling.

Ed gazed at me. 'You're in a good mood today,' he finally commented.

I spread my arms wide. 'The sun is shining!'

Ed looked out of the window.

'So can I have your lighter?' I reminded him.

'Oh, right. Of course.' And he leant back in his chair so he could fish the lighter out of the pocket of his skinny jeans, revealing a patch of taut olive-brown stomach, a jet black line of hair disappearing into his fly. I flicked my eyes to the floor, my belly suddenly fluttering with nerves. These grapes do make a girl feel a bit strange, I told myself.

I was finishing up my shower when I started feeling a bit odd. Sort of hungry-sick. Hungry. No, sick. No. Hungry? I couldn't decide. It was very silly to only eat grapes really. I knew that. Imagine what Dad would say if he knew how ridiculous I was being! Maybe I should eat something a bit more substantial. Some toast maybe. Yes. That'll be all right. Just some plain toast. No butter. Surely there can't be many calories in a piece of toast.

Ed was in the kitchen, making a cup of tea. He turned when he heard me come in.

'Are you OK? You look really pale.'

I didn't answer straightaway and I suddenly felt like I needed to sit. Ed came over to me and sat down.

'What's up?'

'Oh,' I said, holding my forehead in my hands, 'I don't feel that great. I was OK before my shower but now . . .' I placed one hand onto my stomach. 'Maybe I should have some toast or something. I think those grapes might be making me feel a bit light-headed.'

Ed jumped up and set about making me toast immediately and I sat quietly, hoping that the good feeling from the start of the day would return. I didn't feel like I had the energy to stand up, let alone concentrate on beautifying myself. The smell of toast soon filled the kitchen.

'You know, I'll never understand why girls do this to themselves,' Ed said.

'Do what?' I croaked.

'Starve themselves when they're not actually overweight.'

'Well, I'm not exactly a skinny number.'

'You are so.'

Ed came over and put a piece of dry toast under my nose.

'Thanks.'

'Not a problem.'

I withdrew my head from my cradling hands and looked at my toast. It didn't produce the rush of hungry saliva I was expecting – in fact, the opposite. My stomach creaked ominously. I took the toast to my mouth anyway and tried a tentative bite from one corner. Bloody dry, all right. But I ploughed on, taking several bites and forcing myself to swallow them, one by one. Ed placed a glass of water next to me too and I took a sip of water now and then. Halfway through the ordeal I put the toast down and resumed my head-in-hands position, and waited for the food to hit my stomach and for my energy to return.

'So are you looking forward to the party tomorrow night then?' Ed asked.

'Not right at this moment in time.'

'You'll be OK by tomorrow though. You'll have a blast.'

'If you say so.'

There was silence while we both sat in our own thoughts, the clock ticking quietly in the background, the fridge humming.

After a bit, Ed stirred and wandered back to the kitchen counter. 'I'm sure you're going to look amazing,' he said to his coffee maker.

And even in my tragic state I buzzed quietly with pleasure. He really can be a nice guy, can Ed, I thought.

It wasn't long after this that I had to leg it to the bathroom to be sick, after which I went straight back to bed. Ed came in as I lay, buried in self-pity, on my side. He placed some water next to my bed.

'Do you need anything else?'

'No,' I groaned. 'It must have been the Bombay mix.'

'Sorry?'

'The Bombay mix at Kate's. We shared some Bombay mix.'

Ed was quiet for a minute then said in a confused voice, 'I've never had a problem with it myself.'

'They had a bug,' I groaned again.

'The Bombay mix?'

Oh my God, he was being so dense. 'No, you twat, the kids. The kids have had a bug. A bug in the house. Kate had her hand in the bloody Bombay mix and so did I. Geddit?'

'Oh.' Ed sounded hurt. 'Can I get anything else for you? A bowl for beside your bed?'

'I said no, Ed, just leave me alone.'

I lay there in misery. I hadn't meant to be so sharp with him. I could see he was only trying to help. But I felt so horrible. Why couldn't things just come together for me for once, like they were meant to? I had bumped into Charlie for a reason, to be in his life again, and this party was my opportunity to shine. I'd put so much bloody effort into it! I also wished I'd pulled the curtains; the sunshine seemed to make me feel worse rather than better. It was mocking me, streaming so generously in my window, as if I

225

deserved it or something. Which of course I didn't. Oh fuck, here comes the bile.

I ran to the toilet again and after vomiting violently I sat on the cool floor for a bit, getting my breath back. I was vaguely aware of Ed talking on the phone in the kitchen and then I returned to bed.

'Sam,' he whispered from the door.

'Yes?' I croaked.

'That was Kate, she said that the bug should only be twenty-four hours, forty-eight tops.'

'Great.'

'Right. Well, call me if you need anything. I'm around a lot today.'

'Thanks, Ed.'

37

MARA

I was quite busy on Friday morning. It was getting closer to the annual book festival funded by the local council. Most likely, this would be the last time it ran, being one of many things coming under the council's sharp knife. The children's book readings were always at the library and the staff worked really hard to try to make it as welcoming and stimulating as possible, aiming to boost membership on the coat-tails of the festival. It was a fun week but unfortunately it never made significant differences to the membership stats. Yet another reason for the council to close the doors on this place before long. The spectre of closures was looming, bigger and darker every day, over my precious library. Closures that were apparently justified cuts that needed to be made in response to the economic downturn. Downturn, I mused, was a wholly unsatisfactory word to describe the rising tide of misery that those on the bottom of the food chain experienced. I worried that things were going to get so much worse before they got better. And, as for the library closing, I simply refused to think about it. Or at least I tried not to.

Ed called mid-morning to let me know that Sam was vomiting at home with a bug picked up at Kate's. And I surprised myself by having a wave of fury rise up and swamp me. Bloody Sam! Could she not keep her crappy little life to herself for once! No, she had to go and ask Kate for twisted diet advice. I knew all about these grape diets, having witnessed Kate do them for years, feeling torn apart with frustration that I couldn't do a thing about it. And now, silly Sam not only managed to come home with a bag of grapes, she was also infected. It was the last thing we needed in the house. Ed was going away on Monday on this big job. Never mind the big party Sam was going to. Honestly.

I sat seething at my desk and then took myself outside for a walk round the block. What was wrong with me? In normal circumstances, my reaction would have been one of sympathy. Instead I just felt angry with her. I stomped along the road, trying to pound the anger out of myself. The thing was, I realised, I felt squeezed into a corner right now. Worried about Ed, frustrated with Sam. Everything happening a bit too much in my face, not leaving me any space at home just to process life and be quiet.

I smelt him as soon as I walked through the door. Old Vern was back. He hadn't been in for a long time and I'd started to worry. I glanced at my staff, Cindy and Laura. Their faces were scrunched in disgust, which they dropped when I caught their eyes. They were both too young and cosseted to understand why I allowed Vern to read the paper every day, let alone worried when he hadn't been in for three weeks. They were scared of him and repulsed by his smell and couldn't see the human being underneath. But I didn't press the point with them – they'd come across misery in their own lives soon enough and have more empathy eventually. I strode over to them, quietly finding out how long he'd been there. Five minutes. My arrangement with him was for fifteen minutes a day. And usually you could set your watch by him at ten thirty.

I skirted around him to my office and pretended to work while I took surreptitious glances at him through the glass. He was hunched over the paper, his face close to the print. He looked paler and more drawn than usual. Where have you been, Vern? What are my own pathetic worries compared to yours? I wondered. And then I immediately chastised myself – was I just being a condescending, guilt-ridden, middle-class moaner? I sighed and looked at the clock. It had tipped past the fifteen minutes I usually allowed him. I stood up and reluctantly went and put my hand on Vern's shoulder.

'Hello, Vern,' I said quietly. Loud noises often frightened him.

He didn't look up. His stomach was pressed against the table, his hands grasped together, almost in prayer. He looked even more vulnerable than usual and I felt my heart lurch again in sympathy. I looked at the page he had open. He was reading about Syria and the growing number of ordinary people forced from their homes, miserable story after miserable story recorded on the pages of *The Times* in grim little black-and-white type.

'Vern,' I said again.

He grunted to show that he was listening.

'It's time to go now, love.'

Vern sat back from the table, taking his hands away, and sighed.

'Bad news, bad news,' he muttered.

'Awful, Vern,' I agreed.

With difficulty he stood up and bent down to pick up his rucksack. The sum total of his belongings. He took one last, regretful look at the newspaper and then he turned, finally looking at me in the eye.

'There are little ones with no place to be,' he muttered, angry and helpless all at once. I just nodded. Vern turned and shuffled out of the library.

I stood watching him go. I was aware of the stares from my staff and the couple of patrons at the desk, and wanted to shout at everyone to leave the man alone! He might live on the fringes but he cares about the heart of things more than can be said for you lot! But instead I took a deep breath and returned to my office and shut the door firmly behind me.

38

SAM

I put one foot on the floor and stood up, and stretched gingerly. I hadn't vomited since one o'clock that morning, the longest stretch so far. I took one foot towards the door. Maybe that's it then. I hoped so. I shuffled out to the kitchen and saw a note placed at perfect right angles to the edge of the kitchen table. Mara.

> Ed and I are taking the kids out for the day.
> Hope you're feeling better.
> Back around 6ish.
> M x

My heart sank. Mara's disapproval at me bringing a bug into the house managed to ooze from the scrap of paper. I hadn't exactly been up and about the previous night, bar the regular visits to my friend the toilet bowl, but from the snatches of conversation I did hear, even without hearing the content, Mara's annoyance was plain.

It's not my bloody fault! I wailed to myself and then clutched my stomach – greatly reduced, I couldn't help noticing – as a violent cramp took over. I staggered to the toilet and sat down, just in time. Perhaps, I thought to myself, doubled over in pain with my eyes squeezed shut, it wasn't actually a bad thing the others weren't here right now.

When they did come home I was dressing for the party. It felt like it had taken me the whole day just to get showered and have some toast and tea. My visits to the toilet had been frequent, lengthy and painful. A couple of times, I went from the toilet straight to my bed to curl up and sleep.

Mara knocked on the door when I returned and brought in a cup of tea.

'You're not still going!' Mara's face, which had been wearing an expression of something like contrition, flicked into shock when she saw me in my dress.

'Of course I am. I'm fine,' I insisted.

'Have you stopped vomiting?' Mara set the cup on my desk.

'Yes . . .'

Mara looked at me. 'But?'

'Nothing.' I buried my head in my wardrobe.

'You paused.'

'Did I?' I withdrew my head. 'I didn't mean to.'

Mara's lips tightened. 'You still look awful.'

'Thanks! But skinnier, don't you think?' I pulled my dress tight against my stomach.

Mara sighed. 'Do you want some supper before you go?'

'No, I'll be all right. Don't have much of an appetite yet,' I said, and she left the room.

*

The venue was half full when I got there, which was a relief. I leant against the bar, not trying to look cool – although I hoped that's how it came across – but because I was recovering from the effort of getting there. I felt decidedly light-headed and as I waited for my drink I hungrily devoured half a bowl of peanuts before I'd realised what I'd done. I kept scanning the crowd for Charlie, obsessively wiping crumbs from the corner of my mouth as I did so, but he wasn't anywhere. I had spotted the toilet and judged I was within a fast trot of the door, should that be necessary. So far, so good. I wiped the corners of my mouth again.

'Sam,' a familiar voice behind me called, and I turned.

'Ed?' Had I forgotten something? I thought wildly for any other reason why he'd be here. Was something wrong? But he was all dressed up. What was going on?

He walked towards me, smiling, and from behind him, dressed in the most perfect little black dress you have ever seen, was Rebecca. Together they walked up to me.

'Wh-wha—'

'What are we doing here?' Rebecca finished for me, looking smug.

I blinked.

Rebecca laid her pretty head on the top of Ed's arm. 'Dear Ed agreed to come as my date.'

'Oh.'

I felt beads of sweat form over my top lip. My weeks of grooming in preparation for the party felt like they were unravelling before the neat little package that was my sister. And I wished she'd take her damn head off his arm. We all know how gorgeous and petite you are! I felt like screaming.

'How are you holding up?' Ed whispered to me.

'Top of the world. What are you—'

But I didn't get to finish my question. Charlie chose that moment to finally emerge from nowhere. He joined our awkward little party with a few smooth strides.

'Ah, if it isn't the prettiest sisters from Petersfield.'

Rebecca tinkled her practised laugh again. My stomach gurgled. This wasn't the great reveal of Sam looking sexy in a dress I'd been working up to at all! Charlie was looking at me with a gleam in his eye – that was good. But I hadn't imagined

233

this moment with the others there. And not feeling this bad! The room seemed to shudder around me. It sounded like everyone was shouting. I unpeeled my tongue from the roof of my mouth. I had to get my shit together and say something for God's sake.

'Um, Charlie, this is Ed, Mara's brother.'

'Yes, I know, I met him the other day,' Charlie shouted. He reached out and shook Ed's hand.

'You did?'

Ed looked at me and shrugged. 'I was in the wrong place at the wrong time.' Even Ed, who had such a lovely voice, sounded like he was shouting.

Charlie laughed expansively, boom boom boom.

'Now, let me get your drinks. What'll it be, Ed? Rebecca, your usual? Sam, ale?'

'Make it a vodka tonic,' I muttered, excusing myself to teeter to the bathroom at a fast, thigh-clenching trot.

When I returned, Charlie was still standing there with Ed and Rebecca, and I could hear her laughing right across the room. Of course I knew Rebecca was going to be at the party but I hadn't expected her to bring Ed. Stupidly I thought that because no one had mentioned her all week the whole weird thing between Ed and Rebecca was dead in the water. But it obviously wasn't. I couldn't possibly just stand there in that little circle and make small talk, I couldn't.

The lamé clutch Claudia had leant me was on the bar next to them. I joined them long enough to pick it up and then moved a little way down the bar and took a seat. I soon got involved with an important text conversation with nobody. Charlie dropped my drink to me after a little while.

'Here you go, gorgeous.' He nodded to the phone. 'What's that about? Why aren't you with us?'

'Work.' I put the phone face down so he couldn't see it.

'On a Saturday night?'

I nodded and took a sip. Ick, it was strong. I felt like the whole world was too strong, too loud, too intense for me.

'Well, you know what they say about all work and no play.' Charlie looked at me intensely. 'You look so good tonight. Good enough to eat.'

It was working. It was actually working! I just wished I could stand up for more than a minute without feeling sick.

Charlie leant in again.

'Look, I can't hang around talking to you by myself all night. It will happen though, OK? And in the meantime don't be a stranger.'

'OK,' I managed, my voice tiny in comparison with his. 'I'll try.' I said that bit to his back. He had gone, returning into the fray, under cover. I had to bide my time.

39

SAM

It was disgusting and it carried on all night. Rebecca twinkled and twirled and tried her best to outshine me with all the men in the room – in particular Charlie and Ed. It wasn't hard for her – I wasn't exactly able to strut my dress or sparkling personality around the room.

Can't you see she's faking it all! I seethed from the sidelines, sipping vodka on my empty stomach. It's all a big game – she's never going to give a shit about you, about any of you. In fact she's never going to care about anyone at all ever.

Eventually I got talking to some random man who was quite cute and funny, and I slowly began to relax a little. I wasn't going to go desperately pawing after Charlie. Rebecca's tinkling was attention-seeking enough. And there was this cute, funny fellow. I hadn't caught his name and I was missing sections of his banter but I picked up enough now and again to laugh.

I was amusing him with stories from shoots that had gone terribly wrong when an elegant arm wrapped its way around whatshisname's neck.

'Luce!' he exclaimed, smiling a broad and genuine smile.

'Hello, little brother, charming the ladies again are we?'

I swallowed and my insides dropped an inch. It was her.

'This is Sam. Sam, this is Lucy, my sister.'

'Oh, I know who she is.' Lucy looked at me. 'An old friend of Charlie's – we've already met.'

'Hi,' I smiled, terrified.

Lucy launched into a conversation with her brother about people I had never heard of. She was dressed in a simple satin dress the colour of oysters, with tiny little straps that showed off sculpted collarbones. I sat there, my bowels loosening by the second, my body sending out urgent alarm signals. Get to a toilet now! it was telling me. But I couldn't move. The coolness in Lucy's eyes and tone had frozen me to the spot. Eventually though, after what was probably seconds, my body took over and I stood up, muttered my excuses and teetered to the toilet.

Halfway there I felt a hot, wet intruder slip out into my pants.

Oh fuck, oh fuck! I tried to pick up speed, clenching the top of my thighs together even tighter, thankful that I'd decided against wearing a thong. I could see the door to the Ladies, almost there, almost there.

But suddenly he was there, muscling me off track into a dark corridor, his unmistakeable scent enveloping me.

'Not now, I really need the loo!' I pleaded.

'You are such a tease, I've hardly seen you all night,' Charlie admonished me in his smooth voice, taking my hand and pulling me out of a fire exit into the cold night. He had obviously had several more drinks since he saw me at the beginning of the night. It was making him reckless. Dangerous. We were in an alley down the side of the club. He took my wrists and pushed me against the wall, kissing me roughly. I tried kissing him back but the effort of keeping my bum closed and concentrating on his lips was too much. I wrenched away from him.

'You having a good night then?' Distract him, that's what I needed to do.

'It's better now,' he mumbled, his eyes glazed with drink, and he tried launching in towards my lips again.

'Charlie, I'd love nothing more than to ravage you right now but honestly I really need to go to the loo.'

Charlie sighed and released my wrists, confidently running his hands down my body.

'You do look good enough to eat, Sam,' he said huskily, and pushed his crotch into mine, 'but I suppose I can wait a bit longer.'

Then he stood back and sniffed.

'What's that smell?'

'What smell?' I said, stepping into the doorway.

He sniffed around some more, his shirt open at the neck, hands in his pocket, swaying slightly. He was even more handsome, I noted, when he was drunk.

'Oh, it's gone.' He kept sniffing. 'That's strange.'

'Probably something in the alley,' I called and bolted inside.

When I emerged from the toilet, having stuffed my soiled pants in the sanitary disposal bin, the atmosphere had changed. It felt like half the party was missing. The roar of conversation had gone, leaving only music. Those left were looking towards the door, where a bunch of people were all trying to get out at once. I could hear shouting from outside. It didn't sound good. I cast around for Charlie, Ed and Rebecca. No sign of them.

Suddenly Lucy's brother ran across the room and pushed his way outside, his face serious. I felt full of foreboding but my feet took me quickly across the room to follow him. Something was wrong. I had a dreadful feeling it would have something to do with me but I still had to know. Half the party were on the footpath. Someone was shouting in a shrill voice while a low voice rumbled in counterpoint. I skirted around the gawping half-moon of onlookers onto the road, only just getting out of the

238

way of a cab as it pulled in. There – I finally had a view of the scene. It was Charlie and Lucy! He was pleading with her but she was having none of it.

'Get your hands off me!' she shouted as she stepped towards the cab, a couple of her pretty friends trying to shoo Charlie away.

'Lucy, don't go, this is crazy!'

'No it's not,' Lucy yelled from the car. 'It's over.'

And with that the car pulled away from the kerb and into the night, leaving Charlie reeling on the footpath, and his friends heading back to the bar, eager to get back to the main business of the evening.

Instinctively I rushed to him. 'Are you OK, Charlie? What's going on?'

He stood swaying, his eyes still glazed. 'Sheesh a fucking nightmare,' he mumbled, gazing in the direction the cab had gone.

'Come on, come and have a drink.' I tugged on his arm softly.

He looked at me finally then, confused, as if he couldn't understand why I was there.

'Charlie?' I said.

But he said nothing. He turned away from me and gazed at the disappearing cab, as if it was the only thing that existed in the world right then. In the argument with Lucy, his shirt had become untucked, his hair ruffled and his jacket was no longer sitting on his shoulders properly. He looked desperate. He looked totally heartbroken.

I felt the hope I had for that evening and all the desperate weeks leading up to it turn into sharp needles in my belly. I stepped back from him, almost turning my heel on the kerb, just steadying myself in time. This. Was. All. Wrong.

'Come on, mate.' A couple of his friends barged in where I had been and clapped him on his back. 'Come and celebrate, there's plenty more totty inside, come on!' They tried to move him out of the road but then Ed was there, shadowed by Rebecca, her make-up still looking as pristine as it did five hours ago. Another cab pulled up and Ed opened the door.

'Just go home, mate,' he told Charlie as he negotiated him inside, somehow completely ignoring the vociferous complaints from his friends. Rebecca hovered by the door, one arm on Ed's back, like a little nurse guiding the doctor to the patient. She completely blanked me; I may as well have been invisible.

'How do we make sure he gets home OK?' she chirruped to Ed. He didn't answer and leant in to talk to the driver, then shut the door firmly behind Charlie, effectively preventing anyone else speaking to him.

'He'll be fine. He doesn't need any more liquor, that's for sure.' He was using such old-fashioned language but somehow making it sound right. 'The driver knows where to go.'

The next thing I knew I was back inside. I don't remember walking back in. I was reeling from what I had just seen, trying to make sense of it, the furious screams of Lucy still ricocheting around my head. Had she seen us kissing? Is that why she took off? But I had kept an eye on the entrance to the alleyway the whole time and we were only out there for a minute, weren't we? The night was a jumble in my head. All night I'd felt outside of myself. Mara was right, I was in no fit state to be out, and instead I'd put a couple of vodkas on an empty stomach with my feet in heels. No wonder I felt so jangled. And Charlie had never felt so . . . aggressive before. That wasn't like him. It must have just seemed that way because I'd been feeling so unwell, so weak. He couldn't have been so forceful with me really. It was all in my head.

I looked around me at the deflated party, the punters swaying out the door to more exciting venues. I longed for the safety of my own bed more than I'd longed for anything all night.

At that moment Ed came up to me. He was holding my coat.

'Here you go,' he said, gently helping me put it on.

I almost started crying with the relief of having my coat on.

'Thank you. My hands are shaking.'

'I'm not surprised. You look like you need to be in bed.'

'Funny, that's just what I was thinking.'

Ed shook his head at me.

'You look like your sister when you do that,' I said. I managed a small smile.

'For once, I don't mind. Mara's right, you know, you are a worry, Sam Moriarty.' He put an arm round my shoulders and squeezed them.

'You're not going, are you?' Rebecca appeared next to us. She looked as bright eyed and bushy tailed as she had at the beginning of the evening. I looked at Ed. Surely he won't want to stay here will he? The idea of him not being at my side as I trekked home was horrible. At that moment it felt like Ed was the only thing keeping me warm, upright and sane enough to get home to where I should be. But his face was blank, completely unreadable.

'The night is young! Let's not let all that drama ruin Saturday night.' She did a little wiggle. 'What do you think, Ed, time for a boogie?'

I looked at him again. What would he say?

'No thanks. I'm going to take Sam home, she's not feeling well.'

Thank God.

Rebecca gave a little pout.

'Aw, poor Sam. I would have thought you'd be bouncing off the walls seeing Lucy take off like that, not feeling all sorry for yourself—'

'I'm feeling sick, actually—'

But Rebecca ploughed on. She wasn't listening to me. Her eyes had taken on an extra gleam. She was a cat about to pounce.

'Not that you should be getting your hopes up. There's no way he would ever go backwards to you. He's moved on into a different world to you and it's not a world you're ever going to be a part of—'

'OK, that's probably enough, Rebecca. I'm going to take Sam home.'

'Oh.' Rebecca looked crushed for moment then gave a little shrug. She leant up and gave Ed a peck on his cheek. 'Too bad, Ed. I'll get you on the dance floor one day.'

'Bye, Rebecca.'

Ed turned me round and led me to the door.

'Get better soon, Sam. And forget about tonight,' Rebecca called out to me.

I didn't answer. Forget about tonight, she says. Forget about what? About Charlie kissing me roughly? About crapping my own pants? About him being heartbroken when his girlfriend took off? About the horrid words you just said to me?

Ed led me out into the cold night, his arm firmly round my shoulders. It stayed there all the way home.

40

CLAUDIA

I arrived at the café to Sam scowling at me over half-eaten scrambled eggs.

'Where the bloody hell have you been?' she demanded.

'Hello to you too.'

It wasn't like Sam to greet me with a strop and I wasn't sure how to deal with it. I was tempted to turn round right there and then and walk out again. I had enough going on without dealing with anyone else's crap but she must have seen something of that in my face and dropped the attitude quickly.

'Oh bollocks, sorry,' she said. 'It's me who should be apologising. I just can't get my head around last night.'

And she was off, telling me all about Charlie's birthday party. At least I think that was what she was talking about. To be honest, I couldn't really keep up. The story was pouring out of her and it was coming at me at double speed, or that's what it felt like. Of course she couldn't really have been speaking at twice her usual speed but, with my head crammed full, I struggled to process what she was saying.

'. . . so there they were on the footpath and she just leaves him, screaming, "It's over," and goes off in the cab! What do you think, Claud, do you think it really is over?' She paused and looked at me. I realised I was expected to give her some sort of response rather than just a sympathetic noise. What was it that

243

she'd just said? I felt something in my hands. It was the menu. I had been holding it the whole time Sam had been speaking but I hadn't taken any of it in. Maybe I should have stayed home today after all. I couldn't be a good friend right now. This was awful.

'Have you been listening?' Sam said again.

'Yes, of course I was,' I replied. Think. Say something.

'I'm thinking,' I said.

'The thing is,' Sam continued, 'he seemed totally floored by the whole experience, as if it came out of nowhere. But I don't understand that because when he's been with me he's been saying it's not working with her. But I suppose he was really drunk at the time.'

The waitress arrived and took my order or, I should say, I opened my mouth and somehow formed a string of food-related words. I hope they made sense. The pimply girl taking the order wrote them down anyway. It gave me a moment to come up with some Charlie-related words and I strained to remember the content of Sam's download. I took a sip of coffee and Sam watched me place the cup carefully in its saucer. I think I had the gist.

'It could be the end, Sam. Or it could be that they thrive on drama and this is just one of many walkouts by the girlfriend. What's her name again?'

'Lucy.'

'Lucy . . .' What could the name tell me about the woman? Not much, not really. I think of Lucys as being warm and apple-cheeked, with curly blonde hair, none of which was helpful right now. When Sam told stories like this one it was usually my job to give her some context, some big-picture stuff to make the action in the foreground reduce to a more manageable size for Sam to process. At least that was what I'd always thought she needed. What a great big pile of rubbish that seemed like now. Why should anyone come to me for advice? And worse, why should I have thought that what I had to say was of any use?

'Is she a drama queen?' I finally dredged up another question.

Sam shrugged. 'She doesn't seem like one. More the cool, calm, keep-everything-up-my-clean-anus type actually.'

'Nice.'

Sam smiled. 'It's true! Anyway that's why I think this really might be the end. I doubt she'd normally be that out of control in public.'

'So why are you so grumpy then? By what you're saying you should be over the moon, right?'

Sam hesitated. 'That's what I don't understand either, Claud. I should be happy but I'm not.'

Sam worried the side of a finger with her teeth, her face scrunched up in tired confusion.

'What was Charlie's reaction to her storming off?' I asked her.

She rubbed her face and I saw just how miserable she was. It wasn't just a case of being in a hungover grump – the poor old thing was obviously raw about this Charlie character. I finally felt something click into place and I was brought into the moment.

'Did he seem upset or dismissive or what?' I asked.

Sam's eyes brimmed with tears. 'That's the thing I don't understand, Claud. He was gutted. He looked so forlorn, and so . . . lost!'

'Wouldn't that be normal though, Sam? He's just been dumped.'

'Yes, but—' Sam wiped away an escaping tear crossly. She hated showing emotion in public or indeed in private. She liked the wider world to believe she was fearless. She sure had it bad for this guy.

'I thought he might be relieved, that it would mean he could spend time with me and not feel guilty,' she said quietly.

245

'Aren't you really talking about yourself?'

Sam sighed. 'Oh you're probably right, Claudia. I'm going to go and sort myself out in the loo. These tears are really starting to ruin my breakfast. And we haven't talked about you at all yet.'

When she returned, she launched straight back into Charlie and Lucy's break-up again, turning it over and over, examining it for every crack, every blemish. How upset Charlie was and how this didn't fit the scenario Sam had in her head, ready and waiting for just this opportunity. When he finally dumped Lucy he was supposed to run joyfully into Sam's arms. It was never meant to be the other way round.

'What if he pines after Lucy forever?' she asked me, her face white and not at all pretty.

Breakfast came as a welcome distraction and we moved onto some perfunctory conversation about friends and family, but Sam's heart wasn't in it. Any subconscious wish to share my news with her had dropped out of my handbag when she'd started banging on and on.

Finally it was time to pay and just when the teenager returned for our payment – or should I say my debit card – Sam pinged her head up like she'd just seen the light.

'I've got it!' Her face flooded with colour, a maniacal grin fixed on her face. 'Don't you see, Claudia, he's forced her to dump him. Without knowing it, he's subconsciously pushed her away.' She gesticulated wildly, unable to get her words out fast enough. 'The relationship was doomed but he couldn't initiate anything upfront so he was just enough of an arsehole to finally push her away – that's it! That's why she's dumped him. It was him all along; he just doesn't know it yet. I've done that countless times. Claudia? Do you know what I mean?'

And suddenly I'd had enough of her and her two-penny

analysis. She was being a self-absorbed bore. All I wanted was to get away from her endless Charlie talk.

'No, I don't actually.'

'Haven't you ever done that? You know when things are out of your control, and you're not aware that you're doing it, but before you know it you're getting dumped and you're free? It's great!'

'Actually, if something isn't working, I usually just tell them.' Adding in my head that I didn't usually go far enough for something not to work. I stood up and pulled on my coat. I really had to get out of there and I could feel frustrated tears welling up inside. Why were we even friends? She hadn't asked me a single question about myself.

She was still talking out on the street. 'But that's brilliant, isn't it? He won't realise it straightaway but in a day or two he'll be feeling on top of the world. And he'll be free.'

'To be with you?' My tone was harsh and I heard Sam take a sharp breath.

'I hope so,' she said quietly.

I was scanning the street for a cab but forced myself to turn back to her. She looked pathetic, chewing her lip like a twelve-year-old.

'Well, don't throw yourself at him whatever you do,' I said.

'Of course I won't! I'm not silly!' And she punched me playfully on the shoulder. 'Anyway, I'm quickly learning to lure them in, Claud, thanks to your excellent tuition.'

'Well, if you say so.'

I waved at a cab, with no luck.

'Damn.'

There was another one sitting at lights in the distance. I strained to see if its for-hire light was on. We didn't speak. In my head I was already in the cab, not talking to anyone.

In the silence between us Sam finally twigged that perhaps I wasn't the most cheerful person on the block just then.

'Is it something I've said?'

'No.' I paused. It wasn't something you said, Sam – it was everything.

'We haven't really talked about you, have we?'

'No, we haven't. But now I've got to get to my parents' for lunch.'

The cab pulled over. I hugged her quickly and got in, not even asking her if she wanted a lift somewhere, and I realised that what I'd needed all morning was a hug myself.

41

CLAUDIA

I took a deep breath and pressed the doorbell – brass, polished twice weekly. The door opened immediately, almost as if Mother had been hovering behind it.

'Come in, come in, we haven't seen you forever!' She reached up on tiptoe to kiss my cheek before marching down the hall. 'It's been too long, darling, too long,' she called over her clip-clopping court shoes.

I followed her, muttering I'd been flat out with work.

'Oh you girls, such high fliers,' she said in a voice leaking polite disapproval. When Sabrina and I were growing up, Mother had made the same noises as my father about how important it was for us both to succeed. But when it came down to it and we were eventually achieving greatness out there in the shiny corporate world of her dreams, she couldn't understand why we were too busy for 'family time'. She felt, if she was honest with herself (which she didn't generally make a habit of), somewhat miffed.

Sabrina crossed her eyes at me from her perch in the kitchen. I smiled in relief. I hadn't been sure if she was going to make it today and I was grateful for the extra buffer. It was the first time in as long as I could remember that I wasn't looking forward to a family meal. Even while living a life they couldn't possibly understand, I never once felt distanced from my family. But now I did; now I felt like a usurper.

No one seemed to notice my reticence to start with. Mother burbled small talk over her Aga, as if she had been wound up and set off like a small toy. A little bird with excellent manners, I thought. Sabrina provided most of the required noises, dotted with frequent winks in my direction.

'I can see you teasing me, you know.' Mother looked sternly at us as she carried a steaming dish to the table. 'Now it's time to sit up.'

I took a step towards the dining room and I felt my phone vibrating in my pocket. Marco! Not now, not while I was here. But in a moment of recklessness I pressed the call button and motioning to my mother that I'd be one minute. I stepped quickly out of the back door.

'Marco.'

'Oh, lovely lady, nice to hear your voice.'

'Same here but I've got to make it quick, my family are waiting for me to sit down for lunch.'

'Of course, of course! I have good news for you though. My results are back and I'm all clear, baby.' Marco's syrupy voice, which had the ability to become so thick and sticky it could shut synapses down, suddenly became the most beautiful thing in the world. I felt relief whoosh from my stomach to my toes.

'Oh, that's great news!'

'Well, I hate to disappoint the ladies and all. But go and eat, see you at the club sometime, OK?'

'Yes, OK. Bye then.' Brilliant – that narrowed things considerably. And before I could change my mind, I called David. Maybe he'd have his results too. He answered after two rings and this time knew exactly who was calling.

'Claudia.' His voice was hard.

'Hello, David.'

'I'm glad you've called. I've had the test results back.'

'Yes?' I felt sick – it had to be bad news, he sounded so angry.

'They're negative.'

'What?' Did I just hear him right? His words jarred – they didn't sound right.

'I said the tests were negative.' He slowed the last word down as if I was very thick.

'Oh, right.'

'So that's that then. I don't wish to have any more contact with you, Claudia . . . Claudia?' I stood stock still, looking down the pared-down winter garden, its edges butting the neatly clipped grass, a large grey bird bath pulling the whole gorgeously designed thing together.

'Yes, of course,' I finally whispered and hung up before the odious creature could say another thing.

'Fuck me,' I whispered to the garden. So it was John who had given it to me all along. And I was in exactly the wrong place to process this information. I took some deep breaths and then went back inside, steeling myself for lunch.

After lunch, the women cleared the table. I was about to continue into the kitchen to wash up, but my father called me to join him in the sitting room instead. I paused momentarily before joining him on the sofa. He was so good at prising things out of me and today wasn't the day for sharing. But of course I joined him, the pull to obey him as strong as it had ever been. I sat next to him on the sofa so I could look at the fire, rather than at him. That was the problem with him – he always knew when I was unhappy, which was fine when I could confide in him but excruciating when I couldn't.

'I saw a friend of yours the other day, what's her name, the GP,' he began.

'Lily.'

'Yes, that's it, lovely girl.'

'Woman.'

'Yes, yes, you're right.' He smiled.

I waited for him to come to the point.

'She had her husband with her, a well-spoken chap, very confident.'

'He's a builder.'

'Yes, he was telling me about a house he's working on at the moment in Berkshire, has a green oak frame or something.'

I turned and looked at him, suddenly feeling cross. He was pushing tobacco into his pipe, an indulgence that no one could dissuade him from.

'Why are you telling me this?'

He looked up from his satisfying little activity, a poorly executed 'I don't know what you're talking about' look on his face. 'Just making conversation, Snooks,' he said.

Using my nickname failed to placate me. I kept staring at him hard until he crumbled. He shrugged.

'She just seemed really happy, that's all,' he conceded, bringing the pipe to his mouth and starting the protracted huffing and puffing required to light the smelly beast. Eventually he added, 'And it made me think of you, that's all.'

'Right.' I sat back. 'In what way, exactly, did it make you think of me?'

Papa's pipe crackled as it finally took light. He exhaled the smoke in a sigh.

'I was wondering if there was someone in your life, that's all.'

I stared at the wall opposite the sofa, at the fireplace and tasteful paintings, placed just so, and I pictured John, his handsome, earnest face as he sat across from me in that lovely restaurant and asked me if he was seeing anyone while I had sat opposite him, leaden with self-loathing.

'No,' I replied in a small voice, and then was suddenly swamped by anger at my father, at his too-high expectations of me, at the bar he had set for me to aim for. All for what! So I fell short of it just when I met a man I could see eye to eye with?

'It's not as if you've encouraged me either,' I spat at him.

'Excuse me?' he spluttered, pulling his pipe out in a quick, shocked movement.

'Nothing.' I crossed my arms. What was the point anyway? Like he'd understand. No one in this too-good-for-everyone-else family would ever understand.

There was a silence, filled with anger as far as I was concerned. But when Papa broke it, his voice was full of love.

'Tell me what's on your mind, Claudia, please.'

And then, out of nowhere, I felt tears spilling down my cheeks and I covered my face with my hands. Papa shifted closer and put his arm around me.

'It's all right, darling, we love you. There there.' As if he could read my mind and knew that was the only thing I really needed to hear.

I leant against him, his spiky beard poking into my head while he held me, waiting for the tears to stop.

'I'm sorry,' I finally managed, sniffing and wiping my face.

'That's OK. You're right anyway. I know I've been pretty strict in that department. Maybe part of me didn't want to see you grow up. Maybe—' He paused and smoothed my hair off my forehead. 'Maybe I've never wanted to see you settle for second best,' he added, passing me a box of tissues. 'Here, you can stop sniffing in my ear now.'

'Well, I'm not bloody perfect, you know. Why should someone else be?' And I blew my nose noisily.

'You're right, darling. Of course you are but can you blame me for wanting the best for my girls?'

I folded my tissue into a wet square. 'What if what you think is the best for us might create a mountain that's just too high to climb?'

Papa slapped my knee. 'Well, Snooks, how about throwing the hiking boots away and not worrying about climbing any mountains?'

'Are you sure?'

'Definitely.' And he hugged me tight against his smoky chest.

Oh Papa, I thought, if only it was that simple.

42

ED

I sat back in my seat with relief. I didn't expect to be so pleased to be leaving London. I thought I'd feel a bit sad about the prospect of no Sam for three weeks but now I couldn't wait to get away from her. The whole thing had made me feel exhausted and more than a little disgusted. Charlie's party had been an endurance test, putting up with Rebecca as she flirted with her plastic smile, angling for any interaction she could get with Charlie, and making sure her fingers or head were on my arm whenever Sam was in the vicinity. She was witty, I had to give her that, but her humour was invariably patronising, sarcastic, caustic or all three at once and always, always delivered with her Cheshire-cat smile. It made my skin crawl, recalling it. And out of the corner of my eye, dear old Sam, tottering around looking peaky, trying so hard to ignore Charlie and then looking so lost and bewildered after the big scene. It was all a pile of meaningless bollocks.

I stared out the window, watching the last of London dissolve into countryside. She hadn't even remembered to say goodbye to me last night. I'd told her I was off early on Monday morning but she was too busy mooning over that drunken fool of a man.

No more, I thought to myself. No bloody more. It was time to get away, move on, maybe even meet someone who actually cared about me. It was time to leave her and all her pettiness behind me.

43

SAM

A cold wind whipped down the street, made even colder, I thought, by the imposing buildings that seemed to be looking down at me in contempt. What are you doing here, you pathetic, scruffy excuse for a human being? they seemed to say. I scowled back. I was there on an important mission. Something that really mattered. This was about love! One human concerned about another. Something you'd know nothing about, you . . . you . . . buildings. Ha! I told them, all right. I am on a mission. I am chasing Charlie, no less. Operation Chasing Charlie. I liked that. I smiled and then stopped. Focus, focus, focus, girl. My eyes were glued to the main entrance of the hospital, a revolving door simultaneously sucking people in and spitting others out.

Just to be clear, I wasn't chasing him – I just wanted to see his face. It had been three days since his party and he hadn't been in touch. So far I had successfully resisted contacting him but my will was being gnawed away by an impatient and hungry heart. If I could just glimpse him I would be able to get through another twenty-four hours without calling him, through til Wednesday, perhaps even Thursday. But then it would be almost a week since it had happened and surely he'd have been in touch by then?

I needed to see his face for myself. Even a fleeting glance would do. Would he look drawn or happy? I was hoping for happy but, then again, if he had reached that point after the break-up, why hadn't he called? And if he was still depressed – well, I had to hope he wasn't pining after Lucy. A biting wind whipped around my legs and I dug my hands further into my pockets.

After waiting for twenty-two cold minutes he finally left the building. He strode out and turned left, and I felt as if my gaze was somehow glued to him, so intensely was I looking at him. Surely he would feel it and turn my way? But he strode off and turned left towards the nearby Tube – which I dared not follow him on – and was gone. That was it. I'd seen him. And he looked, I thought, decidedly unhappy.

44

MARA

After a cup of tea, and a few minutes lost in *Review*, left over from the Saturday paper, I opened my laptop. I rarely used it, especially during the week. I felt like I got plenty of screen time during the day, thank you very much. But I really should check my bank account to make sure everything was ticking over as it should. While Ed had been around I'd forgotten to look as often as I usually do, letting it lapse for at least two weeks, which was most unlike me. I pride myself on keeping everything very neat and tidy in that department, always putting a little aside for emergencies. I was most definitely not interested in living in a reactionary fashion when it came to money.

So when I saw that my bank balance was in the red I gave a yelp of surprise. George looked at me, confused. He didn't normally hear me yelping, in surprise or otherwise. I scrolled down the history and frowned, then stood up and fetched the calendar from the kitchen wall, placing a finger on the last three Thursdays one at a time, and searching for the corresponding date. The twenty-fifth – nothing. The eighteenth – nothing. The eleventh – nothing.

Nothing! For three bloody weeks!

My mind clattered through the past few weeks, totting up everything Sam had spent money on that wasn't her bloody rent. Toiletries and make-up for that bloody party. And the dress.

And the nights out. God, she was so selfish. So completely and utterly self-absorbed. I logged out and shut the laptop, then went to the toilet (comprehensively scrubbed with disinfectant the day before – and not by Sam either), seething as I peed my tea away and wondering how much longer I could put up with it. How long could I continue living with this child before I'd have to take action?

45

SAM

I had it all figured out. The next step in Operation Chasing Charlie was to view him at home. Not his London flat. No, this mission would take me further afield, to the countryside, to his parents' house. Well, not to the house itself but certainly nearby. My trusty sidekick Facebook told me that was where he was going tonight. I had made do with the single glance of him across the courtyard outside his work and had somehow made it to Friday without contacting him but now I was hungry for more. It was like a scab sitting there on my knee just asking to be picked. I had to know – was he still unhappy? Or had he been having a particularly bad day when I saw him? If he was still unhappy this weekend, I'd feel better about the fact that he still hadn't been in touch. If he was happy . . . well, I didn't want to think about that.

I sat on the Tube, turning over my plan and feeling very pleased I actually had one. It was preferable to giving in to my miserable heart, which was busy feeling utterly lost and really wanted to go to bed and cry for a long time. I was still reeling from the anti-climax Charlie's birthday party had proved to be. But I wasn't going to give up now. Not after all the hard work I'd put into luring him so far. I would keep on moving forwards. I had to get there; I just had to be patient.

A bunch of women sat opposite me, obviously friends going home together after work. They were deep in discussion about a mutual friend and the steamy affair she was having with her boss, completely oblivious to the other passengers on the train.

'She may as well be wearing a sign around her neck—'

'Totally glowing—'

'It'll only end in tears.'

'No, it'll be worth it. Look at her!'

'I saw her workmate the other day, whatshisname, Robert?'

'Is that the cute one?'

'What, the cute gay one or the cute dark one?'

'Aren't they both dark?'

'OMG, stick to your story.'

'OK, so he said that—'

'Isn't Robert the one with the square face? You know. He looks like a Lego man.'

'No! He left ages ago, got a job somewhere else—'

'That's right! He got a job in marketing at Legoland.'

'Really?'

'No!'

How long had it been since I had had time like that with my girls? I thought back. I couldn't remember. Too long. Far too long. I sat up straighter. I had the distinct impression my head had been pulled out of a hole. Had I been so wrapped up in this Charlie business I'd become the kind of girl that dropped her friends for a man? Had I really become that kind of person? I shook my head. I couldn't bear listening to the friends a minute longer so I stood and moved towards the door, ready to leap out at Queen's Park. The need to immerse myself in my friends was suddenly urgent, as pressing as the need to think non-stop about Charlie had been ten minutes ago.

Hurrying along Harvist Road, I imagined a relaxed Friday night in with Mara. I'd ask all about how she was and really listen to her. Be the best friend I could be.

But there was no one there. Not even a note. I frowned. Friday night, and Mara wasn't home? My tummy dropped. Friday night. It was Friday night and no one had called me to organise meeting up. I blinked, thinking back. We hadn't met up last Friday night either. I called Claudia but her phone was off.

46

CLAUDIA

I sat at the kitchen table while Mara made coffee, absent-mindedly running the tips of my fingers across the smooth surface. It was late on Saturday morning and the kitchen was filled with Mara's crossness. I didn't prod her for details. I found that, given space and time, Mara usually got around to talking about whatever was bothering her. Sam had never understood this, which I always thought was unfortunate and remarkably blind of her.

'Where's Sam?' I asked.

'I don't know. She was here this morning, her door was shut before I went shopping but she left without doing her Saturday jobs.'

I raised my eyebrows. 'She has Saturday jobs?'

'Well' – Mara set a plunger and two mugs down – 'I don't mind if she does them on Sunday but I'd prefer she did them on Saturday to get the weekend off to a good start.'

Mara's mouth was pinched as she poured warm milk into both mugs, stirring the liquid aggressively as she added the coffee. She sat down and looked at me.

'What?'

'I didn't say anything.'

'You not saying something usually means something, Claud. Am I being unreasonable?'

'Unreasonable? Oh what would I know? I don't have to share

263

my space with anyone else. I imagine some ground rules would be helpful. But perhaps . . .' I paused, about to rephrase what I wanted to say, then decided against it. 'You might be treating Sam a little bit like a child?'

'She is one though! She missed her bloody rent this week for the third bloody time!' Mara held up three indignant fingers.

I stepped around my thoughts once more. Mara was obviously burning up about all this. But it had to be said. 'Could it be she acts like a child because she gets treated like one?'

'I don't know. Maybe. It's a pain in the neck though, regardless of how it's come about. She's almost thirty years old! Honestly.' Mara took a long sip of coffee and sighed. 'I don't know what to do about it, Claudia. I can't carry her for much longer. She's gone completely silly over this Charlie business. Every day for two weeks there's been a new exfoliator or body cream or something in the bathroom. Not to mention the dress – and the rest. But no bloody rent!'

'I paid for her dress,' I added, instantly regretting it.

'Great! So that was money that could have gone to rent and it didn't. It's disrespectful – to me, to our friendship, to' – Mara waved her arm in circles at George and the kitchen – 'our home!'

I reached out and caught Mara's angry hand and squeezed it. 'Babe, you're really upset about this, aren't you?'

'Wouldn't you be? If one of your best friends gave such a small shit about you?'

'But she does care about you, of course she does. She can just be horrendously ditzy.'

'Call it what you want, Claud. I'm completely over it.'

It always amazed me how effectively anger smothered memory, leaving only a handful of irritating traits to chew over relentlessly, as if they were the only food the angry person had available. I saw it time and again with conflicts I was required to mediate at work

– people who had once been friends, who knew each other really well, pacing around their grievances, completely forgetting that the person they were upset with had any feelings at all – let alone complex ones. And here was Mara, chewing over a few – highly irritating, I agreed – misdemeanours of Sam's, as if that was all there was to her. Completely ignoring her warmth, years of loyal friendship and the highs and lows they'd shared. Forgetting all the weeks she had paid her rent or hadn't brought a bug into the house. Forgetting who she was beneath the dizzy exterior. But what would I know really? I pictured my tidy, peaceful flat. Nobody else to negotiate; no one at all. But in that moment the image of my empty flat was far from comforting and I felt my chest squeeze a little.

'I've got some news, actually,' I said before I could stop myself.

'Good, let's talk about something else.' Mara set her cup down and smiled.

'It's not good.'

'Oh?' The half-hearted smile fell off.

I felt a lump lodge in my throat, out of nowhere. For a moment I thought I wouldn't be able to speak.

'I . . .' I swallowed. 'I've been diagnosed with an STI.'

'What?' Mara looked shocked.

'Don't look so shocked, Mara, you know what I'm like,' I said, more bitter than I wanted to.

Mara frowned. 'Yes, I know you're a grown-up, onto-it woman!' She reached across the table and grabbed my hands. 'And here I am bleating on about Sam, when you've got much more important issues.' Then a change came across her face and she grew paler.

'Wha-what . . .'

'It's only chlamydia,' I finished for her.

Colour flooded back into Mara's cheeks. 'Oh thank God.' She let out a huge sigh through her teeth.

'Indeed.'

'Do you know—'

'Who gave it to me?'

'Yes.'

'Well, strangely enough, yes, I think I do. At least tests point in his direction. But—' I shook my head. 'I can't believe it could be him, he's so . . .'

'Grown-up?'

I looked up at her in wonder. That was it! That was what I had been trying to put my finger on. He was an adult, not a boy in a man's body.

'That guy from work, I take it, John something or other?'

'How did you know?' What was going on? Mara had her ignorant blinkers on thinking about Sam but then turned her head towards me bursting with insight.

'I could tell by the way you've talked about him in the past.'

'I've hardly spoken about him and not very nicely when I have.'

'Exactly. If you didn't care about him you would have got a lot more mileage out of it. And this time, even when you made fun of him, you were holding something back. There was something in your eyes.'

'There was?'

Mara shrugged as if it was completely obvious. If it was so bloody obvious, I thought, why had it taken me so long to realise how I felt about him?

Mara collected the mugs and cafetière and took them to the sink, casually asking over her shoulder, 'So when are you going to tell him you like him?'

47

SAM

This was meant to be a good idea, I said to myself, as I cycled furiously, one eye on the dark sky ahead. I'd set off from Petersfield twenty minutes before with renewed energy for my mission. But the uncomfortable reality of Operation Chasing Charlie soon put paid to my enthusiasm. There was more traffic than I remembered, forcing me to brush along the hedgerows, my exposed ankles at perfect nettle height. And the bloody rain – I hadn't factored that in at all – was nearly upon me. Oh no, here it comes, the first spots. I hesitated slightly and then took the next left. There was no way I could sit in my proposed hiding spot to scope out his family home – I'd have shelter in the pub. The spots turned into fat, rapid drops and then, out of nowhere, a wall of water.

What the hell am I doing? I leant my bike against the crumbling wall of the pub and ran inside, stopping in the foyer to let the worst of the water stream off my body onto the coir mat. I wore a fleece on my top half, which I could shake the drops off, but my jeans – why did I wear jeans? – were absolutely soaked. I gazed at them in despair. All I had in my little backpack was a bottle of water and an apple. Fuck, fuck, fuckity fuck.

Eventually I summoned some courage and went inside. It was a busy Saturday afternoon, packed with people with nothing better to do than stare at my bedraggled state. I avoided all ninety

267

eyes and went straight to the fire to stand as close as I could, and started turning slowly, a damp pig on a spit. Think. I had just enough money (gleaned from my Dad's small change) for a half of cider, which I'd have to make last for as long as it rained. Just. Bloody. Brilliant.

I was so busy ignoring the stares and chuckles of the locals it took me a couple of seconds to register that someone was saying my name. But then, as I turned to acknowledge him, nerves bloomed in my belly.

'I thought it was you!' the man exclaimed, his arms reaching out to embrace me, his face as handsome as ever and shockingly like his son's.

'Mr Hugh-Barrington,' I heard myself say, somehow forming words with my suddenly rubbery mouth. Just when I thought this afternoon couldn't get any better!

'Call me Charles, please,' he said and we hugged awkwardly, him going in for the two-cheek kiss, but I was cold and jittery and consumed with nerves and I completely forgot what to do and attempted a hug. The result was an awkward embrace during which the side of my head was pecked.

'You're soaked!' He looked me up and down, still holding onto my shoulders, and I realised I was shaking. 'You need a brandy. Carla! A brandy, make it a double!' he called over his shoulder, and then motioned to me to stay where I was while he moved – quite urgently, I noted – to his seat in the far corner of the room, coming back with his jacket, which he draped round my shoulders before I could think about protesting.

'Now, as soon as you're dry' – he eyed my legs again with a well-practised gaze – 'you'll come back to ours.'

I felt the colour drain from my face. 'Oh no, Mr . . . Charles, I can't, sorry,' I stammered, scrabbling frantically for a good reason.

'No, you must. Charlie's here – he'd love to see you. And Jimmy. You can have some soup.'

'Thank you for the offer but I've got to get back . . . ah . . . someone is coming to my parents' house and I haven't seen them for ages.' I swallowed. I knew I didn't sound convincing. I tried to smile. 'Anyway, I saw Charlie not that long ago, at his birthday party.'

'You did?' Charles Snr raised his eyebrows and then frowned. 'He didn't mention it.'

My heart sank. He didn't?

Charles remained frowning. 'So you would have seen the old boy getting dumped then. Rather unceremoniously, all told.' He sniffed and then met my eye. 'He's rather down in the dumps and before that he had a lurgy of some sort or another. Horrid couple of days spent on the loo.' Charles brightened. 'Anyway, here I am wittering on, what is it you young folk call it – too much information? I'm sure an old friend visiting him would do him the world of good.'

Oh God! He's had the bug too? Will he know it was from me?

'I . . . er . . . I didn't know her. Lucy, I mean.'

'No? I suppose you've been out of the picture for a long time—' I smiled thinly.

'It's rather strange really. It appears he was smitten with her and has found this out rather too late, the silly old chap. Should have made more of a go of it when he was with her.' He shrugged. 'But there you go, it's always the way. The grass is always greener, until you get there and realise it's not, eh, Sam?'

I tittered feebly and had an overwhelming desire to sit down. I took a wobbly step towards a tired leather armchair near the fire and sank into it, apologising as I descended.

'I say, are you sure you're all right, old girl?' Charles stepped forward and felt my forehead. 'You're awfully hot.'

'I've just been next to the fire for too long, I think. I'll be all right in a minute.'

'Look, you stay right there, I'm going to get the car and bring it to the door, and I'm going to take you home, no arguments!' He was gone before I could even string a sentence together. I leant my head back. Nothing for it then. I'd have to see Charlie, saying what? I was just in the neighbourhood? Yeah right, like he'd believe that. There was no such thing in the countryside – he knew that, I knew that and, worst of all, he'd know I knew that.

48

SAM

Charles – I was struggling to call him that – ushered me solici-
tously through the family's usual entrance, past welly boots and
tweed jackets and wet Labradors, into the kitchen and sat me
down at the table while he went off to find the others. I looked
about, overwhelmed by the familiar smell and surroundings. It
hadn't changed at all. New curtains perhaps. The kitchen table
sat in the middle of the warm square room. Along two walls ran
the kitchen counters – broken up by a deep Belfast sink and a
great big cream Aga rumbling quietly. A huge Dutch dresser
stretched cheerily along one wall, housing floral plates, a jumble
of Emma Bridgewater mugs and random photos, fliers, invites,
cards, all stuffed in and around them, and pinned to the wood.
On the last wall, a three-seater sofa sat under a large window that
looked out to the kitchen garden. The throw was different – the
dog hair covering it looked the same. It felt so homely in this
kitchen, with its happy lemon-yellow walls. I had forgotten just
how homely it was. My memory had held a much more starched
version for all these years.

Lydia interrupted my thoughts. 'Sam, how nice to see you.' I
got to my feet to greet her – this time getting it right. Peck, peck.
'Charles tells me you got soaked, how dreadful.'

Lydia scrutinised me with sharp eyes. She was dressed casually, a soft white cotton shirt tucked into jeans, her blonde hair as

271

ordered as ever. I hovered, standing next to the table as she went to the sink, unsure if I should sit down again or offer to help.

'What can I get you – tea? Some soup?'

'Soup would be great, thank you.' And I sat down again.

'So . . . what are you doing with yourself?'

'I work in film and television.'

'Oh?' Lydia sounded surprised.

'Yes, as a third AD. I help keep things ticking along on time on set.'

'That sounds interesting.'

'It can be sometimes.'

Lydia brought my soup over with a cup of tea for herself and sat down delicately in a chair two spaces away from me.

'What was it you did at university again?'

Oh. That question. I just loved that question. It really made me feel like such an achiever.

'Well, I did a year of a BA in media studies but it didn't grab me so I left and went and worked abroad instead,' I answered, hating how apologetic I sounded. I never sounded that way when I was talking about it with friends but with people of my parents' generation, or older, it was different. It was as if I slid straight to the bottom of the food chain as soon as someone asked me about uni. As if I was a great big waste of money and time.

'Didn't grab you?' Lydia's politely sarcastic tone completed my slide. 'Sometimes it's just about knuckling down, doing what has to be done. I doubt Charlie would be where he is now if he'd just told himself it didn't, how did you put it? "Grab him."'

Lydia smiled a thin smile. I could feel her inverted commas digging into my face. What could I say to that?

'I . . . I guess I was too young, or something,' I stuttered. 'I needed some action, some real work.'

'And now?'

'Now?'

'Do you ever think of returning to your studies now you've had some . . . action?' Lydia looked at me with raised eyebrows.

'Absolutely not!' Suddenly I didn't feel like I was bottom of the food chain, after all. If Lydia thought I was inferior just because I didn't complete my degree then I didn't care. I grinned at her, to show her that she couldn't just press me down into the floor with her pointy questioning.

'Why would I waste money when I've got a good job? So many people go to university not really knowing what they want to do and end up wasting loads of money and time. OK, so it took me a little while to find something I liked doing but I didn't cost my parents any money while I was finding my way. . You were lucky that Charlie loved what he did right from the beginning.'

Lydia gave me an inscrutable look. 'I suppose that's true. I hadn't thought of it like that. Still—'

'Anyway, it isn't like I had the luxury of my parents backing me. They could've helped me a bit but I would've walked away with a whopping big debt if I'd done a whole degree, or more than one or whatever.'

I wanted to press this home to her, shake her out of her comfortable bubble, remind her that not everyone could just do something because they wanted to, or thought it was the done thing. That some people – most people! – have to actually plan things, weigh things up, and a lot of the time decide that, on balance, they can't actually afford to do it. Not that I was thinking about money at the time I dropped out of uni. I left because I couldn't concentrate. I couldn't settle; I had itchy feet and some-thing else – oh yes! My thoughts clarified as I watched Lydia sip her tea thoughtfully. Something about feeling wretched from being dumped by your son early on in the year had something to do with it. Didn't it?

It was about then that the yellow walls ceased to feel cheerful and started to make me feel a little ill. Lydia and I continued to chat about this and that. I was blethering on, filling her in about my family when all of a sudden I lost my train of thought. My head felt woolly, confused.

'Are you feeling OK? You don't look very well.' Lydia put her hand out and for the second time in an hour I had my forehead felt. 'I think you may have caught a chill.'

'I'm fine,' I said but I didn't feel it. I felt hot and buzzy and all . . . swimmy again. Again? Oh yes, that's right. 'Actually I think I might be feeling a bit poorly. I wasn't feeling well last week.'

Lydia sighed. 'And I thought it was just my young men who can't look after themselves. Obviously you women are just as hopeless.'

'Sorry.'

Lydia smiled quickly and stood up. 'You look like you need a rest. Those boys aren't going to be back inside for a bit yet so why don't you go and put your head down for a bit? I'll dry your clothes for you while you sleep and then you can stay for some supper.'

'Oh no, that's too much trouble.'

'Don't be silly, of course it isn't. Anyway, Charlie will want to see you.'

I caught Lydia's eye briefly and I saw the scepticism I was feeling myself at this idea reflected in her eyes. Part of me just wanted to get the hell out of there as soon as possible but most of me had already decided that going to sleep right then was the only thing I was capable of.

'Thanks.'

★

When I woke again it was dark. I fumbled around and turned on the light and took in the pretty bedroom. When I remembered I

274

was at Charlie's house I sat upright in a panic and reached out for my phone. It was six o'clock! I must have been asleep for a couple of hours, maybe more. My afternoon came back to me, a series of embarrassing moments jangling for first place in my head. I groaned.

At the foot of the bed were my clothes in a neat pile. Lydia must have dried them for me and returned them as I slept. The idea of her quietly laying them there didn't half make me feel uncomfortable, like I was living too much on display. It felt like everyone – Mara, Claudia, Kate, Rebecca, Mum and Dad, even Ed – knew how I felt about Charlie, how ardently I was waiting for him to whisk me away. And now his mother had me turn up sopping wet on her doorstep, rescued by her husband, for Pete's sake, and I was so fragile I had to be put to bed and even have my clothes dried for me. This is too much, I thought. I wanted my heart plucked off my sleeve and stuffed into a box, somewhere dark where no one could see it. And to not be lying in bed at Charlie's house where anyone could wander in and see me sleeping!

I dressed and was about to go downstairs when I remembered about Mum and Dad. I grabbed my phone. They'd be worried sick about me. The phone rang and rang; no one was there.

'Mum, Dad, it's me. Just to say I'm at Charlie's. I got wet and ended up staying here for a bit, and fell asleep. I haven't seen Charlie yet. I'm going to see if they can give me a lift home. I'll call you later.' I tried Dad's mobile, and then Mum's. Both went straight to voicemail. For a moment I imagined them driving around the countryside, looking for me in a panic. And then I remembered. They weren't even home! They'd gone to visit Mum's friend in Wales for the night. I let out a sigh of relief. Guilt trip averted.

'Here she is!' Charles Snr announced my entrance in a jolly boom.

I stood in the doorway. Charles Snr was next to the fire, a drink raised in my direction. On the sofa next to him sat Charlie and I met his eye briefly. He smiled politely at me. I pulled my tummy in and smiled back. And then, rising out of his chair, was his brother. I coloured. I'd completely forgotten about Jimmy. He turned and held out his arms.

'Sam! What a lovely surprise!'

I hugged him in a daze.

'Jim . . . you're . . .' I looked him up and down, taking in his strong frame (more solid than Charlie's leaner version), his hair (still blonde), his fully formed features. 'A man!'

'It's nice of you to notice, Sam.' And he wiggled his hips a little as Charlie and Charles Snr laughed.

A man maybe but still the puppyish little brother beneath it all.

'Come and sit down, Sam. You can't stand in the middle of the room ogling my brother all night,' Charlie said.

'I'm not ogling,' I said, feeling myself blush some more. 'I just can't quite get over how different he looks.'

I tried to smile what I hoped was a natural smile as I crossed the room. As I walked past Charlie, he got off the sofa to greet me and I tried desperately to pull my tummy in further.

'Hi.'

'Fancy meeting you here, Sam.' Charlie bent and kissed each cheek. I felt a shiver pass over me, although I wasn't sure if it was him or the lack of oxygen from pulling my stomach up to my lungs. Charlie was dressed in casual country attire – jeans, an old shirt and sweater, his hair ruffled by the fresh air, pink spots on his cheeks, and somehow – how this was possible was beyond me – he looked even more sexy than he did in a suit.

'What can I get you, Sam? A gin and tonic? Or would you prefer wine?' Charles Snr smiled warmly at me.

'A gin and tonic would be lovely,' I answered. A gin and tonic was, of course, the last thing I actually needed. I felt light-headed, and out of my depth. But I had a whole painful evening to get through with Charlie here in the bosom of his family. A well-supported bosom that definitely didn't include me. Oh God, I needed that G&T more than anything else.

'What are you up to now, Sam?' Jimmy asked me, his eyes bright and friendly.

'What, other than crashing your family weekend?'

'Don't be silly, it's lovely to see you again.' Jimmy nudged his brother. 'Isn't it, mate?'

Charlie was staring at the fire. He had the look of someone who had been doing that rather a lot. His tease about me ogling Jimmy just now had obviously been a short break in some serious introspection. Jimmy looked back at me and made a face. There was an awkward pause as we both tried to think of something to say.

'Here we are!' Charles came back into the room, with a drink for me and another one for himself. 'Cheers! Here's to long-lost drowned rats.'

'That's not very nice, darling.' Lydia followed him, with a bowl of fat olives in her hand. She set them down on the coffee table in front of the brothers and sat delicately on a pretty upholstered stool next to the fire.

'Help yourself, Sam,' she said. 'Jimmy! Save some for other people.'

'Sorry, Ma,' Jimmy winked at me.

'Talking of long-lost people in our lives, I saw Bunty the other day at tennis. Did you know her Sarah is just back from Kilimanjaro? Such a marvellous girl, and squeezing it in with her career. Do you ever see her, Charlie? Charlie?'

'What?' Charlie looked up from the fire, bewildered. 'Sorry, Ma, I was thinking about something else.'

Sure, I thought, I knew exactly what he was thinking about.

'Sorry darling.' Lydia looked at him with concern. 'I've got terrible timing sometimes. Here I am talking about women when they are really the last thing you need in your life right now. They've caused enough trouble for the time being.'

'They certainly have. One in particular,' Charlie muttered.

'Well, she obviously has her eye on other things; you're better off without her.'

Charlie looked at his mother in pain, as if she held the answer to all of his problems. I had never seen him look so vulnerable.

'Do *you* think she's seeing someone else?' he asked.

I was sure that if I hadn't been there, Lydia would have crossed the room and gathered up Charlie in a big hug. She certainly looked as if she wanted to.

'I don't have a clue what she's up to, darling. But if she's not there for you, then she isn't worth clinging on to. A man needs a woman who will be there for him. Isn't that true, Charles?'

Charles Snr made a noise that signalled agreement and Charlie sunk back into the sofa, apparently satisfied with her answer. It was quite shocking how much he looked up to Lydia. I just couldn't imagine turning to my own mother for comfort like he did, or respecting her opinion on things as private and as precious as heartache. I doubt I'd turned to my mum with real problems since I was about twelve. But perhaps I should? Perhaps that would bring Mum and I closer? Yet when I tried to picture it, all I could see was Mum giving unwanted advice in breathy tones. It was always too much. Lydia was too restrained for my taste; my own mother was too eager. Something in the middle would be quite lovely.

'You're welcome to tell me all about her.' Jimmy gave Charlie a playful whack on the arm and winked at me. I tittered back nervously.

Lydia looked in mock despair at Jimmy. 'I'm sure *you're* quite capable of reeling in the women by yourself.'

'I don't know, he might not have any that climb mountains for kicks,' Charles Senior cut in. He seemed keen to change the subject. Throughout the strange interaction between Lydia and Charlie, he'd been very busy eating nibbles, with occasional apologetic glances in my direction. Now he turned to me pointedly.

'Sam, what news of your parents? I hope they're not wasting time trying to set you up with people.'

'They wouldn't get a very good reception if they did,' I admitted.

'See?' Jimmy joined in. He reached out and grabbed another olive. 'We are perfectly capable of running our own love lives, aren't we, Charlie?' He nudged his brother again, who just grunted.

'You're quite right, you're all obviously doing an excellent job. I'll be quiet,' Lydia said and laughed, and her boys loyally joined in.

The conversation moved on to the day's shooting and I was glad to be left to my own thoughts again. I've got what I came for, I thought. I wanted to see how he was, and admittedly, coming within spitting distance wasn't the plan, but I knew now. He was, quite simply, crushed. Nothing I could do would change that. I'd just have to wait.

But for how long? my anxious side clamoured.

Oh just shut up, I answered. I took a deep glug of the G&T Charles Snr had given me, almost finishing it in one. It slipped down, heat exploding into my gut and almost instantaneously spreading out through my limbs. Ahhhh. I took another sip. Drink gone. I sat in the soft chair, listening to, but not following, the conversation, feeling warm and adrift, almost as if everything was out of my control now. When I next glanced at the table beside my chair, my drink had been replaced with another one. I smiled in delight and brought the cold crystal to my lips, vaguely aware that they had turned to rubber and were not quite in sync with the few words I had to contribute, but I tried nevertheless, as I suddenly had something hilarious to add.

★

The atmosphere in the kitchen the next morning was confusing, at best. I felt like I'd been run over by several large trucks, consumed by my pounding head and aching joints, and everything felt blurred, as if I was looking through muslin. Most disturbing of all was the feeling I had missed out on something extremely important.

But Charlie gave me a warm grin as I joined him at the kitchen table, looking like he'd just been told an extremely good joke. He was a different man from the sad sack on the sofa last night.

'Well, that was a first.'

'What do you mean?' I felt a sinking feeling as the mirth bubbling behind Charlie's mouth prepared to spill out. His perfect lips, usually so collected, were having great difficulty staying together. They were wriggling all over the place, desperate to smile or even jump right off his face and dance a jig in his cornflakes. I shook my head. What the hell was wrong with me? I'd never known a hangover like it. 'How much did I drink?'

'Well, that's the strange thing, I didn't actually see you drinking much at all.'

'Strange thing?'

'Well' – his lips contorted some more – 'for someone who hadn't drunk much, you were certainly the chief entertainment of the evening.'

'Entertainment?' That didn't sound good.

'Oh, you were in full flight, on your soapbox, railing against everything from public schools to the bankers – it was like having our very own socialist campaigner in the room.'

280

'That must have gone down well.'

'Oh brilliantly. We were all very amused, except for the bit about Sarah.'

'Sarah? Who the hell is Sarah?'

'You don't remember?' Charlie chuckled. 'She's the daughter of Ma's bridge partner. Just back from climbing Kilimanjaro?'

'Ah . . .' Faint bells were ringing in my head.

'You went completely off on one about her, suggesting she sounded like she'd make a good debutante for *Country Life*, that a pretty, privileged girl like that deserved to be celebrated, how fabulous she must be, how perfect, and on and on from there really.'

I sank my head into my hands. 'Don't tell me, all delivered with lashings of sarcasm.'

'Oh, you didn't mean it?' Charlie chuckled again. 'You don't think the Hugh-Barringtons should spend – now how did you put it – the money an average family might spend on a car and all go for a jolly jaunt together with Sarah to Ascot this year?'

'Fuck.'

'Oh there was plenty of that thrown in for good measure, just so we'd understand how fervently you felt about things.'

I shook my head. Please let this be a joke. Having opinions about things was one thing but I didn't usually make a point of shoving them rudely in the faces of the generation above me. People my own age, that was game on, but not my parents' generation. Not people hosting me, people who – it was finally dawning on me – had been nursing me. But the dread that had sat in the pit of my stomach first thing that morning now leached into my whole body. I knew Charlie wasn't making it up. I was unwell, I drank too quickly on an empty stomach and my manners had obviously flown out of the window.

Lydia chose that moment to make her appearance, clipping in

wearing a pale-blue linen suit. I flushed as I made eye contact.

'Good morning, Sam.' Her voice was cool.

'Good morning.' I paused, my heart beating in my throat, but ploughed on, desperate to smooth over some of the damage done. 'Ah . . . Charlie's been filling me in on my behaviour last night. It sounds like I was a right pain in the . . . bum,' I said, just catching myself in time.

'You were fine.'

Lydia had her back to us and was looking through a stack of papers on the dresser using small, careful movements but her words didn't fool me.

'Well, it sounded like I was a complete idiot, I'm sorry.' I watched Lydia's tiny shoulders relax slightly beneath her jacket and she turned to look at me.

'I think, Sam, you probably have the flu and we'll drop you home on the way to church. We're leaving in ten minutes.'

'Oh. Thank you, thank you very much. I'd completely forgotten about my bike!' I giggled awkwardly and caught Charlie's eye. He gave me a small grin and stood up to start clearing things from the table, obviously finished with teasing for the moment. He certainly wouldn't joke around like that in front of Lydia. Just like that, he was back to being the perfect son, the one who had come home for the weekend to have his wounds tended from the nasty woman whom Mummy didn't think was good enough for him. I went to find my coat, glad to be getting out of that kitchen and out of this house where everything felt so loaded and I felt so out of place. It crossed my mind that, on balance, this family might actually be more screwed up than my own.

49

MARA

On Sunday evening, with still no sign of Sam, I stomped around the flat doing her chores. I'd really rather have been reading Margaret Atwood again but I sure as hell couldn't live with this mess staring me in the face all week. Where was she anyway? She hadn't been in touch all weekend and all my texts had gone unanswered. From time to time my conscience kicked in – was she all right? – but it was quickly engulfed by my anger. She's fine, my head grumbled, just off leading her self-absorbed life and not giving a toss about the people around her.

At seven o'clock the phone rang. It was Ed. He was having a great time; the scenery was breathtaking, the air so fresh it froze your lungs.

'I'm so glad, Ed.'

'You sound grumpy.'

'I'm not grumpy!'

Ed didn't say anything and my words hung there in red capital letters.

'OK, I am a little bit grumpy.'

'What's going on?'

I sighed. 'It's Sam.'

'Surprise, surprise.'

'She's missed yet another rent payment and hasn't done

anything around the house all weekend. In fact I haven't seen her at all.'

'Haven't seen her? Where is she?'

'God knows. I'm guessing with Charlie. Her phone's off.'

'Do you think she's all right?'

'Of course she's all right,' I snapped, but my conscience flickered in the background.

'OK, Mars, there's no need to bite my head off.'

'Sorry. I'm just feeling fed up. I'm thinking about asking her to move out.'

'Really?' Ed sounded shocked.

'Maybe.'

'Perhaps you should sleep on it first.'

'Well, she isn't here to talk to now so it looks like I've no choice but to sleep on it.'

There was a pause and I could hear happy voices in the background. The spick and span kitchen suddenly felt lifeless and more than anything I wanted to be with my brother, outside a pub in Scotland, teeth chattering as we looked at the stars, only a couple of paces away from a warm, yellow room full of interesting people whose foibles I didn't know like the back of my hand.

'Did you take your bike in?' Ed's voice pulled me back. My bike. Dammit, I'd forgotten again. Too busy being cross.

'I'll do it next weekend.'

'You'd better, those brakes are really dodgy, Mars.'

'I'll bike carefully, don't worry.'

'It's the other people I worry about.'

I smiled. 'Thanks for caring, Ed.'

'Look, get yourself to bed, Mars. Try not to dwell on things. It's a big beautiful world out there.'

'I will, thanks for calling.'

It was easy for him to say that, thought I, as I brushed my

teeth. Him up north experiencing the beautiful world while little old me was stuck in my little hamster wheel in Queen's Park. But his concern soothed me all the same and later, when I heard Sam's key in the lock and her quiet (for once) steps down the hall, I felt relieved that my friend was home, safe and well. We'd sit down and talk things through tomorrow, I told myself as I snuggled under my duvet. No need to be rash. Not just yet.

50

CLAUDIA

I tried swallowing my nerves as I stood on his front step. It had been a long, frantic day and I hadn't had much time to get ready. A quick change of clothes and extra mascara was all I'd managed, which made me feel even more vulnerable. John lived in a quiet street in Kensington, in a stately Georgian crescent lined with mature ash trees. It would be pretty in summer, I thought, and then pulled my thoughts back sharply. I wouldn't see it in summer because it – whatever it was – would be well and truly over by then. I was sure of that.

As I heard John's footsteps I realised that I couldn't actually remember the last time I had visited a man at his home. It had to have been years.

'Claudia! Come in!' John opened his arms, as if he hadn't seen me less than two hours ago at work. He was dressed in jeans and a simple granddad-style long-sleeved top in a dark aubergine that fitted just close enough to outline his solid chest. His hair was still wet and his feet were bare. I actually felt my knees go weak. I didn't know that was possible in real life. I swallowed again and smiled. Put one foot in front of the other, there's a good girl.

He led me down the hall into the kitchen, which overlooked a garden sitting tidily around a circular patio. Through the dusky gloom I could make out a barbecue sitting under its winter cover in one corner. In another, what looked like a weeping pear stretched its bare arms over the wooden slats of the patio. For the second time I flashed forward into summer and pictured a group of smiling people, their faces splotched prettily with the dappled light under the tree. I sighed.

'It's lovely, isn't it? Keeps me out of a lot of trouble that garden. It's especially nice in the summer.' John came up behind me and gave me a slender glass of bubbles, steadily looking out the window with me.

'I bet it's amazing.'

'Not that long to wait.' He turned and looked intently into my eyes. Why does he have to do that? My insides contracted and I turned away quickly, taking in the rest of the room. The kitchen merged into an open-plan living area that, minus the hall and stairs, ran the length of the ground floor. One entire wall was a dark purple, not dissimilar to John's shirt. It was the kind of colour I was drawn to but hadn't the courage to try myself. Whoever had decorated this place sure had balls. The other walls were off-white, and on them hung various pictures, mostly sketches, all very regimentally framed in white. I walked the length of the room, inspecting each one, my shoes squeaking a little on the warm oak floorboards. Warm in colour but also, I realised after a bit, warm underfoot too. That explained the bare feet then.

John joined me as I came to the end of my nosy tour of his walls and gestured for me to take a seat on one of the large sofas. He paused before sitting opposite me.

'So who did all this?' I waved my hand around the room.

John looked confused. 'What do you mean? I did, of course.'

'Really? Are you sure you haven't got a clever wife tucked away in a cupboard somewhere who comes out and makes this place look so . . . homely?'

John smiled a slow grin. 'Homely, you say?' he said, looking around him as if he hadn't seen it before. 'I've never really thought about it like that.'

'It's not often you come across men who think this much about their homes. Not straight ones anyway.'

'What are you trying to say, Claudia?'

'Nothing,' I laughed. 'You know what I mean. It's usually the women who are in charge of decorating a home. And if there isn't a woman in the house . . .' I slowed down, suddenly feeling self-conscious. 'A man's home can be a bit . . .'

'Barren?' John said.

'I would have said bare,' I answered.

'So what would you do to this house if you lived here?' John asked.

I looked around, feeling his eyes on my face. I knew he had that intense expression without looking at him. It was strong enough to burn holes in my face, I was sure.

'Ah . . .' I looked around some more, finally stopping at the sofas. 'I'd probably choose different cushions.'

'Is that all?'

'I think so. At least going by what's downstairs. Not that I want to see the upstairs,' I added hastily.

'Oh.' John sounded disappointed.

I took the last sip of my champagne and busied myself with looking for a place to put the glass. Anything but meet John's eye. But before I could find somewhere John stood up abruptly.

'Let me fill that for you.'

'I'm OK actually,' I said.

'Are you sure?' John strode to the kitchen. 'Just a little drop?' He waved the bottle at me.

'The doctor said I shouldn't drink while I'm taking my medication,' I said.

John's smile vanished. 'Of course. I shouldn't either really.

How about I go all out and crack open the Evian?' He grinned and rifled around in the fridge for a bit.

I laid my head back on the sofa, grateful for the momentary distraction that took John's piercing eyes off my face. His anticipation had been obvious from the minute I walked in the door. He wanted an answer to his damn question. That or to get me into bed. And I wasn't quite ready for that yet, with anyone, let alone him. I wasn't going there with him anyway, I told myself. I was here to forge a friendship with an interesting man. I sighed. Who was I kidding? This man, this home, felt more right than anyone I'd met in my life. And I'd made a complete dog's breakfast of the whole thing. He wanted to know if he was in a relationship . . . sure he did. I stood up. Do something, Claudia, I thought. Don't sit there stewing.

So I joined John in the kitchen and watched him chop-chop-chop a capsicum into tiny strips, then do the same to mushrooms and spring onions. He asked me about my family and I told him about Sabrina, the family clown, about the neat little package that is Mother, about my father, with the heart of a lion. As I spoke about Papa, his voice rumbled in my head. 'Throw those hiking boots away,' he'd said to me. And I watched John's hands moving happily over the food and wished I could. I really wished I could.

When he was finished he placed a luscious pile of food in front of me and I couldn't help myself.

'There's something deeply sexy about a man who can cook,' I said, biting down on my lip as soon as I'd spoken. John's eyes lit up immediately and I cursed myself as I felt his heat from across the table.

'I'm glad you think so. That was, after all, the intention.'

'Great,' I answered feebly.

We ate in silence for a while, our awareness of each other's movements, each bite, each chew, so acute it was almost more than I could bear. I was racking my mind for something to say – anything, anything – but all I could hear was the blood in my ears, as if I'd been running.

'I enjoy eating with you,' John said after a while.

'Thanks. Me too,' I mumbled through a mouthful of capsicum.

'You still haven't got back to me about my question from last time,' he continued.

Oh great, here it was. The question.

'Claudia?'

'Sorry, I-I just don't know what to say,' I stammered.

'Why not?'

I could hear his voice hardening but still I was afraid to say what was welling up inside me. If I opened my mouth, surely I'd scream? My emotions felt like a tidal wave building up, about to erupt all over the plate. I had never felt this vulnerable, this out of control. My eyes filled with tears and I bit down hard on the inside of my gums. I would not, *would not* share myself with him. He didn't want me, not with all this emotional crap too. He wanted a fuck, that was all.

Abruptly John stood and grabbed his plate from the table and took it to the kitchen, and, after a moment's pause looking out the window, returned to get mine. He stood very close, looking down at me, and I was straining so hard against my tears, I didn't realise that my fingers – white and shaking as they twisted the fabric of my dress – were visible to him as he looked down at my lap. All I knew was that suddenly I was in his arms, being held tight, with John on his knees beside me. I felt myself tilt and the wave spill out, the tears pouring hot and fast onto that purple chest, and my ever-rational, über-controlled mind wasn't doing a single thing about it.

And John held me tight.

Eventually he pulled away from me a little but remained kneeling next to my chair. He reached out and wiped each side of my face slowly with his thumb.

'Claudia,' John said, taking my face gently with one hand. 'Look at me. Can you forgive me?'

I laughed.

'For what?'

'What do you mean, for what? For passing on a bloody STI, that's what.'

'Oh that? Of course! I forgave you the second after I found out it was you. I have literally not given it another thought.' I sniffed loudly.

John looked confused. He stood up and drew his chair around so he could sit back down close to me and he took my hands in his.

'So . . . why are you crying? I thought it might be because you hate me for passing the bug on to you but . . .' Then he stopped. 'Do you know what, I have exactly zero clue why you're crying.'

I started to laugh again.

John smiled back. 'It's because I'm a man.'

'No it isn't, it's because I'm me. Very few people would understand why I was crying. I've probably only just worked it out myself.' Sniff. 'Have you got any tissues?'

John stood and retrieved tissues then sat down next to me again. I blew my nose noisily and surprised myself by not caring a fig. There was no need to be worried about what John thought of me – it was loud and clear, and I couldn't put up walls around this any longer.

'You sure we can't talk about the weather instead?' I asked, smiling.

'No.'

'I thought not.' I gazed out the window and took a deep breath.

Why had I been crying? Why indeed. I had to start somewhere; John deserved some sort of explanation.

'I was really knocked sideways by that STI – or, more to the point, how I felt about having it. I've never had one before but also I've never questioned sleeping around. If I have protected sex, then what's the problem? But then . . . well then when I got it, I felt—'

'Dirty?'

'Yes, I suppose you're right. I felt dirty. Clichéd but true.'

'I felt like that too.'

'You did? I'm so sorry.'

John frowned. 'Why should you be sorry? It wasn't you who passed it on – it was me giving it to you. I've tracked down who gave it to me by the way. It was a woman I slept with a couple of times before I met you. Now it's her turn to work out who gave it to her. My money is on the ex-husband she was rebounding from when I met her. But anyway,' – John shook his head – 'back to you – you felt, totally understandably, fairly gross when you discovered you had an STI. So far, so clear.'

'I felt horrible. And I guess it made me feel like I was letting my family down.'

John's eyes opened wide. 'You told them?'

'God no, of course I didn't. But I still felt like I'd let them down.' I paused. Come on, woman – spit it out. 'And all along, you were such a gentleman, and so solid and kind. And although I was angry with you at times and tried to push you out of my head, I've just thought about you so much. I think about you so much.' My voice was catching but I kept on. 'And I didn't feel like I was worthy of you—'

'Claudia!'

I held up a finger, shush. 'I realised I'd finally met my match – you know, how we see eye to eye, not a match as in . . .'

John's smile was wide. He was loving this. 'Go on,' he said.

'Anyway, I just generally felt like a complete fuck up. I felt I wasn't worthy of you when I didn't know you were the one who gave me the thing, then when I knew it was you, I still wasn't worthy because . . . because . . .'

John leant forward. 'Because, Claudia?'

I sighed.

'You can't come up with a reason because there isn't one. You are more than worthy of me. If anything it's up to me to prove my worthiness to you.'

A tear rolled down my cheek again. John wiped it away.

'But before I do can you please answer my question? Am I seeing someone, Claudia?'

'I think you know that answer, John,' I said.

'I want to hear it from you.'

And finally I took his handsome face in my hands and kissed him.

'Yes you are, John Tightpants, you most definitely are,' I whispered.

John exploded with laughter. 'John *what?*'

51

MARA

I dragged my heavy feet up the stairs. It was late for a weekday, well after nine o'clock. It upset my equilibrium a little getting home this late. I always felt anxious in advance of the next day, knowing I would wake tired, heavy and possibly blue. As soon as I opened the door, however, the smell of cooking – cooking? – snatched my thoughts away from my worrying and led me up the hall and into the kitchen.

'Sam?' I found her sitting at the kitchen table.

'You're late.'

'You've been cooking!' I said, astonished.

'Yeah, well . . .' Sam stood up and huffed three steps to the hob and lifted a lid. 'I don't know what it'll be like now it's been sitting around for so long.'

'I didn't know I was going to be home so late or that you'd be cooking, sorry.'

Sam grunted and stabbed at the contents of the pot with a wooden spoon. I felt a sudden desire to scream with laughter but squeezed my lips tight to stop it. Judging by the set of Sam's shoulders, right now wasn't the best moment to test the girl's sense of humour.

'I'll be back in a mo, let me just take my coat off.'

What is going on? I thought to myself, as I removed my coat and returned my shoes to their place in the line-up under the bed. Sam must finally be feeling remorseful for her singularly selfish behaviour. I peeled off my tights and felt my legs heave a sigh of relief. Then I hung up my skirt and dropped my tights into the washing basket. Without a doubt, Sam inhabiting the kitchen and doing something other than opening a bottle of wine was a loud and clear expression of her love. I pulled on tracksuit bottoms and slid my feet into slippers. Ah, that's lovely. I stood up, relishing for a moment the feeling of soft wool around my tired feet. Time to put my shoulders back and attempt to eat whatever it was that Sam had gone out of her comfort zone to cook. When my hand touched the doorknob, however, an unwelcome thought crossed my mind. Of course it could be that Sam wasn't sorry at all. It could be that she simply wanted something. My heart sank. I really, really hoped that wasn't the case. Not tonight.

The table was laid Sam-style, which involved a couple of mismatching knives and forks being thrown into the middle of the table. 'Can I do anything?' I hovered. It had been so long since Sam cooked, I couldn't remember what to do.

'No, sit down – it'll be ready in a minute. I'm just going to serve it up, is that all right?' Sam answered politely although I wasn't convinced. I could hear that underneath it, Sam was still annoyed about me being so late home. I didn't say anything and sat down obediently, trying very hard not to think cross little thoughts about the shoe being on the other foot.

'Here you go.' Sam put a plate of what looked like pasta with a tomato-based sauce in front of me.

'Thanks,' I said, and I meant it. It was nice to be cooked for, regardless of the attitude or the possible food poisoning.

'You haven't tasted it yet,' Sam said gruffly. She put her own plate down then returned to the kitchen counter to grab a bottle of wine and two glasses.

'Here.' Sam filled my glass – too deeply for my liking but she was obviously trying hard. 'To you, Mara.'

'To me?'

Sam clinked her glass with mine. 'For being a patient friend!'

'Cheers, Sam, I appreciate it.' I took a big sip – anything to line the stomach. 'I know you'll be good for the money when you can.'

'Money?'

'That's not what you meant?'

Sam's face drained of colour. 'What money, you mean the bills?'

'Well, that and the rent.'

'The rent? Have I missed a week?'

'Actually, you've missed three weeks.'

'Fuck.' Sam wiped her face with her hands in a fed-up sweep. 'Three weeks? I had no idea.'

I took another sip of wine. 'What do you mean, then, by being a patient friend?'

'Oh, you know, this Charlie business. Me running around like an idiot after him, coming in all hours, disappearing for days on end, generally losing my mind.'

'Oh, Sam, don't worry about that, at least you've stopped now.'

Sam looked at me with a pained expression.

'What, you haven't stopped?'

Sam sighed. 'I don't know. I think I might stop chasing his tail, I feel pretty down about it all right now, but . . .' She sighed again, another dramatic sweep of her face. 'The problem is it will only take one call, one text, one look from him and I'm right back there, panting after him. Putty in his hands.'

'Is that what happened this weekend? Is he over his heartbreak, ready to jump back in the sack with the next girl in line?'

'Ouch!'

'Sorry, that probably sounded a bit harsh.'

Sam sighed.

The meal was cooling in front of me, goading me to take a bite, but it smelt . . . I couldn't put my finger on it . . .

'You're probably not that far off. I don't know, he was definitely not himself but by Sunday morning he was teasing me again, which is usually a good sign. Oh, I don't know, Mara, I can't seem to let it go.'

I looked at my friend. When was she going to screw her head on again?

'Sam, you're worth more than that. I've said it before and I'll say it again. He doesn't seem to make you happy, which is the point of loving someone, isn't it?'

Sam nodded reluctantly.

'Well, forget about him for a moment and let's eat up. This food is getting cold.'

Sam poked the . . . stuff on her plate.

'I'm not sure it could be worse.'

'Come on chicken, on the count of three . . . one, two—'

At the same time we shoved in a forkful and reluctantly chewed for a few moments before reaching for our glasses at the same time to wash it down.

'Oh my God, that's disgusting!' Sam shouted.

'It's . . . quite weird, Sam, but not disgusting.'

'It's fucking disgusting!'

'Just wondering though, why did you put so much cinnamon in?'

'I didn't.'

'Are you sure? I'm sure I can taste it. It's an . . . interesting choice.'

Sam went to fetch the jar of spice she'd used and held it out for me to see. 'This so isn't paprika!'

'You are such a worry, Moriarty,' I answered, laughing at my silly friend and feeling happier than I had in ages.

52

SAM

It was two days before I saw Charlie again. Two whole days.
Although technically speaking from the time Charlie asked me
out for a drink to the moment I said yes, I'd actually only held
out for thirty-two minutes. But in my head I was sticking to
the two-day gap. I had to hold onto something, some shred of
evidence that I wasn't – how did Mara put it – 'a wet dishcloth,
squeezed by Charlie's big hands'. Thanks, Mara, that's really
adding to my self-confidence here, I thought. Followed swiftly
by: why am I always the first one at the pub, no matter how late
I arrive? I chewed the inside of my lip. He'd just better show up,
and before I lost my nerve.

And there he was, striding across the room.

'Sam! So sorry I'm late, had a devil of a meeting, what can I
get you?' He leant down to kiss my cheek. His coat shifted as he
bent over, releasing a slight puff of man and sandalwood. A killer
combination. I mumbled something about it being all right and
promptly felt annoyed with myself.

Focus, dammit! I am *not* all right. He is most definitely *not*
all right and he doesn't smell good enough to eat. I yawned and
eyed the table. I pictured laying my head on it and drifting off,
there and then, and escaping the task ahead. Battling with my
will was exhausting and not made any easier by this bloody virus
hanging around, sapping my energy. Stop making excuses. I

steeled myself as Charlie returned with drinks. The last drinks we would be sharing as lovers.

'You look miserable,' he said, setting the drinks down and slipping in opposite me.

'Do I? I'm not. Miserable that is. I'm still a bit ill, that's all . . .' I teetered off.

'Well, you don't have the vim you displayed on Saturday night, that's for sure!' Charlie chuckled.

'Oh God,' I groaned, 'please don't remind me.'

'What do you mean? It was hilarious, hands down the funniest scene I've seen at Dunbourne for years. Ma's mouth was so pursed I wondered for a moment if she'd actually eaten her lips!'

I groaned again, head in hands.

'But Dad, he loved it, I think. He's never had much time for Ma's airs and graces anyway, and he loves a good set-to. I haven't seen him that animated for ages. I mean, you really didn't hold back, did you?'

'I don't really remember it, Charlie, and I don't want to.'

'That's a pity.' Charlie paused for a moment. 'Actually I think the old man has a real soft spot for you. He could probably have done with a daughter, especially a fiery one like yourself.'

He was right – I knew it. The ride home the next morning was a one-sided conversation conducted entirely by Charles Snr, his eyes flitting up to his rear-view mirror, constantly hopeful of catching my eye while I sat there mute with shame. Meanwhile, next to him in the Jag, Lydia had sat straight as a post, barely saying a thing the whole way. It had all got so out of hand. I couldn't keep embarrassing myself like this. Chasing Charlie was one thing but shaming myself in front of my friends, and now his parents, was something else. I was turning into someone I didn't recognise.

'Charlie—'

'The thing is, Sam, I know I've always teased you about your political views.'

'Charlie, I—'

'But I've never really understood how explosive you are. You're practically boiling inside, aren't you?'

'Well, I don't know about that, but—'

'It's really very, very sexy. And the reason, I think, that I've always been attracted to you. I like your passion, Sam. That's you, a passionate, expressive, brave person—' Charlie held his fingers in the air as if he was holding something important.

'The way you just rocked up to Dunbourne like that, unannounced—'

'Actually your dad found me in the pub up the road.'

'—and brandished your views around the place, not caring a toss what other people thought. It was gorgeous. You're gorgeous. Do you know that?' Charlie reached across and grasped the top of my arms, staring into my face more intensely than he had in perhaps the whole time I'd known him. Then he let go of me suddenly.

'But I'm being so rude, sorry. You were saying something?'

'Oh, it was nothing.'

'No, please. Say what you wanted to say.'

But my will, no stronger than ten-denier tights at the best of times, had fled the room, leaving my legs – and heart – completely bare. And Charlie waded in, boring those earnest eyes into mine and now, oh no, there he goes with the head shot, clutching my thigh under the table. I sighed.

'Is that a sigh of pleasure?'

'No. Well, maybe a little. Actually it was one of resignation.'

'I'm flattered.'

I smiled at him. 'You really are a smooth bastard, aren't you?' Charlie leant across and kissed me, an insistent, perfect, just-juicy-enough kiss that resulted in an all-too-familiar hot-cold whoosh of hormonal lava, flooding every limb. Then he pulled away, as if kissing like that was a normal occurrence, and asked me, 'Are you free to come to a gig this weekend?'

I was sure that in that moment I'd follow him across any number of sharp, cutting surfaces to the ends of the earth if necessary. Which, if my memory served me right, was exactly the mentality one had to have to survive one of the 'gigs' that Charlie liked attending.

'Who's playing?'

'Only Coldplay,' Charlie answered, completely chuffed he'd beaten the masses to two tickets. I tried to swallow my disappointment. The masses were the important feature here. Masses and masses of boring, soulless twats who couldn't think for themselves. Well, not musically anyway. Not in my book (I chose to ignore the fact that Claudia and many other people I respected love them too). This was music for consumers. Music for conformers. Some of the most irritating, boring music on the planet.

'Sounds awesome, I'd love to go!' I said.

53

ED

From: Ed Minkley <edminkley@gmail.com>
Date: Wednesday, 11 March
To: Covington Green <greenworldcov@gmail.com>
Subject: Fresh air

Hey,

Sorry, mate, you're right, I've been rubbish lately. Been way too long.

In answer to you questions – job's brilliant, loving it. I can't believe I've already been here for more than a week. You've never been to Scotland, have you? You really have to! It is wild – literally. There's an edginess up here and I don't just mean the temperature. Everything feels less tamed than it does down south. It's like the land is darker and stronger and colder than you – and there's nothing us piddly humans can do about it. There is no alternative but to feel alive up here – you can't hide yourself away from what's all around you.

Which is just what I needed. Because no, Sam hasn't been in touch. I know you wanted me to confront her before I left but it just didn't feel like the right time. She's too wrapped up in that toff to even notice me. So, mate, it's good to be away right now. The longer I'm away actually, the more I think I'm getting over her. She's been in my head for long enough! Anyway there's this really hot production manager up here helping me keep my mind off things. Nothing serious but she's fun and it's nice to be the one being chased for a change.

Mara seems OK. Honestly, mate, I really wouldn't get your hopes up about her.

Ed

54

SAM

I didn't intend to be sharing a small table with my mother and Rebecca at Kow Ling's with a dildo in my bag. That wasn't the plan at all. The plan that evening was to find some suitably outrageously coloured fishnet stockings to wear to this damn gig I'd agreed to go to. I was thinking fluoro pink, or yellow or something. Something garish and punky. I knew that no one attending the gig would bat an eyelid but at least I'd feel more like the rebel I wanted to be. I didn't like Coldplay but I sure as hell wasn't going to just wibble along to it unconsciously. No, I was going to be awake and scathing and wearing really ugly fishnets to prove it. And the plan was to pick some up en route to the restaurant.

The complicating factor to the plan was this. I, wandering past a sex shop, had a blinding moment of inspiration and went inside. Sure enough, there had the kind of tawdry stockings I was looking for, lined up in crisp packets, and I chose a pair with a fluorescent leopard-skin pattern on them almost immediately. So far, so 1983 gone wrong. However I had a little time on my hands, which is never a good thing for me, especially when I had cash in my wallet. This is where the plan started to go awry.

The drinks and lingering smooch with Charlie a couple of nights ago had, unsurprisingly, been sloshing around my head ever since. In particular, I couldn't stop thinking about Charlie's observations regarding my abundance of vim vam voom, my passion, my boiling belligerence, as he saw it. I had sighed many times recalling that conversation. I, ever hungry for a compliment, had lapped up the attention and had thrown out my intentions to sever ties with Charlie on the spot. He was keen, he was keen, he was most definitely keen, people! I couldn't walk away from that, not after all the work I had put in to catching him.

But. And this was the rub. I had been thinking hard during the previous sigh-filled days and I was starting to wonder if the gregarious, slightly rude person I had always presented to the world – most definitely to Charlie – wasn't just that, a presentation. Was that really who I was underneath? Was that really who I wanted to be? It was the weekend at his parents that had shaken me up. I couldn't get rid of the shame of my behaviour. I had crossed my own moral line, stepping away from being a sarcastic quibbler into the territory of being downright rude. And it didn't feel right, not one little bit.

So there I was in a sex shop, looking at dildos and handcuffs and lacy fanny floss, when my phone buzzed in my pocket.

Just got off phone from Dad – he was asking if you were
all better.

Oh God, now I had to think about Charlie's dad!

That's sweet of him. Did you tell him the Dickhead H6
virus has almost finished?

Hahaha. You crazy woman.

Crazy woman . . .

'I wonder,' I murmured at the racks of fake penises. And my mind ticked over: if I could be excessively passionate and – what

305

was it – 'boiling inside' in the bedroom, then maybe he wouldn't notice if I was making a complete arsehole of myself the rest of the time. I wouldn't have to be outspoken and bordering on rude just to show off to him. Instead I'd give him fireworks in bed, and then when we were married and spending lots of time with his parents, I'd be as nice as pie and he'd have forgotten that he loved me for being offensive.

I paid for the dildo and tights within seconds. I had it all figured out.

'So what have you been buying? Thought you were broke?' Rebecca gave the bag a swift little kick with a navy suede toe.

'Hey, don't do that!'

Rebecca laughed. 'Well, share then. What have you been buying?'

I recognised that look in my sister's eye. It was stubborn, grade five. I had to throw her something to get her off my back. I bent down and tried to open it without showing the entire contents and pulled out the tights, throwing them across to Rebecca.

'Hmmm.' Rebecca picked them up from her lap and turned them over with doubtful fingers. 'Delightful.'

'Yeah, well, I felt like a bit of trash.'

'For a change?' Rebecca smirked.

'Rebecca!'

'It's all right, Mum, I'm used to it.' I glared at my sister. 'They're to wear to a gig. Coldplay.'

Rebecca looked confused.

'Exactly.'

'God, you're so cryptic sometimes, Sam.' Rebecca threw the tights back, no longer interested.

'That sounds like fun, dear,' Mum offered. I stiffened with annoyance at her bright, encouraging tone and exhaled through my nose violently.

'Well, I really hate them actually, Mum.'

'Oh.' She paused for a moment. 'Then why—'

'Charlie's taking me.'

'Oh! Oh, right.'

Rebecca whipped her head up from intensely studying her nails and gave me a hard, glittering stare that I felt cutting into my middle. It lasted only a moment though and she snapped back to her more normal level of disdain and kicked the bag again.

'So what else is in there?'

'Nothing.' I coloured. What could I say to put her off?

'Doesn't feel like nothing to me!' And Rebecca had snatched the bag before I could stop her and was holding it above the table, reaching in, feeling something and pulling it out.

Fuck.

A shiny gold dildo being held aloft in Rebecca's talons.

'Ooooh! You naughty thing!'

There was a moment – which felt like forever – before Mum realised what was happening, and I thought that perhaps Rebecca would stuff it back into the bag before Mum registered, before we actually had to have a conversation about it, because surely, surely Rebecca wouldn't want to embarrass Mum as well as me?

'I really don't want to know what you're going to do with it!' Rebecca uttered, this time shrieking and shaking the totally fucking transparent box.

'Rebecca! Give it back!'

I desperately tried to snatch it from her but she held it out of my reach, taunting me and laughing.

'Stop it!' Mum's angry-beast voice came out of nowhere and cut through the hysteria with immediate effect. Rebecca sat down, chastened, and passed the dildo back to me.

'Sorry.'

'I should think so, you're making a scene.'

We looked around. People were turning away now, tittering into their noodles. I felt my blood hammering through every vessel in my body. I hadn't heard that voice for many years but it couldn't have come at a better time.

'It's a present for someone at work, a joke for a hen night,' I squeaked.

'We're not discussing it, Sam.' And Mum opened the heavy brown vinyl-bound menu decisively. 'Now what are we going to eat?'

I stared at the menu unseeing, still reeling from the embarrassment of having the only dildo I'd ever purchased waved around in a restaurant in front of my mother. But also, as I turned the plastic pages, I was still hurting from the freezing stare Rebecca gave me when she heard I was going with Charlie to this stupid gig. That was completely unnecessary. Completely.

55

MARA

From: Mara Minkley <marajaneminkley@hotmail.com>
Date: Thursday, 12 March
To: Ed Minkley <edminkley@gmail.com>
Subject: re: Scotland

Ed,

So I've chatted with Sam and things feel better on that front.
She's being paid cash tomorrow so she promised me she'd
hand over some wedge then. It's not the money so much as
the lack of awareness that hurts but catching up on her debts is
a positive gesture. So, my twin, you can see I am trying to see
this glass as half full!

I was so jealous, hearing you having such a good time up
there. I would love to escape these grey, London streets for
some bracing Scottish air. When I imagine inhaling some of
it I can feel my head opening and relaxing all at once – and
the roar of London being left completely behind. I hope that's
what it's like for you. Think of me breathing in lovely fumes as
I bike home as usual! By the way, I've booked my bike in to
get my brakes sorted out tomorrow after work, so you can stop
nagging me.

Speaking of work, I'd better get on with some. I've got lazy Lisa in here today and she's barely removed her emery board from her fingers all day, the little sod.

Lots of love,

M x x

56

SAM

Vic and I were knocking back a coffee while the set was being re-dressed. So far that morning the shoot seemed to be ticking over well. Worryingly well. We stood side by side, having reviewed proceedings on the call sheet, and scanned the set for problems but there just weren't any. Everything had been set up quickly; they were ticking off the shot list ahead of schedule. All going well they would be wrapping shortly after lunch.

'So . . . how's that hot photographer?' Vic said.

'Ed?'

'Duh! Of course I mean him.'

'Apparently he's having a great time – he's on that job in Scotland that Katherine's doing, remember?'

'Oh yeah, I'd forgotten that. Apparently? What does that mean? You don't think he actually is?'

'I'm sure he is. I just haven't heard it from him directly, that's all.'

Vic nudged me with her elbow.

'Do I detect a note of jealousy in your voice? Huh? Huh?'

I frowned at her, annoyed that she was making me blush. She was grinning away like a schoolgirl at me.

'Of course not!'

'Sure, Sam!'

She started giggling in a very aggravating way. I was about to set her straight – not least of all fill her in with all the excitement of Charlie – when I felt my phone buzzing from inside my Puffa. I took it out. Vic had time to wind me up so I had time to check my phone. It was Claudia. Claudia? I was confused, couldn't even think what time of the day it was for a moment, but I was pretty sure it wasn't a time Claudia normally phoned. What did she want?

'Mind if I take this?' I waved it at Vic.

Vic was rosy with laughing and waved her consent to me.

'Claudia?'

'Sam? It's Mara. She's had an accident.'

*

Claudia was waiting for me at the main reception, her face ashen, and I upped my walk to a fast trot to hug her.

'She's this way.' Claudia took my arm and led me to the lifts.

'Is she in A&E?'

'No, ICU.'

'ICU? That means it's serious, right?'

'Yes, it does, Sam. A lorry cut in front of her, and she couldn't stop in time and went into the side of it.'

'But she couldn't have been going very fast – Mara never goes fast!'

'Well, she was going fast enough to put herself into intensive care.'

The lift pinged at us, strangely cheery, when we reached our floor. Claudia led the way down a wide corridor, dodging dazed patients, visitors and brisk-stepping medics. Every step I took down that corridor became more surreal and the chill that had started in my heart when I got the phone call spread down every limb as I walked, until my whole body was fizzing with cold. I realised, as I walked through the decisive doors of ICU, that this must be what proper fear feels like.

Kate was sitting miserably on a plastic chair in the waiting room and I embraced her clumsily.

'Don't you bloody start!' Kate reached out and wiped her hand down my cheek.

'Sorry.' I dragged my hand across my snotty nose and Claudia silently handed me a tissue.

'Have you seen her yet?'

'No. They're doing stuff to her.'

I pushed aside the images my mind conjured of a bloodied Mara being subjected to urgent medical pokings and proddings.

'How did you hear?' I asked.

'Dad called me – the police had called him.'

I looked around the waiting room, wondering if I'd missed him.

'He's at home, the miserable sod. Hates hospitals.' Kate sighed. 'But he'd just need looking after if he was here. I'd much rather have you guys.'

'What about Ed, does he know yet?'

'Yes, I managed to speak to him. He's coming as soon as he can. Maybe even getting here tomorrow morning.' She took her phone out of her pocket and looked at it absently. 'There's no signal in here so I'm not sure what he's managed to do.'

We sat and flicked through magazines without really seeing them and took turns visiting the yellow café on the ground floor to drink tea and choke down dry sandwiches. Hours passed but we lost track of time, suspended in that ziplocked, humming, fluorescent building. All that mattered was seeing Mara. Nothing else, nothing else. By the time the beautiful, quietly competent Asian doctor came out to speak with us we were grey in the face from the suspense.

'Which one of you is Kate?'

'I am.' Kate was suddenly alert, her brown eyes not leaving the doctor for a moment.

313

I shuffled down a couple of seats to give him the seat next to Kate.

'Thank you for waiting,' he began. 'We believe she is stable now but we're going to keep her sedated for the moment. The good news is her vital signs are all doing OK. They're showing signs of being stressed but are within good levels. She has a broken collarbone but nothing else that we can see at the moment.'

'At the moment?' Kate's forehead wrinkled with confusion.

'Well, she may have other broken bones but we have been concentrating on more important issues – whether there is any internal bleeding and how severe her head injury is.'

Kate took a sharp intake of breath and her hand whipped up to her mouth.

The doctor's eyes flickered slightly but he pressed on. 'The good news is that she was wearing a helmet that was securely fitted so that would have taken a lot of the impact. We've done an MRI scan and that doesn't show any bleeding, just swelling, and we would expect her to have some swelling, after all she's had a bang on her head. Just like when you bang your finger, it'll swell.' The doctor mimed banging his finger with a hammer, with all of us following the arc of his hand mutely.

'The important thing is that it doesn't swell any further. At the moment we have her sedated to rest her brain. The swelling appears to have reached its peak but we don't want it to go any further. We may have to put her into an induced coma if it progresses but we are hopeful we won't need to go down that route.'

Blah, blah, blah, coma was all I heard. I couldn't believe I was hearing this. It couldn't be possible. Mara in a coma? Please God, no.

'. . . and so you can come in and see her briefly, one at a time.

We will call your father if anything serious happens overnight but hopefully we won't be in touch and she may even be out of sedation as early as tomorrow.' He stood up, patients to see, things to do.

'Call me if you need to,' Kate cut in, standing with the doctor and placing a small hand on his arm. 'Don't bother Dad, he won't be able to handle it.'

The doctor looked unsure. 'It is usual to keep in contact with a patient's parent if they don't have a partner.'

'Can you see him here?' Kate motioned to the waiting room. 'He really isn't that strong, Doctor. I'll keep him informed but me, my brother and Mara's friends are her main supporters.'

'All right then.' He looked doubtful but made a quick note on the chart he was carrying.

And he took Kate through the carefully controlled doors into the inner sanctum, the sound of life-support machines cheeping terrifyingly, before the heavy doors swished shut behind them.

When it was my turn, I stood next to Mara's bed and held her hand. I was glad to feel it was warm. Machines beeped, monitors tracked her heart rate, plastic tubes ran into her arm, a ventilator covered her nose and mouth. It was like watching TV. But not. Mara wasn't an actor, this was real life, and I was suddenly angry. This was a person, a really, really special person, lying here. And she shouldn't be! At that moment I would have gone into battle with any demon to save Mara's life, I felt so fiercely protective of it.

'Don't worry, Mars, we've got everything under control. You're going to be fine,' I whispered to her from where I stood, too afraid to get too close. Could I kiss her head? I wavered, unsure, but then a nurse bustled up and asked me to leave, and

315

I returned to Claudia and Kate in the waiting room. They were jacketed and ready to go. It wasn't until we reached the front doors and my phone began chiming with missed-call alerts that I remembered about the gig with Charlie.

57

SAM

I had to hurry to keep up with Ed as he strode into the hospital. I was shocked at how awful he'd looked that morning. He'd travelled overnight to get back to London the previous day and by the look of his glistening eyes set in dark, puffy shadows, he had barely slept at all in the past forty-eight hours.

'You know, you could go and do something else for a while if you'd like to,' I suggested, as we entered the hospital together. It wasn't as if Mara was going to go anywhere. She was still out cold – and the doctors hadn't given any more indication how long it would last.

'I can't leave her, Sam.' We entered the lift and he sternly punched the button for ICU. 'I don't want to be anywhere else but here.'

His sharp tone stung and I tried to remind myself he was exhausted and stressed.

Mara was unavailable to visitors when we arrived so we sat down in the now familiar plastic chairs to wait. Ed stretched his long legs out, his bum right on the edge of the seat, his body becoming as close to horizontal as possible. He closed his eyes, quite clearly not wanting to chat. I wondered what they were doing with my friend that meant we couldn't see her. Perhaps they were washing her, her body heavy and unresponsive, or maybe they were changing the bag of urine that sat there, so normal now, tucked down one side of the bed. It was so strange that forty-eight hours ago this would have been so strange, so alien, but now it was all so normal that Ed could stretch out and close his eyes.

'How's Charlie?' Ed cut across my thoughts, catching me out.

'Charlie?'

'What, is there more than one?'

'No.' I felt myself blushing.

'Well?'

'Well, what?'

'How is the fine specimen of manhood?'

'Oh, he's fine, yep.' I peered at him; he had his eyes open but remained stretched out at forty-five degrees.

'And you guys? How are you guys going?'

'Oh, good actually. We've been seeing a lot of each other lately. Before this happened, of course. He's really concerned about Mara . . . now.'

'Now?' He sat up and stared at me.

'Yes . . .' I felt flustered, instantly regretting the use of the blunt clarification of the word now. 'W-well,' I stammered defensively, 'when it first happened, I stood him up without realising and he was really pissed off.'

'He was pissed off that your friend was in hospital?'

'No, of course not! He was angry that I didn't get in touch.'

'And you didn't get in touch because you were at the hospital, right?'

'Yes, but he didn't know that til later.'

'Right. What a delightful guy.'

'He's not that bad!'

Ed's face was hard when he looked at me. 'Whatever you say, Sam.'

I picked up a magazine and opened it purposefully. I didn't

have to listen to this. I knew he didn't think much of Charlie, and I'd shared a little story about something slightly annoying about him, but he wasn't meant to get angry about it. I thought we might laugh wryly together about the incident. No need to take it so personally. I was chewing together a good case for feeling quite cross with him when the consultant came through the door.

'Edward Minkley?'

'Yes?'

'You can come on through. We've taken Mara out of sedation and she's responding.'

I felt my tummy turn over and I raised my hand to my mouth. She was awake! Ed stood up immediately and went quickly to the door. As they were about to go through the consultant turned and caught my eye.

'Do you want to bring your—'

'Friend, she's Mara's friend,' Ed cut in quickly. 'No, I don't think so.'

I looked at Ed, expecting him to say something to me, but he strode through the door without even looking back, leaving me with a large man and his rat-faced child sitting solemnly at the other end of the room. I leant back in my chair and let the magazine fall flat onto my knees, feeling utterly redundant. It was amazing, I thought, how effectively Minkleys made me feel like a child. Like I wasn't mature enough for their grown-up take on life. I wanted to be in there when she woke up and show Mara how much I cared. Well, sod it. Maybe I should just go then, leave them to it. I stood up and strode out of the waiting room but stopped at the first window I came across. It was sunny outside, the kind of glorious, spring-just-round-the-corner day that Mara loved getting out into. I sighed and leant against the window. Of course I wouldn't leave. There was nowhere else I wanted to be. And they were right to treat me like a child anyway, when I could act like one so easily. I stood there for a while then returned to the waiting room to wait impatiently.

Half an hour later Ed came through the door again, and something about his face made me get up and cross the room, and put my arms around him before I could think it through. He held onto me, hard, and I was alarmed to feel him weeping into my hair.

'Ed? Talk to me, what's happened? Ed?'

'She's OK,' he choked, 'she's OK!' He let go and stood back, and wiped his eyes sheepishly. 'Sorry.'

I kept my hands on his upper arms, not sure if he could stand alone quite yet. 'Don't apologise.' I let go of one arm and pulled him out the door by the other, and took him to the window. 'Talk to me.'

Ed took a deep, jagged, breath. 'Oh, Sam. I'm just so relieved, I was so—' He welled up again, unable to speak for a moment. 'Sorry, I was so fucking worried about her. But she's awake now. She knows where she is!'

'Thank God.' I turned to the window, enjoying the relief of good news. When Ed had started crying, I thought the news had got worse, not thinking for a moment he could be crying out of happiness.

'Thank the doctors.' He leant his forehead on the window, a good head above mine, adding in a much smaller voice, 'I don't know what I would have done if she hadn't pulled through.'

We stood silently side by side for a few moments. Then, 'Sam! What am I doing here, looking out the window? I need to go and call Kate and Dad.'

'And Claudia,' I added.

'Yes, and Claudia. I think I'll go downstairs to do that.'

'OK.'

Ed started down the corridor and then turned and smacked

the side of his head with his palm. 'I'm so stupid – I forgot to say go in and see her! Come and find me outside when you've finished.'

'Are you sure?'

'Of course, why wouldn't I be?' Ed called back, a puzzled look on his face.

I could tell as soon as I neared the bed that Mara was different. I couldn't quite see her face yet, with machines and a curtain in the way, but even the way her legs lay under the thin blankets was different. She was present again. Without thinking about it, I started grinning as I rounded the bed and saw her face.

There she was. Dark hair recently brushed, her face pale, but without that freaky mask. And they'd propped her up a tiny bit. I struggled to keep the lump in my throat down.

'Hello, you.'

'Hiya,' Mara replied, very quietly, her voice a little rusty. 'I hear I've given you all a bit of a fright.'

'That's putting it lightly.' I sat down in a chair next to the bed, still warm from Ed's bum, and took her hand.

'Sorry.'

'Shut up with that.'

'How are you?'

'Mara, who cares about me? How are you feeling? Can you remember what happened?'

'No but they told me I rode into the side of a lorry.'

'Bloody stupid.'

'Bloody stupid all right. Ed was just telling me he's been on my case to get my brakes fixed. I can't remember that. I thought he'd flown in from India to be with me but he hadn't. He's been here for a while.'

'He has,' I agreed, not liking the halting way Mara was speaking.

'The doctors said my memory will come back, bit by bit.'

'That's good.'

'Yes . . .' Mara trailed off and closed her eyes. I looked at Mara's face, so beautiful, and normally clamped shut around her thoughts; the tightly controlled face in front of a busy, busy brain. But here, against the starched white linen, Mara had no choice but to acquiesce to her exhaustion, to the drugs keeping her quiet, to a brain and body traumatised. It made me feel very wobbly, and as bossy and annoying as Mara could be, I desperately wanted the Mara who knew everything back. I sat with her for a little while and then stood up slowly, not wanting to wake her. As if reading my mind, Mara's eyes fluttered open.

'Sam?'

'Yes?'

'How is Ed?' And her eyes were suddenly boring into my soul.

'He's good, I think. I mean he's been worried about you, but he's got some work and—'

'I mean, how is he in himself?'

'OK, I think.' I gnawed the side of my lip, not sure what else to say. Because he was OK, I thought. Then I frowned. Did I even know how he was?

'What?' Damn, Mara saw the frown.

'Nothing, nothing. I think he's OK, really. I'll keep an eye on him, don't worry.' I leant over and pressed Mara's arm. 'Anyway, you'll be home soon enough, you just concentrate on getting better, don't you worry about us.'

'Don't patronise me.'

'Ouch.' I withdrew my hand.

Mara sighed. 'Sorry, I don't mean to snap, I just feel bloody awful.'

'It's OK.'

Mara turned and looked at her machines, then turned back and this time her stare was weaker.

322

'I can't help but worry about him, that's all.'

'I know, try not to.' I stood and kissed Mara on the forehead and left her to sleep some more. And as I walked down the corridor to find Ed, I resolved not to wind him up with stories of Charlie or anything else. I would do exactly as Mara had asked and look out for him.

58

CLAUDIA

'Have you decided what we're doing tonight yet, my gorgeous Salad?'

I grinned. He really was the most ridiculous man. I'd never had a nickname before but John had made short work of that, progressing from Claudia to Coleslaw to Salad before I could stop him. He was even starting to call me Crunch, sometimes.

'Why Salad?' I had asked him the first time he said it.

'Because you're a particularly crunchy salad,' he replied, moving swiftly to nibble my earlobes while I shrieked.

To start with, at the beginning of last week, I had made pathetic efforts at hiding the relationship at work but it was futile, as the truckloads of chemistry between us was impossible to shove under the carpet. Even having Mara in hospital couldn't dampen my excitement when I was around him. I knew people were watching us and talking about us but I was so deliriously happy that I didn't give a rat's bum.

'I don't mind, we could see that film you want to see, whatsit? Or . . .' I bit salaciously into a large piece of cherry chocolate cake.

'Or?' He cocked an eyebrow at me. 'Not another night in. Are you sure Salad doesn't need some fresh air? You don't want to get wilted leaves.'

I slowly wiped away a sticky chocolate deposit in the corner of my mouth. 'Oh, I don't know, I happen to know someone who is good at spritzing,' I said, then spoiled the whole effect by snorting into my plate. Through my giggles, I noticed a neat, grey pencil skirt hovering next to our table.

'Hi, Claudia. Erm, hi, John.'

I wiped the grin off my face with my napkin.

'Hello, Rebecca, how are you?'

'Oh fine, thanks. You?' Rebecca smiled her thin smile, her eyes flitting back and forth between John and me.

'Great, thanks!'

'How's Mara doing?'

'Really well, thanks. She's on a ward now and should be home in the next couple of days.' I eyed Rebecca shrewdly. 'Has Sam been telling you about Mara?'

Rebecca's cheeks pinked slightly. 'No, it was . . . Mum.'

'Oh, right.'

'Anyway, John, I just came to tell you that your one thirty is running half an hour late so you don't have to rush your lunch after all.'

John laughed. 'That's lucky because I'd completely forgotten I even had a meeting at one thirty. Brilliant news,' he said, adding, 'thank you, Rebecca.'

Rebecca nodded and hurried off, obviously keen to get away. We giggled together. How gorgeously hilarious everything was in his company.

'How's Rebecca working out for you anyway?'

'She's very good at her job . . .'

'I can hear a but coming . . .'

'She's hard to read. I have no idea what's going on in her head.'

'Plastic?'

'No, too bright for that. Extremely reserved. I never hear about life outside of work.'

'I think her main objective is to be at the right places with the right people, as far as I can tell.'

'Actually' – John put a finger in the air as he remembered – 'last week she did tell me about a concert she'd been to. Surprised me. Seemed a bit rocky for her or something. Who was it . . .' He looked heavenward as he thought. 'I know! It was Coldplay.'

'Oh really? Sam was going to that. But . . .' – my thoughts ticked backwards to the previous week – 'with Mara and everything, I haven't heard her talk about it. Maybe she didn't go . . . What night did Rebecca go?'

John shrugged. 'I don't know. I was only half listening. A Friday or Saturday I think.'

I thought back. Mara got knocked off her bike on the Friday and Sam came straight to the hospital. We were there until quite late. Then, as we were leaving, Sam's phone started up – ping, ping, ping. It was Charlie, wondering where she was. The night they were meant to see Coldplay. How interesting, I thought, how very interesting indeed.

59

ED

It was Saturday and I surprised myself by leaping out of bed, wrapping my Rajasthani lungi around my waist. I was feeling the lightest I'd felt in a week – although this week had felt like the longest week in the world. I folded my bedding neatly away and stowed it behind the couch, then rearranged the futon back into couch shape, carefully arranging the throw over the top. Next I opened the window a fraction. A biting-cold wind came in but I knew Mara couldn't abide fustiness, especially her brother's. She had emptied a trunk for my possessions when I'd returned from India, and from this I pulled clean jeans and my one collared shirt. I sifted through my other clothes on the floor, making a pile of the dirties and neatly folded the rest, placing them in the chest. I stood back. It was a pleasant scene, this order first thing in the morning. I could almost get used to it. Gathering up piles of dirty clothes, and the ones to wear that day, I headed down the narrow hall to the bathroom.

The door to the bathroom was shut. Amazing – I'd never known it possible for Sam to be out of bed before ten o'clock on a weekend morning. Coffee first then.

A little while later, Sam's eyes widened when she saw me with just my lungi wrapped around my waist.

'Aren't you cold?'

I rubbed my bare arms. 'A little.'

'You should have told me you were up – I could have got out of the bathroom a bit sooner.'

'That's OK, when a woman needs as much help as you do to face the world in the morning, I wouldn't dream of demanding that you shorten your shower.'

'Charming!'

She reached out and hit me playfully on the arm.

'Didn't hurt,' I teased, hoping she'd do it again. I ran my fingers over where she'd just touched it in a ridiculous attempt to get closer to her.

She just narrowed her eyes at me and withered.

'Whatever, Indian boy,' she said, gesturing to my lungi.

'You know you love it,' I replied. She just sighed back. Maybe that was trying a little too hard. Still, she hit me. I'll take that.

After breakfast, we both got stuck into cleaning and airing the flat. Mara had made good progress in the week since her accident. The doctors weren't saying yet when she'd be discharged but Sam and I had both taken to keeping the flat immaculate, ready for her homecoming the minute she was allowed out. I suspected that Sam's motive was the same as mine: if the flat was ready it would somehow speed up her return. Sam had also knuckled down big time with her work. She says she's on a mission to pay back the rent she owes – again, trying to get everything in order for Mara.

The times I had seen her I could have sworn she was being nicer to me, and staying away from the topic I hated most. And she kept asking how I was coping. I suspected that Mara was behind this change in behaviour, and for my own sanity I tried not to fantasise it was because Sam was having a change of heart.

That morning, she opted to clean the bathroom – 'as I need

it more than you, apparently' – and I set to work in the kitchen, wiping down cupboards and worktops, cleaning the windows, and brushing and washing the floor. George watched, bemused, from a chair, his tail twitching. I popped my head into the bathroom when I was finished. There was Sam, on her knees, leaning over the bath and scrubbing it fiercely with bright pink gloves. She leant back and pushed her hair out of her face, adding a wet slick down one side of her hair. Of course she hadn't thought of tying it back, I chuckled silently to myself. She looked at me with bright eyes. I leant on the door frame. She really was utterly, painfully gorgeous.

'Cup of tea, ugly?'

'Gasping for one, thanks. I'm almost done.' And she leant back over the bath and scrubbed some more. I had to wrench himself away to the kitchen, as it was too much watching her from behind. Way too much.

'God, that's good.' Sam took a noisy slurp from her tea.

'It looks good in here, Mara's going to love it.'

'She'd better!'

Sam sat back to allow George to transfer from his chair to her lap. She fussed over him for a while. I watched her, enjoying the moment.

'So did you meet anyone nice in Scotland?'

Whoa, that came out of nowhere. I didn't want to talk about other people, not now. Not when I had her to myself. I shrugged.

'There was one woman.'

'Oh, yes?'

'We had some fun.'

'Sounds good.'

'It was.' I nodded. I supposed it had been. She was sexy and funny, and it was nice to flirt with someone. Would I have slept with her if I'd stayed the last week of the shoot instead of coming back? Maybe. Maybe not.

'Good for you, Ed. Glad you had some action.'

I made a non-committal noise in the back of my throat and before I could stop myself asked, 'Have you seen Charlie this week?'

'No, I've either been working or at the hospital, haven't I?' Sam sounded sharp. I knew I shouldn't have brought him up but it was so hard not to. After all, Charlie was the double-barrelled elephant in the room. Maybe she'd change the subject.

'He hasn't been in touch much actually.' Sam's tone was softer, confiding. 'Just a couple of texts asking how Mara is but not responding to me when I suggest we meet up. He sure plays hard to get better than anyone I know.'

My heart soared involuntarily. Maybe he's losing interest!

Sam looked up quickly from George.

'I thought it was women who were meant to be the complicated ones?' she said.

I looked at her and shrugged. If only you knew, Sam, if only.

At one o'clock, the flat was finished, tidied within an inch of its life and smelling of fake lemon. We were super-duper pleased with ourselves. Neither of us had done that much concentrated housework in a long time, possibly ever. The next plan for the day was to grab a sandwich and eat it on the Tube on the way to the hospital.

'Where's the iron?' I was on a roll – this tidy business was going to my head.

'Jesus, I don't know, do we have one?'

'Haven't you gone all girly girly on us? You should know these things now!'

'Yes, well. I'm not sure I'm very convincing.'

'You're lovely the way you are, you know.' The words were

out of my mouth before I could stop them. 'For a troll,' I added hastily.

Sam gave me a look I couldn't read.

'Fuck off,' she said.

'Sorry.'

60

SAM

I came in at the top corner of the park, having run to the cemetery and back. I was fighting every sinew and muscle that wanted me to stop, and by the time I got to the park it was pretty much all of them. But I wasn't going to stop, not until I got to the—

I stopped suddenly and turned around, retracing my steps at a wobbly walk to the park bench I had just struggled past.

'What are you doing here?'

'Oh, hello, Sam.'

She was sitting there, sitting there on this freezing-cold day, casually fiddling away on her phone with purple fingers. Rebecca didn't just sit on a park bench in early spring. The bench might be damp and mark her coat.

'You're good, out running like this. It's been two days since I've been to the gym.'

'Sounds crazy.' I extended one leg behind me to stretch my hamstrings, hands on my hips, and then switched legs, waiting for my sister to answer my original question but she said nothing and kept tapping away on her phone. I moved closer to the bench, grabbed one foot and pressed it into my bottom, feeling the heat of the stretch down my quad.

'So what are you doing here?'

'Oh, just getting some fresh air, people watching.'

'You don't like people.'

Rebecca turned and gave me a sour look. 'You do talk trout sometimes, Sam. Who doesn't like people?'

'But you don't even live near here.'

'So? I like this park – it's pretty. The daffodils.' Rebecca waved a half-hearted hand towards a swathe of yellow.

She was right, of course. I couldn't argue with her on that. I hoisted my other foot up and pressed it into my bum. This one was always a bit more stubborn.

'So have you seen Charlie lately?' Rebecca asked me, keeping her eyes glued to her phone.

'No. I've been at the hospital most days actually.'

'Oh yes, of course you have,' she answered hastily. 'How is she?'

'Getting there.'

'Good, good,' Rebecca answered, not really listening, as she tapped on her phone some more.

'So have *you* seen Charlie lately?' I asked in the lightest voice I could muster, placing one foot on the bench and leaning over it.

'Oh, yes,' Rebecca said casually without looking up, as if to say what a stupid question, of course she'd seen him, she sees him all the time.

I changed legs and leant in, looking intently at my trainers.

'I saw him at Coldplay a couple of Fridays ago.'

'You went to that?' I stood upright, unable to keep the shock off my face.

'Yes.' Rebecca smirked, more than a little contemptuously. 'I love them, they're one of my favourites. It was a great night, Charlie had a brilliant time.'

I had to get away then. I wanted to run as fast as I could, away from this wind-up of a conversation that was making me boil with envy and confusion, excluded from this special club where the same sort of people hobnob happily every evening, not giving a shit about whether someone was in hospital – not caring about anything except having a bloody good time with people like them. Anyway, if I stayed I'd probably be sick on her horrible suede shoes, or hit her or something. I turned and started down the path towards home, muttering I needed to get home.

'Oh, Sam,' Rebecca called to my back, 'you don't know when Ed's home, do you?'

'No idea,' I called over my shoulder, picking up my pace into a fast jog, more keen than ever to get some distance between myself and the poisonous little tart.

61

CLAUDIA

Now we found numerous excuses to nip past each other's offices, and could be seen flitting back and forth from Marketing to HR and vice versa throughout the day, to the enormous pleasure of the office gossips. A tally had started in the marketing department of how many visits per day, while the junior lawyers were taking bets on how long it would take for us to wear a track in the carpet. Usually this would have ticked me off but weirdly it all made me very happy.

Late on Monday afternoon I decided to surprise him rather than making my usual, strident appearance. I took a sheaf of papers with me as an excuse and crept quietly along the wall of the private offices, stopping just short of his door. It was closed so I looked down at the papers in my hand and pretended to read them, stretching my ears towards his office, trying to ascertain if he was in a meeting or not. Directly opposite his door on my left, and hidden behind a partition, Rebecca was speaking on the phone. I was shocked to hear her giggling warmly. Before I could stop them my ears immediately honed in on Rebecca's conversation.

'Oh, stop it, you don't really mean that . . .' Giggle, giggle. 'Well, I might be able to . . . no, I just have to check my diary . . .' Giggle, giggle. 'I am not playing hard to get . . . I'm not!' Titter. 'I'll let you know later . . . OK, bye then, lover . . . Bye.'

I snapped back into my body. Surely that wasn't Ed she was speaking to? I felt hot and a little disorientated, and for a moment I didn't know whether to keep walking and knock on John's door or make a hasty retreat. As I wavered, still staring unseeing at the papers in my hand, Rebecca stood up abruptly, her head coming up over the side of the partition. I saw her appear in my peripheral vision but pretended to be immersed in my papers. I waited for Rebecca to acknowledge me but she didn't. She moved out of sight, and I looked up to watch her wend her way across the floor at a fast clip towards the toilets. Heart beating hard, I knocked on John's door softly and entered, breathing a sigh of relief when I saw him sitting alone, beaming at me.

'Did you know Rebecca was seeing someone?' I asked as I stepped inside.

62

MARA

Sam sat slumped in the chair, her shoeless feet propped up on my bed. Her socks were giving off a slight whiff of sour milk but I didn't mind. Crotchety Chris was on duty that day and Sam's visits, which invariably involved bags dumped here and there, a coat dangling untidily on the back of the chair, socks on the bed, made C. C.'s lips pinch even tighter. You had to take your pleasures where you could find them in this place, I had learnt, and making some fun was even better.

It was very strange to be in a place where I wasn't the one in charge of everything. Everyone kept telling me that all I had to do was concentrate on getting better. That I was in the right place. Wrong! I wanted to say, and probably had done several times over. I was very much in the wrong place – I was in hospital! Not a good thing and not the right place. The last person who had tried to suggest all of this was dear Ed. He even said that it was good for me to have a rest from being in charge, that I spent my time worrying about Dad, about Kate, about everyone far too much, and that I had to focus on myself for change. Bah! I had said. Lying in a hospital bed all day just meant I got to worry without being able to do a damn thing about anything. It was very frustrating. Only one more night and I'd be home. I couldn't wait to get out of this place.

Sam hadn't stopped fiddling with her phone since she'd sat

337

down. There was no doubt in my mind what the source of Sam's preoccupation was but I was delaying bringing him up. It was, after all, one of the most tedious topics of the century. But after ten minutes of non-stop tapping and staring and sighing over the little black rectangle, I had had enough.

'Must you fiddle with that all the time?'

'I'll be done in a minute.'

I waited, grinding my teeth, for a minute to pass.

'Sam!'

'Sorry. I've finished now. Can I show you one thing?'

I sighed but attempted to sit up.

'Look at this pic on his Facebook page from the gig I was meant to go to – do you think that's Rebecca's arm around his waist?'

The camera had caught Charlie halfway though a word, his lips jutting unflatteringly out from his sweaty face. One arm was raised, holding a pint, the other round someone out of shot, whose delicate hand could just be seen appearing around one side of his waist. The flash hadn't done him any favours, in my opinion. I sat back on my pillows. How many of these boring, samey party pics were there on horrid Facebook?

'Well?'

I sighed. 'Maybe, maybe not. Sam – I really don't care!'

Sam frowned at me then went back to studying her phone again. That wasn't the answer she wanted. Oh, she was pathetic, the poor old thing.

'You're not still pining after him, are you? I thought you'd gone off him. You've stopped dressing up.'

'That's because I'm only coming in to see you.'

'Thanks very much.'

Sam pouted. 'Anyway, you're not meant to notice what I'm wearing, you've been under the weather. Can't you just stop being so perceptive?'

338

'I have far too much time to think in this place.'

'Yeah, I suppose you do,' Sam said distractedly, tap-tap-tapping on her phone some more.

'So are you still chasing his tail?'

Sam finally let her phone drop into her lap and looked at me. 'It's the same old story, Mars. One minute I think it's a bad idea but then the next minute not. The last time I saw him I was all geared up to stop whatever it is we've got going on – but I didn't. He was going on and on about why I'm special, and why he likes me. But . . .'

'But what?'

'I just worry I wouldn't ever fit into his world, you know? I'll never be good enough for that. But then I think, why even worry about things like that? This is the twenty-first century, we should be able to be with whoever we want, as long as we . . .'

I didn't fill in the end of Sam's sentence. If I weren't so tired, I'd shake the silly thing. If only it was possible to shake Charlie right out of her system, like shaking the last of the puffed wheat from the box. Wouldn't that be satisfying? I thought, imagining the swift, final crunch of the puffs being squashed beneath my feet.

63

ED

From: Ed Minkley <edminkley@gmail.com>
Date: Tuesday, 24 March
To: Covington Green <greenworldcov@gmail.com>
Subject: She's home!

She's back home, mate. Discharged late this afternoon and we were home around six. Docs said she might be able to get back to work next week on half days but they've given her the all-clear and there's no long-term damage done apparently. A good end to a shit week.

No, Katherine was cool about me coming back early from that shoot. She was really pleased with what I'd done in a couple of weeks, so all good there.

And awesome your project is doing so well, and yes, I'll tell Mara about the progress. She is interested in what you're doing but, as I keep saying, this won't necessarily translate into her being interested in you! Sorry I keep being harsh about it, just don't want to see that pretty heart of yours getting broken.

Ed

64

SAM

With Mara home at last, I would much rather have been at home to look after her but instead Wednesday found me working on a particularly tedious green-screen shoot in the massive, sprawling Pinewood Studios, situated on the wrong side of the M25. It was unusual to film something so small-scale out there. Most of the companies I worked with used more central studios, but this one had got a sweet deal on the hire. Nice for them, but whatever the production company had saved in money, the crew was paying for that day in time. I had crept out of the house at five this morning to be on set at six thirty, something I complained about bitterly but silently, as many of the crew had travelled another hour on top of that to get there. The joys of the production world, I thought as I yawned into my third coffee of the morning. I was always bemused at parties when people found out what I did for a living and then said, 'Ooooh, that must be really glamorous!'

'Yes, really glamorous,' I would answer them, holding out my work-chapped hands for inspection. 'This is what my hands look like after three days on set.' The person trying to make polite conversation with me would look at me, their face blank, and change the subject quickly or find an excuse to wander off. Granted, that really only ever happened when I was out in Petersfield, a rare, once-a-year-at-Christmas cringefest. London parties were infinitely worldlier. In fact it was hard to find someone to talk to who didn't work in the industry in London, which could be equally boring. I yawned again. At least the money from today would get me much closer to being in the black again with dear Mara. She looked so small coming home, a good couple of inches shorter and at least one dress size skinnier. It had broken my heart seeing Ed walking up the stairs slowly with her yesterday evening. She had looked at me as I waited anxiously at the top of the stairs and said, 'These stairs have been vacuumed! Have you completely lost your mind?'

Not hello, no it's good to be home. No, Mara Minkley talks about the state of the carpet. It was brilliant.

The art director was painstakingly arranging the packaging of the erectile-dysfunction treatment on a green plinth, which sat in front of the green screen. With him were three others: the DOP, director and gaffer – all men, all geeking it out together, fiddling with the arrangement of the pill box, the lighting, the camera angle, taking shot after shot after shot. The irony of the men all gathered around the all-important plinth and not being able to quite achieve the shot was not lost on me. I'd crack a joke about it if I wasn't so bored and tired. If I had someone to joke with.

I looked around the room. There were about twenty people all up. No one I was working with that day I could call a good friend, and there was no one I could have a good giggle with. I wasn't working with my usual first – I had picked up the job last minute when his usual third was laid up sick. I knew rationally that if I made the effort I would find someone to laugh with but I just couldn't be bothered. My job felt very stale. I sighed.

The last time I'd really enjoyed my job was when Ed worked with me. I wondered if we'd work together again soon. I smiled as I remembered the look on Katherine's face when he'd sorted out the issue of the car being in the way. Brilliant. It would be so much more fun if he were here now.

'Scene nine wrapped, set up for scene one, thank you,' the first's voice crackled quietly out of the radio on my hip, cutting across my thoughts, and I shoved my phone guiltily into my pocket. I may have been feeling sick of my job but I sure as hell didn't want anyone accusing me of slacking off. I should have seen that coming, been ready for the next scene and prepping whoever needed to be prepped. I glanced at my call sheet. Scene one was the actor talking direct to camera, introducing the product. Shit, the talent! I hadn't even noticed the talent arrive. Had she even arrived?

I hurried over to the dressing room, knocked once and entered. There was the make-up artist, and the wardrobe assistant, and as they glanced up and moved slightly I could see, sitting in front of the mirror, the actor. I breathed out a sigh of relief.

'Hi everyone – oh!' I felt the colour drain out of my face and then flood back at double strength as I took in the pretty face of the woman who had turned round in her chair to say hello. It was none other than the ex. I couldn't believe it. Lucy!

'Oh hello.' Lucy smiled cautiously. She was trying to place me. 'Oh, you're Charlie's old friend!'

'What are you doing here? I mean . . . I thought you were a doctor?' I stammered, my mouth dry.

Lucy laughed lightly and – I realised with shock – nervously. 'Oh, only just, I'm doing a bit of this on the side, to help pay off some student debts.'

Debt? Her? Wouldn't Mummy and Daddy have paid for everything?

There was a rap on the door followed instantly by the door opening quickly, slamming into my shoulder before I could move out of the way.

'Jesus!' I yelled and Lucy's face creased with concern.

'Oh, sorry, Sam. There you are!' It was one of the runners,

straight out of film school and really brimming with energy, the little bugger.

'Here I am, right by the bloody door.' I glared at him, rubbing my shoulder.

The runner looked at me, his head poking through the doorway, not coming into the room any further than necessary. He nodded to my radio. 'Mark's been trying to speak to you on that but you're not picking up.'

I glanced down – no light, dead battery. Not a good look. The radios on set were my responsibility. If I haven't noticed the battery dying then I wasn't paying enough attention, period.

'Tell him I'll have her on set in five, OK?' I said and shut the door. I would have to work really hard for the rest of the day to get anywhere near Mark's good books or he'd always think twice about hiring me again.

'Are you OK?' Lucy was at my side, rubbing my shoulder.

'I'm OK, thanks.' I rolled my shoulder, testing it gingerly. I'll live. The shock was worse than the pain. Recognising Lucy and then getting slammed into by a door was not an ideal combination.

'Are you ready?' I asked.

'Another minute and she's all yours,' Roz, the make-up artist, assured me, while Sian, in charge of Lucy's wardrobe, gave me the thumbs up.

'Don't worry about me, let's just get you ready.' I ushered Lucy back into her chair.

'Are you sure?' She still looked concerned.

I smiled. 'I'm fine really, and I'll be in a much worse state with Mark if you're late!'

Lucy caught my eye in the mirror, letting it linger slightly.

'You'll make a good doctor,' I said.

'I hope so,' she answered.

'Quiet for a sec, Lucy, and close your eyes.' Roz brushed a huge powder brush over her face. 'OK, now open them.'

Lucy looked at her obediently and Roz looked over her work carefully. Satisfied with what she saw, she removed the protective cape from around Lucy's neck and beckoned her to stand up. Sian gave her the once-over, and both women pronounced her ready. Underneath her doctor's coat she was dressed in a crisp white shirt, tucked into a very fitted grey pencil skirt, which ended just below the knee. Her feet were in black heels, which had the mere hint of sexy professional woman about them, not quite sensible but still serious. Her blonde hair was immaculately swept back into a French twist. She looked exactly right: young and fresh, yet professional – someone you could believe.

'You look great!' I said, meaning it, and I led her into the studio.

As we walked over to the director, Lucy confided, 'This is my first time doing something this big.'

'Really? You're so relaxed, I would never have guessed that,' I whispered back.

'I'm scared shitless!'

I patted her on the arm. 'You'll be fine – you're the doctor, remember?' And I smiled at her encouragingly as I handed her over to the director, a squat man with a thick black beard.

My day became infinitely more interesting after that. I tried very hard to dislike her but it was hard when she'd been so nice to me. Not only that but she took her job seriously and didn't spend the whole time flirting with the crew. She was smart and a good listener. Strangely it seemed that everyone around her seemed to blossom in her presence – they became more interesting, warmer and all round better company. The crew I had thought were boring, drab and lacking in soul at the beginning of the day were all potential lifelong friends by the end of it.

Lucy was wrapped at five o'clock. After she had changed and said goodbye to the relevant people (all beaming at her and telling her how wonderful she was), I fought off stiff competition to walk her out to the shuttle bus that ran between the studios and the Tube station.

'You did really well in there,' I enthused, my Puffa making its endlessly satisfying rasp-rasp-rasp as I swung my arms.

'Thanks, it helped to have a familiar face around,' Lucy replied.

We walked through the massive humming complex, chatting about the crew, about the day. Both waiting for the other to bring up the uncomfortable subject that lay between us.

There was a pause in the conversation and finally Lucy brought him up.

'So you've heard about Charlie and me?'

'I was there.'

Lucy wrinkled her nose and then shook her head. 'You were? I can't remember much from that night. After I left I got very drunk.'

'He seemed pretty upset about it. He said you'd split up with him, is that true?' I was surprised I'd said that. The last thing I needed was Lucy feeling sorry for him.

'Did he?' Lucy sounded mildly concerned. Her lips pursed together. 'I expect he was quite surprised.'

'Have you met someone else?' I asked.

Lucy laughed, bitterly. 'No, no. I was quite dazzled by him, haven't even glanced at another man since we got together. It was more that—'

We'd come outside a different way than I was used to and I had to pause to get my bearings, and Lucy stopped talking. We set off again, turning right and right again, getting nearer the bus

346

stop. I hoped I'd hear the rest of the explanation before we had to say goodbye but she'd gone quite quiet. We halted at the bus stop, our arms crossed against the cold.

Eventually I couldn't bear waiting any longer. 'So – what happened with Charlie that made you split up with him?'

'You know, I shouldn't really be talking to a friend of Charlie's about this.'

'We're not that close,' I mumbled.

'Really?' Lucy looked intently at me for a moment and I felt my face grow warm.

'No . . . I mean, we knew each other a long time ago but I-I haven't had much to do with him for ages,' I stuttered.

'Well, I'd had my suspicions for a while. And then at that party, I thought I saw him go outside with a woman – I don't know who – and something snapped inside me.'

I swallowed nervously.

'I didn't know for sure that he was playing around but it just didn't feel right.' She shrugged. 'And if he wasn't then, I suddenly realised it would only have been a matter of time before he did cheat on me.'

I crawled with shame and wished it wasn't me, the worst person possible in the world for Lucy to be confiding in. I'm the one he was playing away with. I'm the one who stood in Lucy's shoes all those years ago in a student pub in Warwick. I'm the idiot who should know better but can't help herself. How did he do it? Charming all these otherwise intelligent women?

Over the top of the puggy lump of shame in my tummy came that familiar wave, the urge to share. Don't do it! my head shouted at me but it wasn't loud enough to stop it. My mouth was already open—

'I wish I'd done the same.'

'What?' Lucy looked at me, confused.

347

It was too late – the sharing was going to just start gushing out. My shoulders sagged in dread.

'I wish I'd got out before he dumped me,' I said.

'Who dumped you—?' Lucy's eyes widened and then narrowed in understanding. 'You mean Charlie. You're another ex-girlfriend. I can't believe it.' She shook her head.

'What do you mean – you can't believe he'd go out with me?'

'No, of course not. I just feel like I've met far too many of them. There are thousands of you littered all over town. It's just that, here I am, having the best day I've had in ages, and the woman whose company I'm enjoying is another one of his bloody ex-girlfriends!'

I coloured again.

'Sorry. If it helps, my life would have been much better if I hadn't gone out with him.'

Lucy snorted. 'That I do believe.'

The shuttle bus pulled in and the waiting gaggle of people shuffled forward. Lucy was pushed closer to the bus by the firm, polite queue.

'It was nice to meet you again,' I said stupidly, self-consciously, as the doors opened and Lucy moved towards the steps. She turned before she boarded and called to me, 'One thing – what were you doing in our flat that day?'

The people waiting behind us sighed a collective sigh of impatience and I scrabbled for an answer.

'We were catching up, nothing more!' I called brightly, willing myself not to blush or look away, and Lucy held my gaze for a brief moment then turned with a wave and got on the bus. I watched her walk down the aisle inside and take her seat. She sat on the side closest to me and was busying herself with her bag. I kept half an eye on her – not wanting to look like I was staring – willing her to acknowledge me – please don't let our talk

348

end like that. The door closed and I looked up one last time to wave. Lucy was inserting earphones into her little ears and she looked down at me, an infinitely more guarded smile on her face. The sort you make out of habit.

'Crap,' I muttered to myself, watching the bus creep out onto the drive and head off to the station. I felt like a dog.

65

SAM

If I hadn't had such an intense day, I would have gone straight home to see Mara. But instead I got off the Tube early, telling myself I needed a drink at the Cock & Bull. Of course I could have had a drink at my local in Queen's Park or picked up a bottle on the way home. But it had to be at the Cock, I told myself sternly.

Sure it does, my voice of reason snapped back. And you're not hoping to check up on him or anything.

I ignored it and entered the pub with my head held high. I spotted him almost immediately, my heart doing a little flip, but I pretended not to see him and walked coolly to the bar.

Ooooh look, here he is before you for a change. When he's not expecting you. Interesting.

Shut up.

From the corner of one eye, I saw he was with a couple of men, who were all braying and doing an awful lot of backslapping. My stomach untwisted a little. So far, so good. After my disturbing day working with Lucy I had prepared myself for seeing him with another woman.

The bar was busy and I had to wait for service but I doggedly avoided looking his way. I concentrated on making my lips look ever so slightly pouty, in what I desperately hoped was a natural-looking way, and waited for him to notice me.

I smiled at the barman. 'A pint of Ringwood please.'

I hadn't thought through what I would have done if he'd been with a woman. Make a scene? Leave straightaway? I took a sip of my ale and turned slightly away from the bar, still studying my phone. The full liquid slid down my throat. After all, this was why I was here at the bar – I had to admit it to myself. I was checking up on him. *But*! I took another self-conscious sip. I was also a sophisticated, grown-up woman, completely at ease with my own company. I must remember that.

I was halfway through my pint when he finally came over. I was getting worried – would I have to take more direct action? I hoped not. I was fairly sure a sophisticated femme fatale wouldn't actually have to bump into the object of desire. He would be drawn to me, his senses overriding his brain . . .

'Saaaaaaam' – kiss, kiss – 'how lovely to see you, what are you doing here?' He seemed pleased to see me.

'Oh!' – surprised face – 'Hello, Charlie. I'm good, thanks. I was just passing, popped in for a vino. Well' – I lifted my glass and looked at it, widened my eyes in a goofy self-parody – 'you know what I mean.' And I laughed a suitably grating hee-haw laugh to add to the goofiness.

That went well.

Charlie chuckled politely with me.

I tried again. 'Had a huge day. Actually' – like I just remembered – 'I spent the day with Lucy.'

Charlie's usual composure fell off his face momentarily and he hastily replaced his smile to cover his shock.

'Why would you want to do a thing like that?'

'I was working with her.' And there it was again, a flicker of shock across his face, plus confusion.

'Working with her? I . . . don't understand.'

'She acted in a commercial I was working on.'

'Acted?' Charlie squinted in concentration and then his brow cleared. 'Oh, she's actually doing it. I remember her wittering on once about earning some extra money doing TV stuff. I thought it was all pie in the sky. I hope they didn't get her to talk. She was an extra, was she?'

'She was the presenter.' I didn't like his tone.

'Christ – really?' he spluttered into his lager.

'She was playing a doctor, talking about the benefits of . . . a product . . .' How much should I say? Oh fuck it. 'She was advertising a drug that helps with erectile dysfunction.'

'Oh that I must see.' Charlie shook his handsome head and then took another sip, finishing his glass.

'Another?'

'Why not, I think I've got time. I can't stay for long though, I've got somewhere else to be soon,' I said, hoping like hell that sounded like the truth.

Charlie grinned at me and leant over the bar to order the drinks.

'So have you had a busy week?' I asked him, feeling more confident with most of a drink on board.

'I suppose I have, you?'

'It's just that you haven't been in touch so I guessed you were flat out,' I said lightly, tilting my head to one side, the way I'd seen Drew Barrymore do in *50 First Dates*, trying for a gosh-aren't-you-cute-but-I'll-forget-about-you-tomorrow delivery. Not where-the-hell-have-you-been-don't-you-care-any more voice. Not that – a million cute miles away from that.

Charlie eyed me for a moment as if he was double-checking my intent. 'Well, I have been pretty busy, you're right.'

I lifted one shoulder and let it drop. 'I don't mind, I've been busy too. Visiting Mara a lot.' After playing cute, there was always guilt tripping.

'I'm so sorry, I should have asked. How is she?'

'She came home yesterday actually. She's going to be fine. Her collarbone will take a while to heal but everything else is fine. I think she'll take a while to get another bike though, her confidence is pretty dented.' As I spoke, Charlie made a discreet investigation of his watch. Which reminded me: I was busy I'd better leave.

'Anyway I've got to get going, I haven't seen her all day.'

'OK.'

'You don't seem upset I'm leaving.'

Damn, that was too much.

'Of course I am, babe,' Charlie said smoothly, running a finger along my jaw.

'You're not seeing someone else, are you?' There, I'd said it. No taking it back. I studied his face. His eyes widened with . . . surprise? Denial? Acknowledgement?

'What makes you say that?'

'I don't know, sorry, it's my big day talking, I'd better get home.' I started bustling about locating my handbag and shucking on my coat, wishing I could keep my feelings to myself for once.

Then I felt my hands being caught by his insistent fingers.

'I love the times we have together, babe.'

OK, that was present tense – I could work with that. But was there a but?

'And you have nothing to worry about.' He cupped both hands around my face and drew it towards him for a kiss.

66

SAM

Kate had a small patch of concrete and weeds outside her front door, on which lay two wet odd socks, a squashed ball, a twenty-pence piece, a blue pen, a pink hair tie and several pieces of junk mail being whirled around by a bitter wind. Ed and I, our hands buried in our jacket pockets, studied them as we waited for the door to open.

'Hi, sorry, come in. 'Scuse the mess.' Kate opened the door to complete chaos inside. But despite the mess – or possibly because of it – Kate looked amazing, dressed in a dark blue jersey dress ending at her knee that showed off her calves and ankles. Luke came running down the hallway, pursued by Rosie.

'Nee naw, nee naw! I'm a fire engine, watch out!' Luke tried storming between us to get out the front door and Ed grabbed him and held him upside down.

'Luke, if you don't behave, there will be no ice cream,' Kate said sternly.

'Ice cream? Are you crazy?' Ed gestured to the freezing air outside the front door. Luke giggled and ran away from him, somehow turning up his fire-engine siren by at least fifty per cent.

'Luke, too loud!' Kate shook her head and led them to the kitchen, shouting over the noise. 'He eats ice cream all year round – they both do. It's like they don't feel the cold. Luke!' She shooed both kids into the living room and then joined us in the kitchen.

'Sorry.'

'What for?' I said.

'Luke, he's . . .'

'A six-year-old boy.'

'A flippin' loud one.'

'We're used to it, aren't we, Ed?'

'You should hear Mara's fire-engine impression.'

Kate gave her brother an ineffectual shove in the arm.

'Thinks he's a funny man. But really you do need to keep an eye on him, he's becoming a real tearaway.' Kate looked towards the living room, where they could hear a fierce squabble escalating. Her face flickered with unease.

'He'll be fine, stop worrying.' I put my arm on Kate's.

Kate took a quick breath and nodded briskly. 'You're right. Of course you are! I worry too much about them. How's Mara doing today?'

'Bossing us both around already, isn't she, Sam?'

I rolled my eyes. 'Yes. It's only been three days and we're thinking of sending her back.'

'Oh, that's great. I just hope she doesn't do too much too soon.'

'I'm sure she will. More importantly, little sis, tell us about this man then,' Ed asked from his customary spot, leaning against the kitchen counter, his arms folded.

'Well . . .' Kate glanced at Rosie, who had reappeared and adhered herself to her mother's side. 'His name is Ben Garcia.'

'You're dating an Italian?'

'His father was Italian I think,' Kate mumbled as she rooted around in her handbag.

'Needa date, Mummy,' Rosie piped up.

'No you don't, Rosie, you've just had some food.'

'Needa date!'

Kate sighed. 'Ask nicely.'

'Pease.'

'He's a friend of Olivia, you know, the girl I used to work with.' Kate took some dates from a container and passed them to Rosie and then to Luke, who had materialised at the mention of food.

'Would that be anorexic Olivia or bulimic Olivia,' I couldn't help asking.

'Funny ha ha.' Kate sighed. 'Not all models are like that. I wasn't.'

'Much,' I replied, and Ed sniggered.

'You guys!' Kate sighed.

'Sorry,' Ed and I said at the same time, pulling a 'whoops!' face at each other. We both knew perfectly well how Kate disliked that joke. She'd heard it too often for it to be funny any more but for us it was like an itch that just had to be scratched.

'You're right, we're not funny, Kate. Very good babysitters, shit comedians.'

'That's true.' Kate smiled.

'And you should go, you're going to be late. We can manage the little tykes, can't we, Luke?' And Ed growled at Luke, advancing his big tickling hands towards him. Luke screamed, delighted.

At the playground, both kids quickly ran off to get on with the serious job of playing. With the coffee having passed Ed's critical scrutiny on our last visit, he was happy to nip into the park café while I perched on a bench to watch. The playground was crowded, the happy energy of kids outside filling the air. I took a deep, cold breath and let my eyes linger on the bare-limbed trees, starkly silhouetted against the blue sky. Soon Ed was there beside me with hot coffee.

'Perfect!' I smiled at him.

'You're in a good mood.'

'It's a lovely day, isn't it? And I love being with the kids.' I turned to find them in the playground, almost getting panicky when I couldn't see them straightaway. So many children. But there they were, by the sandpit, digging away industrially in the soggy white sand.

Sitting there, I was reminded of the last time I was at the park and realised I hadn't told Ed.

'I bumped into Rebecca here last weekend.'

'What was she doing in the park?'

'Stalking you, I think.'

'Really?' Ed turned to me, his voice sharp.

I nodded. 'Pretty sure. She wanted to know if I knew when you'd be home.'

'What a pity I wasn't in.'

'She seemed to think so.'

Ed shook his head to himself, chewing something over in his mind. I waited for him to say something else but he didn't offer anything.

'Do you like her?'

Ed threw back his head and laughed, and I felt something strange – excitement? nerves? I didn't know – spike through my belly.

★

Luke hoped they'd get an ice cream. Rosie would drip hers everywhere but he knew how to lick it all up quickly. There was the playground – what to do first? Slide, then train, then climbing rope, then swings, then . . . he ran around. Come on, Rosie. Their hair whipped around in the wind, and soon their hands were pink and frozen, smelling of the metal of the slide, the chain of the swings. Mummy was going out with a new friend, she said, which meant he and Rosie were out with Uncle Ed and Sam. And they would have ice cream – they promised. He looked over to them. They were talking again. Not looking his way. They were always talking. Luke could feel the unfamiliar weight of the big-boy coins in his pocket.

'Look after this carefully, and you and Rosie will get an ice cream.' Mummy had put the money in there. He wanted to go now. They were still talking. They could go now quickly and come back. Luke knew the way.

★

A boy in the sandpit let out a long wail, his sandcastle crushed by another kid. Ed and I glanced up, looking for Luke, expecting him to be the culprit. No Luke, no Rosie.

'Monkeys, where are they?' I got up and started walking over to the other equipment, with Ed following close behind. Not at the swings, not on the slide, not on the rope, not in the tunnel. Our heart rates increased.

'Luke! Rosie!' we called, glancing feverishly around the playground.

'Ed, they're not here!'

Ed was white. 'You ask around the mums, I'll have a look on the street.'

The mums all shook their heads at me, looking concerned, checking on their own children.

Fuck, fuck, fuck, where are they?

★

Down the street, they turned towards what Luke thought was the ice-cream shop. It was quiet. A big building ran down one side. Luke slowed down. He wasn't sure he could remember that. The wind blew an empty crisp packet past them, turning over and over, almost flying. It made Luke feel uneasy.

'Let's turn around, Rosie.' Luke tried to take her hand but a little orange cat bounced after the crisp packet. Rosie loved cats.

358

'Cat!' Rosie pointed excitedly.

'Rosie!' Luke shouted.

The cat bounced off ahead of him, turning into a door. Rosie ran after it, her nappy wobbling from side to side. 'No, Rosie, that's the wrong way!' Luke shouted again but she kept chasing it, through the door. And she was gone. Luke looked behind him for a second and then ran after her.

Inside it was dark. There were stairs going up and it smelt funny. Rosie was clambering up the metal stairs – clang, clang, puff, puff – after the cat.

'Rosie!' Luke followed her up, up, up. Rosie was fast when there was a cat to follow. Every now and then there was a window, small and dusty. Through the third one he could see the park. He looked for the sandpit but the view was blocked by trees. He could hear mewing. There at the top of the stairs, next to a closed door, was Rosie, squeezing the cat.

'Cat!' Squeeze. 'Cat!' Squeeze.

'Come on, Rosie, say bye bye, cat.' He remembered Mummy saying that lots. Mummy. He wanted to be outside, at the park again. Rosie finally let go of the cat and they started down the stairs. But then there was a loud bang that echoed up the stairwell, and it was a little darker inside and much quieter. Luke tightened his grip on Rosie's hand and tried to hurry her down the stairs but she was slow and uncertain going down, taking them one by one. Finally they reached the bottom. He reached up and tried to open the door. It was locked.

67

CLAUDIA

After much searching, I found the thick woollen hat that had been given to me in good faith by the stolid Tante Helga 'für za English vinter'. It had been languishing unused in the bottom of a blanket box. Far too lumpy and practical for me, scoring a zero on my style scale. As I was rummaging I wondered if I'd actually been brave enough to throw it out but no, there it was. I tucked my hair up inside the hat and then wound a scarf around my neck. Right. Mirror time. I was amazed. I really did look like someone else, plain and tired. I wrestled with myself as I eyed my make-up for the briefest moments, then opened my compact and dabbed a little foundation on. That was a bit better. Still plain but at least I didn't look completely knackered too. I just couldn't bring myself to go out without any make-up on at all.

I dug out an old black coat from the cupboard and pulled it on over the top of my jeans and checked again. Not bad. I looked tidy but nondescript. Most importantly not like my usual self. Exactly what I was aiming for. Stuffing keys and wallet into my pockets, and putting on dark glasses, I pulled the door to the flat closed.

I couldn't contain my excitement. I felt it welling up as I trotted along the road towards the Tube, like it did when I was a child and was being taken out. I checked my phone again. John would be in position now, in a café diagonally across the road from the restaurant where Rebecca was meeting her date for lunch. He would call me as soon as he saw her arrive, at which point I would make sure I was at the window. I had done an extensive recce the day before and discovered a clothes shop opposite the café that was perfect. It not only had the right sort of clothes for a nondescript sort of woman to idle endlessly looking at but upstairs there was a window overlooking the street and the restaurant! Brilliant. With any luck they might even dine in the window – even better. At the very least I would see her enter with her lover or at least leave with him.

I arrived at the clothes shop ten minutes early, passing John, who winked at me exaggeratedly, on the way. I started looking on the ground floor, slowly sliding one garment at a time along the racks. At the time Rebecca was due to arrive, I went upstairs, directly to the rack closest to the window, nervously waiting for my phone to start vibrating in my pocket. And there it was! I stepped quickly to the window, whipping out the phone to check – yes, it was John. I didn't answer – that wasn't the plan. Sure enough, there she was, stepping along in a perfectly straight line but, dammit, alone. I watched her go into the restaurant with absolutely no hesitation whatsoever. She didn't even check the name, I mused. She'd obviously been there before. I hovered for a couple of minutes, waiting to see if Rebecca would take a table in the window. When she didn't, I went downstairs, having a half-hearted look at the sales table – even in disguise I didn't want to be seen as rude or dodgy – and joined John at the café next door.

'Well, the bird has landed,' I said breathlessly as I sat down.

'Indeed, but without her mate. So what's next? Do we wait around for her to finish?'

I looked around me and pulled a face. 'They could be all

afternoon, and I've got other ideas for our Saturday.' I leant forward and kissed him lightly.

John's eyes lit up.

'So . . .' I sat in silence for a while, looking out the window, aware of John's eyes roving all over me, but still wanting to complete this mission. I just had to know if it was Ed Rebecca was having lunch with. Surely all this silly flirting between them hadn't come to anything? Both of them had been playing games. Ed had only spent time with Rebecca to try to make Sam jealous and Rebecca had done something approximating the same thing, although for goodness only knew what reason. That woman. But even if it never happened between Ed and Sam, it would be awful if he ended up with Rebecca. A complete disaster.

Then I had it! I whipped away from the window.

'I'll go in and ask to use the loo.'

'They'll send you down the street to the Tube station.'

'I'll pretend that I'm preggers!'

John grinned. 'Oh yes? You and your enormous stomach?'

'I could be in my first tri-whatsit. When you don't show but need the loo a lot anyway.'

John raised his eyebrows.

'Lots of my friends have moaned about it to me over the years,' I added hastily.

John's eyebrows remained uplifted.

'Don't look at me like that.'

He released his brows.

'Thank you.'

'You know, the night you told me about the unmentionable STI, I thought you were going to tell me you were pregnant.'

'Really?' I squeaked. I thought back to that painful night and, with a start, I remembered his expectant face. 'I'd forgotten all about that. You looked so happy before I told you . . . the news.'

'Exactly!'

I blushed.

'And I was upset,' John continued, 'not because of the STI per se but because you weren't pregnant . . . which meant there wasn't a really good reason for you to be with me. It meant you were, once again, slipping out of my reach.'

I squeaked again and stood up. 'My God, you make a girl go all queer with all of your lovey-dovey talk.' I chucked on my coat.

'What – are you going now?'

'No time like the present.' I couldn't sit much longer in the café. I was burning to find out who this damn date was and after all those intense looks from John's sparkling peepers I had to get the hell out of this café and get my man home.

'But what if Ed isn't there yet?'

'It might not be him.'

'Isn't that why we're here?'

'Yes, but I'm still holding out hope it won't be him.'

'With all you've told me about him, he really doesn't sound like Rebecca's type.'

'Exactly, which is why it's really important his best mates are on to him so we can try to put him off, if he is actually seeing her.'

John shook his head at me. He thought I was mad with all this meddling. But he was smiling.

'It's only been ten minutes.'

I went round to his side of the table and kissed his forehead.

'If it is Ed, he'll be there. He's a Minkley so he's always on time. And I am a woman of action and I can't sit still a minute longer. I will take the plunge!' I extended my arm out straight, fist clenched, in the direction of the door and left, following my closed fist outside. The staff looked on at me bemused.

Inside I could see right away that Rebecca was alone, sitting at a small table, looking expectantly at the door. The fact she was on her own was excellent news but her obvious door watching immediately put paid to the plan to use their toilet. I didn't want to risk her recognising my voice. So, thankful for the dark glasses that I'd kept on as I entered, I took my phone out as if taking a call and went straight out the door again. I almost collided with a very smooth-looking toff coming in but I was so intent on getting away, worried that I might have been recognised, that I only managed a muttered sorry. I scurried back to John, hissing at him to move away from the window.

'I don't think she recognised me – I hope not – but she was looking at the door when I came in.'

'Don't tell me, because she was alone?'

'Yes, dammit. Why didn't I listen to you?'

'I have no idea, Crunchy. But I saw someone interesting.'

'Oh?'

'The guy who bumped into you on the way out . . .'

I shut my eyes in concentration. For a moment I couldn't remember; the adrenalin from my mission was making it hard to think straight.

'Oh, the toff, very handsome, floppy hair.'

'Not too handsome, I hope, but yes, that's the one. I've met him before. He dated a friend's sister, I think. I'll remember his name in a minute.'

'Is that all?'

'Well, I thought it was quite an interesting coincidence.'

'But we don't know if he's got anything to do with her, do we? He could have been going in there to meet anyone.'

'True. I just thought you'd be interested, my sleuth. You were all fired up to know everything a minute ago.'

'I'm over it now. As long as it isn't Ed she's meeting, then great. Anyway, don't we have some other plans for the day?'

John paid up and we headed towards my flat as fast as we could. If Ed was safe from the uptight one then I was safe to enjoy the rest of the weekend without worrying about it.

68

SAM

The plods turned up quickly. A man and a woman. They were very professional and quick, taking descriptions of the kids and then relaying a whole lot of coded gobbledygook into their radio to other officers who were on their way. Ed tried to call Kate but her phone was off.

'When's she due back home?' the female bobby asked me.

'Five o'clock.' It was three thirty. The light was getting low.

Had we seen anyone suspicious?

No.

When they'd finished asking questions we asked the police if we could keep looking ourselves. We had to do something!

'Someone can't have taken them, Ed, surely.' I desperately wanted reassurance as we walked out of the park.

'They'd be mad to, they're a nightmare,' he said through clenched teeth. 'Anyway, I can't bear to think about it so let's imagine they've wandered off and got lost.' He bit the side of his thumb and then turned to me.

'We've got to think like them, Sam. Imagine what they've been doing.'

For a moment, I could almost have been watching an episode of *The Bill* but it was just a moment, and in the chilly air and gathering darkness I felt the same cold fear I'd felt in the hospital with Mara, to the power of ten. Around me was the quiet, unassuming street and in my head was Kate's face when we told her we couldn't find Luke and Rosie.

Ed stopped at the railing of the park. 'Rosie follows Luke everywhere so she wouldn't go off on her own. So it would have been Luke who wandered off, with Rosie following.'

I felt like screaming and clawing at the ground in despair and here was Ed thinking rationally through the problem at hand, trying to navigate a sensible path. I held onto Ed's arm, as if by touch I could have some of his strength.

'Where would Luke want to go?' he asked me.

I pictured Luke's compact little body that morning, in his funky adult-style jeans and red anorak, his hair a blond thatch, roaring around being a fire engine.

'Ice cream!' Ed exclaimed.

'Huh?'

'All day he was on at us about getting an ice cream, the little freak. It's so cold.'

I remembered Kate crouching down next to Luke and putting some coins into his pocket. She was good friends with her kids even though they were little. I loved the way she could hang out with them and loved other people hanging out with them too. My eyes clouded over for the thousandth time in ten minutes.

'Sam? Are you listening to me?' Ed shook me roughly by the shoulder. I looked up, my eyes full of tears.

'Kate – oh my God – she's—' I choked.

'Sam, listen carefully, this is important. Have. You. Taken. Luke. For. Ice. Cream. Round. Here. Before?' He looked steadily into my eyes, willing me to rewind carefully through my memory.

I looked around me, from desolate to feverish in an instant. I was going mad. Where were they? Where were they?

'Sam! Pull yourself together!' Ed shouted.

I flinched but it worked. I began to think a little clearer. I looked at the park. Luke. Ice cream. Of course! I had taken him, lots of times.

'There's a shop just around the corner, this way.'

We set off running to the shop, down the road, then left down a quiet street. There was the corner shop, warm light spilling onto the footpath. My spirits rose as we drew close; they must be here, they must be.

Inside it was warm and smelt of curry. But the barrel-tummied man behind the counter hadn't seen the kids.

Was he sure?

Yes, quite sure.

That boy Luke, such a little character, a pretty mum, very polite, and the little sister like a dumpling. No, not here.

We left the shop, our fear ratcheted up another notch, our heartbeats going just that much faster. Ed stood outside, looking down the street.

'Let's go back to where they came from and think again.'

★

It was three forty-five.

Luke could hear the wind outside, blowing little sticks and leaves against the door. He had banged and yelled at the door for what felt like a long time. Now Rosie sat on the bottom step, quietly snivelling. The cat had come down to investigate and sat a couple of steps up from them, its body a round shape in the murky darkness, its eyes glinting at them from time to time. Luke liked the cat being close. It was almost completely dark at the bottom of the stairs and so, so quiet inside. Further up the stairwell a faint light came in the window but the window faced the park, not the street, so the only light coming in was the London light.

From time to time Luke banged on the door and yelled again. It was very loud in the stairwell but his hands on the door sounded

368

muffled, and Luke had a feeling that when he banged you couldn't really hear it on the other side.

Their tummies gurgled. It was cold. Luke's feet were damp inside his boots. Rosie didn't smell good; she'd done a poo in her nappy. He sat right next to her with his arm around her and sang all her favourite nursery rhymes, all in a row, even the most babyish ones. Then he ran out of things to sing. He tried singing 'Hush little baby don't say a word' but his voice went squeaky and sad, and tears got in the way. That was Mummy's song. He pushed his tears back; he knew he had to be brave for Rosie.

★

Ed and I went back to the park. Police officers were working their way down the street, knocking on doors, asking people for information. Ed stood by the gate to the park again, and then took his phone out and started punching buttons.

'Who are you calling?'

'Mara.'

My stomach clenched tighter. 'You can't do that! She'll completely freak out.' But it was too late.

'Mars? It's me. I can't talk for long, we're at the park with the kids and they've wandered off . . . we were watching them . . . look, Mars, we'll talk about this later but can you think of anywhere they might have gone?' Ed held the phone out from his ear as Mara gave her response. 'Mars, Mars, calm down. Of course we'll find them . . . Look, I'll see you later.'

He stuffed his phone into his pocket. 'That wasn't a good idea.'

'I did try to tell you.'

Ed turned around yet again, scouring the park, the street, the view of the playground they had from the gate, searching, searching.

I was thinking about Luke. About his stomach.

'This has to have something to do with food.' I frowned at the street. 'Maybe they didn't get to the shop but perhaps we should follow their footsteps again in that direction. I just can't see how Luke would leave the playground for anything other than food.'

'OK.' Ed was earnest, desperate for some kind of plan.

I turned towards the shop. 'They had to have gone down this way. It's the only way Luke knows, I'm pretty sure of that.'

We set off, passing the police officer who'd originally answered their call talking to a woman on her front step. The street was a mixture of terraces, interspersed with a few more modern buildings used as offices. From the park, heading towards the shop, there was a terrace of about ten houses.

'They've got little legs so they probably felt like they'd gone quite far by now.' We were walking slowly, at Luke's and Rosie's pace. The terrace stopped; we'd come to a wide driveway that went down to a car-park building. A few yards further down the road was the left turn to the shop. We looked down the driveway to the car-park building and turned to each other.

'What if—' And we sprinted down the driveway towards the building. It was very dark and the building felt big, dark and industrial. Away from the street, it was quiet. We couldn't hear the radios of the police officers, just the wind, eddying around concrete. The car access to the building was firmly shut with large metal grills.

'Rosie? Luke?' we called out, peering around the building, looking for little hidey-holes. The driveway ended in a concrete turning bay and a high solid wall. No way for little legs to get over that . . . and then on the wind we heard a muffled banging.

'Luke! Rosie!' We ran towards the sound. At the end of the building was a door. We reached for the handle but it was locked! Pressing our ears to the door, we could hear muffled banging and yelling – it was Luke!

'Luke, Rosie, we'll get you out of there!' Ed rattled the door while I ran up the street yelling all the way. 'We've found them, they're in here!'

Officers ran over from the other side of the street and three reached the door before me.

'I can't get them out. The door. It's locked.' Ed was straining at the door, his eyes wild. My heart beat faster as I could hear the little voices hollering behind the door.

From the street came the sound of a car driving fast. It turned down the driveway, its headlights lighting up the scene at the door – a frantic uncle, three composed officers and me. A wiry officer got out with a crowbar and with a couple of deft movements the door was open.

There was Luke, holding Rosie's hand, both with tears marking their cheeks. Ed dropped to the ground, tears running down his own face as he held them both tight, and then I joined them, wrapping my arms around all three of them. From the corner of my eye I was vaguely aware of an orange cat scampering away into the evening.

'It's all OK,' Ed finally managed to say as he sat back on his heels, hastily trying to wipe his tears away with shaking hands.

And Luke remembered the most important thing.

'Can we have our ice cream now?'

69

SAM

Ed and I carried the subdued kids through the door. The clock said five thirty but it felt like midnight. The walk home had been very quiet. Neither child had said a word and for once didn't try running off ahead. They studiously licked their ice creams, dripping them onto our jackets, and for once we didn't mind the mess. When they were all gone, Luke announced he was cold.

The police said we could take the children home but had said they'd be in touch with Kate later on.

'I'm glad she's not home yet . . .' I said as we set the kids down in the bathroom and started running the bath. 'But what the hell are we going to say to her? Sorry, Kate, we lost your kids. Can we take them out next weekend? She's not going to let us near them ever again.'

Ed didn't reply and tested the water with his hands.

'Right, kids, time to get in.'

Rosie and Luke obediently let him take off their clothes and put them in the bath, and then he sat very close to the bath and let his hands dangle in the water. I sat on the toilet seat and stared at the kids, still reeling from what we'd just been through.

'Rosie went the wrong way.' Luke was scooting a plastic boat around and around in front of him. Ed became still.

'You mean she went in the door, Luke, the door we found you behind?' Ed asked.

'The pussy cat went in there.'

Ed and I exchanged looks.

'Where were you going, Luke?' I asked.

Luke scooted his boat around and around. Rosie patted the water quietly, her round cheeks red from exhaustion.

'Luke?'

Luke looked up at me blankly.

'Did you leave the park?'

'I wanted an ice cream.'

'You went for ice cream?' Ed asked him very softly, and he nodded gently at the plastic boat.

There was the sound of keys in the door.

'Hiya, sorry I'm late!' Kate called out happily.

'We're up here,' Ed replied. My mouth went dry and my stomach turned over. I scrunched my toes and took a deep breath. Kate stood in the bathroom door.

'Hi, darlings!' she said, all smiles.

'Mummy!' Rosie reached out for her and Luke burst into tears. She reached out to get wet hugs and lifted them out of the bath into big towels.

'How are my darlings – were you good for your uncle and Sam?' Luke buried his face into her shoulder. Kate looked at us sitting there, not saying a word.

'You two look stuffed. Did they run you into the ground?'

'You could say that,' Ed replied.

'I'll go down and put the kettle on.' I disappeared down the stairs, cowardly leaving Ed to explain. I looked at the kitchen cupboards and tried to remember what I was meant to be doing. I felt yet more tears prickling behind my eyes but then Ed was there next to me, quietly getting a saucepan out and emptying some beans into it, putting on toast, finding a grater and some cheese.

'How did she take it?' I finally managed to ask.

'I haven't told her yet. I'll get a cuppa in front of her first,' he whispered. Then he stopped his activity and wrapped his arms around me.

'It's just one of those things, Sam, not anyone's fault.'

I leant against my friend for a moment, trying to hold back the wall of tears threatening, but pulled back when I heard the others coming down the stairs. Ed was still holding my arms and standing very close when Kate and two clean, pyjama-clad children came into the room. A flicker of amusement crossed Kate's face but I didn't acknowledge it.

'How was the date?' Ed asked.

'I'll tell you all about it once these monsters are in bed but, in short, it was great!' Kate replied, beaming.

Before I could say more, there was a knock on the door and Mara let herself in. Her quiet, measured tread in the hall gave her away. She stood at the kitchen door in her long dark blue woollen duffle, the left arm hanging loose with her sling underneath it. It must have been a mission to get ready and out of the house alone. She looked at Kate, at Ed and I, and finally at the kids about to tuck into baked beans.

'Mara! What are you doing here? You should be at home.' Kate rushed over to give her a hug.

'Stop fussing!' Mara held up a hand in protest, and I saw a glimpse of what a cantankerous eighty-plus-year-old Mara would be one day. Kate ignored her sister's obstinacy as she hung Mara's coat over the back of a chair while Mara trained her stern stare on her nephew, who was tucking happily into his beans.

'You gave Sam and Ed a really big fright today.'

'What did you do, you rascal?' Kate joshed her son, her face still rosy from her date, her voice twinkly. She brought her tea up for a sip but stopped when she caught sight of our faces.

374

'You haven't told her yet?' Mara asked us in a clipped voice.

'Told me what? Sam? Ed?' The colour had drained from Kate's face.

'I was naughty, Mummy,' Luke said quietly.

Kate put the children to bed twenty minutes after that. They were almost asleep on their feet. She had taken the news very well, I thought. But I could feel Mara seething across the table, like a volcano, like a tiger about to pounce. And I was right – as soon as the children were out of the room Mara leapt in.

'What the hell were you thinking, Sam?' she spat at me.

'Don't you mean, what were *we* thinking?' Ed asked her.

'No, I'm asking Sam. If you were on your own, Ed, you wouldn't have been distracted by her, you would have stayed close to the kids all the time and this wouldn't have happened!' Mara was furious, each word forced, gravel-like, through clenched teeth. Her eyes were hard and bright and not, for a single second, leaving my face. She looked at me like she loathed me. I felt rooted to my seat and knew with a sinking, sinking heart that nothing I could say would change the way Mara felt. I scrabbled around in my mind, full of shame, for something to say but came up with nothing.

Then there was a knock at the door. I felt Mara's gaze shift as Ed rose to answer it and soon I heard Claudia bustle inside, and Ed thank her for coming. He must have called her but why? So she could come and tell me off too? I wished I could just blink and disappear.

'Well,' Claudia said in her no-nonsense voice as she joined us at the table, 'it sounds like everyone's had a fright.' And she sat down at the end of the table, with Mara on her right and me on her left.

'I think that's the understatement of the year,' Mara said, her teeth still clenched.

'The main thing is that they were found, safe and sound, right?' said Claudia.

'The main thing is Sam wasn't paying enough bloody attention!'

'*We* weren't paying enough attention, Mars,' Ed interjected.

'Please don't fight,' Kate said as she came back into the room. We all watched as she walked to the sink and stood with her back to us, looking out into the inky night beyond the window. Was she imagining what could have happened? Was she about to tell me I could never have the kids again? I waited for her to say something – anything. But she took a deep breath and let it out slowly, then walked to the fridge.

'I think I need a wine, how about you guys?'

'What a good idea,' Claudia agreed.

Mara sighed and muttered her assent.

We sat and sipped half-heartedly. Claudia forged on valiantly with questions about Kate's date, which she answered in a rather more subdued voice than the one she'd used on her return. There was a tacit understanding that we'd just talk about other stuff for a bit, let the air settle. Mara wasn't playing the game though and managed to continue seething. At last Kate brought the conversation round to the children.

'I think this is a blessing, you know.'

'What?' Mara spluttered.

Kate gave her a small, Kate-sized warning look, almost invisible to the naked eye. 'This could have happened to me, to you, to any of us. He's been a real tearaway lately and I think it's given everyone a really good shock – including Luke.'

'How can losing Luke and Rosie be a good thing?' Mara's face was dark. 'It's just classic Sam, this is – deeply irresponsible.'

'Mara, why are you ignoring my part?' Ed's voice was sharp and I almost flinched. I had never heard him speak to her like that before.

'Because you can be trusted, unlike her!'

'Mara, calm down, this is crazy,' said Kate.

And finally I couldn't contain them any longer. My tears spilt out, running like two streams down my face. Mara had opened her mouth to say something more but paused when she saw my face. She stood up.

'I'm going home, and Sam, I think you need to find somewhere else to live. I've had enough!'

'Mara!' Claudia got up and followed Mara's stiff, angry back out to the front door. I didn't watch them leave the room, I simply hung my head, bent over with shame. Someone passed me a tissue and I took it. It was Ed. He hadn't followed Mara to the door; he'd stayed sitting at the table with me. So had Kate. But rather than comforting me, it made me feel even lower. I didn't deserve their kindness. Mara was right – it was my fault. I was irresponsible, ditzy. A fucking idiot.

'Come on, let's take you home. You can come and stay with me tonight,' Claudia said as she returned to the table, half lifting me out from the table onto my wobbly legs.

'What about John? I don't want to cramp your—' I couldn't think of the right word to use.

'She could stay here,' Kate offered.

'No,' Claudia said briskly, 'she's coming home with me. John is at his place anyway.'

I allowed myself to be led out to the hallway by Claudia and helped into my coat. I supposed I had to go to Claudia's. I couldn't stay here, not being reminded about what a fuck up I was.

'Are you all right?' I heard Claudia ask Kate as they hugged.

'Yes, I'm fine, honestly.'

Ed said. 'I'll stay here tonight.'

'What about Mara?'

'Let her own words ring in her head. She'll be fine.'

I looked up as Claudia raised her eyebrows at Ed, saying, 'I didn't know the Minkleys did tough love.'

Ed chuckled. 'I didn't either but it appears we do, eh, little sis?' He put his arm around Kate, who smiled sadly.

I had my head down as I left but I was vaguely aware of Claudia signing something to Ed, something about needing to talk to him or something. I felt utterly, utterly exhausted.

70

SAM

While Claudia made up a bed for me on the sofa, I took myself into the bathroom and called Charlie. I was desperate for comfort, for distraction. He didn't pick up and I left a message – please call me – sounding much more querulous than I wanted. I texted him too, just in case. Hopefully he'd call. Anyway, I tried to tell myself sternly, either way, you're seeing him tomorrow for lunch. He can comfort you then if not before.

Claudia was sitting on the couch when I came out, with two mugs of hot chocolate waiting on the coffee table. She was idly flicking through a magazine but I could tell straightaway she wanted to talk.

What am I going to say to you? I thought. I don't have anything of worth to say. Nothing at all.

'This will help you sleep.' Claudia indicated the mug. I took a sip and winced.

'It's what you need,' she instructed. 'You've had a shock.'

'Not as much of a shock as Luke and Rosie had, locked in that stairwell.'

'Like Kate said, though, it's good to get a fright now and then.'

'Mara didn't see it that way.'

'Of course she didn't, she won't for a while. She's very black and white. But she's not their mother, Kate is, and she's OK. Most importantly, she's OK with you, darling.' And Claudia patted my foot.

I sighed.

'Look, don't feel beaten down. We all love you very much, including Mara. We're family.'

I grunted, unconvinced, and then thought of something.

'Please don't compare my friendships with my sister.' I glanced at Claudia, who was looking troubled or something. But it flicked off her face and she smiled.

'We're even better than family,' she said.

'Some family. Mum and Dad are all right.'

'OK, some family. But my point is, families have bust-ups – it's what happens when you're close – and then you make up.'

'Yeah, right.' I could really see Rebecca and I getting along one day.

Claudia had that strange, troubled look again.

'Well' – she patted my foot again – 'don't dwell on it. It will blow over – it will.'

I really wanted to believe her. I yawned, feeling the exhaustion right down to my toes.

'I'll let you go to sleep. Sleep in tomorrow if you can. Have you got anything on that can't be changed?'

'Only lunch with Charlie.'

'Oh.'

'I want to see him!' I wheedled.

'All right, all right.' Claudia stood up and stretched then looked as if she was going to say something again, that strange, indefinable look on her face again. But again she didn't; instead she leant over and kissed me on the forehead, wishing me sweet dreams.

*

I woke to the sound of Claudia's front door shutting. It took me a moment to remember why I was at Claudia's but then it came back to me in a whoosh of pain. God only knows what Claudia put in that hot chocolate but it worked. By rights I shouldn't have been able to sleep so well last night. My chest felt heavy with shame and once again I ran through every detail of losing the children, feeling my gut twist in fear all over again. How on earth would Mara forgive me? My thoughts ran ahead, through a future where every gathering was uncomfortable with us both in the same room, when I gasped, realising the consequences – I would simply not be invited to things any more, never mind not being able to just pop by. My friends (Claudia was right, actually, they were my family) would have to choose between us. A tear ran down the side of my face. Of course they'd choose Mara over me, fuck it. Most of the gang were bloody Minkleys after all.

I reached out and felt about for my phone. Nothing. Not a single new message. No one gave a shit about me, no one at all.

I woke again a couple of hours later and started when I saw the time. Eleven o'clock? I got up too quickly and had to wait for the black spots to disappear before heading straight for the shower. As I cleansed with Claudia's luxury toiletries I started feeling a little better and my mind started filling with thoughts of Charlie, which for once felt less complicated than thinking about anything else.

I'd vowed I wouldn't be early again for him but I couldn't help but walk quickly down Claudia's street to the Tube. Charlie would make everything OK. He was always so even tempered, with nothing fazing him. And he (almost always) made me feel wanted. When I was with him the rest of the world disappeared. There was, as always, the little niggle of worry. I hadn't seen him since 'bumping' into him at the Cock & Bull but he'd texted me when he could, in-between his round-the-clock shifts. It was hard work when another surgeon on your team was off sick. I was grown-up enough to understand that.

When I got to the pub he wasn't there. Not to worry, not to

worry. He'd be here soon. I counted out coins for half a bitter and sat down, aware as I took a sip of how hungry I was. Thank God he'd be buying lunch.

As I sat waiting, and the beer started loosening my mind, a plan that had been slowly gathering voice in the back of my head somewhere since that morning spoke loud and clear. Of course! It was so obvious. I smiled, pleased with myself and took out my phone.

> Thank u so much for looking after me last night lovely friend xxx yr drugs blinking knocked me out

Claudia didn't reply. I didn't expect her to – she would be in the thick of her workday. On a whim, I texted again.

> I'm going to ask Charlie if I can stay with him, so if I'm not home later, I'll be at his.

There. Send. I hope I haven't jinxed things by getting ahead of myself.

Oh look, here he is. Excellent timing.

'I was just thinking about you.' I smiled in what I hoped was a mischievous way.

'Oh really?' he answered flatly as he took off his coat. His face was tight, like he had a lot on his mind. He took his phone out and checked it before slipping it into his pocket. He still hadn't sat down.

I kept the smile on, determined. 'Busy at work?'

'So so. Another one? I'm going to grab a coffee.' He pointed at my drink and headed to the bar without giving me even a hello peck on the cheek.

It doesn't matter; stop worrying.

Charlie took a sip of coffee and texted something again. It had to be the twelfth time since he arrived. He hadn't even really listened when I told him about what had happened with the kids. It was as if that wasn't even a story, no big deal. This wasn't at all how I imagined it would be.

'Do you have to do that?' I couldn't stop myself.

'What?'

'That . . . texting all the time.'

'It's work, I have to.'

'You said you weren't busy.'

'I wasn't until I got here.'

Charlie's tone was defensive but he slipped the phone back into his pocket anyway. I noticed he didn't apologise. But I couldn't dwell on that – I had to ask him before I lost all enthusiasm for my great plan.

'Charlie?'

'Hmmm?' He was gazing out of the window now. It was like he wasn't actually in the room with me.

'I need to ask you something.'

'Yes?' He turned to me and I tried a smile again.

'Can I come and stay with you for a while?'

'What?' Charlie went very still.

OK, so he's listening. That's a good thing, right?

'Mara's kicked me out.'

'Well—'

'It won't be forever, just while I sort something else out—'

'The thing is—'

'I won't be any trouble. I won't start rearranging your pad or anything,' I hooted awkwardly. 'God no, nothing like that—'

'Sam.'

'I mean, I'm not into having my style cramped either. I'm not trying to take over your life—'

383

Please stop me!

'Sam!'

'Sorry, I was babbling.' I blushed.

'Yes.'

You're not meant to agree!

'The thing is—'

'I do that when I'm nervous.'

'Sam!' Charlie held up his hand, palm flat. Stop.

'Sorry.'

'The thing is, Sam, I can't.'

'Why not?' I felt myself go into free fall.

'I just need my space at the moment. It didn't work out with Lucy and I was living with her, and I just don't want to mix lovers and living together for a bit.'

'Lovers?'

Charlie grinned. 'Sorry, lover. Singular. You pedant.'

I forced myself to grin back. I knew he was right; of course he was. He didn't want to scupper a good thing. But that didn't stop me feeling deflated and, to make matters worse, here he was getting up and putting his coat on.

'Look, I've got to go, sorry. I've got to nip home to meet the boiler man.'

Boiler man? I stood up with him, putting my coat on in a daze, and he embraced me, kissing me briefly on the lips.

'I'll see you soon, OK?' And he was gone, out through the doors of the pub before I even had time to say, 'Looking forward to seeing you . . .'

I stuffed my hands in my pockets and walked down the street in a daze. He'd never been so uninterested in me ever. The further away I got from him, the more obvious the truth was. He didn't want to be there today, not with me. And on the one day I really did need his comfort he wasn't there for me at all. Stuff this,

I thought. I don't need this! I turned abruptly and headed for Leicester Square station. I'd catch him at home right now. Have it out with him – was he into me or not? I suddenly, violently, couldn't bear his wishy-washy fence-sitting a minute longer.

SAM

I stormed down Charlie's street. It felt like I was being pushed along by some frantic force beyond my control but I also knew that I had to get there before I chickened out and let him blow hot and cold for the rest of eternity with me just taking it. Because that's how it would be. This grand plan of winning back the catch of a lifetime would never come to fruition. Mr Charles Hugh-Barrington would have to have me, really have me, or it was all over.

I was almost there when I saw a man slowing down near Charlie's gate. I picked up my pace when I saw him turn into it. He certainly wasn't a plumber and there was no sign of a van in the street. Good, this meant he'd be alone. The man ahead took out his key and I stepped forward, smiled and slipped in behind him through the communal front door, then nipped upstairs to Charlie's flat before he could question who I was.

At the door, I had a moment of immense foreboding but I pushed it aside. You silly cow! I said to myself. You've had enough of all this not-knowing-where-you-stand crap. What is needed now is some clarity! But I trembled as I knocked on his door. Nothing. I knocked again and pressed my ear to the door. There. I could hear steps. The door opened.

'Sam—' He looked shocked but I pushed past him before he could object. I scanned the room. The kitchen was empty, the bedroom door shut. The bathroom door was open with no sign of a boiler man.

'Not here yet then?' I asked him, my heart racing.

'Pardon?' Charlie's voice was almost squeaky.

'The boiler man.'

'Oh, yes, right. No, he's running late.'

I narrowed my eyes. He was acting very strange, kind of flustered, standing there pushing his hands through his hair as if he wasn't sure what to say next. I caught sight of the sofa – our sofa – and remembered our steamy afternoon together. Oh, why did perfectly fun things have to get so serious? Why couldn't my life just roll along like it should for once? I found myself running my hands through my own hair, vaguely aware that I was mirroring Charlie's nervousness. And then it came to me. I was standing there in that damn flat and it was the same place I'd been so many bloody times before. Different flat, maybe, but the same situation. It happened with every single boyfriend who lasted more than five minutes. It was the point where it stopped being light and fluffy and started getting difficult, and it was when I usually bolted. I forced myself to look Charlie straight in the eye, which was difficult as his gaze was skittering all over the room. Not this time, I told myself. I wasn't going anywhere until I had an answer from him. Not after all the heartache and effort and rent money I'd spent trying to win him back. No way.

'Look,' I began, 'I don't want to be here but I just have to talk to you. I—' I became aware that my hands were on my hips and I took them off and folded my arms instead.

'We've had a great time lately.' I looked at him for confirmation and he nodded. 'But I can't go on like this.'

'Like what?' Again his words came out as a little squeak.

I opened my arms out, palms up. 'Come on, you know what like!'

387

Charlie said nothing, just pushed his hands through his damn hair again.

I sighed. 'Do I have to spell it out? We had great sex, some fun times, but—'

But I didn't get any further, as a crash from the bedroom stopped me in my tracks. Did that come from the upstairs flat? No. Charlie's strained expression and the way his eyes darted to the bedroom door brought the situation into a sudden clear focus. Before I'd even thought it through I ran towards the door, reaching the doorknob a split second before Charlie did, and just as he finally found his voice.

'Sam, don't go in there!'

But I threw open the door. There, sitting in the middle of Charlie's bed, dressed in tiny pants and a shirt, was Lucy.

'You!' she cried.

I reeled backwards and stepped onto Charlie's foot.

'Ow!' he said.

I whirled around. 'What the fuck is going on, Charlie?'

'I could ask the same question,' Lucy said from the bed.

Charlie had both hands on top of his head. He looked like he was surrendering, like he was in a stick-up, which he was in a way. In fact it was bloody lucky I wasn't armed because with the amount of adrenaline pumping round my body at that moment I could have done anything.

'Ah—' was all he managed to say.

'Don't just stand there!' I shouted.

'Well . . . Lucy was just here taking a nap,' he said, and then half-heartedly gestured to me while he said to Lucy. 'And Sam just popped in.'

'Crap!' Lucy and I said at once.

'Last time I looked,' Lucy said, her voice icy, 'we were about to have what I thought was make-up sex, when suddenly she' – she stabbed a finger in my direction – 'your . . . hang on, how did you describe this particular ex-girlfriend? Oh yes, it's coming back to me now – your "old friend" was here wanting to talk about all the good times you've been having.'

There was silence. Charlie's face matched his ivory sheets.

'Yes, I did hear what she was saying,' Lucy said.

'It's not what you think,' he said.

'Surely you can think of a better line than that!' I shouted.

Charlie rounded on me then, the colour coming back into his cheeks as anger rose to the surface.

'Why don't you just go, Sam. We'll talk another time. I can't—'

'What,' Lucy interrupted, 'talk to two women at once? It appears you've managed to be sleeping with both of us at the same time.' She swung her long legs over the side of the bed and pulled her jeans on with jerky movements. I couldn't have put it better myself.

I shoved past Charlie and went and stood in the living room. My head and heart were racing, and I found I was gasping for air. Charlie stayed where he was in the doorway, lamely watching Lucy pull on her jacket and then push past him to come and stand defiantly near me.

'Well?' she said. 'This is your cue to explain yourself, Charlie.' She turned to me. 'And you, Sam. I didn't know you were seeing each other.'

'We're not,' Charlie said.

'Well, that clears that up, you bastard,' I said, tears pricking in my eyes. That was it – that's what I came here for, a definite yay or nay. And my God the nay hurt like hell.

'Something's obviously been going on,' Lucy insisted. 'The thing I'd like to know is how long for.'

I glanced at Charlie. He was looking at me, pleading and wary. I swallowed. What the hell was I going to say? I'd got so used to keeping everything under wraps, from Lucy, from Rebecca, from Mara, from Ed. Hell, I'd even been hiding stuff from myself, hadn't I? Wasn't that why I was here? To stop drifting along forever and find out once and for all how Charlie really felt about me? And now I knew that he didn't want me. He didn't think there was anything even happening between us. I meant nothing to him, which meant I owed him nothing.

'The truth, Lucy, is that I've been hanging out with Charlie for weeks. And I thought we were seeing each other again.' Lucy's eyes widened but I kept going, amazed I could talk with the wall of tears banking up in my head. 'We had just had sex that time you came home early from skiing.'

'Here?'

The poor woman looked in so much pain but I couldn't pretend any longer.

'Yes, it was here,' I said wearily.

'Sam!' Charlie said, as if he was telling off a naughty child.

I held up my hand. 'Don't try and muscle in here.'

I turned back to Lucy. 'Look, you can hate me if you want, I'm sure I deserve it. But I never meant to hurt you. At the beginning, you were just another girlfriend, almost identical to the one he cheated on me with eleven years ago, and I didn't care about you at all. But as time has gone on my conscience has been growing.'

'How very mature of you,' Lucy sniped.

I grimaced. She was right to be angry.

'And then I worked with you,' I ploughed on, 'and I realised what a cool chick you are, and that made me feel really rubbish.'

'But you kept shagging Charlie.'

'I kept chasing Charlie's tail, more like,' I said. 'Or maybe it's actually been my tail I've been chasing this whole time.'

Lucy frowned in confusion.

'Look, I didn't want to hurt anyone. I just bumped into Charlie one day and something inside me propelled me to see if we could make a go of it. It's just that—' A ball rose in my throat and I swallowed. 'It's just that I've never loved anyone like I loved Charlie, ever. I had to know if he was meant to be The One.' I wiped my eyes with the back of my hand and sniffed a sniff that was so loud I almost didn't hear Charlie's reply. Looking back, it would have been kinder on my heart if I hadn't.

'Pardon?' I said.

'You can't be for real, Sam,' he repeated. 'Why on earth would I want to be with you?'

His voice was raspy with scorn and each syllable cut through me.

'What do you mean?' I asked in a tiny voice.

Charlie laughed. 'What do I mean? Are you serious? I'm never going to be with someone like you, Sam. You're cute but you're not beautiful. You're not a lady, and you're not like me.'

I couldn't say a thing and I could hardly see from all the tears swimming in my eyes but I did know I had to leave then or I would be screaming and crying in front of the last person on earth I wanted to see that. I made it to the front door and put my hand out ready to open it when Lucy's voice stopped me.

'Hang on, I'm coming too.'

'Don't go, Luce, we need to talk,' Charlie pleaded.

'Get your hands off me!' Lucy wrenched herself from him and came towards me, turning back to him as she reached the door. 'How exactly is Sam not like you, Charlie?'

'Lucy—'

'Well? Do you mean not in the same social circle?' She was gesticulating wildly. 'Or more than that, perhaps she's not in the same league?'

'Well—'

'Because, after all, you are such an amazing person, Charlie, so gracious and well bred and such a gentleman.'

'You know what I mean, Lucy!'

'No, Charlie, I don't think I do. Because it seems to me that while it could be argued that you and Sam are birds of a feather, both being capable of adultery, at least she has a conscience – at least she was actually following her heart—' She broke off and turned to me to add viciously, 'But breaking mine in the process.'

I thought I might throw up.

'It isn't someone who went to the right school that you should be with at all,' she continued. 'It's someone as shallow and callous as you. And that person will certainly not be a lady, and it most definitely won't be me!'

With that, she threw open the front door, making it crash into the wall, and disappeared down the stairs. I followed her straightaway, leaving Charlie standing in the doorway bellowing Lucy's name.

72

SAM

We both clattered down the stairs and onto the street.

Lucy mumbled, 'I've got to get out of here,' and disappeared down the street. I paused for a moment, my head blasted with shock. For a moment all I could think about was why she'd gone in that direction, when the Tube was the other way. And then I must have started walking back the way I came. I couldn't remember any of this part, other than feeling very cold and very shaky. Just before I got to the Tube station I became aware of Claudia and Ed, running towards me.

What were they doing here? When they reached me, Claudia opened her arms and let me fall against her. Then when I'd stopped sobbing so much I couldn't breathe – let alone walk – they led me down the street and into a pub, where Claudia shuffled into a booth and, in lightning-quick time, Ed bought me a brandy. And then another. And then, as the sharpness of the shock eased a little, it dawned on me that it was very strange for Claudia and Ed to have been there in that street at that moment. And running.

'We got there as soon as we heard,' Claudia said.

'That bitch, I can't believe it was her! But how did you know?'

Claudia and Ed exchanged glances.

'What the fuck is going on?' I asked them.

'It's a bit of a long story.'

'Well, I'm completely incapable of doing anything just now so you may as well tell me.'

'OK.' Claudia paused.

'Go on!' What were they stalling for? Ed was sitting looking, what was it . . . sad? Looking serious anyway. He obviously wasn't going to do the talking. I glared at Claudia. There was a whole lot going on here that I had to know. Had to.

'Well, my love, I've been feeling strange about Rebecca for a while.'

I wasn't expecting the conversation to veer off track but my day wasn't exactly running smoothly thus far.

Claudia continued, 'I must admit, I've never really understood your animosity towards her. I've always seen her as a bit pathetic really, a bit of a try-hard, but basically harmless.'

I rolled my eyes.

'When she started hanging around after Ed got back from India I was going through my own stuff, and I guess I didn't think about it too much. In retrospect, I think that should have set off alarm bells immediately.'

'It did with me.'

I turned to Ed. 'Oh look, he speaks.'

'Sam, we're here because we care about you,' Claudia said, her voice edging towards being stern.

'Sorry, I just feel like I'm spinning out here. Go on, Ed.'

After a bit of nervous throat-clearing Ed continued, 'I . . . er, I did think it was strange, all the attention she was giving me. She'd never noticed me before and it's not like I'm her type . . .' The last bit was muttered into his drink.

Claudia picked up the story. 'It's really since she got the job with John that I started feeling something wasn't quite right. I couldn't put my finger on it for quite a while but then last week I overheard her giggling on the phone to someone, obviously a lover—'

I looked at Ed wide-eyed. 'You can't be serious?' But Ed just blinked at me, a strange, vulnerable look on his face.

'Jesus wept, Sam, are you crazy?' Claudia said. 'Of course it wasn't Ed—'

'That's not what you thought at the time,' Ed cut across her.

'I know, I shouldn't have jumped to conclusions, that was really stupid of me.' Claudia squeezed Ed's arm, and he grunted.

What was going on here?

'Anyway, there was definitely something about it that made me feel very uncertain and John and I decided to follow her.'

'Really?' I almost laughed. My friends cared so much about me that they had stalked my sister?

'Yes.'

Claudia was grave and I felt a rush of gratitude to my dear friend – and the mysterious John Tightpants I was yet to meet – who would go to such lengths for me.

'So we watched her arrive at the restaurant she was due to meet this person at. I even went in there, pretending to need the loo, but she was there on her own so I turned and left and, coming out, bumped into your man. Charlie.'

My stomach dropped through the seat beneath me.

'What—'

'I've never seen him before but John told me afterwards who he was. He met him somehow, years ago, at some dinner or something. Anyway that got me even more suspicious.'

Claudia paused, checking to see how I was taking it.

'I don't understand.'

'So John and I both had our ears open for any new developments. Today Rebecca was due some time off in lieu and John had told her she could go home at two o'clock. He noticed her texting furiously through lunch and then he was just passing the water cooler on the way to the toilets when he heard her say she'd meet him at his place for some indoor sports.'

'And you thought it was Charlie?'

'We thought there was a good chance it would be and we wanted to make sure.'

'Right . . .'

'Anyway I was in a meeting so John couldn't tell me straightaway. In the meantime he found out Ed's address and then as soon as I knew, I called Ed and we came. We wanted to intercept you so you wouldn't walk into it. I'm sorry.' Claudia's eyes filled with tears and she reached out and grabbed my hands. 'We really didn't want you to get hurt.'

I sat in silence for a moment, looking from concerned face to concerned face. So many questions were whirling around my mind. I still didn't understand why they were going on about Rebecca.

'I really want you to know I wasn't involved with any of this, at least not willingly,' Ed started up again. 'It's been going over and over in my mind today, wondering why Rebecca made such a fuss of me, and I can only think she was using me as a decoy so you thought she was interested in me. But it was all so fake.'

'There was another reason she flirted with you,' said Claudia.

'Claudia . . .' Ed sounded like he was warning her.

Claudia opened her mouth to speak and then shut it quickly. 'Actually no, I don't think I'll say, it's silly really.'

'Say it.' My teeth were clenched. This was becoming more and more like a dream that made no sense and I really needed everything straightened out.

Claudia shook her head.

'Claud, I cannot bear any more secrets. Tell me!'

Claudia bit her lip, tensing with indecision, and then sighed. 'I think Rebecca was actually flirting with Ed to make you jealous, Sam.'

What? I looked at Ed. His face was magenta and he was frowning at Claudia. I couldn't read what was in his eyes but he wasn't pleased.

Claudia put her hands in the air. 'Sorry, Ed, but that's my theory.'

'Why would that make me jealous?' I wondered aloud and then wished I hadn't. It dawned on me – God, I was slow on the uptake today – that Claudia meant Rebecca was trying to make me jealous of her closeness with Ed so that I'd want him. I blushed with Ed and lowered my head, cringing.

'That's embarrassing.' I managed a weak smile.

'You're telling me.' Ed's frown slid into a sheepish grimace, his eyes flashing at me across the table.

Whoa. This was all too much. Way too many revelations and emotions for one day. I rubbed my face vigorously with both hands.

'The thing I don't understand is why you're sitting here telling me Rebecca's having it off with Charlie when it wasn't her I just walked in on.'

'What?' Claudia and Ed said at the same time. 'Then who the hell was it?'

We all jumped on a bus soon after that and rode towards Claudia's. I was grateful they didn't slag Charlie off the whole way back although I'm sure they wanted to now that we knew he wasn't a two-timing bastard but a three-timing slimeball. The crazy events of the last few weeks kept playing over and over in my mind, all of my encounters with Rebecca coming into sharp focus. Every time I'd mentioned Charlie, Rebecca had reacted. At the time I'd put it down to her being incredulous that I was making a play for someone so out of my league – someone from Rebecca's precious circle. But it wasn't that at all – it was envy! When did it all begin? Was he seeing Rebecca before I even started seeing him? Or did it start after? My stomach roiled in nausea when I thought about sharing him with my own bloody sister, intimately sharing with her. Yuck, yuck, yuck. What was he thinking? What was she thinking? After all, Rebecca knew we were seeing each other – why would she want to see him as well? And the scene in the Chinese restaurant with Mum loomed in all its cringing glory, over and over again. There I was with my sex toys, trying to spice up my love life, to entice Charlie further, and that bloody dildo – it was still in its packet, what a fucking waste of money – was bandied about for all to see, for *Mum* to see, when all along Rebecca was the little sex kitten. No wonder we'd only got it on once over the past few weeks. What the freaking hell was Charlie thinking?

And it kept coming back to that. As the bus stopped and started, with Claudia and Ed boxing me in, protecting me from the rest of the world and quietly letting me process my thoughts in my own time, I ultimately kept coming back to that question. What the hell was he thinking? Yes, Rebecca had crossed a line even I never would have thought she was able to. But Charlie – why? Why the fuck why?

73

SAM

The first couple of days that followed passed in a numb cloud. I went to work mechanically and returned to Claudia's every evening to be distracted with sufficient liquor and trashy television. I ate, I slept (thanks to Claudia's special hot chocolates), I walked, I worked. I did all of these things without trying to think about the horrible truth and, more importantly, without feeling anything. But underneath I knew my anger was rising, like bile creeping up my oesophagus, and before long it would break the surface. It happened on Thursday morning, much sooner than I expected. I awoke feeling significantly thawed. I shook my head, once, twice. The numbness was definitely fading. I stood and stretched and felt fury flood every vessel, warm every limb.

The hurt from his betrayal was there, sharp and hot in my belly, but there was something else in there with it. Something about this not being all about being the sad, thwarted one. If I was really honest with myself, I had been waiting the whole time for this to happen. I was angry and it was a relief to feel it.

I dressed, I ate breakfast, I stared out of Claudia's perfectly clean windows. What was he doing right now? Smarming his way through his morning, completely oblivious to the way he's made me feel. What an arsehole. I wished I had the bottle to throw this all in Charlie's face somehow. But I couldn't. I wouldn't. I had clawed pathetically after him for too long. I didn't want to see him again. I didn't want to get burnt by his smooth tongue. Rebecca was right – I didn't belong in his world and, quite frankly, I was so glad I didn't. I didn't want to have anything to do with him and she was welcome to him. They deserved each other.

74

ED

From: Ed Minkley <edminkley@gmail.com>
Date: Monday, 6 April
To: Covington Green <greenworldcov@gmail.com>
Subject: Why not?

Cov,

Sorry I've been out of touch for a bit. Major newsflash here. Sam may finally be over Smooth Features. She caught him in bed with his ex-girlfriend – the leggy blonde that I've told you about before, I think. Yes, you read that right, his ex-girlfriend. He obviously has a thing for them. It's never going to work for us but at least she's not going to be chasing Charlie any more.

Oh, and more craziness – before any of the above happened, Luke and Rosie ran off and managed to get lost when Sam and I were looking after them. As you can imagine, it was terrifying. And Mara was furious about it all – so much so she kicked Sam out of the flat. She blamed her completely for it, which was completely unfair – although Mara's been through so much lately, and Sam isn't always the easiest of housemates, so in a way I could see why she overreacted. Anyway it meant Mara and I sat down and had a long chat about it all. She came back down off her high horse and admitted that perhaps I had something to do with losing the kids too. It's going to take her some time before she forgives Sam but it was good to get her to see it wasn't all her fault. We sat up late and talked about everything – I might have accidentally let slip about how much interest you've been taking in her . . . sorry, mate! But she was really chuffed actually, in a low-key Mara way. Maybe I've been wrong about her.

But all that drama aside, you must be looking forward to visiting home soon. What about a stopover in Old Blighty beforehand? It's kind of on the way. Why not?

Ed

75

SAM

On Friday morning I was still furious. I power-walked to the Tube, seethed for all five stops, then stomped from Oxford Circus all the way to Katherine's office. When I arrived, Vic and Katherine looked like they'd already been talking for a while already.

'I'm not late, am I?' I surveyed the duo. Katherine was sitting right on the edge of her seat, a bundle of excited energy. Vic was smiling at me.

'No, don't be silly, we just started a little earlier. We had some details to discuss before we all got together,' said Katherine.

I took a seat and waited to hear what she had to say. As nice as it was to see these wonderful women, especially given how I was feeling, it was very strange to have a meeting at this stage of the project. Katherine had just had the green light on a TV series that she'd been trying to get off the ground for years. Vic was down to first on it. It was massively exciting of course. But when I was the third on dramas, it was much more usual for me to get a phone call from Vic to book me in. We'd only meet up further into pre-production to talk details.

I listened as Katherine outlined the project. A ten-week shoot, mostly on location near Inverness, story centres around a small-town medical practice, a couple of child leads, two camera units, a promising cast. I'd completely forgotten about the Scottish connection for this project. Katherine went to film school in Glasgow, had old friendships with people in the Scottish industry and looked for any excuse to film there. It sounded brilliant. Ed loved his time on her last Scottish shoot – I knew I would too. It would be such a relief to escape this town for a bit and there was no way I could bump into Charlie up there.

'When are you shooting?'

'We'll begin the middle of June.'

'Right, that's . . .' I tried counting in my head.

'Ten weeks away.'

'Punchy.'

'Exactly, so I want to get crewed up quickly then we can really get down to business. Most of the HODs are in place but there is something I wanted to run past you.'

'OK . . .' I looked at Vic enquiringly. What was this all about? Vic didn't give me any clues, just smiled at me.

There was a small pause and then Katherine said, 'Would you like to first the second unit?'

I looked at her in shock.

'Really?'

Katherine didn't laugh. She leant forward over her massive notebook and looked me seriously in the eye.

'Yes, really. I think you're ready for it, Vic thinks you're ready for it. What about you?'

'I . . . fuck me, I'd love to!' I laughed.

'Excellent, that's settled then.' Katherine pretended to make a massive tick on her page.

Vic and I walked to the Tube together after the meeting. It felt quite mad that after I had power-walked in edgy fury all the way to the meeting, I was now walking back on a high.

'Thank you for that, Vic.' I put my arm around my friend's

shoulders. It was so kind of her to put me forward for the job, especially as it meant she would have to find someone else to third with her, and she might end up with someone she hadn't worked with much before. Vic and I had such a well-oiled thing going on. Communication was so easy and made such a massive difference to our job satisfaction, especially when we were working under pressure. If Vic didn't get the right person to third . . . well, everyone will know about it if that happens.

'It wasn't me. I mean, I do think you're ready but it was Katherine who thought of you for the job.'

'Really?'

We separated for a moment to dodge a clutch of teenage girls who were hogging the middle of the footpath.

'Why are you doubting yourself?' Vic continued as we came back together. 'Has what's-his-chops knocked the job confidence out of you too? I get that you might be feeing heart sore and everything, mate, but what's he got to do with all the work you've put in over the years to get to this point?'

I had told her about Charlie when she'd called about the meeting. Good old Vic. She'd given me a characteristically blunt reaction and for once I welcomed someone describing Charlie as an effing great waste of space.

'You're right, you know. Why should I feel insecure? I've just got my first first-AD gig—'

'On a hefty-sized shoot.'

'On a blinking hefty-sized shoot, not even in London!'

Vic and I grinned at each other. What fun we were going to have.

'So what are you going to do about him?'

'Do about him? Oh, I don't know, forget about him eventually. Like you said, Vic, he's a waste of space. I just want him out of my head.'

'Fair enough but doesn't that mean he's just going to walk off scot-free to break some more hearts?'

We were at the Tube. We paused once we were inside, finding a spot near a grimy tiled wall, out of the tide of people pouring in and out of the barriers.

'I can't affect what he does in the future, Vic. I'm the last person who should try – I've managed to put myself through the same heartache with him twice now. What more could this muppet do?'

Vic was staring unseeing at all the people going past us.

'I don't know, mate, but wouldn't it feel great to show him up somehow?' She turned to me and her eyes were gleaming with mischief. She gave me a hard hug.

'I've got to scoot. It is bloody lovely you've said yes to that job.'

'It's just what I needed.'

We moved into the queue and beeped our way through the barriers. Vic was heading left along a corridor; I was going right to the escalators.

'We'll speak soon and let me know if you want any help with getting him back won't you?' Vic said as we started moving apart.

'Sure thing,' I said. 'You're a crazy woman.'

'You know it!'

We waved once more and I was just about to step onto the escalator that would take me down into the earth when she added, 'Do you think Katherine might ask Ed on that job too?'

'Put it away, Vic!' I yelled back, and I stepped onto the metal grooves of the escalator step and down I went, grinning to myself, cheeks blazing.

On the train, my head spun out from the excitement of the morning. My first job as a first AD! Running the set on the second camera unit meant I'd be getting up close and personal with the heather, the mountains, the rivers, in all weathers.

Katherine had explained in the meeting that the intention for this story is that the landscape would be more than just the backdrop but a character in itself, a force that shapes and echoes what's going on for the little humans living in the town. The second unit would be shooting all of this while the main unit concentrated on the central storylines. It was a good introductory first job for me as it wouldn't involve huge numbers of people and complicated sequences. I couldn't wait to tell Dad about it.

At Notting Hill Gate I came up to earth. I headed down Pembridge Road towards Portobello, painfully aware of how close Charlie's house was. 'What are you going to do about him?' Vic's words rang in my head. Nothing, I answered. Absolutely nothing. I had been well and truly shown my place by him and I didn't have any bravery left. On top of that, I was still trying to process the whole thing with Rebecca, who was so obviously guilty. She had been pointedly silent for the past few days. Surely by now she would know what had happened with Lucy, and she'd be dying to rub it in my face. Charlie would have told her. I laughed out loud. What was I thinking? Of course he wouldn't have told her – telling the truth to girlfriends was noticeably absent from his skillset. But Lucy would have told her friends – she was bound to have – and they would all be gossiping about it. I shuddered as I imagined them sitting around in their suits laughing at me.

She just wouldn't let it go!

Who was she again?

Oh, she was at his party, in a blue dress I think.

I can't remember her.

No, she's not very memorable.

Gah.

But when I played out this little bitchfest in my mind, I just couldn't put Lucy in there. I tried and failed. Despite the fact

I had found her in Charlie's bed, in my heart I knew she was a decent person. Like me, she'd been swayed by a beautiful charmer but in her core she was much stronger than that. Maybe, just maybe, she could help do something about him.

I was almost at Portobello Road. The pretty gift shop I was on my way to was waiting for me, a little island of loveliness and calm. I wanted to concentrate when I got there so I paused my striding and ducked into a doorway to pull out my phone. In my contacts list was Lucy's number, tapped in the day I'd worked with her. I looked at the number for a moment. Could I do this? Yes. She answered almost immediately.

Mara's birthday was a week away, the big three zero. In the background of all the latest drama, I had been thinking vaguely about what to get her but I couldn't quite find a scrap of head space to think about it. I wasn't sure she'd even want something from me; she still hadn't spoken to me since losing the kids. But quite aside from however Mara felt about me I felt like it was the right thing for me to give her something. I wasn't going to let Charlie get in the way of our friendship any longer. He had monopolised everything for long enough, even affecting my friendships and my judgement. Even though he wasn't around when Ed and I had lost the kids, he may as well have been. My head was crammed full of him, and I was sure I would've paid much more attention if I hadn't been in this stupid shaken-up state that he'd brought on.

I pushed open the door to the gift shop. Mara and I have dawdled in here many times together over the last couple of years. It was full of things you'd never buy for yourself but were always lovely to receive. We have bought notebooks and picture frames and fairy lights and all sorts of things. There was something for everyone in there, even things with clean lines that Claudia loved. I had a long way to go to win back her trust but this felt like the right place to start.

I thought I'd get her a nice notebook and maybe something functional with a link to the past. A letter opener or something. Mara would like that. But then right at the back of the shop I found a print of a tree in silhouette, with little birds and beasts sitting in its branches, in the simple, quirky Scandinavian style that Mara loved. It reminded me of the beautiful bare trees across the road from the house in Harvist Road and for a moment I had a strong pang of yearning for the little home in Queen's Park. It was perfect.

76

ED

From: Ed Minkley <edminkley@gmail.com>
Date: Wednesday, 8 April
To: David Willis <david@griesonbanks.com>
CC: Covington Green <greenworldcov@gmail.com>
Subject: Water project

Hi David,

Thanks for your email about Covington's project. It's great you're still interested in investing. I've cc'ed him here so you can now talk directly. He could be passing through London shortly, in which case you could potentially meet in person. He could do with finding out what proper beer tastes like.

All best,

Ed

77

MARA

I could hear them coming up the stairs.

'It's my turn first!'

'My turn, my turn!'

'MUM, it's my turn! Tell Rosie that!'

'Luke, cut it out, will you? He might not even be around. Now pipe down, we're almost there. Look, there's Aunty Mara now.'

'Hello, Luke. Hello, Rosie!'

I knelt down to give them a big hug each but Luke powered straight past me into the flat.

'Sorry about him, he's got some bee in his bonnet about finding George.'

'That doesn't matter. Now little Rosie-Posie, you can't get away from me.' I reached out and grabbed my niece. She let me hug her squidgyness and she giggled appreciatively. And then she said, 'Nanty Sam?'

'Not again. You're going to have to learn to say hello, not just ask for Sam the minute you see me, you know.' I kissed her and she ran off down the hall, calling for George.

The first time she'd said that to me – the day after they'd been lost – it had not only stung, it had worried me. Rosie shouldn't be asking for the very person who would lose her given half a chance. But she'd kept on saying it over and over, as had Luke, every single time I'd seen them.

411

Kate and I followed Rosie down the hall to the kitchen. Both children were under the table.

'Why the aunty bit? They never used to call her that – she was always just Sam.'

Kate shrugged. 'I don't know, maybe absence makes the heart grow fonder?'

'And I suppose you think that should apply to me too?'

Kate gazed in her peaceful way at me. She didn't have to answer that with words; her position was clear.

'Well, it feels like emotional blackmail to me.'

'They're just children, Mara.'

'I know. It's the most effective sort, coming from them.'

We got lost talking about Dad for a bit after that. The kids were under the table for a while and then they weren't. Then it was much quieter.

'I might just go and check what those monkeys are up to.'

'I'll come with you. I don't really want them in my room disturbing George – oh.'

They were in my room, leaning on one side of the bed. They were gazing at George, who was a fluffy circle right in the middle of my pillow. He didn't look like he was about to run off at all.

'We're being very gentle, Aunty Mara,' Luke said. 'Just like Aunty Sam taught us.'

'Nanty Sam,' echoed Rosie.

'What do you mean, Luke? What did Sam teach you?'

Luke's face was serious. 'She taught us how to say hello to George. You put your hand out like this and put it on him, very slowly and quietly. Oh, Rosie, it's my turn. It was your turn last time!'

Rosie had stretched out her pudgy arm to put her hand on George too. But Luke wasn't shouting, he was saying it all in a whisper so he didn't disturb George. George was staying perfectly still.

After a bit Luke took his hand away, followed by his little mimic Rosie.

'I think George misses Aunty Sam too,' he pronounced.

'Nanty Sam.'

Both children gazed at me solemnly.

'You've done it, you two. Pass me the box of tissues there, would you, Luke? Thanks.'

Kate was right about the absence thing.

78

SAM

I was early but Lucy was even earlier than me. She stood in a patch of gorgeous spring sunshine to the left of the heavy door, painted British racing green. So far, so establishment. She looked as beautiful as ever, her hair pulled casually over one shoulder so it fell like a golden river on one side of her beige cashmere poncho. Her legs were perfect sticks inside skinny blue jeans. Her high boots made her look like she meant business. Which she did. She completely agreed with Vic when I called her. Something had to be done about Charlie. So we were taking it to the top. Well, technically to the second in command but he was the one who would want to see us.

'Hi, Lucy.'

'Hi, Sam.'

Our eyes skittered over each other's faces. My heart was in my mouth and I could see she was nervous too. Neither of us were in a hurry to get inside.

'I'm glad we could do this so quickly. I think I'd chicken out if I had time to think about it,' I said.

'Yes, I think I'd be the same. It's good you called yesterday. Charles comes to this club once a week at the most so if we didn't catch him today it would be another week before he'd be back in town again, maybe more.'

'And there's no way I could face going to the countryside to speak to them.'

Lucy made a face. 'The "them" in that sentence would be the problem. It would be a thousand times harder to lay things out to Lydia. She dotes on her boys and she'd be very hard to convince.'

'You know, I've been going over and over all of this. I don't think I noticed it at the time, or at least didn't think very deeply about it, but even all those years ago, Charlie was always so good around Lydia, never pushing things too far. He never swore, never let on what he'd really been up to. And it is still the same now, isn't it? He is still the perfect son around his mother.' I thought back to the weird visit I'd made the previous month, remembering the power Lydia held over him, how much he'd valued her opinion on things, how his behaviour changed when she was in the same room.

'He's completely still like that. He is such a boy.' Lucy exhaled loudly through her nose.

'Do you think his relationship with Lydia has influenced his philandering? Could it be he's fundamentally a bit scared of women so he doesn't get too close to them, and treats them as disposable items?'

'Fuck it, who cares!' Lucy flashed angry eyes at me and then smiled grimly. She wasn't angry with me. 'I'm sure you could throw Freudian and Jungian and whatever else theories at this and come up with all sorts of reasons to explain why Charlie is the way he is – but at the end of the day what he needs to do is grow up!' She shook her head, as if in disbelief. 'He's a surgeon, Sam. He's thirty years old. He doesn't need to treat people like this. No matter what in his upbringing might have influenced things, at the end of the day he has choices like all of us. You can choose to treat people kindly, you can choose not to sleep around, you can choose to be honest. Millions of people manage to do that every day of the year!'

415

I grinned. My instincts about getting Lucy on board for this were bang on.

'You're right about Lydia though, Sam; he cares what she thinks about him. She's the only person who has any chance of getting through to him.'

'And his dad is the only person who might actually listen to us,' I added.

'Exactly. And talking of Daddy . . .' Lucy pulled her phone out and consulted the time. 'You ready?'

'No, but let's do it.' I felt sick.

'We can do this,' Lucy said. She grinned at me once more then turned and pushed the big door inwards.

She led the way up the marble stairs. The walls were white, the stair rail lacquered black. I was surprised to pass several colourful abstract paintings on the walls. My scant knowledge of what gentlemen's clubs looked like was a mash-up between James Bond and Jeeves and Wooster, and I was expecting to see severe white men in dark oils, their portraits surrounded in gilt frames. Showed how little I knew.

At the top of the stairs, we could turn left into the restaurant or right into the lounge. Lucy led us to the right and then paused in the doorway. This was a beautiful room. It was large, with high ceilings and generous Georgian windows, but it felt cosy. Leather armchairs, sofas and little tables were arranged in clusters to fit between one and about ten people. It was lit by lamps, little Arts and Crafts numbers, on the small tables along the walls, standard lamps next to the sofas. There was a pleasant hum of voices. Some men were reading the paper by themselves, some were playing cards and others were chatting in pairs and small groups. A few were studying tablets. It was warm and comfortable, and it felt like it had been this way for a very long time. I could see why Mr Hugh-Barrington loved it. Even I would be happy to curl up in the corner with a magazine.

'There he is.'

I heard Lucy take a deep breath that I couldn't help but imitate. It felt like I'd held my breath from the door all the way up the stairs. We wended our way to the opposite side of the room. Charles was in a little section that had a couple of high-backed chairs and a sofa. He was alone. He stood up when he saw us coming and smiled broadly, although there was no mistaking the awkwardness in his eyes.

'Lucy! Sam!' He grasped our shoulders – kiss, kiss. 'What a pleasure, please have a seat.'

We all sat down, Charles back in his chair while Lucy took the other and I sat on the sofa. Charles motioned to a waiter and ordered us all coffee. While he did that I scrambled around in my head wondering how the hell we would get started with this conversation. I wondered if Lucy felt the same. I hoped she had it all worked out.

'So . . . here we are.' Charles turned back to us and looked at us both in turn. 'You're both looking lovely, as usual. Although, Sam, I must say you look a lot better than last month. Got your colour back. I couldn't believe it when you turned up looking like a drowned rat, you poor old thing.'

Lucy stared at me.

Not the best start.

'Don't ask,' I said to her.

'Oh. Have I put my foot in it?' Charles looked back and forth between us. 'This was after you'd broken up, Lucy. Charlie was at home nursing his sore heart. And I found Sam at the pub up the road and brought her home. She wasn't stepping on your territory . . .'

We both looked at Charles.

'Oh dear.' He looked very uncomfortable.

'Look, we haven't come to explain all the sordid details of

417

what's been going on in recent weeks, Charles. We've come to speak to you about your son because we hope that you and Lydia might be able to speak to him yourselves and perhaps help him.'

'Is he in trouble?'

Lucy glanced at me.

'He's not *in* trouble, Mr Hugh-Barrington, he *is* trouble,' I said.

Charles sat very still and looked at us again. He didn't say anything for a bit. We looked back at him, one of us in cashmere, one of us in New Look. We both had the same expression on our faces. We'd had enough of the heartbreak and this was serious enough to want to speak to our ex-boyfriend's father about.

'Go on.'

And so we did. We told him all about his son's deceit – leaving out the sordid bits, as promised. The coffee came and I went on to explain what had happened between us the first time around.

'. . . and I believe he's also seeing my sister at the moment too,' I concluded.

'Oh God, really?' Charles's head fell back onto his chair and he let out a long sigh. He was silent for a few moments.

'We have been starting to wonder if he would ever settle down with someone. He's always been so aloof about his love life. We knew you of course, Sam, and have really enjoyed the time we've spent with you, Lucy.'

'You must have met some of the others. I get the sense he's discarded more girlfriends along the way than Hansel and Gretel dropped breadcrumbs,' said Lucy tartly.

'There have been a few over the years but I did get the sense there was a lot he didn't say. I've put it down to a young man sowing his oats and everything. Sorry, bad choice of words. But I never thought he'd be treating women so badly.'

Again he lapsed into silence.

418

'Of course Lydia is going to be very sad to hear all this.'

Lucy and I exchanged glances. This is what we were here for.

'I dread telling her.'

'But you must!' Lucy said.

Charles looked at her balefully. His reaction to listening to our stories had been to rub his head in consternation and now his hair was sticking up like a white halo around his head.

'It's very hard for Lydia to hear bad things about either of her sons.'

I bit my tongue and glanced at Lucy. She uncrossed and re-crossed her legs in an agitated way. It occurred to me that perhaps Lucy didn't feel very generous towards Lydia at all. Perhaps I wasn't the only girlfriend who didn't feel like they made the grade.

Charles continued, 'It's different for the mother. She takes things personally. Any criticism of her children is like being criticised herself.'

Lucy sighed gustily. Charles glanced at her.

'But you're right, I must speak to her and I will. I wish I didn't have to know all of this. I was actually having a lovely day until you two came along.' He gave us a weary smile. 'But you never stop being a parent, no matter how old your children are, and obviously Lydia and I are required to do some parenting. Thank you for speaking to me about him.'

'Thank you for giving us some of your time, Mr Hugh-Barrington.'

'Charles, please, Sam.'

'Charles.'

Lucy stood up. 'Well, we've caused enough waves for one day. We're going to leave you in peace now, let you have your lunch.'

Charles and I both stood with her and we all exchanged awkward hugs and kisses for one final time.

'Shall I let you know how we get on?' he said.

We both shook our heads, caught each other doing it and laughed.

'Don't bother, Charles. Sam and I have heard enough about him, haven't we?'

I nodded.

'You speak to your son. If it helps him treat the next woman he's involved with with some respect for a change, then great.'

'He needs a wake-up call,' I said.

'He needs a boot up the backside,' Lucy added.

And we smiled, and we waved and we got the hell out of there.

Outside Lucy gave me a fierce hug. 'We've done what we can,' she said. 'Now I hope we can both walk off into the sunset and leave this behind us.'

'It's lunchtime, it might be a bit difficult.'

Lucy grinned. 'You know, your hair looks really good like that.'

I put my hand up and touched it. It felt like it always does – or at least as it always did before I tried grooming myself into someone much slicker.

'It's just how it looks when I don't do much with it. Frizztastic probably.'

'It suits you.'

'Thanks.' I felt a stupid smile on my face.

'I'm going to head off now.' She gave me another equally hard hug. 'Look after yourself, won't you? And pick yourself a good one next time.'

'A single one?'

'A single one, Sam. There's an idea. See you around.'

And she headed off down the street into her midday sunset. I walked off the other way. In a matter of days we had twice walked off in opposite directions from a fancy doorway. Both times we had been overwhelmed with emotion but this time we also had clarity. As I walked, turning over the intense conversation in that cosy, privileged club, I realised I'd had another one of those little skips further into adulthood, and it wasn't so much about doing something about Charlie that had made me realise this – it was Lucy's hug.

79

CHARLIE

'Hello you, I haven't had your name flash up on my screen for a while.'

'A nice surprise, I hope?'

'Of course it is, Charlie. It's always a pleasure to hear from you. I was only painting my nails.'

'Good, I'm glad. You don't have company, do you?' I heard Mel giggle a throaty giggle.

'No, I'm all alone. What about you? What's happening with . . .'

Mel paused, as if she couldn't remember Lucy's name. I liked that she couldn't recall it. She could help me forget, too.

'All finished. I don't really know why. She probably wasn't ready for the commitment.'

'And you are?'

Mel giggled again. I loved that giggle: it spoke of dark rooms and good times.

'I might have been.'

'Sure,' Mel purred back. 'But back to reality, are you still living in the same place?'

'I am. Hang on, someone's calling me.' I pulled the phone away from my ear and looked at my screen. It was Ma. It must be important, she never usually called at this time in the evening. 'Mel, I have to take this, but can I ring you back in a minute?'

'Go on then.'

I switched calls.

'Charlie?'

'Hi Ma, are you okay?'

'Can you talk?'

'Sure, I'm home now. Just . . .' – I reached for the remote and pressed the on switch – 'watching some TV.'

'Busy day?'

'You could say that. The list feels twice as long as it should at the moment with Anton still off sick, but we battle on through and stagger home eventually.'

'Good.'

Good? When I complained about being tired, Ma told me I work too hard, or how much good I did for people. She wasn't meant to say it was *good* I'd staggered home that night. It wasn't *good* I was feeling jaded. She couldn't have heard me right.

'Is everything OK with you? You sound a bit . . . quiet or something. Is Dad okay?' I asked her.

'Yes, yes, we're fine thanks, Charlie. It's just—'

'Good.'

'—that . . .'

'Sorry, I talked over the top of you. Go on.'

Lydia cleared her throat. 'I – rather, your father and I – just wondered if you were free to come down for dinner sometime soon. Maybe this weekend?'

'Oh, right. Hang on. Let me open my calendar on my phone . . . can you still hear me?'

'Yes. Yes I can.'

'Right, back again. I could do Friday night, does that suit?'

'Friday would be fine. We'll see you then.'

'Are you sure everything is OK, Ma? You do sound really odd, like you're worried about something. Now you've got me worried.'

'We're fine, honestly, darling. No, it's just that . . . well, we just need to have a bit of a catch-up. We'll see you Friday then?'

'OK, Ma, see you then. Bye.'

'Bye, Charlie.'

I chucked my phone onto the sofa beside me and stared blankly at the screen for a while. I didn't like that conversation at all. I couldn't quite put my finger on it; there was something in Ma's voice. She sounded distant, like she had a lot on her mind and she was fuming. I flicked through the channels for a bit, but there was nothing on that would distract me from feeling that somehow I was in trouble. I picked my phone up again. Dammit, I worked too hard to waste time feeling uneasy about something that hadn't even happened yet. Life is for living, Charlie boy, buck yourself up! I scrolled back to Mel's number. Cute little Mel, only around the corner. She'd sounded pleased to hear from me before. I glanced at the time. Nine thirty. There was still time left in the day. I pictured her in her pants, painting her toenails on the edge of her bed. It was a nice room, that one. I hadn't seen it for such a long time and just thinking about it made me feel a bit better. I pressed on her name to call her back.

80

SAM

I stood at my old front door on Harvist Road with Claudia, waiting to be buzzed up. It was the first time I'd stood there without my own key to get in. It was also Mara's birthday, to which I hadn't been invited.

'Are you sure this is a good idea?' I asked Claudia for the tenth time. Claudia ignored me. Since she'd hooked up with John she had become steadily more and more happy. And even more confident, if that was possible. And having my friend back on form, with her lion heart on her sleeve, made me realise how subdued having the STI had made her. In fact, it was her telling me all about that episode that meant I was standing here at Mara's door. I couldn't say no to her, not after being such a monstrously bad friend when she'd needed me.

I had a different key in my pocket now, one that fitted into the front door of a flat in Kilburn with a friend of Vic's. It didn't have park views but it wasn't far from here. I'd be able to visit for tea . . . if Mara would have me. I crossed my fingers as we waited.

We were buzzed in, up the narrow stairs, which smelled the same – like potatoes (I would never know why) – and then we were at the door. There was Mara, coming down the hall to answer it, expecting just Claudia, and getting—

'Oh!'

We all stood there for a beat.

Then Claudia swept in. 'I've had enough of this. I need my best friends to be best friends again, so sort it out. Oh, and happy birthday, Mara.' She landed a big smacker on Mara's cheek and disappeared down the hall to the kitchen, greeting Ed with a loud holler.

I stood awkwardly and then remembered my present, passing it to Mara just as Mara remembered to close the door, so I ended up thrusting the present into Mara's shoulder.

'Sorry!' we said at the same time and burst out laughing. I stepped towards her and gave her a big hug, and Mara hugged me back, at double the strength.

'Let's not break up again,' I said as we drew apart.

'Promise not to lose the kids?'

'Promise.'

'Promise to pay back what you owe me?'

'It's in my wallet.'

Mara smiled. 'OK, what do you want me to promise?' She paused. 'How about I promise not to give you a hard time about Charlie?'

'That'll be easy because I'm over him.'

Mara raised her eyebrows. God, it was good to see those eyebrows. I almost hugged her again.

'I know something's been going on but no one is telling me a thing.'

'I found out he's been sleeping with Lucy and Rebecca and I dumped him – well, so did Lucy actually – but great, huh?'

'Great? That sounds awful!' Mara's face was clouded with concern.

'No, Charlie and Rebecca deserve each other. It's called social justice, Mara. Each getting what they need.'

'What?'

426

'Mara, have I got a story for you.' I linked arms with her and walked the few paces to the kitchen.

'And I've got the drinks to go with the telling!' Claudia called as we entered the warm kitchen, alive with the sounds of Ella Fitzgerald, saucepans bubbling and bottles uncorking.

Ed turned as we walked in the door and met my eye. I caught my breath and felt a cold tingling all over my chest, like I was missing layers. Not layers of clothes but invisible barriers. I felt peeled back, fragile and open.

'Surprise!' I said.

And then the doorbell went again and in came a broad-chested blonde man, his slightly nervous smile at odds with his patently rock-solid character, and he presented flowers to Mara without a trace of guile then wrapped his big arms around Claudia as if he hadn't seen her in months. I caught Mara's eye and grinning we both turned to Claudia and gave her a thumbs up.

'I know!' Claudia shrieked, while John looked at her like she'd just said something earth-shattering.

Kate arrived next, with Luke and Rosie running ahead of her.

'Nanty Sam!' they chorused and ran straight into my arms. They wanted to see me, stupid children-losing me.

'Nanty?' I said.

'Rosie made it up. It's because she can't say aunty.'

'Nanty Sam.'

'But I'm not—'

I didn't finish what I was going to say; I just had to give them another big hug each. They let me squeeze them for about two seconds and then wriggled off to find George.

Behind Kate came the sound of two men's voices rumbling in the jolly conversation of two people who don't know each other yet. First to squeeze into the already crowded kitchen was Ben, who was as short and lean as Claudia's John was buff, with big

427

brown eyes as kind as Kate's. Following him in was the Minkleys' dad himself, out of his cardi and slippers and, more importantly, out of his house. Kate had the silliest smile on her face, and when Luke and Rosie had finished their tour of the adults, Rosie returned to Ben and took hold of his hand in a firm grasp.

We were all there and when the doorbell went again none of us registered it properly the first time, so it buzzed and buzzed and buzzed. I wasn't in the kitchen and didn't hear the voice on the intercom so I only saw Rebecca when she was standing in the hallway, hanging back from the door into the sitting room, where I was.

'What are you doing here?' I asked her. 'And, Mara, are you sure you want this person in your house?' I strode over to see her out. Like hell was she going to come and ruin this day. But when I reached her I was shocked by how she looked. She was as white as the walls in Claudia's apartment, her red-rimmed eyes looking at me pathetically. No minx-like smirk, no make-up, not much of anything at all.

'Your mum dropped her off. She's coming back in half an hour to pick her up again. She insisted I bring her in. Apparently she's here to speak to you.'

'Well, I don't want to—' But Mara cut me off and pushed the tart into the sitting room with me while Claudia vacated it. She even shut the door! Where was the support now? I wanted to know! They knew how I felt about her, how much hurt she'd caused.

I sat down and folded my arms. I wasn't going to make it easy for her.

'I've come to apologise,' she said in the tiniest voice she'd ever used. It sounded like the whisper of a rat.

'Sorry? I can't hear you.'

'I've come to apologise, I said,' she said again.

'Good for you. Are you hoping it will make you feel better, you fucking bitch?'

Rebecca flinched.

'Actually I want you to feel better,' she whispered.

'Sure you do,' I said.

'I'm not sleeping with him.'

'Get bored of you, did he?'

Rebecca coughed a brittle laugh. 'He's never been interested in me. We've never slept together, not even kissed.'

'Yeah right.'

'It's true!' Rebecca looked at me earnestly and I could see she thought she was telling the truth.

'I find it hard to believe you, Rebecca. People have seen you with him.'

'I know, Claudia told me.'

'What?' Now I was confused. I thought Claudia was *my* friend.

'She bawled me out about it yesterday to get the story straight. Don't worry – she was bloody awful to me. She was only doing it so she could be a friend to you about this mess.'

Rebecca fiddled with a loose thread on the chair arm.

'It's some big mess, that's for sure – no thanks to you,' I said.

'Well, can you please give me the chance to tell my side of the story?' she pleaded.

I sighed. I had nothing more to lose and I supposed listening to her crap couldn't make anything worse.

'You're right in thinking I like Charlie. In fact it would be safe to say I'm more than a little obsessed with him. I've liked him for a long time, long before you bumped into him a couple of months ago. It's been more than a year now and it's the most painful feeling I've had in my life.'

So far, so believable.

'The worse bit of it is that he has never, ever expressed any interest in me whatsoever. He's very charming and friendly, of course, like he is with all of his friends but he just sees me as a little girl – the little girl that I am.'

A tear slid down the side of her face but she kept going. 'I've tried so hard to get him to like me like that – and nothing. And then you turn up and he just skips off – while seeing another woman – into your arms for a good time. It's so unfair.' Her last words came out ragged and angry.

'But Claudia saw you having lunch with him!' I interjected.

'No, Claudia saw me waiting to have lunch with him, and his friend that I'm – was – seeing. He would never ever meet me for lunch or a drink on my own, Sam. I would never dream of asking him, either – I wouldn't be able to bear the shame of him fobbing me off.'

'And the man Claudia heard you giggling at on the phone?'

'Charlie's friend.'

'What's his name?'

Rebecca looked at me, totally resigned and broken. 'It doesn't matter, just one of his friends, the one who was the easiest catch. It was my last attempt at getting his attention. He was awful, anyway, rough and boorish.'

Another tear slid down her face and I knew without being told that she had suffered at the hands of whoever this man was, and I felt sad for her.

'So you're telling me I've got it all wrong, that you were never seeing him?'

'Yes, you had everything, as usual, all along, Sam.'

'What do you mean by that? I had everything? What a load of bollocks! All I've had in the past few weeks is embarrassment and heartbreak!' God, she was so twisted. I really did feel for her for a minute, and then she said such awkward, uncaring things.

She looked at me and sighed. 'You do have everything I've

430

ever wanted, Sam. You've got real friends who care about you, you're sexy, you're brave, you've got a fun job, you're carefree. You get on with life with a smile on your face.'

She looked at me with tears now falling uninterrupted down her cheeks. 'And the most genuine man I've ever met thinks you're the bee's knees!'

'Who?'

She sniffed noisily but didn't say anything and in an instant a chill spread through my chest again as I realised who she was talking about. I stared out the window for a bit, not seeing the bare tops of the trees in the park. My head was full of questions and running ahead imagining a future with real happiness, with someone who could be relied on, with friends who love me so much they will forgive me being totally useless . . . with a sister who actually does have emotions after all.

'Why are you so nasty to me then?' I asked her.

'I don't know! Because I'm a strange, cold bitch! Because I want to have some of your playfulness and don't know how to do it, and it ends up coming out all wrong, all twisted up. Fuck! I don't know but I do know I can't bear having you hate me!'

There was only one thing to do then. I moved over and knelt by this strange, cold bitch of a sister of mine and put my arms around her, pulling her in for a hard, teary hug.

'Come here, you crazy woman,' I said.

81

MARA

There was so much going on that evening that for quite a long time I completely forgot about Covington. Quite why someone would go home to the States via London was beyond me but Ed had assured me that he had a healthy trust fund to back him up. More importantly, he'd said, he was a good friend and he wanted to meet us all. Especially me. It didn't make any sense but I couldn't help but feel quietly thrilled.

'I really don't understand Covington's interest in me,' I'd said to Ed, quite possibly repeating myself.

'You can call him Cov, you know, Mars.' Ed had looked at me with amusement.

'I think if you're blessed with such a grand name, you should use it.'

Ed's mouth twitched. 'Well, that'll be up to you.'

I tried to imagine some American coming to see us. A man who had set up several projects in India, including improving access to clean water for hundreds of people and embedding micro-finance schemes. He was a voracious reader. And I had to admit, going by Ed's photographs, he wasn't bad-looking at all. From the little I knew about him he sounded nothing like the self-absorbed depressive that Mark was. The little I knew about him made him sound quite close to being a saint.

'But why me? Why would he be interested in this boring librarian?'

'Come on, Mara, I've told you already. He's heard a lot about you and thinks you sound pretty amazing.'

'And based on a few conversations had in an exotic location he's going to spend hundreds of pounds more than he needs to and stop over here on his way home?' I'd asked.

'He's probably got a round-the-world ticket or something, Mars.' He'd sighed, frustrated with my sharp tone. 'You're talking as if our friendship is worth less because we met travelling. Like it's some flimsy thing that won't last. We got on really well, you know. He's one of the people I've met who gets me the best in the world.'

I looked at him hard but he was undeterred.

'You of all people should understand that, Mara. What about Claudia and Sam – you met them travelling and look at them, they're family now, right?'

'But that's different,' I said.

'How, exactly?' he asked.

I scowled at him and he put his arm around me, and his kindness made me feel fragile.

'Could it be that you're happy to share your friends with me but not as happy to share me with my friends, Mars?'

I tried to unpick what I was feeling. I knew in my heart he'd hit on the truth but I couldn't logically make it all line up in my head. He had been speaking about this Covington character a lot since he'd come home. Could it be that I'd been feeling jealous of Covington as well as worried about Sam? Perhaps blaming everything that's seemed wrong in the past few weeks on Sam had been unfair of me.

'You know, I reckon you two are going to have a lot in common,' Ed said.

433

So when the doorbell went for what felt like the fiftieth time that evening, I wasn't sure whom to expect. It wasn't until I saw the shadowy figure of a man with a large rucksack behind the frosted glass that I twigged.

I opened the door.

'Hello, is this—'

He was the most beautiful man ever to stand at my door, with warm, intelligent eyes full of truth and a drawing of a bicycle on his T-shirt and—

'Oh, don't tell me, you must be Mara.'

'I— sorry, I'm so rude, please come in—'

'Thank you, I've heard so much about you, Mara,' he said as he passed by me, so close, in the narrow hallway, and I placed my hand on the wall behind me and inhaled deeply to try steadying myself. Maybe Ed was right; maybe this Covington creature and I would have a lot in common. I hoped with all my heart that we would.

82

ED

After Rebecca had been picked up I watched Sam all night, laughing with Mara, with Kate, with Claudia and with John. She chatted with Dad for ages, asking him lots of questions about his time in the navy, before the wife and kids came along, and he couldn't have looked happier if he'd tried. She seemed to be making a point of not looking my way, although when Cov turned up she stared at me pointedly, her eyes flicking to Mara. 'Could he be any more perfect for her?' she was saying. 'I know!' I stared back and felt sky high. But she never sat with me or leant against the kitchen counter alongside me, like I hoped she would. Not until all the food was gone and everyone was piled into the sitting room did she come and find me. I was outside. Ever since working in Scotland, I'd got into the habit of spending a few moments outside at night. Of course Queen's Park at night didn't come close to the in-your-face vitality of the Highlands but after ten o'clock most people were at home and it was much quieter. I couldn't wait for Katherine's project to begin. She'd called me through the week. Yes, please, I'd said. More time in Scotland and ten weeks away from London on a job with Sam. Definitely.

'They're lovely, aren't they?' she said at my arm.

I turned, heart racing. Finally! Then I chided myself – must keep cool, must keep cool.

'What are?'

'The trees. I'm going to miss that park.'

'You should have bought two,' I said.

'Two what?'

'Two of those prints, the one you gave Mara. Didn't it remind you of these trees?'

'How did you know?'

I shrugged and looked at her cute round face, her frizzy hair all crinkly and golden under the street light, and I wondered why I hadn't noticed the faint sprinkling of freckles over the bridge of her nose before.

'So . . .' She looked at me, cheeky and open and complicated and really very simple all at once and my whole body ached with how much I wanted to take her into my arms right there and kiss her like the mad dog I felt. But I wouldn't. Not yet. She had to be completely Charlie-free. I couldn't bear her chasing any part of him, even the whiff of his smart cologne in her mind. No, I would wait, just a little bit longer.

'So?' I answered, and looked out at the park again. I sensed her smiling and felt her lean her head on the side of my arm, and I smiled at the bare trees as they waved at us from across the street.